The Mysteries of Tremont Meadow

MKS Cooper

MKS Cooper

For my new-found Cousin, have fun reading about Bertie & her friends!

Peggy

This is a work of fiction. All names, characters, places, and events are the product of the author's imagination or are used fictitiously. Any resemblance to real people, living or dead, or to places or events is coincidental, unless stated otherwise within by the author.

When a real place is used it is done so with literary license in order to add realism to the story.

All rights reserved. No part of this book may be reproduced, stored in a retrieval system, transmitted in any form or by any means, electronic, mechanical, photocopying, recording, on film, or otherwise, without prior written permission of the copyright owner except for the use of quotations in a book review.

For permission or more information contact the author at cooperbooks72@yahoo.com.

www.cooperbooks72.com

Copyright MKS Cooper, 2023

Cover Designed by GetCovers, 2023

For my baby sister
Julie Bean

One

Bertie

THE SMOKE WERE WHAT woke me up.

The first thing I seen when my eyes popped open were a orange glow comin' in through the bedroom window, an' I knowed right off somethin's burnin'. I smacked Homer's side of the bed an' hollered out at him, "Homer! Wake up! Thar's a fire!"

Course, they warn't no answer, an' I yelled his name agin afore I remembered Homer were dead an' buried a month ago. By now I's wide awake, listenin' to the flames snappin' an' cracklin' as they come closer to the house. Quick as I could, I got over to the bedroom window an' seen the flames crawlin' up the side of the barn like some kind'a giant ivy. Smoke filled the sky s' thick even the moon were shut out.

I heard the sirens, an' faster'n a jack rabbit can run, my yard were full of fire trucks an' lights an' volunteers, some of 'em pullin' on their fire coats an' boots while they's climbin' out of their vehicles. I didn't know what to do or where to go. I headed for the stairs but my legs was shakin' so bad I sat down hard on the top step, an' that's where the young man found me, jist settin' there sayin', oh, oh, oh! He half carried me down the steps an' out the kitchen door jist as the fire reached the porch. That's when my legs give out, an' down I went into the water-soaked grass.

They told me later somebody had saw the smoke an' called for help.

Two

Bertie

I NEVER DID GIT back to sleep. Too much goin' on. The fire department had showed up around two o'clock in the mornin' an' once the word started spreadin' around town, people was in an' out of here like there was a party goin' on. I don't know who all them folks was, but some of the women brought food for me. I know they's tryin' to help me but I don't think I'm goin' to be able to eat for a while. Now it's supper time, an' the last one of 'em jist drove away, thank you, Jesus.

NEXT MORNIN' I'S STANDIN' in the kitchen doorway lookin' out at what were left of the farm. The barn's burnt frame stood out against the sky, lit up from behind by the risin' Florida sun. I had to squint my eyes to see how the rest of the outbuildin's had fared. The silo were gone, jist a heap of ashes an' melted shingles. The remains of the chicken coop lay on the ground, scattered ever' which way by the force of the water hoses. The storage shed leaned at a angle, gittin' ready to collapse on the tractor an' the other farm equipment parked inside it. They was waitin' on the sale I were plannin' to put on next month. Lookin' at the mess, I thought, *well, there won't be no sale now, hardly nothin' left worth sellin'.*

I turned away from the sorry sight an' went to start the coffeepot to perkin', my brain full of thinkin' about last night. Thank God the fire trucks an' volunteers had got here when they did. Once the flames had raced across them dry September fields, they only slowed down long enough to eat up the outbuildin's afore headin' for the house.

When we was first married I tried to tell Homer to do somethin' about the sorry condition of his farm, but you couldn't tell him nothin'. I finally quit talkin' about it. Truth is, though, for over a hun'erd years the farm was left to set in the hot sun, dryin' out more ever' year. I think since 1898 when the last nail was pounded in, there ain't been nothin' done to speak of to keep the buildin's in any kind of shape at all. So now, forty feet from the house, the only part left of the outhouse were the cement base an' the hole in the ground underneath it. Closer in, the pump house done been ate up by the flames afore the firefighters could hook up their hoses to the water truck. The fire had got to the front an' one side of the porch. The posts that had held up its roof was hangin' sideways, leavin' the front wall of the house in danger of cavin' in.

Now I'm standin' here on my water-soaked porch, the smell of smoke pricklin' my nose an' makin' my eyes water, wonderin' how in the world am I goin' to fix this mess?

Headin' back inside, I heard tires crunchin' in the driveway gravel. Through the smoked-up screen door of my kitchen I could see a short, chunky woman walkin' up to the house. It were Mrs. Monk, the owner of the local general store, wavin' an' smilin' real big. I remember Homer sayin' it were bad enough a woman took it on herself to own a store, let alone act s' high an' mighty she'd have the nerve to run for president of the Town Council. Homer didn't hold no truck with women runnin' things he thought was best left to the menfolk. But the woman wadin' through my soggy yard did own the store, an' she had got herself elected to the top position of the Council.

"Good morning, Mrs. Claxton, what a shame," Mrs Monk hollered out to me. "Fast as that fire was moving, you're lucky they got here before the house went, and you with it."

I didn't 'specially feel like bein' neighborly right then.

"I ain't in the mood for company," I said.

"Oh, I'm sorry, I'll keep it short. I'm just checking to see if there's anything I can do to help you. Bad enough Mr. Claxton's gone, God rest his soul, and now the fire. How're you doing out here alone by now?"

I figgered she must be daft, she couldn't see fer herself how I were doin', but I answered her anyhow.

"I guess I'm doin' as good as a body could do right about now, Mrs. Monk. How d' you think you'd be doin' if you was me?"

"Well, you're right, and I apologize. I didn't mean to make light of the situation. I know we've never been friends, Bertha. May I call you Bertha? Mrs. Claxton sounds so formal. And you call me Maxine, you hear? Can we sit at the table and talk for a few minutes?"

The coffee done finished perkin' by then, so I poured us each a cup an' set down across from her. I asked what could I do for her.

"Oh, for goodness sake, Bertha, I'm here to help you," she said.

"Well, you'll have to excuse me, I'm not used to gittin' helped. Whatever I were supposed to do, I pretty much always done it myself, or else it didn't git done. So what d' you want to help me with?"

"Bertha," she said.

I butted in. "You got to forgive me if I ask you not to call me by that name. Only two people ever called me that was my daddy an' my dead husband, Homer. I didn't much care for one or the other, s' if you'll call me Bertie, I'd appreciate it."

I guess I sounded stern, 'cause Mrs. Monk, Maxine, got flustered. She started stutterin', sayin', "Oh, sure, uh, Bertie. I like that much better anyhow. Bertha sounds so formal, doesn't it? Bertie is a friendly name. How come we never got to be friends, Bertie?"

I studied her, figgerin' whether to tell it straight out, or make up some cockamamie story an' send 'er packin'. For some reason, I decided to tell her how it really was.

"Well, first my daddy, then my husband, Homer, kept me s' close to home I never had the chance to make no friends. Why they was like that, I don't know. But they's both gone to glory now, an' I don't have to answer to nobody no more."

"I swear," Maxine said. "You mean to tell me you don't have any friends?"

"Nary a one. Nobody ever come out here, an' ever' time I left the farm I were with Homer. Afore that, I went where my daddy took me, or I were at home, where they said women is supposed to stay. I always felt like they's both wrong about that, but it were jist easier on me to do what I's told. I knowed a long time ago I warn't to cross either one of 'em."

"Well, I never heard of such a thing. If you'll let me, Bertie, I'd like to be your friend. Friends help each other when it's needed, and I think you need help. So, what do you say?"

"I thank you, Maxine. I'd like you to be my friend. But I still don't know what you think needs to be done for me."

"For starters, Bertie, you've got to get out of this house. The front half is damaged pretty bad, it could collapse at any time. You might get hurt. Now, some of us in town talked about getting a crew out here to repair the damage, but Sam Jones made a judgment about that. He's been the County Appraiser and Building Inspector since the last tepee was taken down. He knows every property around here, knows when your house was built, how it was built, who built it.

"This farmhouse was built good according to how things were done back then, but we got to face the facts, Bertie. People who've been in this part of the county for a long time say that your husband, and his father before him, weren't known for keeping things in good shape, you know? The house needed repairs before, but look at the porch! Since the fire it leans a little to the north. The pillars are burned up bad so there's not much holding up the roof. A stiff wind might just blow it down. Probably take the front wall of the house with it.

"The Council thinks it'd be a waste of time and money to try to fix it all. They don't want to issue a building permit for the repairs it would take to make the house safe to live in again.

"The bottom line here, Bertie, is this. We held an emergency meeting this morning. I got appointed to come out here and tell you our decision about your house. It's been declared unfit to live in, Bertie. You're going to have to move."

I set there lookin' at Maxine. I couldn't think what to say.

"Dang it, Bertie, I'm sorry," Maxine said. "I should've eased into it a little bit slower."

Now, I ain't one to cry easy, but I had to fight back the tears. They's jist so much a body can take in, an' I had reached my limit. The tears started an' I couldn't make 'em stop.

Maxine jumped up from her chair an' run around to my side of the table, sayin', "Oh don't cry, Bertie, don't cry!" She wrapped her arms around me an' patted my back, lettin' me cry it out.

When the tears stopped, I reached up an' tucked a loose piece of my hair into the bun at the back of my head. I wiped my eyes with a corner of my apron an' told Maxine, "I ain't cried but a few times in my life. The first time I remember cryin' I were about five years old an' my mama had gone away. The next time I cried was more'n forty-six years ago when they give me my son to hold for a minute right after he were born, afore they put him in the grave his daddy dug for him. He's over in the cemetery outside town. Only one other time I cried was when that baby's daddy got buried next to him in that same cemetery, one year later."

Sudden-like, I couldn't talk no more. Ever'thin' started comin' back to me real clear, like my mama had jist left an' the baby died yesterday. I went still as a scared rabbit, starin' off into space while Maxine stood there, not knowin' what to do. Finally my body kicked in on its own an' pulled in a deep breath.

When she seen I were comin' around some, Maxine said, "Land's sake, girl, you mean you were married before you hitched up with old Homer Claxton? And how did your baby's daddy die?"

I told Maxine I warn't sure what to tell her since I hadn't never talked about none of this with nary another soul. Even if I had ever wanted to talk about it, there warn't nobody to talk about it with, anyhow.

"Well, you just ignore me," Maxine said. "I'm famous for blurting out the first thing comes to my mind sometimes. You don't have to talk about it, unless you feel a need to."

Funny thing, right then I did feel a need to talk about it. I set up straight on my old kitchen chair an' used the other corner of my apron to wipe my drippin' nose an' started talkin'.

"I's jist gittin' to where I could think about the rest of our life together after our baby son died, when my husband, Farley's his name, he were comin' home from town with a load of lumber for the new fence he were buildin'. We had a picnic planned out for that afternoon when our chores got done. I guess he were in a hurry to git back an' unload the truck, so maybe he warn't payin' close attention to his drivin'. Don't nobody know for sure since Farley an' the driver of the other truck both got killed in the crash. All I knowed, I were takin' down the warsh in the back yard when I heard two vehicles pull up. When I walked around the corner of the house, there's the sheriff an' my daddy comin' at me. I knowed right away somethin' were wrong.

"After that, I didn't cry over nothin'. Best I could figger, what good did cryin' do? Didn't bring nobody back, didn't change nothin'. Jist give a body a headache an' made their chest hurt."

Maxine set real quiet, listenin' to me. I had a lifetime of talkin' stored up, an' she didn't stop me, so I kept on.

"After they shoveled the dirt into Farley's grave that day, my daddy took me back to his farm. He told me I were stayin' with him from then on. Said I couldn't live by myself an' I believed him."

"Well, I declare," Maxine said.

"Then I almost cried some years later, when Homer slapped me up alongside my head one day, but I held back, not wantin' him to git the best of me, you know?"

"Well, I declare," Maxine said again. "Why in the world did he slap you?"

"It were my own fault, I guess. Even after all the years since they died, I hadn't got over thinkin' about Farley an' the baby most all the time. Ever' once in a while I'd git lost in my thoughts. That mornin', I's starin' out the window over the kitchen sink, my mind gone to another place, while Homer's bacon burnt up an' caught the stove on fire. Fire. . . Seems like fire is out to git me."

Maxine stood up an' started walkin' around the kitchen real fast, lookin' upset, shakin' her head back an' forth. She put her hands on her hips and stopped in front of me, lookin' like somethin' was botherin' her. "Well, if Homer slapped you around, why did you stay with him?" Maxine asked. "Why didn't you leave him?"

"There warn't nowhere to go. My daddy were dead by then, an' I only knowed some folks from seein' 'em in town once in a while, like at church. I warn't never allowed to talk much to nobody.

"Anyhow, a few years after that, Homer give out, seemed like. He quit slappin' me, mostly didn't pay no attention to me at all, long as I did what he told me to do around the place. I think I figgered out that's why I didn't cry when he keeled over, same as when my daddy died."

Maxine told me some years later she were stunned by what I had talked about that day. Said her life had been hard, but nothin' like what I done been through. Said she decided right then she'd do anythin' she could to make my life easier. Number one on her list were to be the first real friend I ever had, startin' that very day.

Three

Bertie

Maxine stayed true to her word, but I didn't know how to take it all. She come to the farm ever' day bringin' information about housin' for senior citizens, applications for Medicaid an' Section 8. I watched that growin' stack of papers with a grim feelin'.

I finally told her there ain't no way I'm ever goin' to understand all that stuff. I never had to make no decisions in all my born days 'cept which dress should I put on of a mornin', my brown one or my blue one. Maxine thought I were foolin' with her.

"Oh, come on now, Bertie. What are you saying?"

"I'm sayin' my daddy picked out my clothes at the United Protestant Thrift Store over in Sarasota. He braided my hair until I learned how to do it myself. The only thing different about the way I wore it were when I got old enough I's allowed to pin the braids up on top of my head. He didn't let me ever wear makeup, said that stuff made a woman look like a Jezebel. I didn't know what that meant, jist knowed it were somethin' bad from the way he said it.

"We always set in the same back pew at church, an' we left for home right after the last amen got said. On the way out of the church, my daddy always told the preacher he done give a mighty fine sermon, no matter it were a different preacher from time to time, he said the same thing, even when half the time, he were sleepin' through some of the preachin'."

"Oh, Bertie," Maxine said. "This is so sad."

"It warn't always sad. I got to go to the County Fair once a year. Daddy bought me a corn dog on a stick an' a cone of cotton candy. We walked around lookin' at the livestock an' the quilts the ladies from church made for the raffle. The sad part of the Fair, though, were when Daddy heard the fiddles start tunin' up an' the square dancers got to goin', he would take hold of my arm an' steer me back to his truck. Said no daughter of his would be caught up in the worldly corruptions of fiddle music an' dancin'."

Maxine made a snortin' sound an' said, "Oh for Pete's sake! A little fiddle music never hurt anyone!"

"Maybe not, but I wouldn't know, since I never got to listen to it. Then, after I married Homer, life stayed pretty much the same as when I lived with my daddy. Up at dawn, milk the cow, chase the hens off'a their nests so's I could steal their eggs, work in the garden, bake bread. All the chores farm wives do."

"Didn't you ever do anything for fun, Bertie? I mean, how could you stand it, being cooped up on this dreary piece of land way out here in the country all the time?"

"Oh, I got away from here sometimes. One of the best parts of my life with Homer come after you opened up your store. Ever' Thursday we filled up the back of his truck with eggs from our hens an' vegetables from the garden an' drove into town. Delivered it all to your store for you to sell to the townfolk. I set in the truck an' watched ever'thin' goin' on around me while Homer took it all inside an' collected payment from you. That's why you an' me never met face to face, 'cause I warn't allowed to go inside your store or talk to anyone while we's in town. I sure did enjoy the ride there an' back home, though."

"I always wondered about you," Maxine said. "Someone told me once they thought you were retarded because you didn't speak, but now I know. You weren't allowed to talk. Oh, Bertie, I am so sorry."

What I didn't know as I's tellin' all this to Maxine, my life were different from most farm wives. I come to know that later. I had no family 'ceptin' Homer, an I had no friends.

Now Maxine were askin' me to make decisions an' I didn't know how. My world were growin' bigger in spite of the fact that one more person had died. I were confused.

Four

Bertie

"I ain't never had to think about money. The menfolk always took care of that."

Me an' Maxine was lookin' at these little books that showed pictures of places to live when the subject of money come up.

"I don't know how much I'm goin' to need. I got some money put back, though. I sold the livestock an' some of the farm equipment to my neighbor, Jed Bailey, he owns the farm east of here. He come to me after Homer died an' offered to buy some things. I don't know if I made a good deal or not, but it meant I wouldn't have to look after the livestock no more. He took the steer, the cow, the chickens, the goat an' both hogs. I give him the straw an' hay an' chicken feed that were left when Homer died, jist to git rid of it. I'm surely thankful I did that. Made it less for the fire to eat up afore they was able to put it out."

"I agree, Bertie. Jed Bailey's an honest man. I'm sure he gave you a good deal. But where's the money he paid you? Shouldn't it be in the bank? Or did Homer even have a bank account?"

"I don't know if he had a bank account. I put the money in the fruit cellar, stuffed it into a couple of Mason jars at the back of the top shelf, behind the pickles. The freezer is down there, too. It's full of meat from last year's butcherin', so I guess I won't be goin' hungry for a while."

I could see Maxine thinkin'. She said, "I'll bet a dollar to a donut hole, Bertie, that sneaky old man Homer had money stashed somewhere. Whether it's in a bank, buried in the yard, or wherever, there's bound to be something we haven't discovered yet. I'll do some investigating, talk to a few friends in town. One of the Council members, Jake Abbott, is an officer at the bank. He won't be able to give me much information, that kind of thing is confidential, but I can ask him to find out for you if there's anything at the bank with Homer's name on it. As his next of kin you'd be in line to inherit his assets, if there are any."

"Well, I guess that'd be jist fine with me. Seein' as how I don't know somethin' from nothin', I'd appreciate you helpin' me out any which way you can."

"Okay, friend, I'll start the ball rolling in the morning and we'll see what comes up."

I watched Maxine drive away, leavin' me to sit on the fire-damaged porch in one of my old kitchen chairs, waitin' for the day to end so's I could go to bed. Seemed like even though my life was changin', some things was stayin' the same, like, nowhere to go an' nothin' to do, 'cept wait for it to git dark.

Five

Bertie

I heard Maxine as she come up to the back door. It had been two days since she paid me a visit, an' to my surprise, I had missed her.

"Yoohoo," she hollered.

"Hey," I answered as Maxine stepped into the kitchen.

With her git-right-to-it way, Maxine said, "I woke up this morning with the best idea. How would you like to come home with me until we find you a new place to live? What's the matter, you're looking at me like I just climbed out of a UFO."

"Well, I never, Maxine. People don't jist go live in somebody's house. I'm doin' fine right where I am."

"No, you aren't, Bertie. Now, we talked about this. You can't stay in this house much longer. You heard the building inspector the other day when he came out and looked things over. He says the old mortar in the basement is all but gone. There's a big sideways crack in the wall under the front porch, and that wall is about to cave in. The fire did more damage than showed up initially. Burned almost all the way through a couple of the basement ceiling beams where they come out at the porch. If they go, the whole house is likely to come down. Some of the men are going to come out and shore it up to give you a few more days to get everything out of the house, but after that they can't promise anything. Now be sensible and come home with me. To be honest, I'd like the company. I get tired of rattling around in that big old place by myself. You think about it until I come back tomorrow, make your decision then. In the meantime, you got any more of that good coffee you make every morning? I sure could use a cup right about now."

After fillin' up her cup, I said, "This here's a new thing for me."

"What's that," Maxine asked.

"Pourin' a cup of coffee for somebody other than Homer. 'Cept for when Farley were alive, an' we had his preacher uncle to Sunday dinner a couple times, there warn't nobody comin' to visit. Too bad I ain't got nothin' to feed you with your coffee, but with Homer gone, I ain't doin' no bakin'." I couldn't help it, I had to laugh a little bit.

"What? What's funny?" Maxine asked.

"Oh, I was jist rememberin' the time Homer ate all the bread an' I throwed the squash in the creek."

"Now there's a story if ever I heard one," said Maxine. "You going to tell me about it?"

I put the coffeepot back on the stove an' set down at the table. I run my finger through a deep gouge in the porcelain table top.

"See this here place, Maxine? I put that there one day when I's so mad I didn't know what to do about it. One thing I did know, I's afraid to let Homer see me mad like that. He were jist like my daddy, real strong-minded when it come to havin' his way. That's why I married him. Daddy told me I had to, an' I's afraid to tell him no."

"That was a bad thing your daddy did," Maxine said.

"I know that now. Homer were as mean as my daddy. But now they's in the same place together. I hope they's happy, cause they neither one ever seemed like they was happy while they was livin'.

"Anyhow, what made me laugh, Homer come in from the field one day, the heat s' bad he couldn't keep workin'. He made me cut into that bread, hot out of the oven. He wanted it right then, couldn't wait for it to cool. He stood here next to this table an' slathered one slice after the other with apple butter an' ate up most of the loaf. I had to bake more bread in that hot kitchen so's we'd have it for later, but he didn't care. After that day I went to hidin' a loaf away s' Homer couldn't git at it. That way they's always a loaf ready.

"Seemed like he were forever doin' somethin' like that. I almost wish he'd a jist hit me an' got it over an' done with, instead of doin' stuff t' aggravate me s' bad."

"Okay, I got it about the bread," Maxine said. "But how does the squash fit in there?"

I smiled real big. "Well, after the heat let up some, Homer went back out to the field. But he left a bushel of acorn squash settin' on the porch for me to put up. Didn't ask if I had time to do it right then, jist walked out, leavin' me to stare at his back. It wouldn't of done me no good to say nothin'. A few times I got brave enough to say anythin' to him, he didn't pay no attention to me. He never hit me no more after the first few years, but he yelled at me. That day, he jist walked away an' left me standin' there. He knowed I'd do what I's expected to do."

I quit talkin' an' let my mind drift back to that day. I had stood there on that cracked an' peelin' linoleum an' waited until Homer drove his tractor out of sight.

"I don't know what happened to me right then, Maxine. It were like my head went crazy. I started hollerin' out loud an' cussin' at that old man I's married to. It only lasted a few minutes, but when I got done bein' crazy, I got mad. There I were, havin' to bake more bread an' git that squash ready, an' I knowed when he come back later he'd have more for me to put up. I started thinkin' about gittin' all this done an' I knew I couldn't. He'd be mad as a hornet an' I couldn't stand listenin' to him yell at me no more. But then, the craziest idea come into my head."

I had been walkin' around the kitchen while I told Maxine the squash story, wavin' my hands in the air while I remembered that day, but now I plunked myself in the chair an' smiled real big.

"I knowed then I were goin' to do somethin' I ain't never done afore that, an' ain't never done again since."

Lookin' around the kitchen like somebody might be listenin', I said, "I was goin' to lie."

Settin' on the edge of her seat, Maxine said, "You lied? Who'd you lie to? What'd you lie about? I can't imagine you telling a lie to anyone. Well, tell me! What happened?"

"I went out on the porch an' picked out the biggest old squash in the bushel. I's so crazy right then I went to talkin' to that squash like it were Homer. I said, 'You know squash, you look a whole lot like Homer Claxton. Let's see how you like bein' treated mean.'

"I set that squash on the table, right about where you got your hands folded. I took the cleaver I use to cut open them rock-hard squashes, raised it up over my head, an' come down on that squash, splittin' it in two an' takin a chunk of the porcelain out of the table at the same time. "WHAM!" I hollered it out real loud, not thinkin' about how it might scare Maxine. She pulled her hands back real fast an' plopped 'em in her lap, lookin' at me like I was a crazy lady.

I felt bad about scarin' Maxine, but I was wound up by then so I kept talkin'.

"Them two pieces flew in different directions, throwin' seeds all over the kitchen. Then I took the rest of the squash out of the bushel an' put 'em in the wheelbarrow that's settin' out in the yard. I carted the whole mess down the path that goes from here to way out yonder in the meadow. There's a creek out there turns into a small waterfall an' ends in a pond at the back of the farm.

"It were the oddest thing, Maxine, walkin' there. Seemed like the squash didn't weigh nothin' at all, an' I seen stuff I couldn't remember seein' afore. I mean, used to be, when I went down there to empty weeds I'd pulled out of my garden, I's always in a hurry to git back an' finish my chores so Homer wouldn't call me lazy.

"That day, I watched the water goin' over the rocks in the creek. I looked up an' seen the trees was full of all different kinds of pretty leaves. A snake were layin' in the path an' it jist stayed there for a minute all curled up while we stared at each other afore it crawled away. I had to look around to make sure I's in the right place.

"That kind of brought me back to why I were there. I parked the wheelbarrow close to the edge of the waterfall, an' one at a time, I threw them squash as far as I could an' watched while they bobbed up an' down an' disappeared into the pond. When I got back to the house, I cleaned up the mess I'd made in the kitchen an' set out more bread dough to raise. I's real nervous about tellin' Homer the lie I had planned out."

Maxine interrupted me. "What did you tell him?"

"I were goin' to say them squash warn't no good, bugs had got in 'em an' ate out the insides so I threw 'em away."

"Did he believe you?"

"Well, don't you know, that old man never even noticed. All he saw were the empty bushel settin' on the porch an' figgered I got the job done."

Maxine laughed out loud. "That was great thinking, Bertie, but did he bring you more squash when he came in that evening?"

"Yes, he did. But I's feelin' pretty proud about foolin' him once, so I did it again the next day. I canned eight quarts an' had 'em settin' on the sideboard to cool when he come in that night. I guess he figgered I had done 'em all because he didn't say nothin' about it. He never did know the rest of them squash is out there in the pond with the first batch.

"An' after I dumped the second load, I set down under a tree for a spell an' listened to the birds singin' afore I come back to the house."

I were thinkin' hard about them couple of days an' got real quiet.

Maxine watched me for a bit afore askin' if I's okay.

"Yes ma'am, I am okay, but settin' under the trees that day, I made up my mind about somethin'. Didn't know how or when I'd be able to do it, but I planned to set under them trees agin afore I die. I want to put down a quilt on the grass like me an' Farley planned on doin' all them years ago, an' look at a book in the shade an' listen to the water movin' over the rocks. I don't guess I'll ever git to do that though, havin' to move off the farm an all."

Now, Homer's dead an' buried, an' the field where that squash growed is burnt black, like the grass around the house. There were so much to take in it hurt my head to think about it.

Afore she left, Maxine promised to be back in the mornin'. I made myself think about her askin' me to stay at her house for a while. A hour went by, then two, while I tried to come up with a reason to tell her no. I couldn't think of none.

Six

Bertie

I STARTED TALKIN' TO myself a couple of days after Maxine's visit. Seemed like I could sort things out better hearin' the words with my ears instead of jist in my brain. Thinkin' about how my daddy had treated me, I hollered out, "How come you was mean to me, Daddy? I feel real bad about them times. I should of found some way to stop you, but I were jist a little girl. You hit me sometimes an' I's afraid you would do it again, so I jist did what you told me to. That's why I married Homer. You told me I had to, an' I were afraid to tell you no. That were a bad thing you did, makin' me marry him. You was both mean men. I's never happy livin' with you or him. But you know what? I aim to git happy now, an' stay that way for the rest of my life."

I stood there lookin' around, afraid he might answer me.

Course he didn't so I went on. "I'm goin' to go find me somethin' to do now to stay busy so I'll stop thinkin' about this stuff. I don't rightly know that I want to give you any more of my mind than you done took from me already. This will prob'ly be the last time you hear from me."

It had been a hard day, thinkin' on Maxine's offer, but my mind were decided now. I took me a clean pillercase out of the bedroom closet an' packed my belongin's in it. Then I set down for the last time in the chair on the porch where I had set most ever' night of my life as Homer's wife.

In the mornin' my new friend were comin' to take me away from this house where I done wasted too many years already.

Seven

Bertie

Afore we left the next day, Maxine said we ought to make a final search through the house, see if we maybe overlooked anythin' important.

After lookin' in the basement an' the rooms on the first floor, we headed up the stairs to the bedrooms. All we found up there was the beds, the dressers, an' Homer's clothes. We had went through the whole house without findin' nothin' 'cept what's supposed to be there. We had poked into ever' corner an' drawer.

Still, Maxine had a hunch about somethin'. She kept sayin' you never know what might turn up. Her hunch turned out to be a good one.

At the end of the upstairs hallway, Maxine spotted a door that had a padlock on it.

"What's in there, Bertie. Why is it locked?"

I told her I ain't never been in there. Homer always kept it locked. When I asked him about it, he jist told me it were the attic an' it warn't none of my business what's up there.

"Well, it's your business now. We're going up."

It weren't hard to open that door. Maxine were a real sturdy lady with strong muscles from all them years takin' care of her farm an' the store. The door were s' old an' dried out that when Maxine give it a hard kick with her boot, the screws holdin' the padlock come right out of the wood on the first try.

Maxine felt around for a light switch on the wall inside the door. "I'm not finding a switch, Bertie. I'm gonna go on up and see if it's at the top of the stairs. You wait here til I shed some light on this situation."

Two steps up, Maxine let out a loud yell an' started battin' her hands around her face, an' sudden-like, the stairwell lit up bright as day at noontime. She turned towards me an' grinned.

"Sorry, Bert. I thought I'd run into a spider web, but it's a string hanging down from the light bulb up there in the attic ceiling. Didn't mean to scare you like that."

"Well, land's sake, I thought the devil had got hold of you."

We was both shook up, but at least we could see now, so up the steps we went.

Once we was standin' on the attic floor, we looked at each other kind of puzzled-like. There warn't nothin' up there.

"Why do you suppose Homer kept the door locked if the attic is empty?" Maxine asked. "Why didn't he want you to come up here?"

"I don't know," I said. "I always thought he were kind of crazy, but this don't make no sense."

"Well, let's get back downstairs. I'm thirsty and I'm hungry. What do you say we stop at Slick's Diner in town and have some lunch before we head for my place?"

Maxine turned to go down the stairs, but her toe caught on a loose board. If I hadn't of caught her arm, she would of gone down them rickety steps nose first.

She raised her foot up in the air, goin' to smack that board back down with her boot heel. Instead, she bent over an' looked real close at the floor.

"You know, Bertie, it looks like this board has been pulled loose on purpose."

She took hold of it an' yanked. It popped up, an' underneath we saw somethin' grayish colored.

"What on earth?" Maxine asked.

I told her to pull up another board so we could git a better look at what were under there.

The board come up real easy.

"What on earth?" I repeated.

Sometimes the stuff Maxine said come out soundin' funny and made me laugh, an' I was tryin' to talk more like she talked, so I said the same thing.

"I think it's some kind of metal box," Maxine said.

She pulled up the next loose board, an' a few minutes later she had enough of the boards pulled out s' we could see it were a fair-size metal box with handles on both ends. We took hold of the handles an' lifted the box out of its hidin' place. The lock still had a key in the keyhole.

"Look there," said Maxine. "He was so sure of his hiding place, he didn't bother to take the key with him. Do you want to open the box, Bertie?"

I sure did. I turned the key an' lifted the lid. Riflin' through the contents, Maxine said she saw what looked like important papers.

"What is it?" I asked.

"I'd say we've found Mr. Claxton's buried treasure, Bertie."

"Buried treasure? What you talkin' about, Maxine?"

"Haven't you ever read a book called Treasure Island? These guys go looking for some loot that was buried by a pirate a long time ago. They finally find it, but not until they go through lots of trouble and danger. Kind of like you've had to do, Bertie. Just from a quick look in this box, I'd say there might be some buried treasure in here."

It took a minute for this to sink into my brain, it were so full of all the new information I had took in lately. But real quick I caught on an' I started laughin' an' my eyes got to waterin'. I took hold of myself long enough t' say, "One time, prob'ly the only time I got up the gumption to speak out to him, I told Homer I were goin' to git back at him somehow for all the mean aggravation he done give out t' me. I told him, 'Homer Claxton, some day, some day. . .'

"I couldn't think right then what that day would be like, I jist knew some day! But now, Homer's gone to a place where he cain't bother me no more, an' ever'thin' of his belongs to me, right? You think, Maxine, this might be the day I start gittin' back at Homer?"

WE SKIPPED LUNCH AT Slick's an' went straight to Maxine's attorney's office. I liked him right off. He were a tall man with white hair. He stooped a bit in the shoulders an' had a real kind smile. He brung to my mind the preacher I had heard one summer when Daddy took me to a revival meetin' at the fair grounds.

When Maxine interduced us, he smiled at me like we was old friends, like he were real glad to see me. He held my hand in both of his, an' talked directly to me, not to Maxine.

He said, "What can I do for you, Mrs. Claxton?"

I were next to bein' speechless. All I could think to say were, "I don't know." I looked at Maxine for help. She jumped right in there an' explained how things was for me now.

"We found this box in Mrs. Claxton's attic, Mr. Downing. She'd like for you to take a look at the contents and tell her what she should do with all this stuff. Do you have time for this right now?"

"Actually, I have to be in court shortly, but if you'd like you can leave it with my receptionist. I can get at it this afternoon but it may take a few days to go through the box. I'll work it into my scheduled appointments and call you as soon as I know what you've got here. Would that work for you, Mrs. Claxton?"

I hadn't got my voice back yet, so Maxine answered him.

"She's going to be staying with me for a while so you can reach her at my home number or my cell phone. Thanks for taking this on with no notice, Mr. Downing. We'll wait for you to call."

What with searchin' the house, then makin' a trip to the attorney's office, we hadn't ate no breakfast or lunch, an we's both starvin'. So on the way back to Maxine's we stopped at the Oriental Palace for supper. Maxine said it don't pay to cook for jist one person, so she ate out most of the time. The food were tasty, but different from what I were used to.

When we got to her place, we watched TV for a while. I had no idea what any of it were about. Homer didn't believe in watchin' TV.

The bed she put me in were bigger'n mine at the farm. Ever'thin' were different. I didn't sleep much that night.

Eight

Bertie

AFTER A WEEK AT Maxine's house, she dropped me off at the farm one mornin' afore goin' to open her store. Once she got the clerk ready for the day's business, she planned on comin' back to meet me at the farm an' wait for Mr. Downing's call while we started packin' the contents of the house.

It done seemed strange to be in my own house again. I hadn't wanted to spend any more time at the farm, but the movin' van would be there Friday mornin', so here I stood in the middle of the kitchen, lookin' around at where I used to live.

I needed to git this done so's we would be ready to tell 'em what to load up an' take to the storage unit we had rented. I were goin' to stay the night here by myself since Maxine had a meetin' that might go on late. I felt shy about doin' this on my own, but Maxine told me I would be jist fine.

"I can't be in two places at the same time, Bertie. I have a store to open up in the morning, remember? You can do this. Just pack up everything and we'll go through it later when we have more time. You don't have to make any decisions, just keep it all for now, okay? Start pretending you know what you're doing, and before long, you will. I mean, after all, how did you learn to bake bread when you were a little girl and no one there to show you how?"

"Well, I had watched my mama do it lots of times, so I took down her cookbooks an' follered the pictures. Took a bunch of times where we couldn't eat the mess I made, but after a while I got the hang of it."

"Same thing now, Bert, only easier, because we don't have to eat the stuff that gets packed. You can't hardly make a mistake. Talking about eating, don't forget to take a break once in a while and eat that fruit and sandwich we brought along for you. I put everything in the refrigerator, along with the carton of milk."

I stood in the doorway an' watched Maxine drive away. Funny, I thought, how easy it had been to forgit what life had been like here. I done settled into a new way of livin' real fast. When Maxine said my possessions had to be packed an' stored, I didn't take kindly to the idea. But today was the day, an' I were wantin' to git it over with.

MAXINE PULLED INTO THE driveway somewhere's around noon the next day, her car loaded down with lunch from the deli in town an' more packin' boxes. I met her at the door.

"Come on in, Maxine. I's jist settin' here thinkin' an' doin' a lot of smilin'. You wouldn't 'spose a body could smile after sech a life as I done had, but the more I think about it all, the more I smile. Ain't that peculiar?"

"No, not at all, Bertie. As a matter of fact, I think it's a good sign that you can still smile after living so long with that old coot

Claxton. Who, by the way, was even more of a scoundrel than we've known about so far. Are you ready for some bad news and some good news, Bertie?"

"Well, sure. I mean, I don't see how it could git any worse than it already is, so anythin' else can only be good news, right?"

"It's great you can think that way, Bertie, but just in case this all comes as a shock to you, maybe you better hold on to your hat.

"Here goes," Maxine announced. "Mr. Downing did a quick look-see through the papers in Homer's safe box, and he says you'll come out of this mess a fairly rich lady."

"What you talkin' about?"

"He says there's all kinds of stocks and bonds and stuff like that in there, most of them, he says, you should just leave alone for now. They bring in pretty good dividends every month or so, and most of the stock is valuable stuff, some of it's getting ready to split pretty soon."

"What d' you mean, split? Ain't they no good?"

I didn't know nothin' about stocks an' money an' all that. When Maxine told me what it meant for stock to split, I was standin' in the doorway, holdin' the screen door open from when she had hurried through it to give me the news.

"Good thing summer's over, Bertie, or we'd have a kitchen full of flies by now," she said. I let the door slam shut an' took a seat at the table

"I's confused, Maxine. Homer were jist a farmer. That's all he did in his whole life. How in the world would he ever know anythin' about the stock market, how to buy and sell stuff an' invest his money?"

"That's a mystery for sure Bertie. Might be a side to Homer Claxton we'll never know. On the other hand, they say the truth will always come out."

"What does all this mean, Maxine? I cain't hardly take no more in. I'm a ignorant old lady."

"No, you're not ignorant, Bertie, just uninformed. But I'm here to inform you of some bad news, and then I'll tell you the rest of the good news, and then you will be very well informed. So listen up.

"As Homer's only surviving relative, you will inherit his entire worldly goods, hereinafter known in legal terms, according to Mr. Downing, as his estate. Homer had investments that bring in roughly two thousand dollars a month in dividends and interest. He also had a bank account with a current balance of twenty-five thousand dollars, give or take some depending on what checks he may have written that haven't cleared the bank yet. The house itself is of little or no value since the fire, but if you decide to sell it, somebody will want it. There's lots of interest out there from people who want old farmhouses to fix up so they can live in the country while they commute back and forth to work."

"What? You mean to tell me I been livin' in this run-down house all them years with no indoor plumbin', wadin' through bad storms an' lightnin' jist to git to the outhouse, an' all the time Homer knowin' we was rich? Why, if I ever were mad at him for treatin' me s' bad, not talkin' to me an' actin' like I were nothin' to him, now I'm really mad. It's a good thing he's dead, Maxine.

"You suppose he would hear me down there where he's at if I's to yell real loud an' tell him what I think of him right now?"

I were walkin' around the kitchen in circles, shakin' my fist in the air, yellin' at a dead man, 'til Maxine thought I might git dizzy an' fall over.

"Bertie! Bertie, sit down. You're working yourself into a fit."

She pulled out a chair, took me by the arm an' pushed me into it, clampin' a hand over my mouth to stop me from shoutin'. After seein' what that part of the good news did to me, Maxine said she warn't sure she wanted to tell me anymore about what the attorney had found in the box. But I had to know, an' Maxine figgered she might jist as well git it over with all at one time.

"You got any whiskey, or wine, anything with alcohol in it, in the house," she said.

"Homer didn't keep alcohol around, Maxine. Why would you want a drink of that stuff anyhow?"

My question must of been funny 'cause it started Maxine to laughin'. I guess we both been needin' a good laugh after all the serious stuff goin' on, 'cause even though I didn't know what were funny, I started in laughin' along with Maxine until the tears was runnin' down both of our faces.

When we finally got hold of ourselves, Maxine said, "Whew, that probably did us both some good. I don't want a drink for me, Bert. I thought it might help you relax some, seeing as how you're so wound up and mad at Homer. But now, I have more to tell you, and I'm half afraid of what it might do to you. You sure you want to hear anymore today?"

"I got to hear it sometime, might as well be now. Go on ahead an' spit it out."

I smoothed the skirt of my dress over my legs an' folded my hands in my lap.

"Okay. I'm ready."

"Well, the bad news is this. Seems Homer saved everything. One of the papers in the box showed that about fifteen years ago, a real estate developer approached him and offered a lot of money for this property you're sitting on. Sounds good, huh? The bad news is, Homer sent him packing. There's a letter in that box from the developer thanking Homer for his time. The letter said the developer could appreciate Homer's reluctance to give up the property, said he understood the farm had been in the family for a long time and Homer didn't want to break it up into little pieces and sell it off to a bunch of city folks. He assured Homer he had no plans to do anything like that, but evidently Homer had made up his mind not to sell, seeing as how you're still living here."

I said that sounded like Homer. "He never trusted nobody. Didn't want to be around people, couldn't stand havin' 'em even come here to visit. Well, what's done is done, but I know this, Maxine, I don't want to live here no more. Too much work for me to do by myself, too many bad memories. I'm wantin' to be gone from here. How does a body go about sellin' a place like this? I don't know where to start, can you help me?"

Maxine's eyes lit up an' she broke into a big grin. "Well, here's the other half of the good news, Bert. Homer put that man's business card in the safe box with all the other papers. A phone call from Mr. Downing was all it took to discover that the developer is still interested in buying Homer's, uh, I mean, your farm. The man's name is Thaddeus Manning, he's a big real estate developer. Owns a bunch of properties in Manatee and Sarasota Counties. He was surprised but excited to hear you might want to sell out.

"Mr. Manning told Mr. Downing maybe Homer knew something a lot of other people didn't know about real estate back then. Mr. Manning offered Homer two-hundred-fifty thousand dollars for his farm, but these days it's worth a whole lot more than that. My attorney said without coming back out here with surveyors and a real estate appraiser, he's thinking the property might be worth, oh, say, somewhere around..."

Maxine stopped talkin' an' looked at me, jist set there wearin' a big smile.

"What? Why'd you stop talkin', Maxine? How much did he say? Tell me."

"You won't believe it, Bertie. He said don't hold him to it, it's a guesstimate. Could be less, could be more, but he's thinking you could get four, five-hundred-thousand dollars for the farm. Maybe more." Maxine set back in her chair an' waited while I stared at her.

"Are you foolin' me? You are foolin' me ain't you, Maxine Monk? Who'd give that kind of money for a run-down old farm? Who is this man? That's way too much, why I never heard of sech a thing?"

Maxine held up her hand an' signaled for me to stop talkin'.

"I'm telling you the truth, Bertie. And the beauty of it is, you don't have to do much of anything to sell it, if that's what you decide to do. Mr. Manning wants it real bad. You won't have to put up a sign, or advertise, nothing. Mr. Downing says he'll walk you through the whole deal from getting an appraisal to the closing of the sale. He wants to see you tomorrow to go over the details, if you'll come in. I'd be glad to drive you to his office if you want to talk to him."

Somethin' didn't set right with me about all of this. It was happenin' too fast an' sounded too easy. Years of livin' with Homer, guess I didn't trust good news. I had some questions needed to be answered.

"What does Mr. Downing git out of it, if I sell the place. He seems awful eager. He must git somethin' out of it."

"Well, sure, that goes without saying. I don't know what his fee would be for handling the sale, doing all the paperwork. I know that without a real estate agent you wouldn't have to pay a commission, so you'll save a whole bunch of money that way. So the attorney, whatever he charges, would be a bargain."

I waited for a beat or two, but Bertie just sat there.

"You're not saying anything, Bertie. What're you thinking?"

"What about you, Maxine? How come you're so willin' to help me with all this? What would you git out of it?"

Right off I were sorry for havin' said sech a thing. I seen the look on her face an' knew I had spoke wrong. But like I had told Maxine when she first come to the house right after the fire, I warn't used to bein' helped. If I couldn't do it for myself, it didn't git done. Since then, I had been lettin' her an' some others help me, but there warn't no money involved in none of their helpin'. Truth be told, I were alone in the world now, an' I were afraid of what might come down the road to me later. This here were a whole different thing.

"Well, all I'm askin', Maxine, you must stand to git somethin' out of the deal?"

"No, I won't get anything out of the deal, Bertie, except the satisfaction of helping you live a better life. I like to think we've become friends in the past month, and friends don't take advantage of friends, especially when it comes to money. I know you had a hard life being treated the way your daddy and Mr. Claxton treated you. But it's time you learn that most people in the world are not like they were." Maxine stood up an' headed for the door.

"I'll come back in the morning. If you want to see the attorney, be ready to go at nine o'clock. You can let him know what you decide to do. If you don't want to sell, he'll give you back Homer's safe box and you can do whatever you want with all his stuff."

Maxine let herself out, pullin' the door shut hard behind her. She didn't say goodbye, an' neither did I. Figgered it would be stupid to say goodbye to a closed door.

I didn't sleep good that night, either.

I GOT OUT OF the bed at dawn an' dressed in a hurry, finally gittin' excited about goin' home with Maxine. I stepped out onto the porch to wait for the sun to come up over the meadow one last time. I knowed it would be hours afore Maxine come to take me to the attorney's office.

I had stayed awake most of the night, starin' into the dark, thinkin' about what that attorney would tell me in the mornin'. Thinkin' about what my life had been like in the seventy years

I had lived on this earth. Wonderin' what my life would be like for the rest of my years. Wonderin' how long I had left to live.

I hadn't talked out loud to myself for a while, but now the words jist popped out like I was talkin' to somebody. After only a few sentences, I knowed I were talkin' to God.

"How come you let me live when Farley an' our baby boy died, God? How come I didn't die when my daddy took me back to his house, an' then made me marry old Homer Claxton? I tried to quit breathin' once, God, did you know that? I held my breath 'til I couldn't keep from lettin' the air come into my nose? I ain't never been no good to nobody, so how come you kept me alive all this time?

"I warn't even good 'nough for my mama. She jist left me here an' never come back for me. The only person in the whole world ever thought good of me were Farley. He said he could see me bloomin' right under his nose, like a flower. He loved layin' his head on my middle, feelin' our baby kick, an' he said that baby were another flower. Jist a bud, waitin' to git out of there an' open up, so then he'd have two flowers. We was goin' to be a bouquet, Farley said."

I thought on that a while, seein' in my head the flowers I brung in from the yard while Farley were alive, puttin' 'em in a jar on the kitchen counter. I started yellin' at God agin.

"They made the kitchen smell so good, an' they was so pretty. But you know what I learned from them flowers the first time I picked some after Farley got killed, God? One mornin' they was dead. I cut 'em off from their roots an' moved 'em into the house, an' they died. Jist like Farley an' the baby. Cut off an' dead. I decided, lookin' at them dead flowers, I warn't goin' to pick 'em anymore. I'm goin' to leave 'em be where they could live, growin' on they's stems.

"The way I figger it, God, flowers is like people. They do pretty good long as they's growin', but when they gits cut down, they die. I ain't goin' to cut no more flowers."

A thin line of light come up over the trees out in the meadow while I was standin' on the back porch, lookin' out at my new world an' yellin' at God. It was all different, now the barn an' the silo was gone.

Everythin' is changin'. I wonder what's next, I thought.

I HAD STEPPED INSIDE to put on the coffee when I heard the car door slam. I went to the door to wait for Maxine. I were goin' to apologize for the things I had said yesterday.

I held the door open for her, an' stepped back as she scooted past me. I poured out two cups of coffee an' set down across from her at the kitchen table.

I were the first one to say somethin'.

"I shouldn't of said them things yesterday. I'm sorry. You done so much for me an' I should of knowed you wouldn't hurt me no way. I'll git used to nice people after I'm around 'em for a bit, I reckon."

Maxine started to cry. She had to clear her throat afore her voice would work.

"Bertie, I feel lower than a snake's belly right now. You didn't do anything wrong, you've got no reason to apologize to me. I walked out on you last night.

"I did some hard thinking after I left here, and I figure I was kind of lifted up in my own pride, believing I was doing some wonderful thing for a person who needed help. I guess I had the idea you should be grateful to me and instead you questioned my motives. You are one of the most transparent people I've ever met, Bertie, and you saw right through me. Only it wasn't money I was after, it was recognition of my so-called goodness I was seeking. I'm asking you to forgive me, Bertie."

"You're the first real friend I ever had, Maxine. I don't never want to do nothin' agin to hurt your feelin's. Lord knows, they's been enough of that done to me, so I know how it feels for someone to think bad of you. An' I want you to know I appreciate ever'thin' you done for me. If I had to take care of all this stuff by myself, I'd still be settin' in this house ever' day, smellin' smoke an' wonderin' what in the world to do next. Let's jist forgit about yesterday an' go on bein' friends. I'm willin' if you are."

Maxine wiped her eyes with the back of her hand. She lifted her coffee cup in the air an' told me to do the same.

"We're going to make a toast to our friendship, Bertie, and pledge to always be there for each other."

I thought Maxine wanted to eat some breakfast, so when she explained what it meant to make a toast, I said I wanted to make a toast, too.

"I think that's a great idea, Bertie. What do you want to toast?"

"Put your cup back up in the air, Maxine. Give me a minute to think what I want to say."

I studied it out in my mind, then said my toast. "Here's to Homer Claxton an' my daddy, William Knight. I ain't mean like they was, so I'm not goin' to say nothin' bad about either one of 'em. I jist want to say I hope they both don't mind if I forgit they was ever part of my life."

Maxine almost laughed out loud, but she knowed I were serious, so she put her hand over her mouth an' said amen.

THE NEXT DAY I give Mr. Downing the go-ahead to git started on the sale of the farm. Thaddeus Manning, the real estate developer, said he couldn't hardly believe his luck. His idea for the farm, Mr. Downing told me, were to turn it into a senior livin' facility. He had been thinkin' on the plan in the back of his mind for fifteen years, ever since he first saw the place an' made his offer to Homer.

Mr. Downing went on to explain the situation to me.

"When your husband rejected Mr. Manning's offer, Mrs. Claxton, Mr. Manning was disappointed. There aren't too many places in this area that have all that your farm offers. Lots of trees, the good kind that can stay put and not have to be pulled down. The creek, and that little waterfall.

"Mr. Manning told me yesterday when I called him, he has plans to expand that waterfall into something really lovely, maybe use it as the central theme for a park inside the compound. I think he's leaning in the direction of making the property into a multi-purpose facility. You know, independent living, assisted living, maybe even adding a wing for folks who need more help than assisted living.

I didn't know what none of that stuff was.

"Um, can I answer any questions you might have, Mrs. Claxton? You look a bit confused."

"Well, yes, I do have some questions. I lived on the farm for sech a long time, I guess I don't know about all this kind of stuff. What is assisted livin' an' independent livin', what would them places be used for?"

I left the attorney's office that day a wiser woman than I had been that mornin'.

Nine

Bertie

I WARN'T FEELIN' REAL spry the next day an' told Maxine to go on ahead to breakfast without me. My stomach felt like chickens was flappin' around in there.

Maxine said she thought my upset stomach had somethin' to do with my emotions.

"After all, look at what you've been through," she said. " First, being made a widow, then the farm burning, learning about Homer's secrets. Now you're about to sell your home and start all over this late in your life. Why, if it was me, I'd probably be in the bathroom throwing up, but if you don't eat, Bertie, you'll get sick. What good will all this money do you if you're too sick to spend it?"

"Well, I don't feel like eatin', is all. My mind's so full of information, it's all pilin' up in there, Maxine. 'Sides all what I'm learnin' about money, an' sellin' the farm, do you know what today is? I woke up this mornin' rememberin' that two months ago today Homer come in from the field halfway through the mornin' complainin' he were sick. Now, I couldn't think of the last time Homer complained about bein' sick, much less leave off workin' an' come back to the house. I didn't know what to do about it, seein' as how nothin' like that had ever happened afore.

"I told him to go git on the couch for a spell, maybe he jist got too hot out there. You know yourself how hot it can git in August around here. 'Specially when you're out in the middle of the field with no shade around 'cept under the brim of your hat.

"Anyhow, he surprised me. Did what I told him to do for the first time ever. He got down on the couch an' fell sound asleep right away. Least I thought he were sleepin'. About a hour later I took him a glass of cold water thinkin' maybe it might help him feel better, but I knowed the minute I seen him layin' there so peaceful, he were dead. Even sleepin', Homer always had a mean look on his face, but this time he almost looked like he were smilin'. I tried to wake him up, but he were gone.

"Funny, Maxine, I stayed calm as ever I could be. I went out an' started up the pickup truck an' drove it over to the Bailey's farm an' asked Mrs. Bailey to call the doctor. Told her I thought Homer were dead."

"Good grief, Bertie, I didn't know you could drive," Maxine said.

"I cain't drive, never did learn how. I guess watchin' first my daddy an' then Homer doin' it, I knowed what to do, how to shift. But up until then, I never did drive for real. It jist kicked in. Course, I stalled the truck out a couple times on the way over there, forgot to mash down the pedal afore shiftin' gears. Half-way there, I almost drove into the ditch, but I made it."

"You had to be scared out of your wits by all of this," Maxine said.

"You would think so. But I warn't. What were interestin' to me, Maxine, it didn't seem to bother me that Homer were dead. Don't that say somethin' as to how I felt about him? When I git to thinkin' over the whole event, I feel like I should be ashamed of myself. But I ain't. I's jist relieved he's gone. I wish somebody would tell me I don't have to be ashamed to be shed of that man who were so mean to me."

"I'll tell you what I think," Maxine said. "I think God knew you'd put up with enough nonsense in your life, and took old Homer home with Him to teach him what was what."

I looked at Maxine real queer-like, an' spit out what I were thinkin'.

"You mean you're sayin' God's goin' to give Homer a chance to learn how he should of been? I never heard nobody talk about somethin' like that. Our preacher always said you git one chance an' you better git it right that time."

"Well, there's all kinds of religions floating around in this big, old world, Bertie. Some of them say bad people go straight to hell when they die and stay there forever. Some religions say you go to sleep when you die and don't know anything in your mind then until the day of resurrection. Others say when you die, that's it. It's over. Nothing else after that. And some religions believe that God, in His mercy, lets us be taught the things we didn't get while we lived on earth, and we can then accept God's teachings or not.

"So, who knows the real truth until we die and find out for ourselves? Me, I like to think we get another chance. Whatever the real truth is, my friend, I'm going to suggest you quit worrying about any of it and just enjoy whatever time you're going to have on this beautiful planet God gave us. Let Him sort it out. That's His job. You just be happy now, and make someone else happy whenever you can. How about it? Think you can handle that assignment?"

"I'll try, Maxine. I like what you jist told me. Makes me feel better already. How about I take you up on the breakfast offer? Where we goin'?"

We went where we mostly go to eat. Slick's Diner in town. On the way there, I told Maxine agin I were sorry for bein' so rude yesterday.

"I jist ain't used to all what's happenin' to me, I guess. It's a lot to take in so fast. But thinkin' on it after you left yesterday afternoon, I made me some decisions. You want to hear what they are?"

Maxine pulled into a parkin' spot at the diner an' turned to face me.

"Sure I want to hear them. What've you decided?"

"Well, for starters, I ain't never goin' to let somebody else tell me I got to do somethin'. If I don't want to do it, or I think I shouldn't do it, I won't. Next, I ain't never goin' to live in Homer's house agin. I need to ask you to help me find a place to stay, if you would."

"You know I will, Bertie. Anything you need that I can help with, I will. How soon do you want to move? If you want, you're welcome to stay with me as long as you need to, until we find a permanent place for you. Shoot, I always enjoy good company, and you're about the best I've had at my place since the last time it snowed in Florida."

"I appreciate it, Maxine. I like bein' around you, an' we're gittin' on real good, so I'll stay with you for a while. An' I thank you.

"The other decision I made, I'm goin' to go to school somewhere. I don't know nothin' about how a body my age could go to school, but I figger with all this money I'm goin' to have now I can pay for me to git a teacher to help me learn to talk better an' read better'n I do.

"I love books, Maxine, I had me some when I were real young. They was books for young'uns who was jist learnin' to read, but I read them books over an' over until they fell apart. I asked my daddy could he git some new ones for me, but he said what's a girl need to be readin' for? He said I should jist stick to doin' the work I had to do around the place.

"He stopped me goin' to school when I were about eight years old. The school sent people out to the house to check up on me, but he always took me out with him to the fields early of a mornin' so when the school people showed up they warn't nobody home. Lunchtime, he brung me back to the house so's I could do my chores an' fix us somethin' to eat.

"By an' by the school people didn't come around no more. It were farm country, an' most of the kids back then had to help with the plantin' an' all. I guess they figgered what's one more little girl out of all them other kids didn't come to school. When the books I had left from them days wore out, Daddy throwed 'em out an' I never had no more after that, 'cept for my mama's bible. I couldn't read most of them big words, an' the ones I could read I didn't understand what it were talkin' about, mostly. But I looked at that book til I about wore it out, too. Now I want to learn to read books that ain't so full of 'thees' an' 'thous.'"

"I'll bet we can find a tutor for you, Bertie, if that's what you want. I'll put a notice on the bulletin board in the store. That's where people advertise when they're looking for something or have something they want to sell. Would that be okay with you?"

"It sure would be, Maxine. Another decision I made is, I'm goin' to find some little girl what needs help like I needed but never got, an' I'm goin' to see she gits it. What good is havin' so much money if it jist sets in some bank an' rots. If I die without a penny to my name, I'll spend all it takes to keep somebody else from havin' to live like I done. I'm goin' to need help figgerin' out how to do all this, Maxine. I'm countin' on you to show me. I know I don't need to ask if you will, but I'm askin' jist to be polite. Will you help me?"

"You know I will, Bertie. I love your decisions. I'll do whatever I can to help with them."

"Thank ye, Maxine. I knowed you would. But there is one plan I ain't told you about yet. I'm excited about it, but I'm also dreadin' it. I know my mama is prob'ly gone to glory by now, but she were somewhere after she left me with my daddy an' went away. I want to find out where she been all them years.

"That's where I'm goin' to need you most. To help me find my mama."

It's a good thing we was at the diner by now, 'cause hearin' my last plan, Maxine's eyes was so full of tears I don't think she could of seen to keep drivin'.

Ten

Bertie

AFTER SPENDIN' THE NEXT few weeks off an' on at the farm packin' my earthly possessions, how Maxine called my stuff, we took a break on Thanksgivin' day an went to some of her friends' for a turkey dinner. I cain't remember havin' sech a good time since afore Farley died.

The friends turned out to be Sheriff Joe Turner, his wife, an' their growed-up kids an' grandkids. Mrs. Turner kept bringin' food out of the kitchen 'til I didn't think the table could hold it all. Ever'body were as stuffed as the turkey by the time we finished off the punkin pie an' coffee.

Sheriff Turner kept us laughin' with stories about his days in law enforcement, an' somewhere in the tellin', he asked me had I give any consideration to what might of started the fire out at my place.

He wondered if there might of been somebody holdin' a grudge against Homer, might of wanted to git even with him for somethin'.

"Did you ever hear Homer talk bad about anyone, Bertie? Or hear him talk about someone he thought maybe didn't like him?

If there was someone like that, maybe they thought by starting a fire, you know, arson, they could even the score."

"Well, Sheriff, I cain't think of nobody right off that Homer did like. As for who liked him, I cain't rightly say, seein' as how we was never around people all that much.

"I did notice whenever we was in town, though, there warn't too many folks even bothered talkin' to him, other than sayin' a polite hello. Other than that, I warn't privy to none of his business, so if he had a enemy, I wouldn't know it, I guess.

"I also don't know what that word "arson" is, Sheriff. Does it have somethin' to do with bein' a friend to somebody?"

"No, it has to do with not bein' someone's friend, Bertie. It means setting a fire on purpose with the intent to damage something. You think you might know anyone would want to damage Homer's farm for some reason?"

"Well, like I said, I can't think who would want to start a fire on purpose."

Sheriff Turner said if I didn't mind, he would do some lookin' into it, see if he might come up with anythin' suspicious.

I told him to go ahead an' do what he thought needed to be done. Tryin' to go to sleep that night, all I could think about were the fire. Land's sake alive.

Arson?

Eleven

Bertie

THE MOVIN' VAN ROLLED up to the farmhouse early that Friday afternoon, an' real quick the men had ever'thin' loaded. We followed the van to the storage unit to make sure the right boxes was put in last so's they'd be easy to git to later for sortin' out an' throwin' away the stuff I warn't goin' to keep.

Maxine said later as we drove into her driveway, "Now, doesn't it feel good to have that job done?

"I think a hot shower and a BLT sandwich would hit the spot right about now. Then we'll spend the evening sitting on the porch watching the sun go down. A sound night's sleep between sun-dried sheets, and tomorrow we'll both be good as new. What do you say to that plan, my friend?"

I had to say that sounded real good. Maxine said for me to go take a shower, she were goin' to go pick one of the last tomaters on the vine. She called it a November survivor.

Right about then I got homesick. Imagine that. Thinkin' about pickin' a tomater that I had growed from a seed, pullin' it off the vine an' puttin' it in my apron pocket, then holdin' my hands together an' smellin' the odor of the leaves, why I declare,

THE MYSTERIES OF TREMONT MEADOW 57

I had to hurry an' git in the bathroom so's Maxine wouldn't see how sad I was feelin' right then.

I guess no matter how bad things is, what it comes down to is our home is still where we want to be. I felt like I didn't have no place to call my own.

After we et our BLT's, we set in the rockers on Maxine's front porch, waitin' to watch the sunset. We was gittin' to know each other pretty good by now, so I spoke my mind.

"I been wonderin' about somethin', Maxine."

"What's that, Bertie?"

"Well, you never talk about yourself. So far, we jist talked about me an' my troubles. You surely have been helpful to me, gittin' ever'thin' straightened out. But I don't know nary a thing about you."

"I don't talk much about myself, Bertie. It's been a long, hard road from where I started to here. It's not pleasant to think about the mistakes I've made along the way, the things I could've done better. Compared to my awful decisions, you are a saint. I've done so many things wrong, I've kept God working overtime in the forgiveness department."

"I cain't hardly believe that about you, Maxine. You're a good person, I know you are, jist from all you done for me since we met."

"You're easy to do for, Bertie. I'm talking about mistakes I made, bad decisions, that have had a lasting effect on my life as well as on my children's lives."

"You got children, Maxine? That's wonderful! I always wanted children, but after losin' our baby, an' then Farley, I done got stuck with Homer."

"Well, you could still have had children, Bertie. I know you weren't especially fond of Homer, but if you wanted kids, you should've had some. You'd have been a good mother."

When I chuckled, Maxine asked me what were funny.

"Homer Claxton, that's what's funny. See, I never really knowed him afore we got hitched. I guess my daddy bein' by hisself on the farm after I married Farley, he were feelin' lonely. So when he met up with Homer at a cattle auction one night, they started socializin' with each other a bit. Their families knowed each other from way back, but hadn't never been real neighborly. Anyhow, he started askin' Homer over to the house to set on the porch of a evenin'. An' Homer would have Daddy over to his place once in a while to help with balin' the hay, like farmers do sometimes. Homer stayed to home, mostly, after I moved back in with my daddy, so there warn't much chance to git to know him. They warn't nothin' big between 'em, they warn't real thick, but if Daddy ever had a friend of any kind, I'd say it were Homer.

"So, ten years after Farley died, the two of 'em come up with the idea to marry me off to Homer. By the time he married me, Homer were used to bein' alone, if you know what I mean."

I seen Maxine shift in her chair, uneasy-like, but I jist kept on talkin', hopin' she wouldn't be put off by what I were tellin' her.

"We was married afore I knowed what were happenin'. But the real truth is, Maxine, nothin' happened. Homer warn't interested in bein' a real husband, I don't think. Me an' Homer never talked much about anythin' unless it had to do with what he expected me to do around the place. He never talked about nothin' personal. You know, havin' no wife, maybe he jist wanted someone to cook for him an' keep his house clean an' do the farm chores the women in a family kept up with.

"The thought crossed my mind a time or two that my daddy might have give Homer some money to marry me. That way Homer had someone to look after him, and my daddy wouldn't have to worry none about me after he were gone. So, early on, I knowed I warn't never goin' to have children."

"Oh, Bertie. After the heartache of losing your baby at birth, didn't it make you sad that you'd never have another child?" Maxine asked.

"At first it did, but after gittin' to know Homer, I were glad. I didn't like to think what kind of daddy he might be, so I put it out of my mind. I didn't want no children I might of had to grow up with a daddy anythin' at all like William Knight or Homer Claxton.

"But, now, here I go, tellin' you more about my life when you're supposed to be tellin' me about yours. I'm goin' to be quiet an' let you talk for a spell."

"Well, okay. I guess if we're going to be friends, real friends, you ought to know who you're dealing with here. It's not a pretty story, and you may be sorry you asked. Where would you like me to start?"

"I don't know, Maxine. I guess how far back you go depends on how much you're wantin' to tell."

"How far back? I'd like to go all the way back and do it over again. Only the next time I'd like to remember everything I did wrong so I could finally do it right. That's impossible, I know. Maybe the best any of us can do is help some young lady along the way, teach her how to avoid the mistakes we made. My problem is, I don't know any young ladies who'd listen. Why is it, Bertie, we all seem to resent it when someone older tries to share their wisdom with us?

"Anyway, before I get on my soapbox, let's get back to where we were with our stories."

Twelve
Maxine

AS FAR BACK AS I needed to go with my story was high school in Chicago. Before that, I was pretty much like any girl, but then, at the beginning of the tenth grade, this kid sat down next to me in our history class. Black hair, big brown eyes, wrestling team captain.

We were crazy in love with each other from the beginning. so much so that we went through high school together and then on to college. The week after we graduated college we were married. We did it all the right way. He gave me a big, beautiful engagement ring for Christmas, and in June we had the big, beautiful wedding.

Our parents helped us with the down payment on a big, beautiful house. Everyone said it was a perfect match. A match made in heaven. It didn't last. After five years of marriage and two babies, he left.

"He left? Why?" Bertie asked.

"Well, Bertie, my theory, after the shock wore off, was that being tied down to one girl from the time he was fifteen years old until he was twenty-seven was too much responsibility for him. He had to go sow his wild oats. When I finally came to my senses and analyzed how he went about the whole thing, I realized he was an out-and-out rascal."

"How'd he go about it?"

"As I said, he left. He left me with the two kids, he left me with the house payment, he left me with the dog, and he left with his girlfriend in the front seat of his convertible and the contents of our checking account and all our savings in his briefcase.

"The only time I heard from him after that was when I finally divorced him for desertion. He called once, to tell me he was broke and couldn't pay the child support the judge ordered. Never heard from him again, haven't seen him, either. That was back in the day when the courts didn't do much to enforce child support, so I forgot about him and moved on.

"It took me a few years to stop defending him. I was a real wimp back then. Right about the time I had to sell the house, though, my thinking changed. We hadn't had the house long enough to build up any equity, so after I paid the real estate commission and closing costs, there wasn't any money left for me. I worked at whatever I could find, but it's almost impossible to raise two kids on minimum wage."

"Well, you had went to college, Maxine. Why couldn't you earn any money?"

"My degree was in art history. That was the easiest course I could find. I went to college just to be where my future husband was. I realized after he left the only reason I went to college was because I thought someone else might nab him while he was away from me. Try to find a job where a degree in art history comes in useful. Ha.

"Anyhow, I sold the house and moved myself and the kids into one of the housing projects on the outskirts of Chicago. I think it cost somewhere around twenty-five dollars a month to live there. Tiny little rooms, but the neighbors were great. There was a family who lived there, the mom and dad started a church, went around and picked up anyone who needed a ride. They got the neighborhood kids involved in vacation bible school, lots of activities like that, so it was good for my kids to be there.

"The bad thing about living there though, no pets were allowed. So I gave the dog away. Now I had to listen to my three-year-old son cry because he thought his pal, Rex, was lost. He finally quit crying over the dog, but he still cried all the time because he missed his daddy.

"One of my neighbors was a woman who was going to college on some kind of a grant. That's money you can get under the right circumstances and you don't have to pay it back after you get your education. Told me I should look into it. Sounded good to me, so I applied, and the next thing you know, I was back in college, this time working for my degree in nursing."

"So you're a nurse. How come you ain't workin' at the hospital?"

"Well, for one thing, Bert, I've got the store to run. That's enough for an old lady like me. I did work as a nurse, though, at a hospital in Illinois. Little Company of Mary. Loved it, eventually. But the first day on the job was tragic. I ran into a nurse's aide who was carrying a bedpan to the bathroom to empty it. That's what they were called back then, nurse's aides, nowadays they're CNA's. Anyhow, I was in a hurry, nervous would be a better word, trying to do everything right, and I literally ran into her. The bedpan went flying.

"Man, I hate to even remember that day. Of course, the contents of the bedpan slopped all over the nurse's aide, me, the floor. Housekeeping had to be called, the Director of Nursing showed up. I was the talk of the whole hospital. Word spread like the fire on your farm. The aide and I both had to go home, we were a mess, and I was so shook up I couldn't concentrate.

"The next day I think I saw more of the floor than I did of the patients. Couldn't look anyone in the eye. When I went to lunch in the cafeteria, I found the table farthest away from everyone and sat by myself. I wasn't hungry, so I just bought a carton of milk. There I sat, drinking my lunch, thinking about quitting the nursing business before I was barely started, when someone asked if the empty seat at my table was taken. I looked up and saw this guy standing there with a tray full of food. He had the kindest look on his face. I recognized him. He was one of the resident doctors who'd been on our floor the day before and witnessed my bedpan incident.

"I asked him if he saw anyone sitting there. Told him it's a free country. Sit where you want to. I'm finished here, anyway. I stood up to leave, and he said I didn't have to go, as a matter of fact, he said, he could use some company. Said he was new at the hospital, too, and asked me to stay.

"I hadn't gotten over my bad experience with my husband, and I sure didn't want any more men in my life right then. Maybe never. But I sat down because I didn't know what else to do.

Neither one of us said anything for a few minutes, he just gobbled up his food like he was starving. He kept smiling at me. Finally he pushed his plate away and stared me straight in the eyes.

"'Look,'" he said, "'everyone makes mistakes, especially when they're the new kid on the block and trying too hard. Give the others a break, okay, and forget about what happened yesterday. I've always found if you let them, other people can be pretty nice.'

"Then he sat back and waited. I didn't say anything, I cried. The past four years had been all hard work, going to school, raising the kids by myself. If it hadn't been for the kids I would have caved in.

"I sure surprised myself, because that resident and I became friends, and then we started dating. Within a year of meeting him, we got married. Had a small ceremony at City Hall, and then, the same people I was so afraid of when I started working at Little Company pitched in and threw us a reception in one of the conference rooms at the hospital.

"I won't tell you his name, Bert, because he's a pretty well-known doctor by now, retired from practice, but still involved in research at a private lab."

"Well, I ain't never been in no hospital, 'cept when I had my baby. An' I ain't never been to Chicago, so it's for sure I wouldn't know his name. But I promise, Maxine, I won't never say a word about him."

"Anyway, he moved in with me and the kids in our tiny little apartment. Both bedrooms were so small there was barely enough room to walk around the beds, and what with all the stuff that comes with raising kids, the place was really crowded. Sometimes I would get cabin fever so bad I had to go outside to get away from it all for a few minutes. My husband promised me as soon as he finished his residency and started his own practice, things would be better.

"So, now I had two kids and myself to support, and a new husband to take care of. For the next two years my life consisted of getting the children up, packing their lunches, putting them on the school bus, packing myself a lunch and getting ready for work, while my husband slept for a few hours between shifts at the hospital. After work, I picked up the kids from after-school care, fixed supper for the three of us, supervised their homework and school projects, and fell into bed when they did. I was exhausted all the time."

"I thought I had a hard life, Maxine, but all I had to do for was me an' Homer. What happened to that husband? I'm guessin' you ain't still married to him, since you live by yourself."

"Yep. You guessed it. What happened to him is, I came home unexpectedly from work one day, so sick with the flu I couldn't keep anything in my stomach. I opened the bedroom door, stepped inside, and stopped dead in my tracks. My husband was in our bed with a student nurse. I'm not sure if it was the shock of seeing him there, or if it was the flu, but I lost it. Literally. I had an emesis basin in my hand, planning to lay down before I up-chucked again, but I never made it into the bed, since it was already occupied. I did vomit, though. All over the sheets, my husband, and the cute little nurse in the bed next to him."

Bertie busted out laughing, but stopped real quick and said, "I'm sorry, Maxine. That ain't funny."

"You haven't heard anything yet, Bert. He jumped out of the bed and her right behind him clutching at the sheet. He started yelling at me, said, 'For Pete's sake, Maxine, what's the matter with you'?"

"His girlfriend tripped over the sheet, she was in such a hurry to get out of there. She fell in the doorway to the bathroom just as I was headed there myself. There we were, her on the floor all tangled up in the bed sheets, and me trying to get around her and into the bathroom before I lost it again. I didn't make it. Guess where the rest of my breakfast landed?"

We both knew this shouldn't have been funny, but we were laughing real hard anyhow. It took me a few minutes to get serious again, and then I said, "Sad, isn't it, Bertie, that we would laugh at something so sinful." She nodded yes without saying a word.

"Anyway, the first thing he did after he got dressed was give me some medicine to stop the vomiting. While we waited for that to work, he put the student nurse in the shower and sent her home as soon as she put her clothes on. Then he cleaned up the mess in the bedroom.

"I felt a little better and was sitting at the kitchen table sipping a glass of ginger ale when he came out of the bedroom with the sheets in a basket and put it outside the door to take to the laundromat. I thanked him for cleaning things up, and that did it. He got really worked up, telling me what had been on his mind for a long time, said he should be apologizing to me, I shouldn't be apologizing to him. He said I was such a martyr, it was driving him crazy. Said I made him nuts, always putting him in the position of trying to make me feel good about myself. He asked me why I was like that, always thinking I was at fault for everything.

"He told me he'd been seeing other women because they made him feel important. Said he spent so much time trying to make me feel good about myself, there was nothing left over for him. He knew it was wrong, but there it was. He was leaving, he said, not because he was in love with that student nurse. He didn't even know her last name, how about that? But she made him feel like he was important.

"I told him I thought he was important. 'You're a doctor, for crying out loud, I'm just a nurse.'" He said, 'Maxine, I'm a self-centered, lowlife, cheating, dependent piece of scum who treats you badly. And you are a very good nurse. You know why I married you?'

"I couldn't answer him, Bertie. Just stood there crying and finally shook my head no.

"He said he married me because my neediness appealed to him. Said I made him feel like that young girl made him feel today. Pretty quick into the marriage, he said he realized that feeling sorry for someone wasn't good enough, wasn't the same as loving someone. He said my putting him before the kids and myself started to get to him, made him realize I didn't have any self-esteem. He didn't respect me.

"I asked him if he wanted to stay, or was he leaving. The one thing I had going for me back then was I usually went right to the heart of a matter."

"You still do," Bertie told me.

"Well, he said he left a long time ago, he just forgot to tell himself he was gone. Said as soon as he found a place of his own, he'd be out of there. Then he told me to go to bed. Said he'd pick up the kids. Said he doubted they would miss him after he left since they hardly ever saw him, with them being in school and him at the hospital most of the time. Said he wasn't like their real dad, or anything, but I was thinking, '*Oh yes you are, you're just like him*'.

"Then before he left to get the kids, he asked if I wanted him to pick anything up for me while he was out. You know what I did?"

"No."

"I swore at him. Something I almost never do. I said, 'Just get the bleep out of here. Stop trying to help me.'

"I slammed the bedroom door shut in his face and fell into the clean sheets he had just put on the bed. I bawled like a baby until I fell asleep."

BERTIE AND I SAT there for a few minutes, me lost in my thoughts of the past, Bertie probably not knowing what to say that would be a comfort to me.

Finally, I stood up and said, "Well, speaking of falling into clean sheets, that's what we ought to do, Bert. Let me finish this some other time. What with the moving van today and all this telling we've been doing, I'm drained. I think we both need a good night's sleep."

Bertie said, "Go git in the bed an' rest now. Don't be frettin' over the past. Like you told me the other day, what's done is done, an' now we move on. Ain't that like you said it?"

"Yes, it is. Thank you for reminding me. And I want you to know something, Bertie. I love you."

I couldn't remember anybody sayin' that t' me since Farley died, an' I couldn't bring myself to say it back, not even to Maxine.

Instead, I said, "Well, thank ye, Maxine. G'night now."

Thirteen

Bertie

LIFE THESE DAYS WAS like goin' to school. Ever' day I learnt somethin' new, jist not what I had planned on.

Once Maxine opened her store of a mornin', two clerks kept it up an' runnin', so 'cept for a Town Council meetin' once in a while, most days she had lots of free time. She spent some of that time educatin' me to the ways of the world.

One mornin' she announced our plans for the day as we was eatin' breakfast.

"Bertie. We're going shopping today."

"What you need to buy, Maxine?"

"I don't need to buy anything, my friend. You, on the other hand, need everything from the skin out."

In the two weeks I been stayin' at Maxine's, she had seen ever' piece of clothes I owned.

"Your wardrobe needs a serious overhauling. First we're headed for Guilford's Lingerie Shoppe and you are going to find out what today's woman wears for undergarments."

The first time we did our warsh together, Maxine couldn't hardly believe I had been wearin' the same two brassieres an' the same six pair of cotton underwear for as long as I could recall. She most had a tizzy fit at the sorry shape they was all in. I had to tell her not to go on so.

"What in the world do I need with more'n that? Nobody see's 'em but me, an' I don't look at 'em, I jist put 'em on of a mornin' an' cover 'em up with a dress."

"Yeah, and that's another thing, Bertie. You wear one of two dresses every day. Your brown one or your blue one."

"Now that ain't so, Maxine. I got my pretty pink dress with the little flowers in it for Sundays. I reckon a body don't need more'n that."

"Well, humor me, dear one. I get tired of looking at the same two outfits all the time. My eyes are starting to burn."

I laughed. "You say the funniest things, Maxine. I guess if you want to, I'll let you gussie me up some. Jist don't go gittin' too fancy, you hear?"

We walked out of Guilford's, both of us carryin' a shoppin' bag in each hand. Puttin' 'em in the trunk of the car, I eyed what we had bought.

"Mercy. How many of them underpants did you tell 'em to put in there? I think you got ever' color of the rainbow in that bag, Maxine. Why, I ain't never had nothin' but white underwear afore.

"An' I were only goin' to git two brassieres. What'd we wind up with, about ten? An' panty hose. Where in the world am I goin' to wear them things?"

"Stop fussing, Bertie. Once you get used to looking like a lady, you're going to be happy to have all this stuff. Now get in the car, we're heading over to Joan's Boutique to look at clothes.

And if I hear you mention the United Protestant Thrift Store one more time, I'm going to tape your mouth closed."

Maxine run around the Misses section at Joan's, pullin' clothes off the rack an' handin' 'em to the sales clerk while I stood in one spot an' watched.

"Okay, Ms. Claxton," Maxine joked. "Get in that fitting room and try some of this stuff on. Uh-uh-uh, I don't want to hear it," she said, when I started to object.

"Remember, you are humoring me. And I don't want to hear anything about the slacks. Just put them on with that purple blouse and the taupe sweater."

I stuck my head out the door of the dressin' booth. "What is tope? Should I tuck in the blouse or leave it hangin' out over the slacks? I don't know how to put this stuff on, Maxine."

"Taupe is the only sweater in there, Bertie, and leave the blouse out. That's how it's supposed to be worn."

Two hours later we walked out of Joan's loaded down with more bags, an' headed next door to the Shoe Shoppe. By now I didn't have no energy left to complain.

Back at Maxine's, bags an' boxes ever'where, we set at the table sippin' a cup of hot tea an' munchin' on shortbread cookies.

"I'm so tired, I don't think I have 'nough energy to put all this away," I complained. But I were smilin' when I said it.

AFTER SETTLIN' IN AT Maxine's, I got restless. I missed the chores that had kept me busy on the farm. I missed the steer, the goat, an' the squawky chickens. I even missed the ornery hogs an' their noisy squeals, rootin' through the slop I throwed at 'em ever' day.

Mostly though, I missed the cow. She always come to the fence an' rubbed her head on my back an' mooed when I walked away an' left her standin' there after I done finished the milkin'.

'What can I do around here? I feel useless jist settin' all day, lookin' at the walls." I was walkin' around the room talkin' to Maxine.

"Yeah, I know," Maxine said. "I've been watching you. You look like that willow tree out in my front yard when the wind blows, the branches moving around and around without going anywhere.

"I have an idea, Bert. Now, don't take this the wrong way, you hear? I'm not trying to get rid of you. As far as I'm concerned, you can stay with me for as long as you want, but I see you chomping at the bit. I'm going to suggest we start looking at houses and apartments for you. I have a few places in mind to start with. Would you like that?"

"Yes, I would. Let's git at it."

"Okay. Hot dog. One stop we need to make before we head on out, Mr. Abbott from the bank called while you were putting on your new duds. Said something about the bank account, getting your name on it. You need to sign a card so your signature is on file at the bank."

"Well, I don't know how I'm goin' to take care of a bank account, Maxine. Homer did all that kind of stuff."

"I bet Mr. Abbott will be more than happy to teach you whatever you need to know, Bertie. We'll talk to him about helping you while we're there. In the meantime, let's get going and see if we can find you the perfect place to live!"

Mr. Manning was settin' in the waitin' area as me an' Maxine walked into the bank. Standin' up, he smiled at the two of us.

"Hello, Mrs. Claxton, you're looking lovely this morning. I like that taupe sweater, it really complements your hair color."

I reached up an' patted the thick braids on top of my head.

"Well, thank ye, Mr. Manning. I never think about what color it is, jist the same old browny-grey stuff been up there all them years."

When I thought nobody was lookin', I reached up an' tucked in a stray piece of hair.

Mr. Manning was talkin' to Maxine now.

"Hello, Mrs. Monk. Is this a coincidence, or are you two here to meet with me? I have so much on my mind lately, I sometimes forget my appointments."

Maxine said, "No, we didn't know you were going to be here, Mr. Manning. Bertie came in to sign some signature cards for her bank account, then we're headed out to look for a new place for her to live. She's decided she doesn't want to be out there in the country any longer.

"She's staying with me for a while. I don't mind her being there at all, she's great company. But she's eager to be on her own, you know?"

"Yes, I can imagine," he said. "Listen, if you want I can arrange a showing for you today at a condominium complex I own, Egret Gardens. It's a lovely place. In fact, Mrs. Manning and I live there. I feel certain you'd be comfortable there, Mrs. Claxton. Would you like to see it?"

Me an' Maxine looked at each other, waitin' for the other one to answer. Finally, Maxine spoke up.

"What do you say, Bertie? At the very least, it's a place to start."

Turning to Mr. Manning, Maxine said, "We have a few places lined up to look at today, but we ought to be done with them before lunch. Where is this place?"

"It's the new building on Siesta Key. We're at about eighty percent capacity now, with new people coming in every day."

He wrote the address down on one of his business cards an' held it out to Maxine.

"Oh gosh, Mr. Manning. You need to give that to Mrs. Claxton. She's in the process of learning to take care of herself, you know. I'm real proud of the way she's taking over everything she can."

"That's right," I said. "I'm even thinkin' of lookin' for a job, once everthin' is settled about the farm. I don't have the least idea what I could do, but I figger there must be somethin' out there for me to work at. All I ever done were housework an' cookin' an' sech as that, so I might look for a job keepin' house. Must be somebody out there needs a person to clean an' cook some tasty meals for their family."

Real quick-like, Mr. Manning said, "Mrs. Claxton, you will be very well off financially in a short while. Why in the world do you want to work? There will be no need for that, you know."

"I do know that, but I ain't ready to sit down an' not git up agin 'ceptin' to take care of personal needs, or git a drink of water. Why land's sake, I'd be dead afore long if I jist set around with nothin' to do all day but watch the television. If I can make somebody comfortable, fill up their belly with good, hot food, maybe comfort a sick person once in a while, that's more'n some people's able to do. Until these old bones won't work anymore, I aim to earn my keep. An' there ain't nobody goin' to talk me out of it, so don't try."

"I admire you, Mrs. Claxton. Many people in your situation would do as you say you don't want to do. They would take advantage of their new wealth and quit functioning. I think it's a wise choice you're making. I'll keep my eyes and ears open, let you know if I come across something that you might want to look into.

"In the meantime, I'll call ahead so when you go to look at the condo it will be open. It's on the top floor, six stories up, and gives a marvelous view of Sarasota Bay. I think you might like it."

"Oh, thank ye, Mr. Manning, but I don't think that would work for me. Some days out at the farm I had a time gittin' up the steps into the hen house, an' them stairs up to my bedroom, why I was thinkin' of movin' my bed down to the parlor. I know I couldn't git up all them steps to the top floor of your apartment buildin'."

Right then, Mr. Manning turned his head to look at the paintin' on the wall. He must of liked the picture, 'cause he was smilin' at it.

Still lookin' at the picture, he said, "No need to climb steps, Mrs. Claxton. The building has a lovely elevator that will take you straight to the top."

As we was walkin' to Mr. Abbott's office, I said to Maxine, "Well, if I didn't feel dumb. I should of knowed a fancy buildin' like Mr. Manning owns would have a elevator in it."

OUR MEETIN' WITH MR. Abbott put me in charge of Homer's bank account. I told him I would need lots of help doin' whatever needed to be done, 'cause Homer never told me nothin' about his money.

Mr. Abbott said he'd teach me what I needed to know, but more'n that he said he would be happy to continue takin' care of Homer's portfolio, if I wanted him to do that, also. 'Course, he had to explain to me what was a portfolio!

What me an' Maxine learned that day answered the question we been askin' – how did Homer know to buy them stocks and stuff, invest his money an' all he did to git so rich?

Mr. Abbott said Homer done overheard a few of the men talkin' at the cattle auction some years back about their investments. One of the men mentioned a Mr. Abbott from the local bank. Said this Mr. Abbott knowed a lot about that kind of stuff.

About a week after the auction Homer come and asked Mr. Abbott to take a look at his bank account, see if he had enough to do somethin' like those other men was doin'. Mr. Abbott was surprised at the amount he had saved up over his lifetime. Homer told him he didn't buy nothin' that warn't necessary, which kinda explained the shape his farm were in when it caught fire.

Well, they got busy with investin' and now that Homer's dead, I got all this to manage. One more thing I don't know what to do with.

It only took me a real short time to tell Mr. Abbott I didn't want nothin' to do with a bunch of stuff I don't understand and I wanted him to sell ever'thing.

Another big decision for my new life.

I felt like a load been lifted off my brain an' left behind at the bank! I was ready to start lookin' for a new home, so me an' Maxine headed for Mr. Manning's condominium to see what he had to offer.

I hadn't never seen a room like the one we walked into at Egret Gardens. Maxine said it were called the vestibule. I told her I didn't have no words to describe sech a pretty place, so she did it for me.

She stood up real straight an' started pointin' at parts of the room like them fancy young girls do on some of the television game shows I been watchin', talkin' like the announcer talks when he's describin' stuff to the audience. She were so funny, it made me laugh.

"The cream-colored tile floor is divided into sections by rich area rugs woven in yellow, pink and magenta hibiscus flowers. Giant tropical plants, scattered here and there at random, seem to grow out of the floor. At the edge of the lobby in a caged atrium, water flows out of a fountain into the foliage below, forming a pool at the foot of a huge snowy egret carved from white marble. The egret stands poised on one foot, head cocked to one side, with its plumage spread in full regalia atop its head."

"That statue looks like it's goin' to take off flyin' in a minute," I whispered to Maxine.

"Bertie, Look." Maxine pointed.

Three big birds come walkin' across the lawn like they was in slow motion an' went right into the atrium. A lady walked out from behind a desk an' joined us.

"How do you do, I'm Julie Rae, the receptionist here at Egret Gardens. Mr. Manning called and said to expect you. I'm to show you around.

"Those two large birds with the plumes are Great Blue Herons, and the one with red on its head is a Sandhill Crane. Aren't they beautiful?"

Julie Rae told us why the atrium were inside the vestibule.

"Mr. Manning's wife, Grace, enjoys the out-of-doors, especially the lovely birds of Florida, so when he built Egret Gardens, he decided to bring the outdoors inside to her.

"The Mannings live in this building, you know, and whenever he has time, Mr. Manning brings her down here. She loves to sit and watch the birds wander around inside the atrium, coming and going from the lawn behind the building.

"We back up to the bay, and there are plenty of fish in the water. It's what keeps the birds coming back. That, plus the bread our residents give them. Mr. Manning has a rule that bread can only be given to the birds at certain times. He doesn't want them to start depending on human food, so the bread is considered a treat for them.

"The birds have learned the bread schedule, as the residents call it, and they come flocking around at those times. It's quite a sight. You should come some time to watch."

Julie Rae said they was two residences on the top floor. The Mannings was in one of 'em, an' the other one were still available. She had went up there an' unlocked it, an' said we should go on up an' make ourselves at home.

STEPPIN' OUT OF THE elevator on the sixth floor, we decided it were as beautiful as the vestibule, an' Maxine started describin' ever'thin' agin, sayin' she were goin' to be my tour guide an' explain things to me as we went.

"The yellow, pink and magenta colors in the carpet are blended together, giving the effect of a renaissance painting. The walls are covered in pale, textured wallpaper, intercepted here and there with mirrored panels that reflect light from the overhead crystal chandeliers."

I asked Maxine how she knowed all them big words an' how to describe what we was lookin' at.

"I haven't always lived on a farm, Bertie. I studied art history in college. I'll tell you about a different part of my life someday when we get back to talking about our past. Right now, let's go have a look at the rest of this place."

I follered her across the wide hall an' looked through the open door at the empty condominium, as Maxine said it were called. She drawed in a deep breath an' blew it out in a quiet whistle. Slappin' me square in the middle of my back, most knockin' me off my feet, Maxine declared, "I think you've arrived, Ms. Claxton. Welcome home."

Walkin' through the door of the condominium onto soft cream-colored carpet, I gawked at the windows. Maxine described 'em for me in her tour guide voice.

"Arched at the top, the panels travel from ceiling to floor, filling the room with light as the sun shines through the leaded glass." Maxine had her head back, starin up at the cypress beams hangin' from the ceilin.

"Look!" I nudged Maxine with my elbow an pointed to the left of what Maxine called the foyer.

"Tell me how you would describe all this, Maxine, I ain't got the words for it."

The tour guide was back. "In the living room, sliding glass doors open into an atrium, reproduced on a miniature scale to the one in the downstairs vestibule. Hanging in midair, the atrium clings to the side of the building. Filled with tropical plants, and open above a wrought iron guard rail, it provides shelter and food for the birds that eat from the feeder attached inside the opening. Benches around the edge of the atrium's deck provide a place to sit and observe the birds as they fly in and out, while a screen keeps the birds from entering the condo when the sliding doors are open."

Maxine's eyes was as wide as mine, an' her mouth were hangin' open when she finished talkin'.

"Close your mouth, Maxine, afore you swaller one of them birds."

Maxine pointed up at somethin', an' when my eyes follered her finger all I could say were, "My word, ain't that somethin'?"

"How in the world did they do that?" asked Maxine.

A hint of blue color covered the ceilin', sprinkled with clouds so thin they's almost invisible.

"Now, that is pretty," said Maxine. "Let's look at the rest of this place, Bertie."

"That's white granite on the countertops of those cherrywood cabinets in the bathrooms," Maxine said. "The place fairly glows from the aura produced by diffused sunlight on golden wood and white stone."

"This is how I imagine Heaven's goin' to look like," I said.

Maxine said, "If I was to write the copy for an article in a magazine about this place, here's what it would say:

"Pale seafoam-green tile, splashed throughout with what can only be compared to the white foam that washes ashore the beach at high tide, covers the floors in all three of the generous bathrooms. Beveled mirrors hide the shelves inside the natural cherrywood cabinetry. Walls vary in color in each bathroom, the hues taken from Florida sunsets. On one side of the master bathroom, a walk-in shower is fitted with brushed stainless steel handrails for residents who might need assistance."

"You make it sound so pretty, Maxine."

"That shower's as big as my bedroom," Maxine said. "Let's go check out the kitchen, see what it's got to offer."

I stood in the kitchen doorway, thinkin' about the kitchen in my daddy's house, an' the even plainer kitchen at Homer's. They would both fit into a corner of this one.

Maxine went on with her magazine article.

"Following the theme of the rest of the condo, the kitchen cabinets are the same cherry wood, but are topped with deep stainless steel counters that match the stainless steel sinks."

She opened the refrigerator doors an' went on writin' her article.

"The double refrigerator doors hide an array of extensive shelving. Tug gently on a handle below, and the bottom drawer glides out effortlessly, revealing a generous freezer. A pebbly black finish, set off with stainless steel trim, matches the cooktop and double wall oven."

I interrupted her. "I don't think I could ever bring myself to cook in here an' git food on anythin'. I'd hate to mess it up, it's so pretty."

We tore ourselves away from the kitchen an' headed down the hallway to a bedroom so big I wondered what kind of furniture you'd put in it to fill it up. More of them cypress beams was on the ceilin', connectin' at the wall with what Maxine said were crown moldin'. Arches like the ones in the livin' room was stretched over the top of the glass doors that slid open to a balcony.

They was two more bedrooms. Both of them looked like the first one we seen, only smaller, an' each one had its own bathroom jist as fancy as the first one.

Back out in the hallway, waitin' for the elevator to take us down to the first floor, Maxine started in with her jokin'.

"So, Bert, when you moving in?"

"Oh, Maxine, I don't think I could live in sech a fancy place."

We walked out of the elevator into the vestibule an' run into Mr. Manning. He was standin' there, waitin' his turn to ride to the top floor.

"Hello, ladies. I assume you've been looking at the condominium that's for lease. What did you think of it, Mrs. Claxton?"

"Mr. Manning, I wouldn't know what to do with myself in a place like that. I'll keep thinkin' on it, but if I was you, I wouldn't wait around for me to make a decision, I'd rent it to the next person comes along."

Mr. Manning were the smilin'est person I ever did meet. I swan, I don't know what he found so funny about what I jist said, but he were smilin' when he answered me.

"I think I'll wait a while and see if you change your mind. That unit you just looked at is right next to ours. Most of the folks who've bought or leased one of the condos here are quiet people who stay pretty much to themselves, and you would be a breath of fresh air.

"Anyway, I'm here to check on Mrs. Manning. She's been sick so I try to come home often to be sure she's not in any kind of trouble."

"Oh gosh, I'm sorry she's sick, Mr. Manning. Is it a bug of some kind?" Maxine asked.

"No, Mrs. Monk. I don't talk about it much, but the truth is, Mrs. Manning, Grace is her name, has trouble remembering things sometimes. At first I thought it was the problem most of us have as we get older, but lately I've noticed she sometimes looks at me like she isn't sure who I am. We have an appointment this week to see a friend of ours who is a geriatric physician.

"He specializes in the kind of thing Grace is going through. I'm praying he'll find out she's having some kind of temporary illness that's responsible for her symptoms. In the meantime, I make several trips a day to check up on her."

"That must be terribly inconvenient for you, Mr. Manning, to leave your business and come home so often," Maxine said. "Can't you get someone to come and stay with her, at least until you find out what's going on?"

"Yes, I've thought about that, but the problem is finding someone suitable. You know, the interviews, checking references. It just seemed easier to do it this way and hope for the best."

I had stood quiet, hearin' Mr. Manning an' Maxine talkin', an' a idea had come into my head. Afore I knowed it, I spoke out.

"Mr. Manning, you know I'm kinda at loose ends right now, stayin' with Maxine an' lookin' for a new place to live an' all. If it would be helpful to you, I wouldn't mind comin' of a mornin' an' keepin' Mrs. Manning company while you was at work for the day. Seems to me that would take a load off your mind, at least for the time bein'."

"Why, I couldn't impose on you that way. You hardly know me. Besides, my wife can be somewhat difficult to handle sometimes. I couldn't put you in a position like that," he said.

"You want to talk about somebody bein' difficult to handle, you never knowed Homer Claxton, did you, 'cept for the time you tried to buy the farm off'a him. The way I hear he talked

THE MYSTERIES OF TREMONT MEADOW 87

to you that time warn't nothin' compared to livin' with him all day ever' day for all them years. I guess I know how to handle difficult.

"'Sides, I think you got the wrong word for how your wife is right now. Maybe she's jist mixed up, or afraid about what's happenin' to her. Maybe she jist needs somebody to help her think on somethin' other'n what's different from how it used to be, you suppose?"

I thought Mr. Manning were goin' to be mad at me for speakin' out like that. He had a hard look on his face an' were starin' over my head, lookin' real uneasy. After a bit, he got a funny sort of half smile goin', an' he started talkin' agin.

"Mrs. Claxton, I hadn't thought of it that way. Maybe I've been too close to the situation. I must admit, I haven't realized how Grace might be feeling. I've been so busy trying to take care of her by myself..."

He were tryin' to say somethin' but havin' trouble with it. Me an' Maxine let him be while his brain went searchin' for the right words.

"I'm afraid I have been sorely lacking in compassion for my dear wife. I haven't been there for her like I should have. The truth is, I've been confused and afraid myself, but I guess I never thought of Grace in those terms. How frightening it must be for her to not know what might be ahead of her.

"Mrs. Claxton, I thank you for opening my eyes to my wife's situation. I appreciate your directness. I think from knowing you even for this short time, you might be good for her. If you meant it, I'll take you up on your offer to come and stay with her once in a while until we can figure out what her problem is and what needs to be done about it. I think Grace would enjoy your company. If you really want to do it, I'd like that."

I looked at Maxine for a answer, but real quick I made up my own mind.

"I'd be proud to keep Mrs. Manning company for a while. Truth is, for me, it would be a welcome chore bein' helpful to somebody who appreciates it, 'stead of always tryin' so hard to please a person, like Homer, who don't even know you done somethin' for 'em.

"I'd be right glad to do it, Mr. Manning."

Mr. Manning took me an' Maxine back up in the elevator with him to meet his wife. She were real nice to us right off, puttin' out a pot of tea an' a plate of hot buttered biscuits, fresh out of the oven. Mr. Manning said that were one of her favorite afternoon snacks. He interduced me as a client who's lookin' at the condo, as he called it, next to theirs, an' Maxine as a friend who come along to drive me, since I don't know how to run a car.

Mrs. Manning were real surprised at that.

"My goodness, you don't drive? Why, I don't know what I would have done my whole life if I couldn't drive. With Thaddeus gone from home so much on business, I would have been stranded."

"Well, I aim to learn how soon's I get settled in my new life. My husband died a couple months back so I'm learnin' how to live on my own. Maxine is helpin' with all kinds of stuff until I'm able to get by."

From there, the talk atween the three of us went to furnishin' the condominium next door, if I decided to live there. Right about then, Mr. Manning excused hisself to go back to the office, leavin' his wife in the company of her new friends.

A hour later, me an' Maxine told Mrs. Manning goodbye, promisin' we would come back later when we was done lookin' at the other two apartments on our list.

"That was a nice visit, wasn't it, Bertie?" said Maxine, as we drove away in her car. "I'm glad we agreed to take her up on the invitation to come back for supper, aren't you?"

"I'm up for it if you are. I wonder can she still cook? Mr. Manning'll be surprised to see us, I bet."

Fourteen
Thaddeus

TO SAY I WAS surprised would be putting it mildly. I was also extremely pleased with what I found when I arrived home. Following the smell of fried chicken, I found myself in a kitchen full of activity. Maxine wielded the hand mixer, beating a very large amount of half and half and butter into a bowl filled with steaming hot potatoes. I lifted a lid and the delicious aroma of bacon and green beans wafted into my nostrils. Bertie was stirring the gravy to keep it from sticking, and my sweet wife, Grace, leaned over and offered her cheek for me to kiss as she sliced a big, white mushroom to add to the salad that was sitting on the countertop in front of her.

"We hoped you'd be home in time to eat with us, Dear," she said. "The girls and I have had great fun getting to know one another. I don't know when I last enjoyed myself so much. We've agreed, we need to get together from time to time. In fact, Bertie wants to come back in the morning, if that's all right with you, Dear."

I was stunned. Where did these two lovely ladies come from who fit so easily into the present circumstances of my life? And

Grace's, I should say. Especially Grace's. I hadn't seen her so content and happy in over a year.

Because our children live so far away, I had tried to be everything to her. Truth be told, even if the children were closer they probably wouldn't be much help. I do have to admit I hadn't told them of their mother's condition, though. I couldn't bring myself to let them know how serious it might be. That would be facing my fear head on and I wasn't brave enough to do that yet. Wanting to wait until I knew for certain caused me to put off telling them what was happening.

But now, seeing how improved Grace seemed after spending a few hours with these two women, I began to hope my imagination had been working overtime. Maybe she wasn't as sick as I'd thought. I resolved to encourage this new friendship and see where it took us.

"I think it would be wonderful for her to come back, Grace," I said. "Will you need a ride in the morning, Mrs. Claxton? Can I take the two of you anywhere before I go to the office?"

Maxine spoke up before Bertie had a chance to think about it. "I'll bring Bertie over in the morning on my way to the store. You'll be surprised to hear what their plans are for the day, Thad. Tell him, Grace."

"Thaddeus, I am so excited. Bertha spied our book collection in the library and told me how she envied people who could read well enough to have all those words right at their elbow, waiting to get into their head. Why, I can't imagine not being able to read well, you know how I love to read. Maxine told me how Bertha recently made a vow to go back to school and learn everything she didn't learn as a young girl.

"I've offered to tutor her! We found my high school math book in the library and Bertha was fascinated with it. She wants to learn algebra, can you believe that? We are both so excited, we can barely stand it, isn't that right, Bertha?"

I suddenly realized that Grace was being allowed to use Bertha's Christian name without being corrected. The ladies weren't the only ones who were excited.

As Grace and Maxine busied themselves cleaning up the kitchen, I invited Mrs. Claxton to follow me into the library to look at the books. I used that as an excuse for us to be alone so I could talk to her.

"How did you do this, Mrs. Claxton? She's a different woman than I left here this morning. It's a miracle."

"It ain't no miracle, Mr. Manning, she jist needed somethin' to do, keep her mind off her own troubles. It's a honest thing she'll be doin', too. I aim to learn to read good, an' she is a good reader, so we decided to put them two things together. That way, she's helpin' me an' I'm helpin' her. See?"

I saw more than Mrs. Claxton thought I did. This woman, put down for all her life by a domineering father and an abusive husband, had a spirit of self-preservation that was contagious. It seemed to me she had passed some of that same spirit along to my wife in the short space of a few hours spent cooking a simple meal and asking for help in learning to read. Bertha Louise Claxton didn't know it, but she was smarter than any therapist I had ever met.

Fifteen

Grace

DEAR ME. I WAS so excited about my new friends and the prospect of helping Bertha improve her reading skills, I'm afraid I chattered non-stop the whole evening after they left. Thaddeus, as always, listened patiently while I went on and on about the adventure scheduled to begin the very next morning. He helped find my schoolbooks from my grade school days. I save everything, you know. He went right to where they were, tucked up in the corner of the top shelf in the library. He gathered the materials we would need. Pads of paper, pencils, the dictionary. By the time we retired for the night, Thaddeus and I had set up a little schoolroom. I could hardly contain my enthusiasm. Why, I hadn't looked forward to an event so eagerly since – well, I don't know when.

THE NEXT MORNING, MAXINE dropped Bertie off at the entrance to Egret Gardens. When I answered our doorbell I found a beaming Bertie standing there.

"I think I pushed the wrong button at first, Grace. I stood there waitin' for the elevator to move, an' finally a lady got in there with me an' asked what floor I was goin' to, an' then she pushed a button an' up we went. I looked real close at the buttons an' seen the one I pushed was for the door to stay open. Next time I'll know better."

The day was spent helping Bertha review the alphabet. It occurred to me after a few minutes of working with words that Bertha had forgotten much of what she'd learned up to, and including, the third grade.

"We won't get very far learning to read, Bertha, if you can't tell me what letters are in the words," I said.

We poured ourselves a cup of the tea I had just brewed and got started. Bertha was a quick pupil, remembering in a rush what she had learned during the time she was allowed to attend classes. She explained to me that her father had pulled her out of school to help with housework and the garden and the animals.

She recalled her lessons so quickly that by the end of the day she was able to sound out words from the story I had chosen for her, *Snow White and the Seven Dwarfs*. When Maxine arrived to pick her up, Bertha joyously intoned "Once upon a time. . ."

A big smile lit up her face as I wiped the tears off my cheeks. I gave Bertha a big hug and sent the book of fairy tales home with her, instructing her to practice reading that evening. "I'll see you in the morning?" I asked, as my two new friends stepped into the elevator across from our front door.

"Yes, ma'am, I'll be back," Bertha said.

Sixteen

Maxine

I picked Bertie up at 2:00 pm and headed home, listening to her excitedly chattering about her day with Grace. She wanted to stay later, but Thaddeus planned to take Grace with him to a dinner party that night. I was praying it would be a good experience for her.

That night Bertie was tuckered out, as she put it, from her reading lesson, and went to her bedroom, telling me she was too tired to eat the leftover chicken from supper the night before that Grace had sent home with us.

I took the rest of the evening off to be by myself. Unlike Bertie, I was famished, so I dug into the chicken and ate every bit of it myself. I love cold chicken.

Licking my fingers on the way, I headed for the kitchen to put my plate in the sink. As I passed Bertie's bedroom, I heard a strange sound coming from behind the door. I quietly pushed it open and peeked in. There, propped up in the bed with pillows, Bertie had opened her book and prepared to read for a while. I don't think she realized just how bone weary she was. The new schedule of sleeping later in the morning and going to bed later at night was different than her former farm schedule. The result of her new schedule saw her in bed early, sound asleep, sitting up with the light burning brightly on the bedstand as she snored in blissful slumber.

"Sounds like a flock of geese in here," I whispered, taking the book out of Bertie's hands and shaking her lightly on the shoulder.

"Hmmmmn," she murmered.

"Lay down, Bertie," I said, as I clicked off the light. Pulling the door closed, I tiptoed out of the room. The snoring began again. Knowing I wouldn't be able to sleep until the house got quiet, I wandered into the living room and nestled into the sofa cushions. Kicking off my shoes and raising my feet to the hassock, I leaned back and closed my eyes.

That's when my mind went into overtime. Funny, isn't it, I thought, how life could take so many twists and turns without a person realizing what was happening. Here I was, an old lady, three times married, three times divorced, without chick nor child to help ease my loneliness. At least none that I could count on. All my plans and dreams as a young woman had faded to nothing, and here I sat in my dead grandparents' house in Florida wondering what the next part of my life would bring to me.

I felt weepy, thinking of Grace's condition. Or was it Bertie's situation? I missed my daughter, Dina, every day, and the fact that my child wanted nothing to do with me was devastating. And my son. I could barely remember his face, he'd been dead for that long. Everything combined, and grief took over.

I broke down and cried bitter tears over the futility of an unfair life.

I WOKE, DISORIENTED, WHEN I heard Bertie in the shower. Still on the sofa, I yelped with pain as my back refused to straighten up. Shuffling to the kitchen, I started a pot of strong coffee. What in the world was Bertie doing awake so early? Peering at the clock on the stove, I read the time. Four forty-four a.m. Bertie walked into the kitchen, dressed and ready for the day.

"What are you doing out of bed this early, Bertie?"

"This is what time I git up, or did git up, all them years on the farm. This past couple of weeks with s' much goin' on all the time, I been goin' to bed later an' later ever' night, until I started gittin' used to it that way. Course bein' up so late ever' night, I got to sleepin' in mornin's. But last night, I was jist plumb tuckered out from runnin' here an' there, lookin' for a place to live. An' then spendin' two days with Mrs. Manning, cookin' an' tryin' to keep her busy, studyin' on them letters an' words. Why, when I got home last night, I didn't think I'd be able to keep my eyes open any longer'n it took to git my night dress on. When you said you wanted to take a little time for yourself, I about shouted hallelujah. I wanted to read for a spell, but my eyes closed soon as I got on the bed. I had me a good night's sleep, an' when I woke up, I were woke up. I done got slept out, an' that were that. I was hopin' you'd stay asleep, though. I peeked at you sleepin' on the sofa when I got up an' figgered you must of been as tired as me, prob'ly fell asleep on the sofa an' jist stayed there, right?"

"Yeah, I stayed up pretty late. That wasn't what made me so tired though. I got to thinking about my kids and got all depressed. I wound up bawling like a baby. You ever cry about stuff, Bertie?"

Seventeen

Bertie

I HAD GOT TO where I were real fond of Maxine an' felt I could talk to her. "Well, it's another long part of my life to tell. But, not havin' a mama while I growed up, leavin' school when I were only eight years old, havin' no childhood friends an' then havin' no real contact with other people only when I went somewhere with my daddy, I didn't know how to talk to nobody.

"When me an' Farley, my first husband, got together, he let me talk 'til I got tired of hearin' my own voice. I used to ask him did he care that I talked so much? He said to never stop talkin', he loved hearin' the stories I told him. He wanted me to learn to read an' write better, so's I could put my stories about the animals on the farm on paper, how I thought I could tell what they was thinkin', how it seemed like they understood when I were sad or lonely. He 'specially liked me tellin' about the cow, how she would stand at the fence waitin' for me to show up, how she laid her head on my shoulder an' stood there like that until I walked away.

"The best ones he said was about the deer comin' out of the woods into the yard, lookin' for me. They knowed I had feed for 'em, but even after they ate what I give 'em, they stayed there in the yard, follerin' me around while I scattered scratch for the chickens. Farley said he bet if I wrote all that stuff down, we could find somebody in the book business who'd want to buy them stories. Even if that never happened, he said don't stop talkin' to him about it all.

"I didn't have a chance to do what Farley wanted me to do, because of our baby dyin', an' then Farley gittin' killed in the wreck. After that, I went back to havin' no one to listen.

"My daddy moved me back to his place an' then married me off to Homer. They didn't either one talk much to me or nobody else, let alone listen to anythin' I had to say."

"It's hard to hear you tell about your life, Bertie. How did you stand it?"

"I don't know, Maxine. I figgered it out some, now I done had time to set an' look back. What I think, they neither one knowed how to be any different. They was jist two old men didn't know nothin' but farmin', didn't know nothin' about little girls or how to be with a wife. An' they warn't interested in bein' anythin' else.

"In the meantime, I thought I could be a good wife to him, I were always tryin' to do things to make him happy, but he didn't want nothin' from me. He told me to jist keep his clothes clean an' do some tasty cookin', don't go to rilin' him up none. So that's what I tried to do.

"Them first couple of years was the hardest. I never knowed what were goin' to rile him up, so he slapped me around some. I got it right after a while, though, jist learned to do what he said an' not argue with him.

"Lots of times I thought about my mama when Homer were hittin' me. My daddy smacked her a lot an' Homer did the same to me if I crossed him, so it didn't take too long to learn to keep still, not talk at all, jist to be sure I didn't say the wrong thing."

"Didn't it ever occur to you, Bertie, that you could've asked someone for help? Anyone? One of the women at church, or Mrs. Bailey? Someone?"

"No, it never did. That's how I saw my daddy treat my mama, an' then that's how Homer did me. I thought that's jist the way it's supposed to be."

"But Farley treated you real good, you said. Didn't you ever wonder why he was different than your daddy?"

"Yes, but the one time I told him how my daddy was, Farley said to forgit him, said I didn't live with him no more, an' if I didn't want to, I didn't never have to go visit him. So I didn't. But I got to tell you, there's a time when Farley were at odds with me for keepin' a distance atween us. I were afraid of him for a little bit in spite of him bein' good to me. Took me a while to trust him."

"Well, I don't wonder," said Maxine. "So, you didn't visit your daddy. Ever?"

"No, that's why I knowed for sure somethin' were wrong the day Farley died an' my daddy showed up with the sheriff. The only time I seen him were when he come to the cemetery the day we buried the baby. Farley had gone over there an' told him I'd had the baby an' he died, told him we was buryin' him the next day. Even then, he said next to nothin'. Stood in front of me after the buryin' an' said he were real sorry about the baby an' he left. Jist walked away."

"Bertie, I hate to say bad things about a dead man, but there was something wrong with that man. He was sick in the head."

"You're right, Maxine. He were sick somewhere's else, too, though. He must of knowed it even then, 'cause after I went back to livin' with him, he warn't right in his stomach. He didn't talk about it, but I could tell somethin' were wrong. I think he married me to Homer 'cause he wanted someone to take care of me in case he got real bad sick."

"Well, that kind of makes sense. By the way, Bertie, where did you and Homer get married?"

"Daddy had invited Homer for supper one night. After we finished eatin' an' I were clearin' the table, Daddy said for me to sit down s' he could talk to me. He told me I were goin' to marry Homer. I said I didn't want to marry nobody, but him an' Homer wouldn't listen, said I had to marry him an' that were that. Two days later we went to the courthouse an' got married in front of the judge, me wearin' my ever'day blue dress, an' Homer wearin' his denim coveralls. We went back to my daddy's farm long enough to get my things, an' that were the last I saw of my daddy until the day Homer come home from bein' gone somewhere an' told me to git in the truck, we was goin' to see my daddy.

"It turned out Homer had been kind of takin' care of my daddy whenever he had a spell of bein' sick, an' that mornin' when Homer went over to check on him an' saw how bad off my daddy was, he had drove into town an' told the doctor to come out an' tend to him.

"We pulled up in front of his house in time to see the doctor goin' in the front door. I asked Homer what the doctor were doin' there, but he jist took me by the arm an' pushed me inside. The doctor looked up an' shook his head at me an' Homer. Daddy were still livin' when Homer led me over to the bed, jist layin there lookin' at me, tryin' to say somethin', but he couldn't make any words come out. I watched while his eyes took on a stare an' his mouth stopped workin'. Homer took me by the arm agin an' steered me out of the room while the doctor covered my daddy's face with the sheet. After that, it were jist me an' Homer.

"Right about then, I started regrettin' not havin' kids to love, but best I could see, warn't too many people was all that happy, why bring more into the world to be miserable along with the rest of us. That's when I decided to jist live what days I had left, an' try not to cry while I were waitin' to die.

I could see tellin about my life were makin' Maxine sad, but she had asked, an' the truth cain't be changed by ignorin' it.

Eighteen

Bertie

MR. MANNING WERE IN the lobby when Maxine an' me showed up the next mornin'. He didn't want to talk to me in front of Grace, he said, so we set at the atrium watchin' the birds.

"I need help, Mrs. Claxton. I have a friend coming into town Friday. I'm picking him up at the airport and I don't want to take Grace with me. He's an old friend, in fact he introduced me to Grace all those years ago. I haven't told him about her illness, and I don't want him to see her like she is without first preparing him. Do you think you could come again on Friday and stay with her? It's an imposition, I know, to ask this of you when you've spent so much time with her this week. But do you think you could do it?"

"You know I will, Mr. Manning. We git along real good, me an' Grace, why, I ain't heard a cross word out of her the whole time I been comin' here. You jist tell me what time an' I'll be here."

"Will you bring her, Mrs. Monk, so I don't have to leave Grace alone so early in the morning?"

"I surely will. I'll just pull up in front and let Bertie out. Your doorman is good about seeing her into the lobby before I drive away. Is that okay with you, Bertie?"

"It is, an' I'm glad to do it, Mr. Manning."

"Good. Well, I'll see you tonight when I get home. By the way, I'll be taking Grace on Thursday for the first of the tests the doctor wants to run on her, so I won't need you then, only on Friday. I will never be able to thank you enough, Mrs. Claxton..."

I put my hand in the air an' wiggled my pointin' finger at him. "I been meanin' to ask you to stop callin' me Mrs. Claxton. I feel like we's gittin' to be friends, me bein' at your house s' much an' all lately, so please call me Bertie, won't you?"

"I will, if you'll call me Thad. It's a deal, then?"

Maxine chimed in. "And you all can call me any time you're having fried chicken for supper. Let's get upstairs and see what Grace is gonna want to cook today.

Nineteen
Tomasso

"Joe's Bar and Grill. Who ya' lookin' for?" I always answer the phone with one of my crazy sayings, and Thad's used to that after all these years. So I shoulda known right away somethin' was wrong when he didn't joke back. Instead, he said, "Hello, Tom, it's me, Thad."

"Hey, you old so-and-so. It's good to hear from you," I said into the phone. "Long time, no hear from. What's going on?"

Thad skipped over my question and rerouted the conversation to me.

"We can talk about me later, Tom. Tell me where you're at right now with things. What's the decision on the house?"

"Well, I've made it final, you'll be glad to hear. I'm sellin' out. I've thought about this for years, but now that it's here, it doesn't seem real. You ever have that feeling?"

"Yes, I'm going through something like that right now myself," Thad said.

"And..." I waited, but Thad evidently wasn't going to elaborate. "Anyhoo," I went on, "the realtor will be here tomorrow to sign the listing agreement and put a "For Sale" sign in the yard.

The neighbors'll complain, they don't like anyone advertising that they want to move out of such a wonderful part of the world. Me though, I figure without a sign, who's to know the place is up for grabs? So, if they don't like it, they can tell it to the Marines.

"So, Thad, what's the call for? Everything okay in the land of snakes and alligators?"

Twenty
Thaddeus

TOM AND I WENT back a long way. High school buddies, different in characteristics but drawn together by similar circumstances. Tom owed his heritage to parents who, after twenty-five years of residency in the slums of New York City had moved to San Diego. They still spoke broken English laced through with Italian words, with accents so heavy some people had trouble understanding them.

I was a kid from the wrong side of the tracks. My father had died from working in the Pennsylvania coal mines that poisoned his lungs. The summer after he died, my mother brought my three sisters and I to California to be near her sister's family, but our circumstances were not much better here than they had been in Pennsylvania. With four children and no father, money was always scarce.

Tom and I felt like misfits among the population of a high school where many of the boys drove the family car to pick up their dates on Saturday night, and the girls wore red lipstick and page boy hairdos. Tom's mother didn't own a lipstick, and neither of our families possessed a car. Both families lived in substandard housing, me in a slum complex at the edge of town, Tom in the local Little Italy section of the city, not far from where I lived.

After passing each other on the sidewalk the first week of school, I worked up my courage and said, "Hey," as I passed Tom on the way home one day.

Tom kept walking without answering.

"I see you go this way every day," I said.

"Yeah. What about it?"

"Nothing. I live about a mile from here. Where do you live?"

"Little Italy. You walk to school every day?"

"Yeah."

"Your old man won't let you drive his car?" asked Tom.

"I haven't got an old man," I said, "and we don't own a car."

We walked along for a few minutes in silence. Then the subject that most boys our age were interested in came up.

"You datin' anyone?" Tom asked.

"You have to be kidding. No car, no money, who's going to go out with me? How about you?"

Tom gave a snort and threw his hands out to his sides. "Look at me, man. I'm short, I got a face full of acne, an' no dough in my pocket. Whadda ya think, am I seein' anybody? These girls, they like the guys with a car and a fat wallet. They like the jocks. I don't play no sports. These babes here, they wanna see you wearin' a sweater with a big letter on da pocket.

"You ever take a good look at Janine Brooks? The short blond one sits with those other girls in the lunch room?"

"Yeah, I've noticed. What about her?"

"I asked her out once," Tom said. "Her and her girlfriend standin' there with her, they laughed at me. They couldn't get outta there fast enough. Last time I tried that. How about you?"

"Nah. I haven't lived here long enough to ask anyone out. Don't have the nerve. Anyhow, my mom says to just concentrate on my grades for now. I'm going to follow her advice."

"Sounds like you and your ma are like this," Tom said, crossing his fingers and holding them up for me to see.

"Well, maybe not that close, but we talk. She's pretty cool most of the time. Plus, I only have sisters, so if I want to talk to anyone, it has to be a girl. Good thing they all love me. If they were one of those girls at school, I'd be talking to the wall most of the time."

By the end of September Tom and I were good friends.

Twenty-One

Tomasso

Thad just missed bein' six feet tall. At one hundred-seventy pounds he outweighed many of our classmates. He was built like I could only dream about. I resembled a fire plug. Short and pudgy. Thad had broad shoulders, skinny hips. He shouldda had the girls all over him, but he was shy and the girls stayed away.

A couple weeks after school started, me and Thad walked past the football field on the way home after school. We stopped to watch the team practicing, when we heard someone yell, "Hey! You over there!"

Thad looked around but we was the only ones in sight. He yelled back, "Who, us?"

"Yeah, you! Get over here!"

It was the coach yelling' at him from the forty-yard line of the football field.

"What the heck is he yelling at me for?" Thad asked. "I'm not doing anything wrong. I'm just walking home."

"I dunno," I said, "but you better get over there. Come on, I'll go wich you."

The coach walked around Thad, checkin' him out. Finishing the circle, he stood lookin' up into Thad's face. Thad was taller than the coach, even at the age of sixteen.

"You ever play football, young man?"

"No sir."

"Manners. I like that. You want to play football?"

"I don't know, sir."

"You know anything about football?"

"Sure."

"Not very talkative, are you?"

"No sir."

"Okay. Here's the deal. I been watching you for a while. You look like you might make a good football player. You wanna give it a try?"

"Sure."

"Right now okay with you?"

"Sure."

The coach laughed. "You ever say anything but sure?"

"Yeah."

"By the way, I'm Coach Watson. I know who you are. I asked at the office."

"Glad to meet you."

"Well, well. The boy can speak. Now, if I was to give you a shot at this, you got any idea what position you might wanna play?"

"Sure."

They stood there, lookin' at each other. I could tell Coach Watson was gettin' irritated by the way he was just starin' at Thad. Finally, he exploded.

"Well, help me out here, boy! You a running back, a guard, you must have some idea. . ."

Thad interruped him. "I'll try kicking."

The coach looked at Thad for half a second, then he turned and yelled again, this time at a kid walking off the field. "Hey, Lewis. Get over here and hold the ball for this kid. He's gonna try to kick it for me."

Lewis hunkered down and teed up the ball. Thad backed up, took in a deep breath and blew it out, breathed in again and took a run at the ball. He came at it from an angle instead of straight on, swung his foot forward at exactly the right time, and connected the instep of his shoe with the ball. A solid smack, and the ball sailed over the middle of the goal post, thirty-seven yards away.

Turning to walk back to the coach, Thad grinned when he saw the look of amazement on my face and Coach Watson's.

"That was one of the prettiest kicks I seen in a long time, Thad," the coach said. "You say you never played football. Was you kiddin' me?"

"No sir."

"Oh, stop it with the 'no sirs'. Talk to me. Where did you learn to kick like that?"

"I've been kicking since I was a little kid. My dad wanted to play football in high school, he was a kicker. His dream was to play pro ball, but he had to go to work before he finished school to help support their family. They were so poor, all the kids had to go to work in the coal mines as soon as they could. It was a huge thing for him, not to be able to play ball. But he played in the street every chance he got, and he taught me to kick."

"Yeah," said the coach, "but you kicked the ball like you kick a soccer ball, at an angle, and you do it with your instep instead of your toe. The ball covers more distance that way."

"Sure. I think my father was ahead of everyone else. That's how he taught me to kick."

"And he was right, wasn't he?" the coach asked. "That ball went right between the posts, easy as you please. Tell me this, Thad. You're a sophomore in high school, you're a great kicker. How come you never played ball?"

Thad shuffled around, looking at the ground, embarrassed.

I knew Thad's story by now and spoke up. "Hey, coach, lay off. He don't like talkin' about stuff. He can kick, okay? You want him on the team, give him a uniform. You wanna know his life story, tie him to a chair and shine a light in his face."

Coach Watson swiveled around, ready to bark at me. Instead, he studied me for a few seconds, then said, "You look like you could tear into a bulldog and come out the winner. What's your name, boy?"

"Tom Pellegrino."

"Attitude. You got attitude, boy. You always this ready to take on the world?"

"Listen, Coach. I was raised on the streets in one of the toughest neighborhoods in New York. Lost a brother in a gang fight. Got a sister, fourteen, be fifteen by now, run away from home when she was told to pack up, we was leavin' for California. We don't know where she is. So, yeah, I'm tough. And yeah, I got attitude. You wanna make somethin' of it?"

He came right back at me. "Yeah yourself, Pellegrino. I'd like to make you into a football player. I need some guys with attitude like you got. You want a uniform, too?"

"I can't play if it costs me. Took everything we had to make the move here from New York. Don't even have a car yet. So, if it costs one red cent, my old man won't let me. And he won't tell you hisself, but Thad can't play either if there's money involved. In fact, that's why he never played ball. He has to work, like his old man had to work. They're worse off at his house than we are, 'cause at least my old man brings home what's left of his pay when he's done drinkin' up the rest of it. Thad's old man's dead."

Coach Watson sent us home with forms to be signed by our parents. "Bring these back tomorrow and we'll get you suited up and into practice right away. And tell your folks not to worry about the money. We'll take care of it."

Twenty-Two
Coach Watson

I WATCHED THE BOYS walk off the field. Tom, built like a pudgy brick wall. Considerably shorter than Thad, he also weighed less. Thad had longer, thinner legs, and Tom was more muscular under the pudge.

After working with him for a few days, and discovering his running speed, I put Tom to work as a cornerback on defense, and the rest is history. Both boys' lives changed as a result of the discipline and teamwork, and their prowess as football players brought the girls flocking around them like flies on dead meat. Thad avoided most of them. Naturally shy, his reservation was a put-off to most of the young ladies. Tom, on the other hand, gave his Italian heritage full reign, causin' me more than a few close encounters with the Dean of Boys and several angry parents. The threat of being kicked off the team finally straightened Tom out, and I started sleepin' again at night.

During the homecoming game of their senior year, Tom played his position so well that he shut down an entire side of the field, and the label of "shutdown corner" was used to define him in the San Diego Evening Tribune sports section. Little did anyone know that he was being scouted by the University of Southern California that night. Since he was determined to stay near his family, it was a no-brainer choice when they offered him a full football scholarship to USC, a little over a hundred miles from home. His future had been cast in stone, and he didn't even know it.

Neither of them had given much thought to what they wanted their future to consist of, other than football. Coming from similar backgrounds, they'd struggled through life dealing with uneducated parents who were concerned mostly with keepin' the heat turned on in their small apartments and feedin' their kids. Until football came along, college had been a dream. Now, because of their athletic abilities, both were headed for a life they had thought impossible.

Twenty-Three
Thaddeus

I ACCEPTED A SCHOLARSHIP to Ohio State University, even though I hated the idea of leaving my mother and sisters behind, but Mr. Anderson, Dean of Boys at my high school, counseled me that I would be of more help to my family if I had an education that would enable me to earn a good salary and provide for their future needs. In the meantime, with one less mouth to feed, life would be easier for my mother.

In the end, I was convinced, and two months after I graduated from high school, I found myself immersed in a new life that revolved around a football scholarship, subsidized by a part-time job, and a heavy load of subjects that would one day lead to a degree in architectural engineering.

That was my life for a long time. Study, football, work, and a little sleep now and then, year-round. No summers off for me. It took a little over eight years to earn my Master's Degree. In my absence, my mother and three sisters had buckled down and picked up where I left off. They discovered if they wanted to eat they had to work. My mother even found enough spare money to get herself a bus ticket several times and came to Ohio to see me. By the time I graduated tenth in my class, I was a different person than the shy, broke and lonely boy who had left California. I'd been offered a contract to play pro football for two ball clubs, but turned them both down in favor of a job with a large architectural firm in Cleveland, Ohio.

Things were good for a lot of years. My job provided me with a lifestyle I'd never thought possible. I had a steady girlfriend, but lately she'd been pressuring me to make the relationship permanent. I wasn't sure I wanted to do that. I enjoyed my freedom, and she wasn't the kind of person I thought I'd be happy with for the rest of my life. As a matter of fact, I often wondered if I'd be happy with anyone, or anything. A streak of melancholy that became evident in my teen years became more prominent until I sometimes thought I would go mad. I broke up with her, and then, in spite of the new feeling of freedom, I grew lonelier by the day. I was thirty-seven. It was past time to settle down. I didn't want to do it alone, but there was no one I wanted to settle with. Or for.

I finally confided this state of mind to Tom during a phone conversation. Months had passed since we last talked with each other, and when Tom heard my voice, he knew something was wrong.

"Hey," I began, "how's it going out there in sunny California?"

"Great! Really great! Life is good. How's things up there in sunny Ohio?" This was our standard joke, but when I didn't laugh at it this time, Tom knew the melancholy that had hounded me for most of my life had taken over again. The conversation ended awkwardly, with me not wanting to admit how bad off I was, and Tom not knowing what to do about it. We left it hanging in the air somewhere between Ohio and California.

Twenty-Four

Tomasso

THE FIRST YEAR OF college wasn't too bad. Most of the professors knew I was there to play football, so they looked the other way when I sauntered through the door after class started or didn't show up at all. Lots of times I handed in test papers with blank spaces where answers should've been. Nothing was ever said about it, and a fake grade was marked down in the record books. One day, though, the coach held a meetin' in the locker room, telling all the players this was an "invitation" they wouldn't want to turn down.

The locker room was full of guys laughin' and jokin' around when the coach barrelled in. He caught our attention right off. "Okay, ladies. Listen up. Here's the scoop. So far administration's been lookin' the other way, ignoring stuff. But some busybody reporter from the L.A. Times has got a bee in his bonnet and started watchin' us. We're winning too many games, he says. Says our players are so good because they don't have to spend any time in class or studyin', leavin' 'em plenty of time to practice. He's accusing different colleges of falsifying grade records, ignoring empty seats in lecture halls. There's also a rumor goin' around that some of our players are gettin' paid for playin' football at our prestigious institution. We all know that's not legit, don't we? I hope none of you are involved in that. If you are, get out of it now.

"Admin's not happy with this situation. Everyone wants our team to win, but jobs will be lost if any of these accusations can be substantiated.

"Startin' today, here's the deal. You guys are intelligent, honest people, right? Right. So, the minute this meetin' is over, you will all be sittin' in your seats for every class. You miss a class, you better be sick. If you miss a class and you ain't sick, I'll see to it you get sick. You all gonna show up for every practice, and you all gonna obey the rules of training. No booze, no girls, no tobacco. Just hard work, study, and practice when you're supposed to practice. You don't wanna abide by what I say, you don't play. You guys here on scholarships might lose 'em. Got it? Okay. I know you can play, I know we can beat any team they throw at us. But you gotta do it the right way. You get out there now and prove me right."

Once the screws were put to me, I settled into it like I'd been waitin' for someone to sit on me and make me behave. On January 1, 1953, USC added another win to their long record of Rose Bowl wins, beating the Wisconsin Badgers 7-0. It so happened this was the first nationally televised Bowl game and the first nationally televised college game of any sport, which meant, as a member of the USC Trojans, I was giving my debut performance to a television audience. Little did I know at the time that seven years later my career in front of a camera would begin in earnest.

In '54 I graduated with a degree in marketing. I couldn't settle down and decide what I wanted to spend my life doin', so I changed my major and started over a few times. Took me some extra years and my final GPA put me in the middle third of my graduating class. By then that was good enough as far as I was concerned, and it kept me playin' football!

By 1960, my life was going in a different direction than I'd ever dreamed it would. The last six years I'd worked for a marketing firm in Los Angeles, going nowhere fast with my career. I couldn't seem to get into the marketing game, couldn't find my niche there. But it was a living and I was able to take care of my Ma. She wasn't gettin' any younger and she kept at me to find a young lady and settle down. She wanted grandkids, but I wasn't sure that was where I wanted to go right then. I had lots of girls, but never one that meant that much to me, so that was a disappointment to my Ma. My old man, he couldn't care less. He was dying from cirrhosis of the liver after all the years of heavy drinkin'.

At the same time, my love life, like my career, was also going nowhere. I was trying to make an impression on my most recent would-be conquest, but she wouldn't cooperate.

"Why won't you go out with me? Because I'm just an ordinary guy and you're goin' for your PHD in physics? You think I'm not good enough for you?"

"Oh, don't be silly, Tom."

"Well, so what's the real reason?"

"Okay, how about this. I'm too busy."

"All I'm askin' for here is a cup of coffee after you get out of class today. Come on, Judy, gimmee a break!"

"You don't believe I'm too busy, do you? Well, you want to hang around with me, Tom, I'll tell you what. Follow me for the rest of the day, and maybe then you'll see why I don't have time to date anyone, you included."

We wound up at the corner of 83rd street and Hindry in Westchester somewhere around 4:30 that afternoon, and by the time I flopped into bed late that night, I knew why Judy had no time for dating.

The Kentwood Players, a local community theater organization, had purchased an old warehouse that year and was in the process of transforming it into a theater. Lots of work remained to be done, and manpower was short. Every member of the Players put in as many hours as they could spare, tryin' to get the one-hundred-twelve-seat theater ready for its first production in a few months. Judy's life consisted of painting sets, sewing costumes, rehearsals, and pounding nails. Nobody asked who was the new guy, but the next thing I knew, I had a hammer in one hand and a tape measure in the other. Someone showed up with burgers and soft drinks, and we ate while we worked.

What started out as an effort to impress Judy turned into a passion for theater. After a few months, Judy was long gone from my life, but I found myself at Kentwood Players whenever I could break away from the rest of my mundane existence.

"We need someone who looks like you for the lead in the Spring production."

"You talkin' to me?" I looked over my shoulder as I held a board in place, and found myself looking at the director.

"Yes, you. We're doing *Guys and Dolls*. You'd be perfect to play the part of Sky Masterson."

All through high school, Thad and me had haunted the movies in our spare time. I loved the world of make-believe, and had memorized word for word entire roles of the leading characters in my favorite films, dreaming what it would be like to be an actor.

I was about to find out. The kid I was in high school didn't exist anymore. That short, pudgy, acne-ridden kid was now a few inches taller and muscle-bound from long hours of lifting weights. The hair had always been good. Black and wavy. The long-lashed, dark eyes and a deeply cleft chin added up to a popularity I never dreamed of as a teenager. Along with the looks, I'd developed an arrogant confidence. I tried out for the part, and got it.

"Tom, come into my office and let's talk," the director said to me one day as I was taking inventory of our stage props. "You know, Tom, we've had some success on the local level with the productions coming out of Kentwood Players. Most people don't know it, but scouts are all over the country, looking for new talent. We've lost a few of our actors to the big screen. Our box office presence rivals some Hollywood productions."

"Yeah," I said, "I hear all the time how good we are, how much talent you're able to pull out of some kid, new to the stage. What about it, though? You call me in here to tell me that?"

"I guess I'm trying to lead up to what I want to tell you, Tom. I'll stop beating around the bush and get right to it. There's a scout that's interested in giving you a screen test. Thinks you have the kind of face she's looking for. Would you be interested in talking with her?"

I laughed out loud. "This is a joke. You're kiddin', right? I mean, I'm not that good. You got people acting for you that could be famous, they're that good. Why me?"

While the director studied me, I could almost hear his thoughts. *Yes, the face is good. Very good. The personality is there. He has charisma, charm. And he's right. He's not that talented.*

The director confirmed my thoughts. "Well, Tom, you see, fortunately for you, it's not always about talent. Sometimes it's about a little bit of talent and a lot of what else you have that makes up the whole package. A persona, you know? You have that, and this scout is interested. Are you? It could change your life, Tom."

It did. The screen test showed me to be extremely photogenic, and the taped audition proved to be just what the movie studio wanted for the lead in a string of upcoming films for the under-thirty movie-goers. I signed the contract, and headed for Hollywood, California.

My first few films appealed to the high school kids because I could still pass for one of them. The good looks didn't hurt things, either. The money they paid me to star in these pictures added up to what I considered to be a huge fortune, which I blew on expensive cars and clothes. Despite the luxuries, there was enough left to send home. Life was good.

I thought I earned more than anyone should be paid for wearing tight pants and sporting a ducktail haircut while driving up and down a beach in Hawaii with four girls in the back seat of a convertible and my supposed best buddy in the front seat, looking for the next big wave. I figured they had it backwards. At least one girl should be in the front seat with me. But that was back in the day when a boy didn't even kiss a girl in a film, they just laughed and roasted hot dogs over a campfire while their friends swam in the surf.

Eventually, though, I became too old to be believable in the teeny-bopper movies, and the search for more suitable roles by my agent proved fruitless. The problem, of course, became obvious. My acting skills hadn't improved in spite of my experience, so for the next few years, bit parts in minor movies paid the rent and bought food, while I continued taking acting classes, trying to find my place in the world of entertainment.

During this time I continued lifting weights at the studio gym. A daily run on the sun-drenched beaches turned my naturally swarthy complexion to a deep tan, and I morphed into the guy in a black, turtle-necked sweater with a devil-may-care, lothario attitude.

I was becoming desperate.

"Hey, Vinnie, you got anything for me?" I called my agent the third time in a month, but the answer was still the same.

"Nah, you know how it is these days, Tom. The studios are all looking for big names right now. Just hang in there, though. Something's gonna break for you one of these days. I feel it in my bones. I'll give you a call as soon as there's anything out there for you.

"In the meantime, there's a casting call out for a commercial for that new underwear company. Something called Smooth-Fit. They're looking for a guy with a great physique to model a line of personal wear for men, you probably heard of this outfit, no seams, no tags, nothing to show under the new style of tight trousers the guys are starting to wear. You interested? Just say the word, I'll set up an audition for you."

"Vinnie! You nuts? I show up in my drawers on some billboard hangin' over the San Diego freeway, I'm dead, man. That's the end of my career. Thanks, but no thanks."

DISCOURAGED BY LIFE IN general, I almost called and cancelled my lunch date with a cute little starlet. *Ah, just go,* I thought. *Get your mind offa your troubles.*

I swaggered into the studio cafeteria that afternoon. I saw this guy look up from his bowl of soup. His spoon stopped in mid-air and he stared at me, but at the time I thought he was just another person recognizing me from my movies, so I swaggered some more and took a seat at my date's table.

I was shoveling food into my mouth with an intensity comparable to a voracious shark, all but ignoring the girl. The idea that I would never lack food again hadn't sunk in yet, and every meal turned into a feeding frenzy. It was not a pretty sight to watch me eat. The man who stared at me earlier was now smiling as he walked up to our table.

He slid a business card onto the table next to my tray. Looking up as I chewed, I swallowed hard and wiped my mouth with the back of my hand.

"Yeah? What can I do for you?"

"Well, for starters, you can look at my card. Then we can talk."

I read his card. I told my date to find another table. As she walked away in a huff, I offered her chair to my new best friend, who, according to his business card, was a talent scout for MGM.

"Have a seat," I said. "Talk to me."

"You are cocky. Sure of yourself. Rude."

I interrupted him. "Hey, wait a minute. Where do you get off talkin' to me like that? You don't..."

He interrupted me. "All traits of one of the main characters to be portrayed in my next movie."

He came right to the point. "I'd like to run a screen test on you for a movie we're casting. You have what we're looking for as far as looks go, so if you can act, we might be able to work with you. You interested?"

It was later, after we'd worked together a while, he told me what he was staring at as I walked past his table that day in the cafeteria.. A square-built, swarthy man of medium height, thick black hair combed back from a darkly tanned face, a heavy roman nose above a beautifully formed mouth. A cleft chin jutting out from the second-skin black shirt, showing off the sculpted muscles of the flat six-pack abdomen, and thigh muscles that bulged through the fine wool fabric of his designer slacks. The man thought he had died and gone to heaven.

As it turned out, my lack of acting skills was not an issue. The role called for a rough-spoken, mono-toned criminal. I tested perfect for the part, and the movie was a box office hit. This time around, I had enough sense to put most of the money in the bank, believing that it would need to last me for the rest of my life. I was wrong. The sequel to the movie made sure that not only would I never need to worry about money again, but if I was smart, I could make it grow into a nice little fortune. Which is exactly what I did. Following my old friend Thaddeus Manning's advice, I began investing heavily in California property. Most of my investment properties were in San Diego. I didn't want to stay in Hollywood forever, and once I retired, I figured I might as well be close to my family.

Several more semi-major roles came my way in the following years, but never again a part like the gangster character I portrayed in those two major films. As I aged, my lack of acting ability reduced me to doing some local theater work. Finally, after a few years of total inactivity in the entertainment world, I had to face the question of what to do with my future.

What I decided to do was take advantage of an offer made to me by Thad to invest in a condominium facility in Ohio. Thad hadn't married, and at the age of thirty-seven, his money was already invested in various real estate deals. So, when I called Thad to tell him to count me in on the Ohio condo deal, he whooped with joy.

I told him I'd need to liquidate some of my California properties in order to do it though.

"Come out here for a few days, Thad, and look 'em over. Use your real estate expertise and tell me what to do. Should I keep them all, sell them all? Keep some, sell some, what? I got a good real estate agent here, you know, but I trust you to be straight with me. I figure you didn't get where you are without knowing somethin' I don't know.

"How about it? Can you come? This weekend is the Fourth of July. The fireworks here will be spectacular. Do you good to get away from everything there, anyhow. From the way you sound, you could use a break. Play hookey for a few days and come see me."

It's funny how life works, I thought, many years later. The call had come from Thad right after I decided to sell my house. I knew from what Thad told me about his depression that something was wrong in my friend's life. I was glad he accepted my invitation to come for a visit.

Thad caught the early morning plane out of Cleveland the next day and was at my house in time to go to dinner with me and my real estate agent. Between them they convinced me I was doing the wise thing to sell my house. It was too big for one person and by now it was worth three times what I had paid for it. The equity I would realize from the sale of it could be put to better use by investing in more real estate. I signed the listing agreement before we finished dessert.

Witnessing me making a leap of faith into my future, Thad's melancholy worsened. He told me he was single, bored, going nowhere, and fearful of doing anything about any of it. He'd thought of chucking it all, he said, getting out of the grey, overcast weather that Ohio offered, moving to a sunny environment, maybe Florida. But he didn't relish the idea of being alone in a new place. He'd be even more depressed. He was confused, and unable to make any kind of decision about his circumstances. However, being around me for one day had already improved his mood, and more than ever Thad longed for a change.

The next day was the Fourth of July. I'd planned a picnic on the beach with a few of my friends to watch the fireworks, and Thad found himself excited about a social event for the first time since he had broken up with his girlfriend more than a year before.

When I introduced him to my friend, Grace Griffith, that night, I was surprised at his immediate and strong attraction to her. I watched them as they sat on a blanket in the dark. The fireworks exploded over their heads, lighting up the area surrounding them. I saw Thad turn to steal a look at Grace, only to find that she was already looking at him. It was no surprise after the last of the fireworks sputtered and died that Thad sought me out.

"Say, Tom, I know you and Grace see each other socially, but are you an item? I mean, are you dating, or what?"

We sat in a cabana on the beach sipping frozen margaritas, the fireworks display finished, the smell of sulfur still hanging in the air. Grace was involved in an animated discussion about movie trivia, so Thad took advantage of her distraction to talk with me. Grace and Thad had been at each other's side the whole evening, separated only by this trivia enthusiast who had targeted Grace once he knew she was my friend, assuming she must know everything there was to know about my movies.

I sensed there was more than idle curiosity in Thad's question and played it for all it was worth. "Well, we date, off and on. I think she's nuts about me to be honest, but I hold her at bay. You know, not wanting to hurt the poor little thing. She's seventeen years younger than I am, pretty impressionable, I think. Why do you ask?"

Thad spit it out. "I don't want to do anything to hurt our friendship, Tom, but I think I could fall for this girl. I know she's lots younger than I am, but there's something about her. I don't know, Tom, I feel like I've known her my whole life, like she's part of me. Isn't that the strangest thing you ever heard?"

"Hey, Thad, I'm kiddin' you, man. Grace is probably the best friend I've had next to you. But as far as anything romantic goes, no way, I think of her as one of my sisters. She's too young for me. She's too young for you! What are you thinking, my friend?"

"I don't know at this point. But I do know there's something there, Tom. This is pretty forward of me, but is there any way I can take you home and then borrow your car? I want to spend some time with her and talk to her some more. Would you let me do that?"

"Yeah, I'll do that, but you gotta let me ask Grace if it's okay with her. After all, she just met you tonight, and she don't know you from Adam. I'll tell her it's okay, but only if she's interested. That way she won't be put in the embarrassing position of telling you face to face if she wants to say no to the whole thing. I'll go talk to her now. You disappear up the beach a little way so you won't be visible while I talk to her."

Twenty-Five
Thaddeus

TEN MINUTES LATER, AS I waded in the surf away from the crowd, I heard footsteps crunching in the sand behind me. I turned around and saw it was Grace.

"Hi, coward." Her voice was playful.

"I'm not a coward. That was Tom's idea. He didn't want you to be embarrassed to have to tell me no to my face."

"What made you think I would say no?" Grace asked.

"I didn't think you would say no, but Tom thought that was a possibility. Should I assume, then, that your answer is yes?"

Grace stood facing me. Water swirled around her bare ankles as the tide surged in, then back out, causing her feet to sink into the hole left behind by the eroded sand. She lost her balance, and I reached out to keep her from falling just as she reached for my arm to steady herself. I lifted her out of the wet sand, walked sideways three steps out of the water, and without setting her on her feet, lifted her up close to my chest and kissed her, not at all surprised that she kissed me back.

We drove Tom home, waiting long enough to watch him disappear through the front door before we drove away.

Twenty-Six
Tomasso

I HEARD THE FRONT door open, then shut. I squinted at the illuminated hands on the clock. Ten in the morning. I rolled over, tried to go back to sleep, rolled over again, and finally gave up when the smell of coffee wafted under my bedroom door. *What in the sam hill is goin' on?* I thought. Pushing off the blankets, I put on my slippers, threw on a robe and plodded down the hall to the kitchen. Thad poured coffee into his mug just as I came into view.

"Good morning, my friend. Do you always sleep this late, or just on weekends?"

He seemed way too cheerful for a guy that was down in the dumps yesterday afternoon. "Well, for your information, it's Thursday, and where have you been all night," I grumbled. I sounded like his mother.

He ignored my question. "You might want to sit down and I'll bring you a cup of java. I have news that will knock your socks off."

I took the offered cup and looked warily at him. "What?"

"I'm getting married, Tom. Day after tomorrow." Thad stopped talking and waited for me to say something. Anything. The first response he got was a blank stare.

Then, like a fool, I blurted out, "Married! To who?"

"Who? I'm marrying Grace!"

I'm sure I looked as stunned as I felt. Sometimes I'm slow on the uptake, and this was one of those times. I couldn't talk.

"Say something, man. Aren't you going to congratulate me? Us, I mean?"

I tried my voice again. This time it worked. "Oh, come on, Thad. I mean, she's a great gal, I love her to pieces, but she's twenty years old. You're thirty-seven. You've known each other, what, fifteen hours? You can't be serious. What are you thinking?"

"I don't know at this point. I just know this is the real thing."

Twenty-Seven
Thaddeus

IT WAS OBVIOUS TOM would not be easy to convince. "I know all your objections, Tom. Grace and I have spent the whole night agonizing over this. But the truth is, we couldn't be more sure of our feelings if it had been fifteen years since we met. Did you ever meet someone and you just knew? I never did until last night. Grace feels the same way. I'm leaving here to go back home in three days, and she wants to come with me. Don't tell me how foolish it sounds, but I'm going to quit my job and we're heading for Florida. I hate my job. I've saved up quite a bundle, enough to get us started down there. I plan on buying up as much real estate as my savings will allow, and we'll both find jobs. We'll go from there and see where we land. It's what we want to do, Tom. Please, wish us well."

He didn't have a choice, and he knew it. So he went with it. "I know this, you are braver than I ever thought of being. All I can do at this point is wish you luck. You're going to need it."

Now, after all these years, Tom was coming to our neck of the woods. Grace was safe at home with Bertie looking after her, and I was at Tampa International Airport waiting for his plane to come in.

I watched him swagger up the incline past security. The years had been kind to him. Everything about him was the same, only older. But a good older. Mature. He had the look of a dignified gangster. I caught myself checking his jacket for the bulge of a gun in the armpit.

I greeted him with a bear hug as he came out of the security area, and he hugged back, adding a few back slaps to cover up his emotions. We didn't care that people watched as we embraced one another, holding on longer than necessary.

"You can't know how glad I am to see you, Tom. I have so much to tell you. Are you hungry, did you eat anything on the plane?"

"Nah, you know how airplane food is. I'm starved. Do you have time to eat something, or do you need to get back to the office?"

"I've taken a few days off, Tom. They don't expect me back until Monday, so we have plenty of time. I want to spend some of it with you alone, though, before we see Grace."

"What is it, Thad? What's wrong?"

"Let's eat first, then we'll talk. There's this seafood restaurant out on the end of a pier. The food is plain, but the fish is fresh out of the water every day, and delicious. You'll love it."

Waiting for our order to come, I steered the conversation to the sale of Tom's most recent home.

"Seems like you get settled in somewhere nice and cozy, then up and sell your house before you have a chance to really enjoy it. You must like moving."

"Yeah, well, a buck's a buck. I buy low, sell high, make some money and move on. It's just me, don't have anyone to worry about, so when I get a good offer, I take it."

"Did you have any problems with the movers this time? I remember one move you made, the movers took your furniture to the wrong address and had half of it unloaded in the driveway before they wondered where you were. All that time you were at the right house wondering what was taking the van so long to show up. I forget who called who, but they had to reload the van and drive a few miles to where you were waiting for them." We both laughed at the memory of that fiasco.

"No, this time most of my stuff went to storage. I haven't found a house I like well enough to buy, so I'm renting a small apartment for the time being. I'm considering your suggestion to come here, Thad. We're not getting any younger, and the idea of spending my old age hanging out with you and Grace is appealing to me."

"You couldn't possibly know how much it would mean to us to have you here, Tom. I pray you turn that idea into reality. Soon."

We ate our food, as delicious as I had promised, reminiscing about the past, neither of us mentioning whatever it was I was obviously reluctant to talk about.

As the waiter cleared the table, Tom said, "Okay, my friend, now tell me what it is that you're avoiding. You've asked me questions about every aspect of my life, and when I try to talk to you about you, the subject gets changed. What's up?"

"It's Grace." I set my coffee cup on the saucer and finally looked at Tom instead of everywhere else. "She's not well. I didn't want you to see her until I explained how she is, didn't want you to be so shocked that it would show. She knows something is happening to her, but she doesn't know what it is. I don't know what it is, either. In fact, the doctors don't know what it is yet. One doctor has an idea, but until they test her and get the results back, it's only guesswork on his part."

"Thad, it sounds serious," Tom said.

I stirred my coffee too long before answering. "I'm beginning to suspect that it's more serious than I previously thought. This doctor, he's a geriatric specialist, he deals with older people who, ah, who, um, might have some serious memory problems."

"For Pete's sake, man, spit it out. What are you trying to tell me? I'm your oldest friend. You oughta be able to tell me what's wrong. Is she dying?"

I looked up quickly at Tom. "I don't know, Tom. I hadn't thought about that. Lord help us all, I hadn't thought about that."

"Oh, Thad, I'm sorry. I shouldn't have even suggested such a thing. So how bad is this?"

"Well, she's seriously ill, but I think she's a long way from dying. I haven't talked to anyone else about this, but I'll admit it to you. I'm afraid it might be Alzheimer's. It took me a while to put the pieces together, Tom, but I started noticing things. She struggles to remember the name of her best friend. She misplaces her car keys, a string of pearls. One time she forgot to sign a check, and when it came back from the bank for a signature, she didn't remember ever having to sign them before. But the day she drove to the grocery store and forgot how to get home was the day I knew something serious was happening.

"I got her to the doctor's by telling her it was time for us both to have a checkup. She got concerned for me, thinking I was ill. She submitted to the tests so I would, too. Some of my test results were questionable, but I told her they found nothing wrong with me. I could tell she was relieved to hear that, but she never asked about her own results. I suspect she didn't want to know, and I didn't want to tell her, so we haven't talked about it."

"What were the results of her tests, Thad?"

"Not good. Physically, they found nothing. Psychologically, the doctor is leaning toward a diagnosis of some form of dementia. You're the only one I've told this to except the two women who are helping take care of Grace. Bertie Claxton and Maxine Monk. You'll meet Bertie tonight when we get home."

"How is Grace dealing with having someone taking care of her?"

"She thinks Bertie is just a good friend who enjoys spending time with her. Same with Maxine, although she's not around as often as Bertie is. But Grace is noticing that she's not on top of things like she used to be. Lately, she's been asking what's wrong with her. I don't know what to tell her, Tom."

"Well, I know I wouldn't tell her what it is, Thad. I'd want her to have peace of mind for as long as possible. If this is what they think it is, by the time it gets really bad, maybe she won't know it, and you won't have to tell her anything."

I decided Tom was right. I'd been thinking the same thing, so it was a relief to hear him agree with my thoughts. Grace would never know from me that pretty soon, she would not be the person she used to be, and she would not be the wife I had married all those years ago.

I PUT OFF LEAVING the restaurant that afternoon, drinking three cups of strong coffee before Tom finally suggested that we should head for home. He was eager to see Grace, no matter how ill she might be. She'd been his closest friend in those early years in Hollywood, and they'd kept in touch over the years.

"Hey, Thad, I know this has gotta be hard for you. I got no idea how I'll react when I see Grace. But puttin' it off won't make it any different. Let's go. Maybe seeing me will perk her up. After all, it's been how many years now since we seen each other?"

In the car on the way to the condo, we searched our memories, trying to dredge up the last time Grace and Tom had seen each other. I'd made several trips to California in the past fifteen years but Grace, it seemed, always had something planned that kept her from going with me. She belonged to this club, and that organization, she played bridge, and volunteered at the hospital. And always, she stayed busy working on some project or another to send to our grandchildren who lived so far away and were so young that they didn't comprehend who it was that sent the gifts. Our daughter always sent a thank you in the children's names, but her notes somehow conveyed her true feelings toward us. Grace never complained, but the last piece of mail she got from our daughter, thanking her mother for her latest gift, said, 'Thanks for the baby's hat, it didn't fit.'

That was a sore spot with me. You give your kids every advantage you never had as you grew up, and it seemed the more you gave to them, the less they appreciated it.

At any rate, all this had kept Grace at home, so it would be interesting to see how she reacted to Tom after all these years. We fell silent as I drove the rest of the way home, each of us lost in our thoughts.

My thoughts settled on our son, John. For a long time it had been hard to have a decent conversation with him. All he'd wanted to talk about was the current status of his favorite football team, or what was happening in the stock market. He'd married a social climber who was more interested in shopping than she was in maintaining even a shallow relationship with her mother-in-law.

Their children were strangers to us. The last time we went to Oregon, I called John's home phone number. A recorded message told me that it was no longer a working number. A call to the operator told me the new number was unlisted.

I finally hailed a taxi and gave him John's office address. On the way there, my usually controlled temper went whacko, and I lashed out in anger, frightening Grace by the depth of my feelings.

"I'd like to know, if someone can tell me, just what we did to these kids that they think so little of us. What went wrong, Grace? Why do they hate us so much that they wouldn't even let us know when their phone number changes?"

Grace sat in silence, looking bewildered.

"Well," I shouted, "I'm going to his office and confront him. He can tell us to our faces what the problem is. I want to hear from his own mouth if we should try to contact him in the future. The way I feel right now, I might be the one who tells him to get lost and not come back!"

We found John at his office, irritated at having his work disturbed in the middle of the day. He invited us to sit down anyhow.

"Can I get you anything to drink? How about some coffee, or a soda?" He stumbled over his words, trying to seem casual as we sat across from him in stony silence.

"So, what brings you to Oregon," he asked, putting his fingertips together, making a steeple of them, which he held in front of his face as if to hide behind them.

"I'll get right to the point," I said. "We called your house and were told by a recording, a *recording*, John, that it was no longer a working number. Then I called information to get your new number and was told by the operator that it's unlisted and she couldn't give it out. We came here in a taxi, John, not knowing if you were even still in this building. We're your parents, and we couldn't get your telephone number, for crying out loud. What if it had been an emergency? Why didn't you let us know you have a new number? What are we to think of all this, Son?"

By now, John was sitting up straight in his leather swivel chair, with his hands folded in front of him on the broad expanse of his obviously expensive desk. The expression on his face told us that this visit was not going well.

"What is it you came here for, Dad? My days are always booked weeks in advance, and right now I'm thirty minutes late for my next appointment. I usually don't take unscheduled visitors, but I could hardly turn away my parents, could I?"

Glancing at his watch, he smiled at Grace. "You're looking well, Mother. Life in Florida must agree with you." It was something you would say to an acquaintance if you ran into them on the street after not having seen them for a while.

We sat frozen in our chairs, unable to think of anything else to say to our son. When he stood and began gathering papers to put into his briefcase, I also stood. Taking Grace by the elbow, I helped her stand up on shaky legs. Putting my arm around her waist, I guided her out of John's office without a backward glance or word of farewell.

That was five years ago, and we have neither seen him nor heard from him since then.

And who could figure out what had happened to our daughter? She and Grace went through the angst that mothers and their teenage daughters often go through, but somehow, they never got beyond all that. Our daughter, Alicia, was headstrong and rebellious as a young girl, and her personality didn't change as she grew to womanhood. She and Grace seemed to always be at odds with one another, and try as she might to please Alicia, Grace always came out the loser. As the years sped by, their relationship became more and more strained. Alicia moved out on her own as soon as she graduated from high school. While she lived close by and they saw each other from time to time, the day came when Alicia met George Humboldt, and faster than we approved of, they were engaged. Their wedding had been planned by Alicia with the help of her future mother-in-law, leaving nothing for Grace or I to do except pay for it all. We almost didn't go to the ceremony, but Grace insisted.

"We can't embarrass her, Thad. What would people think if her own parents weren't there. You're supposed to walk her down the aisle.

We went, and I did what fathers do, but Alicia and George had written their own ceremony, and the part where the minister asks who gives this woman to be married to this man was conspicuously absent, and I had been uncertain when to take my seat next to Grace.

With his first big promotion in the software company that he worked for, George was transferred to Maryland. From the day the moving van pulled out of the Humboldt's driveway and headed northeast, seven years ago, contact with Alicia and her family dwindled to cards at Christmas, a birth announcement when the twins were born, and two years later when their daughter came along. Pictures followed of the babies, recording their growth, and later, school pictures with the dates and ages of each of our grandchildren duly noted on the back. Each Christmas, a package arrived with gifts from the grandchildren with handmade cards addressed to a grandma and grandpa that none of the kids would know if they bumped into them on the street. The card that came from Alicia and George was the same card that was sent to all their friends and business contacts. A professional portrait of the Humboldts and their dog, all gathered on the hearth of a beautiful fireplace with the branches of an extravagantly decorated Christmas tree showing in the background. The printed message read, *Happy Holidays from the Humbolt Family.*

"Maybe my thinking is jaded," I told Grace one Christmas, "but I can't help wondering if the setting for the picture is really their own, or a photographer's prop to make it look like they're doing that well in life. I don't think the dog even belongs to them!"

Then there was Michael, our youngest. He always seemed to be at loose ends. After a few years in the military, he settled close to us in Florida, becoming restless within the year. I urged him to enroll in the local junior college. "Just take a few courses, Michael. Things that appeal to you right now. You don't have to decide what you want to do for the rest of your life. Just test the waters, see where a year might take you. You know, there's always a place in the real estate business for you. Is that something that might interest you?"

"Dad. I'm not you. I don't want to sell houses. Actually, I was thinking about taking up commercial fishing."

"Commercial fishing," I said. "What do you know about fishing, Michael? You couldn't stand to bait a hook when you were a kid."

"Well, I guess I didn't expect any encouragement from you, Dad. It seems no matter what I get interested in, you discourage it. All you can talk about is real estate. I told you, I don't want to sell houses. What does it take to get that across to you, huh, Dad?"

"Michael, Michael. I would love to encourage you in your efforts to figure out what you want to do with your life. But be realistic, Michael. So far, your aspirations have been, uh, I don't even know what word to use for the things you've wanted to get involved in. First there was the organic farm you and your high school friends wanted to start. Not one of you knew the first thing about farming, none of you had the least idea how to go about starting a business like that. I tried to help you, Michael, remember? There was that piece of farmland out east of Arcadia that I had listed. I offered to buy it and hold the mortgage for you guys for a few years, give you a chance to get started. Do you forget all that, doesn't that count as encouragement?"

"Yeah, well, Dad, all you were willing to do was wait for us to pay you back in a few years. Without financial backing, there was no way we would have been able to pay for seed, and equipment, fertilizer and all that. You could have thrown money into the deal to help us out there, but you told all of us to get jobs, if we had to sling burgers at a hamburger joint, so we could pay for that stuff ourselves. How did you expect us to learn the ropes, at the same time we tried to work the farm and still hold full-time jobs? I don't call that very encouraging."

I cringed inside, hoping my disappointment in my son wasn't visible on my face. Where, I wondered, did Michael ever get the idea that he didn't have to work for what he got? How had he come to the point of expecting someone to always hand him what he wanted without having to work for it? Counting mentally to ten, I went on.

"Okay, but what about your next endeavor? The construction business, when neither you nor your buddies had ever so much as driven a nail into a tree house. How did you expect to build anything?"

"Didn't you ever hear of hired help, Dad? Boy, for a man who runs a supposedly successful real estate development business, wouldn't you think that point would be obvious? How many nails do you drive in a day, Dad?"

Michael has an answer for everything, I thought.

"You know, Michael, this is a pointless conversation. You weren't even born yet when I started buying cheap Florida property. No, I've never driven a nail into one of my development projects, but I drove plenty of them into all those little cracker-box houses I bought and fixed up. They're called fixer-uppers for a good reason, because they need to be fixed up!

"I fixed up plenty of them, and then I sold them for a pretty good profit. After a while, when I saw how Florida was booming, I started thinking like you were thinking. The difference was, though, I had quite a few years of experience behind me by then. I didn't just jump into it and expect to get rich overnight."

I could tell Michael had lost interest in anything I had to say. He had that sarcastic, *'yeah, yeah, yeah'* look on his face. But I pressed on, hoping to get through to him.

"Eventually I knew how to keep the books and handle the hiring and manage the operation. I didn't just set up shop one day and have everything go smoothly. When I tried to share my expertise and knowledge with you and the boys about the work involved and the expense of setting up such a business, you got mad at me and said I was being negative. Honestly, Michael, it seems to me that you don't want anything from me except a pat on the back and money to finance whatever scheme you feel like getting involved in next."

That had been the beginning of the end of whatever good relationship Michael and I shared as father and son. He found a job on a dairy farm in the eastern part of the county, and worked there until the rodeo came to Arcadia in the spring. He and some friends went to see the bull riding one Friday night, and the next morning, he announced to us that he had taken a job with the rodeo. When their stint in Arcadia was finished, Michael planned to ride out of town with them, intending to become a bronco-busting cowboy. For the next three years, we heard nothing from him.

The day Grace ran into one of Michael's high school pals, Joey Morton, she was shocked at his news.

"Hi, Mrs. Manning. I bet it's good to have Mike back in town, huh? I haven't seen him myself, but Al Smith has, remember him from school? He saw Mike a few nights ago out at the beach. Mike says he's just here for a few days, he's leaving for Hawaii next week."

Grace is a kind and open person by nature. The truth always surfaced before she could think to lie, and she responded to Joey's news with a stunned look on her face. "I haven't seen Michael, Joey. Did Al say why Michael is going to Hawaii?"

"No, not really. But I heard from some of the other guys that the girl Mike was with at the beach is from Honolulu and wants to go back to see her family. I guess she and Mike are pretty serious about each other and she didn't want to go without him. Gosh, Mrs. Manning, I wouldn't have said anything if I knew Mike hadn't contacted you guys. What's wrong with him, anyhow? I always wanted parents like you and Mr. Manning, but Mike acts like you're terrible people. I really am sorry he hasn't contacted you. If I see him, do you want me to ask him to call you?"

"No, Joey, thank you. I guess if he wants to see us he'll call or come over to the house."

When Grace told me about Michael, I figured we were batting three for three, and for the life of me, I couldn't understand why. When all was said and done, however it had come to be, the bottom line added up to one thing – Grace and I were empty nesters of the saddest kind.

Twenty-Eight
Grace

"Tell me again where Thad is tonight, Bertha. For some reason, I can't remember where he said he was going."

"He's meetin' somebody at the airport, Grace."

"Oh, yes, I do remember. Who is it? Did Thaddeus say?"

"He said it's a old friend, Grace. He should be home in a few hours, an' then you can ask him who it were. By the way, Grace, you was in the middle of tellin' me the other day about how you an' Mr. Manning met, but we got interrupted when it were time for me to go home. You feel like pickin' up on that story an' tellin' me some more? I don't think I's ever goin' to git tired of hearin' people tell me stories about places I ain't prob'ly never goin' to see. You was talkin' about how nice it were on the beach that night. I'll never git to Californee, so tell me about it."

"I'm so glad you like to talk, Bertha. Most people just want to talk about unimportant things, like politics, or the weather. But you really want to know about thoughts and feelings. I haven't had these kinds of conversations for the longest time. All Thaddeus wants to talk about is business.

"Anyhow, where did I leave off? Was I telling you about the beach party where Thaddeus and I met?"

"Yes. You was gittin' to the part where you an' Mr. Manning met up for the first time."

"I believe you're right, Bertha. Well, my mother didn't want me to go. She said, 'No, and that's that.' But I went anyway. I guess I was headstrong, but I wasn't doing anything wrong so I didn't see any reason not to go.

"It was a Fourth of July party with fireworks. A friend of mine was giving the party. Mother disliked him because he was a much older man. I guess she thought he was a bad influence on me, especially since he was a movie actor, but he was only a friend, and very protective of me. He had a sister, two sisters, actually. One of them had run away years before and they never heard from her again, so he thought of me as a younger sister, and watched out for me.

"Mother thought he had ulterior motives for our friendship, but he didn't. She threatened to call the police if I went. I will remember that night for the rest of my life. After all, everything that happened, even before I left my parents' home to go to the beach, led up to the beginning of my life with dear Thaddeus.

"I can still picture the living room of the home in which I grew up. The brick fireplace covered one wall of the room. A massive mantel held pictures of judges, attorneys, a state senator, all members of our family. Scattered in among them were pictures of me on horseback, Queen of the Rose Parade when I was only seventeen; me in my beautiful gown on the arm of my parents' best friends' son, as Senior Homecoming queen and king; me, the night of my debut into California society, my white-gloved hand tucked into the crook of Father's arm as we walked along the spotless white runner.

"They doted on me, you know. I was their only child, and they wanted what was best for me. I understood that. But I went to the beach that night in spite of my mother's threats.

"I've never been sorry I went.

"My father told me later about his conversation with Mother after I left for the beach.

"He asked her, 'What are you thinking, dear?'

"She told him she would be glad to see the end of summer and me back in school.

"Don't you think the summer has dragged on," she asked him.

"'You're leaving a lot of your thoughts out of your speech, Dear. What I hear you saying between the lines is, you'll be glad Grace will be far away from Tom Pelligrino. Right?'"

"'Yes, but Claude, she's a wonderful young woman with a bright future ahead of her. How can she consider throwing it all away on the middle-aged son of uneducated immigrants, an actor, of all things. She spends so much time with him and his movie friends. Once she's back in school, I'm afraid that old saying might be true, the one that says absence makes the heart grow fonder.'"

"'Well, first of all,' Father said, 'do you forget that my great-grandparents were uneducated immigrants? They came to this country and worked hard to give their children the chance for a better life than they would ever have had in Russia. So I, for one, admire Tom's parents for their efforts.

"'Besides, I think whoever coined the phrase about absence forgot to finish his sentence. It should say, absence makes the heart grow fonder *of someone else.*

"'Remember, she's only twenty, and the guys at school are crazy about her. One of these days she'll meet some handsome young man who'll sweep her off her feet and take her away from us. Then you can add another picture to our collection on the mantle, one of her walking down the aisle of the biggest, fanciest church you can find in all of California. How about that, mother-of-the-bride?'"

"'Oh, Claude, we're a long way off from that day, I'm sure. But you're right about the picture. I hope she'll want to wear the wedding dress that mother and grandmother and I all wore, and the veil, as well. We'll have her and her new husband pose in the same way as the rest of us did, three generations of brides with their husbands, and they'll be the fourth generation.'"

"My father said the next day that conversation came back to haunt them.

"The funny part is that I understood why my mother and father didn't care for Tom. He and I had little in common, but he was fun. He made me laugh. His lifestyle was totally different from mine. He lived in a small beach house and had a life free of responsibility. He was a good enough actor, I suppose, but the truth was he got along in the acting business more on his looks than on his talent. If my parents had left me alone, my friendship with Tom might have tapered off. But this was the first time I'd gone against them, and it felt good. I was reluctant to give in and give up. I enjoyed my new independence, and they didn't have enough sense to let me decide on my own to quit seeing Tom. So, I went to the beach, and now here I am!"

Twenty-Nine

Tomasso

MEMORIES OF MY CHILDHOOD in the slums stuck in my mind so strong, I knew I'd never go back there. I'd live on the beach for the rest of my life. That thought kept me from getting serious about any chick I dated. No snotty-nosed kids runnin' around in a three-room, tenth-story tenement walkup for me. I'd told Grace at the start I wasn't lookin' for nothin' serious in a relationship. She wasn't either. We were just two people enjoyin' life, havin' fun together. Her folks, though, they thought I was some kind of old lech, hangin' around their baby girl. The only time I met up with them face to face, Grace took me to a pool party at their yacht club. There's all these guys dressed in white slacks, lime green linen jackets; and the ladies – *whoo-hoo!* Breezy little dresses with big hats. And here I come walkin' in there in my usual outfit, you know, black everything with pleats down the front of my trousers, lookin' like the stereotypical gangster. Her old man almost dropped his bloody mary in the pool. I thought her ma was goin' to faint.

You just know they all thought I was some poor I-talian hood Grace picked up somewhere along the way. What they didn't know, I had a college degree in marketing, I had a college career in football, I was a movie star, and by the time I met Grace I owned enough California real estate to retire on and live a better life than some of them could.

I will say, they all made the best of it, but we didn't stay long. Figured we'd give the folks a break and get outta their way. We could hardly wait to get to the parking lot before we busted out laughin'.

About the real estate thing? That movie agent who gave me my first break was still my agent. He was heavily invested in waterfront real estate around San Diego. He helped me get started doin' the same thing, right after the movies about the gangsters hit the big screen. He had a hunch about how huge a hit they was gonna be, and steered me in the right direction.

"Listen, Tom," he told me when he seen I was goin' to earn a lot of moola. "Do what I've done. I own twenty, thirty properties now. Mostly houses I rent out, but I got a couple big commercial buildings that bring in a lot of money every month. When the time is right, and I want to get out of show business, well, California real estate is going to go to the moon. I figure by then I can sell out and never worry about money again. Why don't I hook you up with my real estate broker, see what's out there right now, huh?"

"Yeah," I said. "Set me up with this guy and we'll see. How about dinner one night next week, the three of us. Let me know."

Thirty

Grace

I HAD DOZED OFF on the sofa. I woke with a start, looking at a strange lady standing beside me, and said, "Yes, may I help you?" I thought I might know her, but couldn't think who she was.

"It's me, Grace. Bertha. You was tellin' me about when you an' Mr. Manning first met, an' you fell asleep. I didn't mean to wake you up, I was jist checkin' on you. You sure you're okay, you was asleep so long I started to worryin' about you. We don't have to talk about this anymore, if you're too tired."

"Oh, Bertha, I'm sorry. I get lost in my thoughts sometimes, that's all. No, I'm enjoying telling you our story. Let's see, where was I? Oh, yes!"

WE DROPPED TOM OFF and then came to my house. My parents were just sitting down to breakfast when I dragged Thaddeus into the dining room and introduced them. I'm afraid I wasn't very subtle about it. I simply announced that I'd met someone and we were getting married. Mother almost fell out of her chair, and my father told Thaddeus to leave.

As Thaddeus closed the door behind him, father forbade me to see him again. But I stood my ground. I told my parents if they made him leave without me I would follow him, with or without their consent.

They knew me, they knew I meant it. They had a choice to either be part of our wedding or miss out on the whole thing. In the end, they only asked that we be married before Thaddeus left to go back to Ohio. They didn't want me running away and living in sin, as they put it, they wanted to make sure it was all legal.

I threw my arms around them both, crying and saying 'thank you' over and over while I ran out the door to get in my car and go after Thaddeus. I didn't have to go far to catch up with him. He had been sitting in the driveway trying to work up enough courage to come back inside. He said later he wasn't sure if he would have tried to talk to my parents again, or throw me over his shoulder and carry me away in spite of their protests. It was so romantic.

Anyway, we went back inside. When mother asked if Thaddeus could extend his vacation until the next week, he said he could extend it forever if he needed to. He had already planned to leave his job soon, so if he got fired, it wouldn't bother him in the least. Of course, that sent mother into another tizzy fit to think Thaddeus might be unemployed right after the wedding. When he announced his plan to move to Florida and go into the real estate business, and then I told them that I agreed with that plan, they both thought we had lost our minds. They were sure I would be back home in California within the year.

"I guessed we fooled them, didn't we Bertha?"

"You did, an' that's for sure."
"Well, to go on with the story..."

THADDEUS LEFT ME THERE with my mother. He knew we had plans to make, and he had to get Tom's car back to him.

"Call me later, Grace," he said, "and let me know what I need to do."

Then he was gone and I was facing the music alone.

"Oh, I have to tell you, Bertha, I felt so frightened at what I was about to do, but I didn't dare let on or my parents would have found a way to stop me. So I put on a brave face and forged ahead."

That morning, Thaddeus asked Tom if he would be his best man. Tom was flabbergasted. His best friend had come to San Diego for a vacation, a thiry-seven-year-old bachelor, and would leave in a few days, a married man with a wife young enough to be his daughter. I can't say I wouldn't have felt the same way. After all, by the time we married, we'd known each other less than a week.

Bertie interrupted my story. "Well, land's sake, I knowed Homer a lot longer time than that afore we got hitched, an' look at how that turned out. Don't guess the length of time makes all that much difference. Did you do like we did, an' git married at the city hall?"

"No, we didn't. I'll say this for my mother, once it became obvious I wasn't going to change my mind, she put herself in charge and planned a lovely ceremony at home with my family and Thad's mother and sisters. Many of our friends were out of town for the summer, but we gathered around us the ones who were still at home. We had about fifty guests, all told."

My father escorted me down the staircase that curved around from the second-floor balcony, ending in the marble foyer, where the wide doors leading into the living room had been left open for our guests to watch our progress. I wore my great-grandmother's wedding dress and veil and carried a great bouquet of orchids and tulips. Someone had taken Thaddeus and rented him a tuxedo. He looked lovely! The music director of our church played the wedding march on our baby grand piano, which originally belonged to mother's uncle who had been a concert pianist, and the vocal music was sung by the daughter of one of Mother's bridge partners. She was a student at Julliard at the time but happened to be home for the summer.

Mother gave Thaddeus my grandmother's platinum wedding band to give to me. Of course, being mother, she had to hint that the band would go well with the diamond that Thaddeus would eventually buy for me."

I held out my left hand for Bertha to see the lovely ring Thaddeus bought for me when he sold the first Florida house.

"It does go well with the band, don't you think, Bertha?"

Diamonds meant nothing to Bertha, but she told me it was lovely anyhow.

"At any rate, Bertha, if you're still interested, I'll go on with this long tale I'm telling. Shall I?"

"Well, sure I'm in'erested, Grace. It's a real good story, an' to think it's all true. Why, I declare, it beats anything I ever did hear. Go on, now."

Well, after the reception in the back yard by the pool, we were whisked away in the limousine Tom sent, and stayed at the Hotel del Coronado for a few days before leaving for Ohio. I hear my mother cried for days after we left.

"What I git out of all this," Bertha said, "is that you an' Mr. Manning must of been in love for it to last this long. How many children did you have, you done told me once, but now I'm the one forgittin."

We both laughed at Bertha's remark, but I grew sober quickly.

"We have two sons and a daughter. I'm not sure where they all are now, though. I ask Thaddeus every so often if we've heard from them, and he tells me no, they're busy with their own lives. I guess that's the way it is with children, isn't it? They grow up and go away and we don't see them anymore. Like with me and my parents. We didn't stay in close touch after I moved away. Now they're both gone, and I wish we'd been closer."

Thirty-One
Bertie

Grace put her head back on the sofa an' dozed off again, leavin' me to my own thoughts. Seemed to me even with the fancy condo an' the yacht they owned, sometimes the Mannings warn't much happier than I had been, livin' with Homer, 'ceptin' for different reasons.

I were tidyin' up the kitchen when I heard Thad at the front door, talkin' to somebody. Untyin' my apron as I went, I met him an' his visitor comin' into the livin' room, an' motioned for them to be quiet. It were too late, though. Grace had heard 'em.

Settin' up on the sofa, she looked at Tom an' smiled, an' said, jist like it had been yesterday she had saw him, "Why, hello, Tom. Thaddeus, hang Tom's coat up and you two come sit down. Bertha and I were just going to have coffee and dessert. Do we have enough for all of us, Bertha?"

"Well, I'll tell you what, Maxine, it were somethin' to watch, that's for sure. Grace actin' like it were yesterday, the last time she saw Tom. There warn't no surprise about him bein' there."

I's relatin' the events of last night to Maxine while we was eatin' our breakfast. "It upset me so, the way she did, I almost cried. Thad, he didn't know what to do or say, but Mr. Pell..., oh shoot, I cain't say his name, I'll call him Tom, like they do. Tom acted like it were the most natural thing ever. She started talkin' to him about their friends in Hollywood, askin' him how his sister were doin' with the new baby. Thad told me in the kitchen while we was gittin' the coffee, that baby is thirty years old now. He seemed real worried, said this were the second time Grace went back in time an' thought it were today.

"An' it's gittin' harder for her to remember ever'day stuff now, too. I had to tell her my name a couple times last week. I don't know what he's gonna do, he's so upset."

"Well, I know sometimes I forget things, Bertie. Haven't you ever forgotten things, and later wondered why in the world you hadn't been able to remember them?"

My fork stopped afore it got to my mouth when I heard Maxine's question.

"What'd I say, Bert? What's wrong?"

I put my fork on the plate. "Maxine, I done had a dream, or somethin', a few nights ago, an' I been tryin' to sort it out so's I could tell it to you afore I forget it agin."

"You look like you just met a bear goin' to the outhouse, Bertie. What is it that could make you look so afraid? Talk to me, my friend. Whatever it is, get it off your mind."

"Well, if I tell you what I been rememberin', or dreamin', or whatever it were, you got to promise not to tell it to nobody, 'cause I don't know if it really happened, or did I dream it. You promise?"

"I don't like to make promises I can't keep, Bertie. Are you sure this isn't something that needs to be told to someone other than me? I mean, what if it's something psychological, you know, like bothering your mind to where you need counseling? Or medication? With all that's happened in your life, I wouldn't be a bit surprised if that was the case. Can I wait until I hear what this is before I make any promises?"

"You're the only person I know I can tell this to, Maxine, so I guess I'll jist go ahead an' do it. It's about somethin' I'm pretty sure happened when I were about four or five years old. An' now I been havin' these real bad dreams for about a week."

"You go on and tell me, Bert. I won't interrupt, it sounds like you need to get something off your chest. Go on, now, don't be afraid."

"Well, I am afraid, but I'll tell it to you anyhow. Here's what I been dreamin'."

"I WAKE UP SHAKIN' all over an' sick in my stomach. I don't want to remember the dreams but they's startin' to come back to me.

"In one dream this little girl is settin' in a rockin' chair lookin' out the screen door into the early summer mornin'. She is waitin' for somebody, I think, to come through the door an' fix her breakfast. Seems like she been settin' there a long time. Jist waitin'.

"I'm rememberin' more of the dream ever' day. I recollect the little girl had cried most of the day afore, an' finally got out of

the rockin' chair an' fell asleep on the hot linoleum floor in the kitchen, wakin' up hungry the next mornin'.

"Rememberin' that her daddy had told her to set in that chair til he say she could come down, she gits up off the floor an' climbs back into it an' is settin' there when her daddy walks into the kitchen. He stands in front of the sink, starin' out the window into the yard.

"In the dream, the little girl hollers out, 'Daddy, I gots to pee!' An' then, 'I want my mama.' He turns around an' raises his hand like he is goin' to hit her. 'Don't you never say her name agin, you hear me? Don't never ask for her agin, either. She were a bad woman, an' she ain't never comin' back here. You go on up to your room an' don't come out til you done forgot about her. Now git!'

"IT TOOK MOST OF this week for me to remember the awfullest part, Maxine. The little girl in the dream were me."

"Good grief, Bertie, what a horrible dream. If it's true, how could you remember back that far? I can't remember anything before the age of ten or so. That had to be a bad dream, is all."

"Yes, it were a bad dream, Maxine, you're right about that. But it seems like that dream is bringin' back what I done forgot about the day my mama went away. That mornin', my daddy come an' got me out of my bedroom an' took me down to the kitchen an' set me down hard into the rocker. Told me to stay right there an' don't git up. Then he went back up the stairs, an' in a few minutes he come down, carryin' my mama. She were all limp, an' I hollered out, 'What's wrong with my mama?' He jist kept walkin' an said she's sick is all, an' told me to set in that chair an' be quiet til he say I can climb down.

"He carried her outside, headin' for the meadow, an' when he come back inside he were alone. I asked him where was my mama an' he said she went away an' warn't never comin' back. I started to cry an' he hit me real hard, said to quit my cryin'. Said I warn't to ask about her ever agin or he'd hit me some more. I never saw my mama after that."

Thirty-Two
Maxine

MY MIND WAS RACING so fast I could barely keep up with my thoughts. Somewhere along the way I could swear I'd heard that Mrs. Knight had deserted her husband and child and left town under cover of darkness. Rumor back then had it that she left William Knight for another man. A different rumor told a story of Mrs. Knight being admitted to a sanitarium, or asylum, and Mr. Knight covered up the situation by saying she had left him. 'Course, those rumors had been passed around town for such a long time they became like a legend, so by now it was impossible to know for sure where she'd gone.

Now, though, here's Mrs. Knight's grown-up daughter telling a whole different story, and making it sound like it could've really happened. She was a small child then, how could she remember back that far with any accuracy? Maybe her mama did leave after Mr. Knight took her outside. But why was he carrying her? I was confused. What was the real truth here, I wondered.

Bertie interrupted my train of thought.

"All them years I believed my daddy's story about her leavin' us. That's why I don't know what to make about what's in my mind from this dream."

I didn't think I wanted to hear any more of this story, but I'd gotten into it, and Bertie needed help sorting through things. "Well, keep talking, Bertie, and we'll see if we can figure it out."

"This next part were like a dream in a dream, Maxine. In my dream I was sleeepin' an' dreamin' that my mama had come back home to git me, an' my daddy started beatin' on her agin. It made me s' mad that when I woke up I asked my daddy about my mama.

"The part of all this that I forgot is what the dream were about that I had the other night. Ain't that strange, dreamin' you had a dream? But I don't think it were a dream, Maxine. I think I were rememberin' what really happened when I asked him about her.

"See, when I were about ten years old, thereabout, I noticed my daddy drinkin' a lot of whiskey, an' for the next couple a years it got to botherin' me real bad because the whiskey made him mean-natured. I think he'd been drinkin' hard that mornin' when I asked him about my mama, an' he started yellin' an' wavin' his arms around in the air, an' cursin', but then he went to cryin'. I think I'm rememberin' what he told me for real, an' if it's true, it's awful."

I could see that Bertie was shaken. She was trembling.

"Hey, hey, it's okay. You don't have to talk about this, just forget it."

"I cain't forget it, Maxine. I done forgot it all them years, now I got to tell it to somebody. Please listen to me, Maxine."

"Okay, okay, Bert. Calm down. You tell me whatever you want to and I'll listen. Just take it easy, you hear?"

"All right, Maxine. I'll slow down an' try not to cry while I talk.

"At first it were hard to understand what my daddy were sayin', he's so drunk. But after a little bit, he settled down some. Seemed like he needed to tell somebody, like I'm tellin' you now, an' I's the only one there to tell it to.

"He said right from the start she were a wicked woman. I can hear him now, like it were yesterday. Said she didn't want to do things the right way. Come into his home the day they was married, right away started tryin' to change things. Puttin' up curtains at the windows, blockin' out the light so's a body couldn't hardly see. Wantin' to put in a better stove, anythin' to spend his hard-earned money.

"He said ever' time he took her to town, she'd wander off an' start talkin' to people, laughin' an' sech, carryin' on like one of them girls what hung around at the Silver Dollar Bar downtown.

"Last time he took her to town, he said he left her settin' in the truck while he went in for a shot of whiskey to see him home. He come out an' she were gone. Found her in the feed store talkin' to some lady, invitin' her to ride over sometime an' drink a cup of tea with her.

"Daddy said he yanked her out of there an' on the way home he give her a good talkin' to about lettin' strangers come into the house, but she wanted to argue about it. By the time they got to the barn, he said he were so riled up he told her to shut up talkin' bout stuff like that. He said she told him she wouldn't live like that for the rest of her life, she were goin' to leave him soon's she could find her a job.

"Oh, Maxine, I wish she had jist done what he told her to do. She wouldn't of had to go away then."

"Hush, Bertie, you be still and not tell me anymore of this stuff, you hear me?"

"I have to tell you, Maxine. Let me go on."

I hesitated. This was so horrible. "Okay, go ahead, but I have to tell you I'm having a hard time with this."

"Well, the next thing he told me, he said he beat the snot out of her that day with his belt, hit her in the stomach with a tree limb that were layin' on the ground. Told her if she wanted some more she knew where she could git it. Told her if she left, he'd come an' find her.

"He never had no more trouble from her after that, he said. Said she was always sickly from then on. Kept wantin' to see the doctor. He figgered it were jist a plan she made up to get him to take her back to town so's she could try to git away. Said he watched her like a hawk from then on."

"You know, Bertie, I've wondered why you just did what your father told you to do without making a fuss or standing up to him. Now I understand why. Even though you haven't been able to remember all of this consciously, it's been in your mind ever since you were a little girl. Do you think you were afraid he would do the same to you if you crossed him?"

"Yes, Maxine. 'Specially because of the next part he told me. I were too young to understand it at the time, I jist knew this next part made me believe my mama didn't want me even afore she left."

"What did that mean old man tell you, Bertie?"

"My daddy said when my mama found out she's goin' to have a baby, she took some herbs she knew about, tryin' to get the baby to come out too early, but they didn't do the job."

"Oh, Bertie, it wasn't you your mama didn't want. I think she just didn't want to bring a baby into a world where its daddy was so mean."

Bertie had to stop for a bit to blow her nose. She tucked her hanky into the pocket of her new slacks and went on.

"Time come for the baby to be born, she didn't tell him it were happenin'. She waited for him to go to plowin' that day, then she went into the barn an' stayed there by herself until it were all over. He didn't know 'til he went to muckin' stalls an' put fresh straw down what a hard time she'd had of it. The straw bales was soaked with blood clear through to the floor. He said she never did git her strength back after that, jist dwindled away.

"He said he couldn't keep track of my age, what with takin' care of the farm an' all, but I were somewheres around five years old when he found her one mornin', layin' there in the bed with her eyes open, lookin' up at the ceilin'. He knowed she were dead, so he buried her out back in the meadow. Right then, he said he decided he warn't goin' to let me grow up to be like her."

"Oh, my dear God in Heaven! Bertie. This isn't something you can keep to yourself. What if it's true?"

Bertie was crying hard by now.

"I know, I know, Maxine. My poor mama, I think he beat her until she jist give up an' died. All them years, he lied about it, said she went away an' left us. I been thinkin' for my whole life that my mama didn't love me, she went away an' left me behind."

I pulled Bertie into my arms and rocked from side to side, patting her back gently, and for the second time since I'd met her, I let Bertie cry until there were no more tears left to shed.

We sat at my kitchen table, Bertie stirring sugar into her cup of coffee, waiting for the sheriff to show up. She had resisted calling him at first, but I finally persuaded her.

"Bertie. If this is true, what we're thinking, your mama died because of what your daddy did to her. You've got to find out the truth and somehow make it up to her. I know it's sixty-five years too late, but if you don't tell what you know, you're going to go to your grave still thinking – wondering, I guess is a better way to put it – did your mama leave you behind and go away, or was she. . .?"

I couldn't finish the sentence, couldn't bear the thought of saying the word '*murdered*'.

Neither of us heard the sheriff walk up to the door. He peered in through the screen and said, "Hey. You two okay in there?"

We must've been real wired up because the sound of his voice scared me so bad I about jumped off my chair. I let him in.

"Yeah, we're better now than we were an hour ago. Glad you could make it out here so quick, Sheriff Turner. It's been a rough morning."

"From what little you told me on the phone, I'd say that's an understatement, Maxine."

He put his hand on Bertie's shoulder and gave a squeeze. "You just relax now, Mrs. Claxton. Maxine tells me you're havin' a real hard time over this. Can't say as I blame you.

"Maxine, fix me a cup of that coffee, smells good. Let's sit for a few minutes and just visit, give us all a chance to pull ourselves together before we head into this."

Sheriff Turner asked Bertie how the sale of the farm was coming along. He told us his cow had calved during the night. Told us how proud he was of his oldest granddaughter, she'd won another certificate for getting all A's on her report card last time. He drained his coffee cup and set it on the table with a firm clunk.

"Okay. Let's see what we got here. Maxine told me on the phone what you told her, Mrs. Claxton. You know, we're just now getting acquainted, but could I call you Bertie, maybe make this situation a little less formal that way."

"Yes sir. That'd be all right with me."

"Okay. Bertie. Now, what I gather, there could be some chance that your mama didn't run off and leave you behind. And by putting two and two together from what you told Maxine, there's a possibility your mama died that night. If all that's true, the final conclusion from your story is, no matter how she died, your mama might be buried on the property that used to belong to your daddy. Is that right?"

"Yes sir."

"Who owns that property now, Bertie?"

"I don't know. After my daddy died, Homer, Mr. Claxton, told me it were goin' to git sold. That's the last I ever heard about it."

"Well, if it got sold, wouldn't the money have come to you, seein' as how your father, Mr. Knight, had no other living relatives?" The sheriff looked at me, then Bertie, puzzled, and shrugged his shoulders.

"Wouldn't a sale be recorded in the public records for real estate transactions, Maxine?"

I said, "You know, I never thought about Mr. Knight's farm being sold. It's been deserted all these years, no one living on it. Some of us talked about it a while back, maybe twenty years or so ago, but decided it wasn't any of our business what he'd done about it. For all we knew, he had family up north or somewhere, deeded it to them or whatever. We finally decided he'd just given it to Homer and Bertie."

I stopped short and was surprised at the thought that popped into my head.

"What you thinkin', Maxine," Sheriff Turner said.

"I just remembered the keys. When Mr. Downing, my attorney, he's Bertie's attorney now, when he was going through the metal box me and Bert found in the attic after the fire, there's some keys in there that don't fit anything in the house. I'm wondering, Sheriff, if maybe they fit something at Mr. Knight's house. What would it take to get in over there and check that out?"

"Well, to be on the up-and-up about it, we'd have to find out who owns the house, then either get their permission to search around in there, or we issue a search warrant. Problem is, we wouldn't know who to issue it to, would we? Now, on the other hand, do we know anyone gonna object if we go in there and look around real gentle-like? If the property never got sold, like as not it belongs to Bertie now. Would you like to give us permission to go over there and take a look-see, Bertie?"

"Can I do that? I cain't hardly believe that farm is mine. Land's sake, Maxine. I don't know what to say."

"Say yes, Bert. It's the only way to figure out what's going on here."

"We'll be careful not to disturb things. Bertie," the sheriff said. "If we don't find anything, we'll close it back up tight, and start searching to find out who owns the place now. What do you say?"

"I guess that would be all right, but do I have to come with you," Bertie asked me.

"Not unless you want to," I assured her.

Me, the Sheriff and Mr. Downing trooped over there the next day, keys from the safe box in the Sheriff's hand.

One of the two keys opened the front door of Mr. Knight's farmhouse. The smaller key opened a desk drawer in the living room. In the drawer, we found the deed to the farm, along with a handwritten statement signed by William S. Knight, and witnessed by Homer J. Claxton.

Bertie's daddy had left the house and its contents, along with the land and all the farm equipment, to his daughter, Bertha Louise Knight Kenner Claxton.

All those miserable years she'd spent living with Homer could have been avoided. She'd had a home of her own, but Homer had kept that information from her.

Thirty-Three
Thaddeus

I drove Bertie to Maxine's, leaving Tom and Grace to visit with each other.

Maxine confronted me as I escorted Bertie to the door. She said she felt like I should have stayed home. "I declare, Thad, I could have come and gotten Bertie. Here you leave your company and drive all the way out in the country when I could have saved you the trip."

"Well, I wanted Tom to spend some time alone with Grace, see for himself how she is. Who knows, maybe seeing him will help get her back on track. Anyhow, I do need to get back there. I don't want to leave him alone with her for too long, just in case. These days, I'm never sure from one minute to the next how she'll be."

Tom heard my key click in the lock and met me at the door, holding his finger to his lips. "She's asleep," he whispered.

"How'd it go?" I asked.

"Really well. We had a great time. Talked about the good old days at the beach. I brought her up to date on my ma's death. Grace was right there with me on everything. Frankly, Thad, I didn't see anything out of whack with her. You sure these docs know their stuff?"

Right about then, Grace called out. "Thad, are you home now? Come and say goodnight to me." I guess we weren't quiet enough.

"I'll go in and talk to her for a few minutes, Tom. Why don't you pour us a cup of coffee and I'll be right back?"

I tucked the sheet around Grace and leaned over her for a goodnight kiss.

"Are you sure you boys will be all right now? I would have changed the sheets in the guest bedroom if I had known Tom was coming, Dear. It's lovely that's he's here, but you should have told me."

"He wanted to surprise you, Grace. Now you get to sleep. We have a few days of visiting ahead of us, and you know how tired you get if you don't have enough rest. I'll leave the night light on in the bathroom in case you need to get up, but I'll bet you anything you'll be asleep in two shakes, and that's the last we'll see of you until morning."

I pulled the bedroom door shut tight behind me. She'd be in dreamland very quickly, but I wanted to be sure Tom and I could talk without worrying that she might overhear our conversation.

I leaned on the frame of the open doorway to the guest bedroom and watched in silence as Tom went about emptying his suitcase into the dresser and hanging his garment bag in the closet. Tom knew I was there, but neither of us wanted to be the first to speak. Finally, Tom was finished unpacking and followed me into the living room.

"This is a great place you have here, Thad. How long now since we've been together? Three, four years?"

"Aha, my friend, your memory is failing you, too. It's been seven years."

As soon as I said it, I wished I'd worded it differently, and started to say so to Tom. A few times over the years I had tried to get him to come our way, but he was always so busy he never seemed to find the time. I was as busy as he was, so the years flew by. Neither of us had any good excuse for neglecting our friendship, and we both knew it.

"Hey, don't worry about it. But while you were in with Grace just now, I remembered the one thing she said right after you left with Bertie. We're in the kitchen, I'm makin' coffee while Grace is talkin' about the last time we was together at my place in California. So, I guess I do see what you been tryin' to tell me. Seven years, huh? She thought it was last week. Is she like that all the time?"

"No. Much of the time she's right there with the rest of us, like you said. But it seems like she's having bad times more often. The strange thing about whatever this is that's happening, she can remember from her early childhood all the way up to when our kids were teenagers. After that, things come and go."

"So, what do you do now?"

"Well, she's been through all the tests, and the diagnosis is Alzheimer's. She's on medication, but I've got to tell you, Tom, somethimes I think the doctors don't know for sure what this disease really is, or how to treat it. It's guesswork. But it's better, I think, to do something than nothing. We don't have a choice except to wait it out and see where it goes.

"Anyhow, it's so good to see you. Tell me what's happening with you. Made a decision yet about our last phone conversation?"

"Yeah. I'm leavin' California, Thad. There's nothing holding me there. Ma's gone. My sister, the one that left home just before we moved from New York to California? We been in contact for a couple of years now. She's happy where she is, doesn't wanna leave New York. Got a couple of kids, married a nice guy, according to her. But it's been so long, we're having a hard time reconnecting, you know?

"And my other sister, the one that came with us when we moved? We talk once in a while, but after our pa died and then our ma, we kind of drifted apart. Don't have a lot in common anymore. She's married, grandchildren, that whole scenario.

"I miss being around you and Grace. If I'd had any sense, I woulda come wich you when you left California. I can't complain about the movies, it was a glamorous way to live, but if I had it to do over, I might not have done it."

"You ever regret not getting married and having kids?" I asked Tom. "Not that our kids filled our life with joy, but even so. You never know how your kids are going to turn out. You have them and hope for the best. Yours might have been great."

"Yeah, now that I'm an old geezer, I think about that. But I guess it's hard to miss what you never had. I get lonely sometimes, Thad. I don't need to tell you, I've had my share of lovely ladies in my life, but after a while, they all start to look alike. Put a bag over their heads, can't tell one from the other pretty soon. 'Course, there's a few out there would say the same thing about me, if you asked them."

I laughed. "That's not funny, Tom, but it made me laugh, which is saying something these days. So, where are you headed after you leave sunny California?"

Tom stared out our living room window, which overlooked Sarasota Bay. I knew he was nervous by the way his fingers drummed on the back of the sofa.

"Come on, spit it out. Where you going?"

"Here." He turned his head to look at me for my reaction.

"Well, it's about time. What took you so long, you old so-and-so?"

We reached over the coffee table that separated us and clasped hands, mine covering Tom's and holding tight. I was reluctant to let go.

We talked long into the night, catching up on seven years of being apart. Tom planned to put his business affairs in order when he got back to California and head to Florida as soon as possible. We decided to sell the Ohio condominium building right away and put the equity into the new senior facility I was working on.

"Wait until you get to spend time with Bertie Claxton, get to know her, Tom. She's straight out of another century. Her mother left when Bertie was real young. She only went to the third grade. Her father, then her husband, kept her pretty cloistered for almost her whole life. She was married for a few years to her first husband, had a baby that was stillborn, then her husband died in a truck wreck. Except for those few years, she had very little contact with the public. She went to church with her father, so she knew people by name, but basically, she stayed at home and took care of her father's farmhouse until she remarried, then did the same with her second husband. He's been dead for a few months now, and honestly, Tom, her life story would make a great movie. You sure you want to give up Hollywood?"

Tom laughed. "Lots of people think they've got a book, or a movie. Run into them all the time. Most of them turn out to be so ordinary, or so made up, you have to wonder what they're thinking. I'll admit, when I saw her tonight, I knew she was different. Her speech, it's like she's from some backwoods swamp."

"What I gather so far, her father's family, mostly uneducated, have lived in the deep south, one place or another, all the way back to whenever. Stuck out there on the farm, that's what she heard, so that's all she knows. But she's persuaded Grace to help her learn to read better, and she wants to improve her speech, too. Grace is loving it. I think Bertie Claxton is going to turn out to be a huge blessing to us."

"That's great, Thad. Hope it works out for you and Grace.'

"Now though, I need to hear about this new facility you're planning. If I'm going to be an investor, I wanna know everything. Tell me whacha got!"

"I'm more excited about this than anything I've done so far, Tom. Fifteen years ago, I was riding around the eastern part of the county looking at acreage for possible development. I drove into this little farming community where a sign at the edge of town said :

WELCOME TO CREEK, FLORIDA
Population 1,020 souls

"I drove through the town and came out the other end where it all turned into farmland. There was a man plowing up a big field. walking behind two large draft horses. I pulled over to the side of the road and waited there until he got to the end of the row in front of where I'd parked. Pulling the horses to a stop, he stood there, watching me. I think he thought I'd leave, but I waved my hand in the air and yelled hello to him. I know he could tell I wanted him to come over, and he did, but he wasn't happy about it.

"I told him I was driving around looking at the countryside, said I stopped because this was such a pretty place. He seemed pleased to tell me he had one-hundred-forty-seven acres. I could see a grove of trees way out on the edge of where he said his property ended. Looked like there was a creek running through. He even threw in the information that the creek ended in a waterfall that dropped down about three feet into a pond, then continued over into the field that belonged to the next farm."

Tom interrupted. "Wait a minute. A waterfall? In Florida?"

"That's what I said to him. Here's how he explained it. Said when his grandfather was a little boy the creek originally went through their property which was mostly flat, but when it got to a low spot in the ground, the water started collecting. After a while, the family noticed that the water was eroding the sandy soil until a ditch formed. Over the years, the ditch got deeper, the dirt on either side caved in and leveled the ground out around it, the creek worked its way through the sandy soil, and now, today, it's actually a little waterfall with a pond at the bottom. From there, it just sort of wanders through the fields onto the next farm.

"I asked him about his family, did he have children, and he seemed to close up right about then. Said no, no children, then he asked me what it was I was doing out there.

"I explained that I was a real estate developer and that I was searching for acreage on which to build a senior complex. He had no idea what that meant.

"'You know, Mr. Claxton, a place where older people can live and be taken care of when they can't take care of themselves any longer.'

"I offered him two-hundred-thousand dollars for the farm, a place to live while the complex was being developed, and the first choice of the apartments after completion for him and his wife to live in, free, for the rest of their lives."

"Sounds fair to me," Tom said. "I take it he didn't accept your offer."

"No, he sure didn't. He ordered me off his property, started cursing and yelling, said he wasn't going to let his family's farm get broken up into little pieces and sold off to a bunch of city slickers. I gave him my card, which he accepted. Put it in the bib pocket of his overalls.

"When I got back to the office, I sent him a letter repeating my offer, and reassured him that the property would not be broken up but kept whole and used for development of the senior complex. I included another card, in case he'd thrown the first one away, and sent it off to him. I never heard from him again."

"I can imagine what a surprise it must have been to hear from Bertie's attorney fifteen years later, right," Tom said.

"That's putting it mildly," I said.

Having heard how Bertie Claxton and I had met, Tom now put the pieces of the story together.

"Man, you are right, Thad. This would make a great movie! Mr. Claxton is dead and buried, you're in the process of buying the Claxton farm from his widow, and the dream you've had for that acreage all these years is about to come true. Wow."

Our voices had gotten louder with excitement. We were slapping each other on the back and laughing when Grace walked into the room in her nightgown.

"Thaddeus? What's all the noise about?" Looking at Tom, she said, "Why, how nice. You have company. Who's your friend, Dear?"

Thirty-Four
Maxine

"You don't mind, do you Bert, if I sit out here in my p.j.'s? I do that sometimes of an evening. I clean my face, brush my teeth, and sit on the porch until bedtime, just listening to Florida at night. And watching. A few times I've seen an alligator crossing the road. Lots of deer around, too. They come almost up to the house to eat the plants, if I sit real still. One time I counted twenty deer in the yard munching on the crepe myrtle tree. Mostly though, they'll be in bunches of six or seven."

"I surely don't mind if you set out here, Maxine. That's what I did most nights, at home. Only difference was, I's jist settin' there waitin' to go to bed so's I could get on with the next day. Waitin' for my time to leave an' go be with Farley an' the baby."

I started to apologize to Bertie for bringing up bad memories, but she stopped me.

"No need to feel bad, Maxine. I got to where them poor feelin's eased up some an' I's able to set quiet, like you, an' watch the sunset an' the wildlife. So you go on tellin' me your stories. Go on now."

"Well, then, there's the gopher tortoises. A whole civilization of them. They live on my property because it's mostly sand, very little water. They dig down into the sand and make homes there, but they come out and roam around a lot. They don't seem to be afraid of me, even the little bitty babies. No bigger across their shells than five or six inches. The grownups, though, they can get huge. One day I spotted the granddaddy, his shell must have been three feet across. He turned his head and stared at me while he lumbered across my lawn. Looked like a throwback to some prehistoric creature.

"Once in a while we'll get a bear if someone leaves their garbage dumpster open overnight, and then there's the armadillos and raccoons. You ever have any of those on your place?"

"Oh, sure, we have all them critters. Homer kept a rifle handy, too, for when he went to the barn. Lots of times there'd be snakes around. One time he found a open place under the cement slab of the pump house. Must of been ten snakes livin' under there. One of 'em were a coachwhip, big feller. He shed his skin right outside the back door of the house, an' after he crawled away, Homer went out there an' measured it. He were a inch or two longer'n seven foot.

"The rest was black snakes, big ones, they don't hurt nothin', but I didn't like havin' 'em that close t' the house, so Homer waited 'til they left for the day to go find food an' lay in the sun, then he filled in the hole under the slab with gravel from the driveway. Them poor critters couldn't figger out where the hole went. One big one kept raisin' up an' bangin' its head where the hole used to be 'til I thought it were goin' to mash its nose in.

They finally give up an' went away an' we never seen 'em agin, 'cept once in a while out in the yard. No poison snakes around, though. Homer said the coachwhips kill rattlers. I pretty much don't like snakes in general, but when he told me that, I didn't mind havin' that big one roamin' around out there."

"I know what you mean, Bert. I hate snakes, too. Especiallly the kind with two feet."

"You seen snakes what had feet, Maxine? I never knowed about no snakes what had feet."

Laughing, I said, "No, I don't mean real snakes, Bertie. I'm talking about people who are so mean and nasty they're lower than a snake's belly. It's just an expression, a way of calling someone a bad name without swearing. Someone like my third husband. We never did finish that conversation, did we?"

"No, we never did. You sure you want to talk about him?"

"Yeah, I don't mind. We'll call it therapy for me, and educational for you. You want me to keep on with my tale of woe?"

"Shucks, you been listenin' to me tell my sad stories, I might's well listen to yours."

Telling all this to Bertie brought back some real bad memories, but I figured I might as well get it all off my chest. I realized talking about it was cathartic, like laying on a therapist's couch in order to be rid of the guilt, but without paying a huge amount of money. So I plunged in and picked up where I'd left off the last time we talked.

I WAS SINGLE FOR a long time after the doctor husband left. By the time the kids were in high school, I'd worked my way up to DON, that's Director of Nursing, at a local assisted living facility, kind of like the one Thad's planning, only not so fancy as his will be. My son, Simon, was graduating from high school and he asked me if I would mind sitting with the father of his best friend, Jeff, at the commencement ceremony. Jeff's mother had died the year before and his dad, Frank, said he felt awkward being out in public alone. He didn't even want to be at the graduation, but Simon and Jeff persuaded him to go and told him I'd sit with him.

THAT'S HOW IT STARTED, at our kids' graduation. They sat me down next to Frank, and Frank picked it up from there.

"Thanks for keeping me company, Sweetheart," Frank said. "I know it might seem strange to some people that I didn't want to come tonight, but Jeff's mother always arranged everything. I just showed up wherever she told me to, and it all worked out fine. Now, though, I'm lost. If the kid doesn't tell me where I'm supposed to be, chances are, I won't be there. It's different, you know, going to this stuff alone. I never realized while she was alive, how my wife took charge of it all and kept me company. I feel like people are staring at me when I show up alone. It's been great having you with me. Thanks a lot for doing this."

A small red flag went up in my brain. A warning. This is the same kind of guy I seem to be drawn to, men who need help. *Well, now I know better*, I thought.

So when Frank invited me to go for a drink after the graduation ceremony, I went, prepared to spend a few hours with the father of my son's best friend. Frank turned out to be charming, witty, and a great conversationalist. When he confided that his wife had usually done most of the talking during their marriage, I asked him why that was.

"Well, Baby Face, I guess she didn't think I had anything intelligent to say. She finished most of my sentences for me. People said they thought it was great that she could always tell what I was going to say. The women liked that I let her speak for me without interrupting her. Made me look like a real nice guy, I guess. Anyhow, it was easier that way than trying to get a word in. You though, Darlin', you're real easy to talk to. You let a person finish a sentence without butting in. I like that," Frank told me, as he motioned for the waiter to bring us another round of drinks.

"Oh, no more for me, Frank. One is almost too many, and I've already had two. I'm afraid I'm not much of a drinker," I said.

"Oh, come on, one more won't kill you. These Brandy Alexanders are real smooth, taste like a milkshake, almost. Just have one more, Sweetheart."

Frank's habit of calling me by anything except my name had begun to irritate me early in the evening, but true to form, I found it hard to voice my displeasure about anything. I drank the third cocktail against my better judgement and found I couldn't stand up without listing to one side when it was time to leave.

"Hey there, Sweet Thing, you better let old Frank drive you home. I'd hate to have to tell your kids I let their mom get drunk and drive home that way. The boys will be out all night, but when they get home in the morning, they can come back here and get your car. How about that, Little Girl?"

The three strong drinks had hit me hard. I wasn't thinking clearly, or I would have seen what was coming.

I woke up the next morning in Frank's bed with him beside me, snoring loudly, his mouth hanging open and drool trailing down his cheek onto the pillow.

Holding my aching head with one hand, I pounded on Frank until he sat up, looking blankly at me.

"You wake up and take me to my car this instant." He listened to my tirade all the way to my car. "Don't ever call me again, you rotten snake in the grass."

The boys didn't know I'd been out all night, but my sixteen-year-old daughter, Dina, did. She had sneaked in through the back door the night before, three hours past her curfew, expecting me to be waiting at the door to ground her for the next five years. What she found was an empty kitchen and a dark house. When she checked the garage, my car wasn't there.

Dina told me later she waited up for me until four o'clock in the morning and finally crashed on the couch. A few hours later the sound of the front door creaking shut behind me as I tried to sneak in without being heard woke her up. Leaping off the couch, she hurried to greet me as I tiptoed down the hallway. I'd slept in my clothes, the same ones I'd worn to the graduation, and I was a mess.

Unprepared to face my daughter, I blurted out the first thing that came to my mind. "It's not what it looks like so don't even ask."

Frank sounded sincere on the phone when he called me later in the day.

"Hey there, Sweetie Pie. I really enjoyed myself last night. How would you like to get together for dinner tonight? I know this great restaurant out at the lake. . ."

I cut him off. I was furious. I was finally beginning to see a pattern here in my choice of men. Rather, in their choice of me, and me letting them do the choosing. I decided I wanted to confront Frank face to face and let him know what I thought of him.

"Sure, Frank, just tell me where and I'll meet you there." When he began to object to meeting me instead of picking me up, I cut him off again.

"No, I insist on meeting you. I have somewhere else to go afterward, and it won't be convenient to have you with me. Just tell me where to meet you and what time."

I realized after I hung up that I was still letting other people make my decisions for me. Why didn't I pick the time and the place and tell him to meet me? Was I some kind of wet dish rag to let people always be dictating my life to me? Well, that was going to stop, starting tonight.

I located Frank's car and pulled into a space on the opposite side of the parking lot. I didn't want to be anywhere close to him when it was time to leave. Entering the dining room, I spotted him sitting at a table overlooking Lake Michigan. He was gazing out at the water and didn't see me come in. The Maitre d' offered to escort me to the table, but I insisted on walking by myself. *Confidence, that's what I want to convey here*, I thought.

Frank looked up as I approached the table, then looked in the diredction of the Matre d', puzzled as to why I was alone.

"I didn't want to be escorted, Frank. Starting right now, I'm on my own, and we have a few things to get straight before we go any farther."

He started to say something but I stopped him. "You just be quiet and listen to me." Pulling out a chair, I sat down across from him and slammed my purse onto the seat next to mine. Frank jumped, startled by my abruptness.

"First of all, Frank, I'm beginning to understand why your wife did all the talking in your marriage. I think she wised up to you early on. Which is what I've done. You are an insincere, self-centered, lying son-of-a buck. If I was a swearing woman, I'd use stronger language, but I'm all through letting other people, men in particular, change me to suit them. From now on, I intend to be who I think I ought to be."

Frank sat, spellbound by my tirade. Until yesterday he didn't know me from a load of hay, but he acted as though I was a woman who could be molded to his will. Now, he didn't seem to know what to think of me.

"Second thing on my list of what I want to say to you. My name is Maxine and I want you to quit calling me something else. Do you call everybody by those endearing names you call me so you won't have to remember what their real name is? Well, if you can't remember my name, I won't have to remember yours either, will I? What would you like to be called? George? Or maybe Father Goose? You were honking like one this morning, it's what woke me up. Maybe Drooley would suit you better. You had lots of that running off your face with your mouth hanging open. Any of those names suit you, huh, Baby Cakes?"

"Well, I, uh, I'm sorry, Sweet, uh I mean, Maxine. That's just how I talk, I didn't mean any harm by using those names."

"Well, see to it that you don't do it anymore, if you even get another chance to address me after we leave here tonight. And number three on the list - you are a snake in the grass, getting me drunk then driving me to your house instead of mine, like you said you were going to do. Did you enjoy yourself while I was passed out in your bed?"

Frank sat there, looking out the window at the water. I took a deep breath and stopped talking, trying to compose myself.

"Maxine," Frank began. "I am so sorry. I don't know what came over me. I think since my wife died, I've been so overcome with loneliness, I lost my head. You're a very attractive woman, Maxine, and I guess once we'd had a few drinks, things got out of hand. Before I ask you to forgive me, I ought to let you know that nothing happened last night. I had more to drink than you did, and by the time we got to my house, all I wanted to do was go to sleep, but I was too embarrassed to tell you that.

"Besides, you didn't know the difference because you passed out as soon as your head hit the pillow. All that aside, Maxine, I need to ask you to forgive me. Please say you will. And say you'll give me another chance, Maxine."

Suddenly, I began to laugh. "Do you realize in the space of two minutes, you've called me Maxine four times? You're a fast learner, Frank. Okay, I've blown my stack and I feel better now. I'm hungry, I haven't eaten all day, I was so mad. Why don't we order some food and see where we go from here?"

Where we went from there five months later was to the court house to be married by the judge in his chambers. My two kids and his son stood up with us, and went with us on a Thanksgiving cruise to the Caribbean, calling it our honeymoon.

Bertie interrupted my narrative.

"I cain't hardly believe you done married him that quick, after bein' on your own for so long," Bertie said.

"I can't either, when I look back on it. I thought it was going to be a wonderful life, but it turned out to be one of the biggest mistakes I ever made. By then, the kids were almost grown, and had minds of their own. We all moved into Frank's house with him and his son. At first, my kids liked the new arrangement. We weren't all crammed into the small apartment we'd been renting. I discovered Frank was well-heeled when he insisted on paying for Simon to go to college along with his own son. I'll say that for him, he could be generous.

"I kept my job at the ALF, and the next year, Dina headed for college loaded down with scholarships and grants, on her way to becoming a doctor. The next few years, everybody came and went, while I worked my way up the ladder to Assistant Director at the ALF. Frank stayed busy conferring with his stock broker and his investments.

"Those early years together, we were all so busy, I guess I missed a lot of what was going on with Frank. Oh, I thought he drank too much at parties, and there was a side of him I hadn't seen before. Frank liked to tell smutty jokes. Not cute ones, not the kind of bathroom humor that people roll their eyes at and moan, ohhhh, but the kind that made people cringe even before he got to the punch line, because the punch line was usually so obvious, and so nasty."

"What is bathroom humor, Maxine? We didn't tell jokes at our house, so I don't know what kind of jokes are funny."

"Oh, Bertie, Bertie. You are a gem. How wonderful it would be if the whole world was as innocent as you are. I hate to explain stuff to you for fear of changing you any. But you're going to learn about real life sooner or later. Might as well be me that explains it to you. Probably the best way to explain it is to tell you one of Frank's jokes so you can hear it for yourself."

Trying to digest the joke I told her, Bertie sat for a bit before she responded.

"All I can think to say, Maxine, is, I'm thankful I never had to listen to none of that kind of talkin'. Maybe Homer had the right idea about television an' books an' goin' to parties an' sech as that. If that's what some people think is funny, I'm glad I don't know them people."

"Well, there's lots of people feel the same way you do, Bert. It took me a while, but I began to realize that Frank and I weren't being invited out with our friends as much as we used to be. I finally cornered my friend, Lillian, and asked her what was going on.

"I don't know what you're talking about,'" Lillian said. "Your imagination is working overtime."

She tried to make me believe we were all getting older, slowing down, not getting together as much as we used to do.

I still got asked to go to lunch with the women, and one day someone mentioned something that happened a few nights before when the women and their husbands were together at the

Smith's house. They laughed and started talking about it, when suddenly they shut up and it got quiet at the table. I asked what the occasion was at the Smith's house. They tried to pass it off as an impromptu get-together. Nothing planned in advance, they said, just word of mouth at the last minute.

I said if it was word of mouth how come I didn't hear about it? I have a mouth, and I have ears. One of the ladies, Mabel, said, "Oh shoot, Maxine. How do you think we all feel trying to hide something like this from you? But you've cornered us, so we might as well come out with it. What do you say, girls?"

Nobody would look at me except Mabel, who was my best friend at the time. She laid it on the line. "For crying out loud, Maxine. You know as well as we all do how Frank likes to tell those raunchy stories and dirty jokes. It's gotten so bad, we hate to see him headed in our direction at a party. Seems no matter what else is being talked about, Frank takes over and real quick starts in with that stuff. Now, none of us minds a little joke once in a while, you know that. But we're talking heavy porn here. The only thing missing is the pictures, and Frank's so graphic, we don't need them."

Once Mabel had broken the ice and confessed, the rest started adding to it. They didn't know what to do about it. A couple of the guys tried to talk to Frank about it one day, and he brushed them off, said they were a couple of prudes, said they let their wives tell them what they could or couldn't talk about. The guys didn't want to be around him anymore, and the ladies felt like they couldn't invite me without him wanting to come along, so they just didn't tell me anymore when they were getting together with their husbands.

The whole time Mabel was telling me this, I kept thinking about Frank's dead wife. Maybe she butted into his conversations, finished his sentences for him, to keep him from talking that way. Instead of thinking poorly of her, I began thinking maybe she was pretty smart. And maybe I'd been pretty stupid, again, marrying another man with problems.

I guess it was self-defense, but I got mad at my friends and told them thanks for letting me in on the secret. I didn't mean to be sarcastic. I was hurt, and it came out as meanness.

I told them I'd try talking to Frank, see if I could do anything about the problem. Then I said, in the meantime they should all have fun at their parties! I threw my napkin into my half-eaten lunch and walked out of the restaurant. I didn't look back, and not one of them stopped me.

I was sitting in Frank's favorite chair when he walked into the living room that afternoon.

"Hi, Cupcake."

He was back to calling me by anything other than my name. He knew it irritated me. I think he meant it to. He says to me, "Can I have my chair, Darlin'."

"It wasn't a question, Bert, he was telling me to get out of his chair. I was already upset over the lunch thing, and now I got more riled up. Frank could tell somethin' was up."

He said, "What is it this time, Maxine?"

I told him what was on my mind, and then he told me what was on his mind.

"I put up with a lot from my wife because we had a kid together and a lot of years behind us," he said. "If she hadn't died when she did, I don't know if we would of stayed together for the long haul. When you came along, I was so used to being hushed up by her, I stayed in the habit for a while of keeping quiet. When I realized you weren't telling me to shut up all the time, I started being myself and loving it. But lately, it seems everything I say is wrong.

"You're always telling me not to joke around, not to tell funny stories, and I know you've been talking to your friends about me, because a few weeks ago, Joe and Ron asked me not to be telling jokes anymore. Ron reminded me, for the gazillionth time, like I never heard it before, that he's a Christian, said he didn't like to hear that stuff himself, let alone have his wife hear it. Said it makes his skin crawl. Joe told me to either cut out the potty talk when I'm around them, or I wouldn't be around them anymore.

"You're all a bunch of old ladies, even your men friends. I think they'd be happy if we stood around and told knock-knock jokes, or Bible stories, for entertainment."

I was still sitting in Frank's chair at that point, but it didn't matter, because he stormed out of the house and came home at three o'clock in the morning, drunk. The last thing he said to me before he slammed the door behind him was the final straw for me.

He said, "Another thing, Sweetheart, just remember whose house this is and get out of my chair. And if you don't like the way things are around here, you can take your little paycheck and go back to living in that stinking project apartment you was living in when I found you. Think about that, Missy Maxine."

"My, seems like he were a real mean man," Bertie said.

"You're right. But I was a wimp back then. I didn't have the courage I needed to stand up for myself. I was worried what people would say about a third broken marriage if I left Frank. But my thinking was about to be changed."

The next day at work, I ran into the psychologist who came to help the residents who were having problems adjusting to their new environment at the facility. She and I got to talking and before I knew it, I was telling her my problems, how confused I was, how guilty I felt about messing up my life so bad.

What she told me changed not only my thinking, it changed my life. She said I didn't need to feel guilty. She thought my decisions had been made in good faith, thinking each time I was doing the right thing. The most important piece of counsel she gave me that day, though, was something I'd never realized before. She said I didn't know how to make a good decision about men. I needed to learn to see what a man was for real, not what I thought he was. Said I needed to stop thinking I could love him so much that I could change him into what I wanted him to be. It was an eye-opener for me.

"I guess I was lucky, Maxine. I never had no trouble seein' Homer for what he was. Jist plain mean."

"I should have been so fortunate, Bertie. But then the psych said I stayed with Frank way too long because by the time I realized I'd made another poor judgment, I didn't want to admit my own part in the situation."

She asked me if I knew what my biggest fault was, and then she told me what it was. She said I didn't have enough faith in myself. She said I didn't need a man to take care of me and my kids, and I realized she was right. I had a good job, two great kids, some friends. Why'd I think I needed Frank? So he could boss me around, make me feel bad about myself? I knew then if I got out of that marriage with any pride left in me, I'd never make that mistake again.

I thought Bertie looked uncomfortable, listening to my sad life.

"You had enough, Bert, or should I go on?"

"Well, I know I felt better after I told you about my daddy an' Homer an' all, so you go on ahead an' unload. Seems like you been carryin' a heavy burden in your mind. In spite of you jokin' around an' laughin' a lot, you seem sad sometimes. Maybe gittin' it all out in the open, you'll git to bein' a happier person."

"Bertha, Bertha! How did you get to be so wise? You just seem to go straight to the truth of a matter. I'm glad you're my friend. At any rate, the story continues. . ."

By now I realized my marriage to Frank wasn't going to work, that I'd find myself on my own again. At first I blamed my poor decisions on a lack of self-confidence. Maybe that was the truth, maybe it wasn't. But by then I had learned enough to know that life at its best is uncertain, and I made the decision to get into a position where I could take care of myself if it ever came to that again.

Neither Frank nor I knew it at the time, but he did me a huge favor when he told me on our wedding day to keep my little paycheck for pocket money. He said he could afford to keep his wife in style. He was so disinterested in me as a person that he had no idea that my paycheck was anything but little. At first I had frittered it away on clothes, stuff to make Frank's house prettier. I couldn't tell you now what all I spent it on, except for my investments. I'll tell you about that later. But the day after I confronted him and he reminded me whose house I lived in and all but told me to get out, I did a total turn-around.

I will say that Frank had a generous streak, but I know now it was motivated by how it made him look to others. He paid for all four years of college for my son, and provided a home for my children. The fact that they were both almost grown by the time I married him didn't seem to occur to Frank, though. He often bragged about how he had raised my children and provided for them. Simon and Dina both disliked Frank intensely and avoided being around him as much as possible, a fact he never seemed to notice, just as he seemed not to notice that their friends didn't hang out at our house.

I spent our entire married life putting much of my money in our joint account, so I didn't feel at all bad about what I did next. I began taking what I could filter out of my household allowance and adding it to my entire paycheck every week. Being as absorbed as he was with himself, Frank totally missed the fact that I was a darn good nurse who had steadily moved up the ladder. He was so busy being out and about that he didn't even know I was taking college courses in nursing and business administration. No one could have been more surprised than I was when they offered me the position of Administrator of the ALF where I had worked for all those years.

Here's the part about the investments, though, Bert. Early on in our marriage, I began paying attention to Frank's bragging at the dinner table about his investments and started to think about doing something with my own money. I didn't use the same brokerage firm that he used though. I did some research and found my own, and then every spare penny I could get my hands on got invested into stocks, bonds, certificates of deposit, a savings account, and a high-interest-yielding IRA. I had a pretty solid portfolio built up.

So, the day Frank told me to take my paltry paycheck and move back to the project apartment where I lived when he found me, I did him one better. I cashed in or sold everything I could, and I bought the land the apartment used to sit on.

"Why in the world would you want to buy the place you worked so hard to git out of, Maxine?"

"That's what makes this story so amazing, Bertie. By then, that section of town was part of a city-wide renovation program. The apartments had been abandoned for a number of years, and the land was being sold off for commercial and single-family use development. I bought the property that fronted the main street on one side and the Metra tracks on the other."

"What's a Metra track, Maxine?"

"The Metra is a train system that runs all over the city of Chicago and its suburbs. People leave their cars in parking lots and board the train in their local areas, and that fast train takes them to locations close to where they work or want to shop. You have no idea how many people live away from the city but work there. The Metra makes it easy for them to avoid driving as much as two hours each way just to get to their jobs. Anyhow, after all the old apartment buildings had been torn down, a strip mall went up in its place."

"What's a strip mall, Maxine? I swear, I don't know nothin', it seems."

"Oh, Bertie, you're getting smarter every day. You've just not been exposed to ordinary life, that's all. A strip mall is a bunch of buildings lined up in a row. Spaces in the buildings are rented to owners of shops and restaurants, that kind of thing. All the businesses share a parking lot in front of the mall and pay rent to the owner of the property. Since I was the owner of the mall, I got to collect all the rent. I leased out space to an upscale thrift boutique, a book store and an antique shop, keeping the corner space for myself."

"Did you live there? Why would you want to keep some of it for yourself when you could of got rent for it?"

"I kept it because the door opened up right in front of where the train stopped to pick up and let off its passengers. I opened a little coffee shop there, a café I called it, a straight shot from the door of the cafe to the train. People in a hurry ran in, grabbed their morning newspaper and a cup of caffeine to get them going for the day, then elbowed their way onto the train hopin' to grab a seat before they all got filled up. That little café was one of the best ideas I ever had. When I decided to move to Florida and sold everything, the money I got for the café practically paid me back for my initial investment in the whole mall. Selling the rest of it put me on easy street. But I'm getting ahead of my story."

I WAITED A FEW months to move out of Frank's house to be sure my kids would be on their own. Simon was off somewhere enjoying his freedom for the summer. He'd graduated from college that spring and was out kicking up his heels before he settled down. Dina would be starting her third year of pre-med in August and was already on campus working at her summer job. In September, I moved into two rooms on the second floor of a run-down Victorian house in downtown Chicago. I came home late one night to find a for sale sign in the yard.

I shared one of the upstairs bathrooms with another renter, a guy named Vic, who was sitting on the front porch steps having a smoke when I climbed out of my car.

"What the heck?" I said to Vic. "Did you know the house was going to be sold?"

"Yep."

"Why didn't you say something? I had no idea. I don't have time to go looking for another place to live."

"Would've said somethin', but you're never home. No time to look for a new place, why don't you buy this old heap of shingles? Then you won't have to move." Vic was laughing as he walked up the steps and disappeared through the door.

Vic had said buy the house. I thought he must be nuts. What would I want with a big old house like that? I walked up the front steps and put my key in the lock when the thought hit me like BLAM. I went back to the curb and took a good look at the place I'd been living in for the past six months.

Three stories high, gabled and loaded with gingerbread trim. Funny how I'd never really noticed it before. I looked at the front door. Make that plural. Solid oak, leaded glass, hand-carved double doors. I didn't like the pink paint, but paint's cheap.

I called the real estate agent the next morning.

Yes, she said, the sign went up yesterday. She'd spoken with a few of the other tenants several days ago and let them know the house was for sale. She was real up front about its condition. The owner died last month at the age of ninety-eight. Her grandchildren had been renting it out for her but they weren't interested in keeping it going now that she was gone.

She said we all must know from living in the house that it's in very poor condition. She wasn't supposed to tell us that the grandkids were eager to be done with the whole thing. Renting it had been a burden to them, but they had loved their grandmother. Now that she was gone, whatever they could get out of it would be profit for them, so they were extremely motivated. The realtor told me it wouldn't last long in spite of all that needed to be done to it. Just since the sign went up she'd had several calls.

"I lucked out, Bertie. I bought it for pennies on the dollar and evicted the other tenants. By the time the renovation restored the Painted Lady to her original beauty, I had been asked to have it listed on the annual Christmas Walk of Historic Homes."

"Why, I declare, Maxine, you're the one should write a book. I ain't had nowhere near the kind of life you had."

"I've thought about it, Bertie," I said. "Then, I think, who'd want to hear about the tragedies and mistakes of an old woman? I'll bet you could talk to anybody in this town and you'd hear the same kind of tales I'm telling you."

"Maybe. Anyhow, what happened next? I know they's more, 'cause you ain't moved to Florida yet in the tellin'."

"Yes, sad to say, there's more. This next part was the worst time in my life. I still hadn't learned how to judge people. I was so gullible, all the way up to where Jack came into my life."

Bertie looked at me, frowning. "Now, don't tell me you went an' got married agin?"

"No, that's not it. Might as well be, though. It was almost as bad, Bertie. Let me go on with my story and you'll see what finally made me see the light."

Thirty-Five

Maxine

THE SUMMER HE GRADUATED from college, my son, Simon, got in with a wild crowd of young men. One of them was taking flying lessons, and somehow he got hold of the keys to a small two-seater plane, so they all went out to Gary, Indiana, to the airport, and took the plane up in the air. Only two people should've been in the plane, but they squeezed in five, and Simon was one of them. They'd been drinking. All five boys died in the crash."

"Oh, Maxine, I am sad for you. I know how awful it were for me t' have my son die, but he were jist a baby. It warn't like I'd had him for a lot of years, like you had Simon."

"You musn't think like that, Bert. What you have to remember is I lost my son, but I still had memories of life with him, all the good as well as the bad. At least I had something to hold on to. With you, you lost all promise of the future with your baby son. You tell me which one is worse, if you can. Me, I wouldn't be able to choose. One is as bad as the other, as far as I'm concerned."

We stayed quiet for a few minutes, both of us thinking about our children. It was Bertie that broke the silence.

"I guess I agree with you, Maxine. You still feel like talkin'?"

"Yeah. After all these years, it's easier to talk about this stuff. It never goes away, but it does get easier."

"By this time, my daughter, Dina, and I were on the outs. She finally told me what she thought of having three fathers before she was out of high school. I couldn't blame her, Bertie, I knew I had messed up my kids' lives, but I was working real hard, trying to make it up to them since I'd left Frank. Didn't make any difference, though. After Simon died, Dina finished getting her MD degree, then up and left. Went to Alaska on a break and decided to stay. She's got a clinic she runs for the Inuit Natives. I doubt she'll be coming back any time soon."

"When I hear things like this, makes me think I were the lucky one, not havin' children to worry over," Bertie said. "How did you ever git through them times?"

"Well, it was hard, I'll say that. I'd been a churchgoer off and on in my life, but it was always superficial. You know, on the surface, knew a few scriptures by heart. Took the kids to church on Christmas, Easter, but it never really meant much to me. I knew who God was supposed to be, but He wasn't real to me, I wasn't sure what part Jesus was supposed to play in all of it. I muddled through my life repeating what few scriptures I could remember, and it helped enough to get me through it, but I was bitter. After a while, though, life goes on, you know? That awful ache in my heart got better, little by little, and one day I realized I hadn't thought of Simon for almost a whole week.

"I went to the cemetery that day because I felt guilty, thinking I'd forgotten him. When I looked at his grave marker, I had what I called at the time a revelation. The scripture I'd had engraved on his headstone spoke to me, and I figured that subconsciously, maybe I'd been using it to deal with the pain. It was two brief verses from Proverbs, the third chapter, verses six and seven. It says. . ."

"Oh, don't tell me what it says," Bertie interrupted. "I'll look it up later an' try to read it for myself. I'm practicin' my readin' at bedtime an' that can be my assignment for tonight. Ain't that a good word, Maxine, assignment? I learned it from Grace the other day when she give me some homework to do. I'm learnin' all kinds of good words from her.

"Another thing, Maxine. We ain't talked about God, have we. You prob'ly think I don't know nothin' about Him, but I do. All them years my daddy made me go to church with him, I listened to ever'thin' the preacher said. I can still remember how to say lots of verses from the Bible, that's what got me through my own hard times, I believe. I think it's a blessin' that God give words to you that helped."

"Yes, well, it didn't last, Bertie. I guess it was always in the back of my mind somewhere, but the truth is, I never did anything about it. Quit goin' to church altogether after that. I even doubted for a long, long time if God was really out there. Eventually I got to the place where I never gave Him a thought at all. It was many years before He found me and whopped me up alongside my head with His Word."

"But I thank you, my friend, for your kind understanding. Not everyone would think the way you do. You are a blessing to me, Bertie."

"Well, I thank you for that, an' the same's true about you, Maxine. You been the biggest blessin' in my life since Farley an' little Tremont, our son, died."

"Why, Bert, that's the first time I ever heard you say the baby's name. Tremont, did I get it right?"

"Yes. We named him after my mama. She were a Tremont afore she married my daddy. Since he were a boy, we couldn't give him her first name, but Farley said, heck, his name were unusual, might as well give his son a unusual name, too, so we give him my mama's last name. He were Tremont Louis Kenner. We was goin' to call him Tree."

"Bertie, I want to thank you for loving me, and for letting me love you."

"You are welcome, Maxine."

"Okay, enough of this crying. Do you want to hear more, or should we save it for another time?"

"Shoot, no, Maxine. You're on a roll, keep on a'goin."

I laughed out loud. "Where did you pick up that phrase, 'on a roll'?"

"I heard it on the television the other night. I'm startin' to learn lots of things from watchin the TV. Go on, now, tell me some more."

IT TURNED OUT THAT I was a financial wizard, a Queen Midas, once I got started. The strip mall was a shot in the arm for the old neighborhood. The anchor store was the coffee shop, or café, as it became known. The Metra train would screech into the station thirty feet away from the café entrance, throwing open its doors just long enough for the travelers to jump aboard, then lurch away at top speed to deliver its human cargo to their various places of employment in the city and surrounding areas.

I'd found a local baker who was eager to expand his business. He delivered sticky pecan buns, cranberry-orange muffins, all sorts of tasty baked goods to the café every morning in time for commuters to sit with a scalding cup of flavored coffee and a hot buttered yeast roll before boarding the train for the ride downtown. The passengers who were in a hurry just took their goodies with them on the train.

By spring of the next year the café took on a new name, The Rail Café. I added sandwiches and soup to the menu for those commuters who didn't want to cook once they arrived home.

One evening as the diners lingered over the final cup of coffee, one of the commuters, a young man who didn't usually ride the train, approached the counter to pay his bill. Slung over his back was a guitar case.

"What you got there, son?" I asked? "Looks like a guitar. You play that thing?"

"Yes, Ma'am, I do. I was downtown today looking for work. I only been here a couple weeks, living with my ma a few blocks away. Heard they was hiring at a club in the city, but I guess they filled the gig just before I got there." He looked glum.

I continued mopping up the counter while I listened to him. I'd had some thoughts about opening up the café on weekend nights, maybe having local authors and poets come in to do some readings. I'd heard about that one time, how some coffee houses did that sort of thing. Now here I was, thinking about doing the same, and adding music to the mix. The thought excited me and began to take form in my mind real fast! Since those days when I had to worry about my husband, Frank, drinking too much alcohol, I didn't want any part of that scenario again. But what about a non-alcoholic bar where people could come and socialize, listen to good music, hear local poets and authors read their work, all without the effect of so-called adult beverages spoiling the atmosphere? It sounded interesting, but I was so busy getting everything else set up I hadn't taken the time to look into it.

I reached across the counter and offered my hand. "My name is Maxine Monk, and I own this place. The soup's on me tonight, and how would you like to help me with an experiment?"

Shaking my hand, he introduced himself. "I'm Jack Jordan. Thanks for the soup, but I don't know about any experiment. What do you have in mind?"

I told Jack about my idea to have something like a mini nightclub in the café on weekends.

"I was thinking of using local talent, like you, Jack. You know, give the people who live close by a chance. We're all getting off to a new start in these parts, what with all the renovations and tearing down.

"I used to live in one of the apartments that sat on this very ground, lots of years ago. When I found out this area was part of the renovation plan, I jumped on it. I knew how bad it was to live in these tiny little apartments when they were pretty new, and it was hard to think of people living in them when they were old and falling apart. But out of nowhere came the idea to put a business in their place. That's what I did, and so far it's working out good. If I decide to give the club idea a try, are you up for helping me out?"

"How much would the job pay?" he asked.

I threw my head back and laughed real big.

"That's what I like, son, someone with no job, no money, no prospects, but enough gumption to ask right up front how much I'll pay him. Well, the answer is, I don't know. How about if we start out paying you a flat fee of, oh, say, twenty bucks each night you play. After a few weeks, I'll keep paying you the twenty bucks, plus a percentage of the take for the night. That'll give you some incentive to put on a good show, pull more people in and plump up the profits so you'll get more pay. How's that sound to you?"

Jack agreed to give it a try for a few weeks while he continued looking for gigs that paid better money, but as it turned out, his run at the Rail Café grew into something pretty permanent. As the place prospered, due in large part to Jack's music, and as my other financial ventures took off and became more time-consuming, I made Jack manager of the Café. As the crowds grew bigger with each passing week, I did something wonderful. Or stupid. I told Jack if the business continued to grow and he stuck with it for a year, I would enter into a contract with him. The contract would stipulate that I would make him a partner in the Café and he would pay me a percentage of the profits every month as a sort of buy-out fee. The contract would stay in force until he was able to buy the business outright, with a limit of two years for the deal to prove good. I hadn't forgotten how hard life had been for me, how I had struggled to get somewhere with very little help. Now, I saw this young man wanting a better life for himself, and it sparked a vein of generosity and benevolence in me.

Much, much later, I realized I had subconsciously replaced my dead son with Jack.

After a few months of working together, I met Jack's mother. She was a frail old woman, and except for a small social security check, Jack was her only means of support. They lived in a run-down area not far from the Café, and I knew from my contact with the developer who was renovating much of the area, that their apartment building was slated to be demolished within the year.

"So, Jack," I asked him as he locked the café door behind us one night, "where are you and your mom going to move?"

I think Jack had avoided talking with me about his situation because he didn't know where they were going to go. His paychecks were starting to look better each month, but I knew from our conversations that after paying rent and utilities, buying his mother's medicine, and food for them both, he didn't have enough left to start saving toward getting them a better place to live. His answer was short.

"I don't know."

"Well," I said, "something will turn up."

And then my heart started to work overtime.

I missed my kids. Maybe that's why I took to Jack so easily. He made me think of how my son might have been, if he hadn't died in the plane crash. And my daughter, Dina. I guessed it was a combination of things that drove her so far away and kept her there. Who could figure out, anyhow, what makes any of us the way we turn out in life?

As far as I knew, Dina was still providing free medical care for the Inuit people at her clinic in Alaska. Before she left Chicago she told me how she felt about everything.

She was angry with her father for deserting her when she was two years old. She hadn't cared all that much for her first stepfather, the doctor, and she hated Frank, her second stepfather. She didn't think much of me, either, she'd confessed, and didn't intend to take care of me when I got old and sick. Dina told me I should have settled down with one man instead of flitting around from one husband to another. I tried to defend myself, tried to make Dina understand what these men were really like, but she wouldn't listen. All she knew was she'd been an unhappy child. Consequently, she wanted nothing to do with me now that she was grown.

A few weeks after our conversation about housing for Jack and his mother, I approached him as he was closing the café for the night.

"Jack, I need some advice. Got a minute?"

"Sure do, just let me finish stacking these chairs so the cleaning crew can get in here."

Jack had recently hired a cleaning crew to come in after the café closed each night. He'd been doing it himself, but things were looking up financially now, and he felt we could afford to pay to have the place cleaned professionally. All he had to do was get the chairs stacked against the wall so the crew could get right to work with the floor buffer. I'd advised against spending the money at first, but I had to admit, the shiny floors and polished woodwork gave the café a much more professional look.

Finished with the chairs, Jack sat at the desk in the office and swiveled his chair around to face me. I was comfortably seated on the leather sofa he had recently purchased from a customer who was redecorating her home.

"Okay, Max, what's up?" Jack had nicknamed me, and I wasn't sure I liked it. Sounded too masculine to me, but I humored him. I'd lost my own two kids, I wasn't about to alienate Jack over a little thing like a nickname.

"Well, I'm rattling around downtown in that big house all by myself and it's lonely. I've been thinking I might rent part of it out. What do you think, would I be foolish to open my home to some stranger, take a chance on getting myself into a real pickle?'

I hoped my plan wasn't so transparent that Jack would see right through it.

"Gosh, Max, I think that would be good for you to have someone in the house with you. Got anybody in mind?" Jack asked.

I waited a few seconds to see if Jack had caught on to my scheme, but it didn't seem as if he had.

"I don't know anyone right off. Thought maybe you might know someone who needs a place. Any of your friends looking?"

"I'll ask around," Jack said. "In the meantime, Maxie Mum, I need to get home. Time to get my mother's pills poked down her throat and tuck her into bed. I'll see you tomorrow."

With that, he was gone, leaving me to wonder if I shouldn't just come right out and ask Jack if he and his mother would like to be my new renters.

Come morning, Jack was waiting for me on the porch steps as I opened the door to retrieve the Sun Times from the shrubbery. He didn't even say hello, just jumped in and started talking.

"I would have come back last night, Maxine, but I thought you might have already gone to bed by the time it hit me. I don't know what you'll think of this idea, but you did ask me for advice, and I know you wouldn't ask unless you meant it. So here's my solution to your renter problem. How about me and my mother? We're looking for a place. I don't know if we could afford the rent here, but if you think this could work, I'd scrape it up somehow. What do you think?"

I had to try not to smile. Jack was an innocent person in some ways, I thought.

"Come on in and have a cup of coffee, Jack."

He walked in through the big double doors and I thought his jaw was going to hit the floor. He looked amazed. The hallway alone was huge. Restored to its original beauty, the house was breathtaking.

"Great gobs of goose grease, Maxine! You could rent out this whole house and probably get whatever you wanted for it. This is a great place! How much are you gonna want for it," he said.

I could tell he was impressed. "Come into the kitchen, Jack, and we'll talk about it." I'd given this quite a bit of thought, so I plunged in.

"I'm not getting any younger, Jack. Eventually I won't be able to live in this house by myself. I'll more than likely have to give up my investment property, too. But for as long as I can, I want to stay here and run the café. I've watched you grow in the past year. You have a good head on your shoulders and a gift for managing things. That, along with your musical talent, could take you far in this old world of ours. So I'm willing to help you get where you want to go.

"How does this sound to you? You and your mother can each have your own bedroom and bath on the second floor. We'll install one of those chair gizmos to take Mom up and down the stairs, but aside from that, the rest of the house will be shared by all three of us. As far as money goes, I'd even be willing to forgo rent if you'd manage the place for me. Now that all the renovations are finished, I planned to start looking for household help. I could leave it up to you to find the people we need to do housekeeping, window washing, that sort of thing. You could keep up the lawn, it's not that big. I haven't the time nor the inclination to do that stuff anymore. That could be your job, and it would pay the rent for you. What do you say?"

"Wow, I'm almost speechless. Except for one thing - when can we move in?"

As I related this part of my story to her, Bertie's arms were crossed over her chest. Her mouth was puckered up and a frown pulled her eyebrows down to the bridge of her nose.

"Didn't take him long to make up his mind, did it? How'd that work out, Maxine?"

I knew Bertie was being sarcastic, but I ignored her and went on with my story.

THE RENTAL AGREEMENT LASTED for one year. Every month that went by I regretted more and more my offer to Jack and his mother. They say if you feed a starving animal, eventually it will bite your hand. It proved to be true.

At first, it was little things that irritated me. I knew she was sick, but Jack's mother, Gladys, did nothing to help around the house. Instead, she added to the workload. She left candy wrappers everywhere. Any place she'd been at the time she unwrapped the candy, that's where the wrapper would lay until I picked it up and threw it in the trash. I thought the woman was just old and absent-minded, but as time wore on, and other habits were added to the list, I came to realize the woman was lazy and selfish.

Dishes were left in the kitchen sink overnight, and after Jack went to work, I cleaned them up, knowing if I didn't they'd still be there the next morning, along with a new batch. Laundry would still be in the washer when I went to use it, smelling faintly of wet mold, so I would run it through the cycles again before I could use the washer myself. Then I would put it in the dryer to keep it from getting moldy again, and because I couldn't stand to just toss the dried clothing in a basket to lay around waiting for Jack to fold at some unknown time, I would fold it and leave it in the basket at the foot of the stairs for Jack to put away. There it would sit until he carried it up to their rooms. I never said a word about all this, and one day Jack fell over the basket. He hollered out real loud, 'Who left this basket here? I almost broke my neck.'

One month the lawn went unmowed until I reminded Jack at breakfast on a Saturday morning that it looked pretty shabby out there. He was condescending and patronizing in his answer.

"Yeah, yeah, landlord. I'll get to it, don't get your shorts in a bunch. It's not the end of the world if the lawn gets a little longer than you think it should be. Tomorrow, okay, I'll do it tomorrow."

Of course, another week went by before he got to it and then he ran the mower around the yard, leaving the edges untrimmed where the grass met the shrubs, which grew taller and more raggedy looking every day.

When the housekeeper quit, telling me she hadn't been paid in over two months, and she couldn't get Jack to talk to her about it, I went into overload.

I sat down across from Jack as he nursed his third cup of coffee, reading the morning newspaper. When he didn't look up over the paper, or lay it down, I reached over, and taking hold of the center crease of the paper, I squashed it to the table in a crinkled heap.

"Hey, what do you think you're doing?" Jack yelled at me. "I'm reading the paper here!"

"Not anymore, Jack." Working up my courage, I asked him, "What's the matter, Jack? Seems to me you're not happy with our arrangement anymore. You're not holding up your end of the bargain, and to boot, the Café isn't doing well anymore. I'm told you don't come in there much, just when it's time to collect the contents of the till. And you've stopped entertaining on weekends, you have some teenage band that shows up and plays their kind of music instead of what our patrons like to hear. The customers are beginning to stay away. Are you tired of it, Jack?" His answer didn't surprise me.

"Yeah, Maxine, I'm tired of it. Sorry, but I'm tired of taking care of my old lady, I'm tired of trying to please both of the old ladies I live with, I'm tired of managing a little café that's never gonna be anything more than what it is right now. I want to sing and play my music and be famous someday, and it ain't never gonna happen if I stay here." Jack stared out the window as he told all this to me.

"Well, I wish you'd told me right up front when you started feeling like this. Could have saved us both some grief. But, if you'll stick around until I can find another manager for the café, I'll start looking today for your replacement. I'll take over the household management as of right now. You give me the checkbook and the bills and let's plan on a meeting sometime in the next few days to go over the books for the Café. Then I'll be prepared to pitch in until I find someone else to do it. As far as your mother goes, what do you have in mind for her?"

He hesitated. I thought I might know what he was thinking, but I didn't want to admit it. "Come on, Jack. What's on your mind about her?"

He faced me. I saw shame, guilt, helplessness, rebellion, all mixed together on his face. Struggling to find the words he needed, Jack finally blurted it out.

"I can't take care of her anymore, Maxine. I'm twenty-four years old, she's seventy-five. I was the only kid she ever had, and she waited until she was an old lady to have me. Fifty-one. Who ever heard of a fifty-one year old woman havin' a kid? All the way through school, I had the oldest ma of anyone.

"All my life, I been taking care of her. Even before my old man died, I was taking care of her, and him, too. He was sixty-two when I was born. Is that disgusting, or what? These two old people makin' a baby together, I can hardly stand the thought of it. But they did, and by the time I was twelve, my dad was dead and I was takin' care of her. She should've been takin' care of me, you know?

"But even then, she had so many medical problems, it was hard for her to get arond, money was tight, seems like I always had to work. My dad didn't leave any money behind, they was always poor. She only had social security to live on, plus she got food stamps. You want to talk about poor, I guess we were really poor. As soon as anyone would hire me, I worked. I set pins at the bowling alley in our town, I bagged groceries at a little mom and pop store on our block. If I didn't work, sometimes we didn't eat after payin' for her medicine and the rent and all that. But now, I guess I'm just burned out. I can't do it anymore."

"So, what do you plan to do, Jack?" I asked again.

"I don't know. Can she stay with you for a while, until I figure out what to do with her?"

Whoa, I might have a real bad situation on my hands, here, I thought.

"I can't take care of her, Jack. I'm gone from home most of the time working on different projects I got going. You know that. And none of it's anything I can walk away from and leave hanging to take care of a sick old lady. You're going to have to check in with the Senior Services Center downtown and see what kind of advice they have for you. Their office is only a few miles from here, why don't you take today off from work, go down there and see what they've got to offer?"

Jack sat with his head hanging down. Without looking up he said, "Yeah, okay, that's what I'll do. I'll make sure she has something to eat for lunch, then I'll head on down there. I'll let you know later what I find out. Thanks for everything you've done for us, Max. It may not seem like it, but I appreciate it."

"You're welcome, Jack. And if it's any comfort to you, I do understand how cornered you feel. Time or two in my own life I felt the same way. We all just have to work through those times best we can, and in our own way. Good luck with it all."

I watched as Jack headed up the stairs to supervise his mother's morning routine. "Oh, Lord," I prayed out loud, "help the poor kid get through this tough time, because sure as spiders have hundreds of babies at one time, he'll have hundreds of days to come yet in his life when he has to figure out what to do. Thanks for helpin' him, Lord. Amen."

I drove off, headed for the first meeting of my jam-packed day, and thought only briefly a time or two about Jack and his problems. The last meeting on my schedule went overtime, and then I joined a few friends for a late dinner downtown.

Arriving at home, I found the whole place without lights. Fumbling with my keys on the dark porch, I pushed open the door and flipped on the hall lights. Tossing my keys on the table, I glanced at the grandfather clock that stood beside it. Ten o'clock at night, and I was exhausted. Calling out for Jack as I walked, I went from room to room turning on lights.

Maybe he's in bed, I thought. *Nah, couldn't be, he never goes to bed this early. Did he take his mother and go out for the evening?*

Fat chance. Talking to myself, I headed up the stairs. Halfway up, I stopped. "What in the world is that odor," I said out loud. It smelled like urine. And..."

"Oh, no, it can't be."

Opening the door to Gladys' room, I found her sitting in the dark in her chair. I located the source of the odor as soon as I turned on the overhead light. Under Gladys' chair was a dark puddle saturating the antique wool carpet. Gladys turned her head in my direction. In the sudden bright light she squinted her eyes to see who it was standing in the doorway to her room.

Running down the hall to Jack's bedroom, I found it empty. Not only was Jack not there, neither was anything else that belonged to him. Other than the furniture that was part of the room when Jack moved in, everything was gone. His guitar, his music, clothing, personal items, everything.

I pulled my cell phone out of my pocket and called the Rail Café, only to be told that Jack had not shown up for work that afternoon. The teenage clerk hadn't called me, she said, because Jack often didn't show up until almost time to close, so she figured he'd be there later. She asked what she should do about closing down for the night, they only had a little over an hour to go before it was time to close. I told her as soon as the last customer left she should just lock the cash register, turn out the lights, turn the lock button on the door handle and pull the door shut behind her.

"I'll be down later to take care of things," I told her.

As I stood there trying to make sense of it all, Jack's mother began calling for him.

"Jack, where are you, son? I think I've had an accident, I'm all wet. Where are you? Helllp, helllp, Jack. Somebody, help me."

Her cries shook me out of my state of shock. I hurried back to her room and leaned over her, trying to comfort her while I thought of what to do. Suddenly, I understood. Jack had abandoned his mother. Anger welled up in me, replaced quickly by my take-charge nature. Remembering my counsel to Jack regarding the Senior Services Center, I called information and asked for their number. An after-hours crisis counselor answered the call.

"I'm pretty sure he's abandoned her," I told the counselor. "He's nowhere to be found, all his belongings are gone from his room, and it appears the mother has been here alone since at least lunch time. I can't handle her by myself, is there any way you can get someone here as fast as possible?"

The counselor told me it's the law in situations like this to call Adult Protective Services and report an abandoned senior citizen. APS is then required to call the police, who would accompany APS personnel to the site to investigate. They would bring an ambulance with them to transport her to the hospital for a full physical and any needed treatment. From there, a determination would be made as to the next step for her.

Sitting beside Gladys, holding her hand and trying to comfort her, it took about half an hour before the doorbell rang.

"I'll be right back, Gladys, I need to see who's at the door."

"You come right back, you hear me. Don't you leave me alone again. And don't turn off those lights," Gladys instructed.

When I opened the door, there stood a police officer on my porch, followed by a police matron, a woman counselor from the APS Crisis Center, and two paramedics with a medic's bag on top of a collapsible gurney, waiting for a thumbs-up from the police to move in and take charge of Gladys.

I filled out the police report in the hallway while the paramedics examined Gladys, checking her vital signs and looking for open wounds, bruises, anything that would indicate physical abuse. In answer to the questions the police matron asked me, I told her I'd never known Jack to be abusive physically to his mother, and until today I'd never known him to neglect her.

"But truthfully, we're not always home at the same time. I run several businesses and keep long hours. As far as I know, Jack is here with his mother off and on during the day and evening. Up until recently, I think she's been able to do some things for herself. She can stand up but she needs a walker. We keep a wheelchair up here and another one on the first floor. She needed the stair chair because all those steps were too much for her, but using the wheelchair and walker she could get around some. Jack fixed her meals and left things in the refrigerator for her, and she knows how to use the microwave.

"I noticed when I got home tonight, though, that both wheelchairs and the walker are in the kitchen. She's been stuck in this bedroom since lunchtime. This is the first time I've known him to do anything like this."

By now the paramedics had lifted Gladys to the bed, wrapping her in a soft cotton hospital blanket, soiled clothing and all. Transferring her to the gurney, they carried her to the waiting ambulance and took off for the hospital.

The police report included Gladys' and Jack's names, ages, and address. I didn't know much else, except the information

Jack had given me that was in his employee file at work. The officers escorted me to the Café, but as I searched the office files I found Jack's employee records were missing. The safe was also empty. The only money on the premises was in the cash register, proceeds from the day's business left there when the counter clerk pulled the door shut behind her that night.

"Well, ma'am, looks like you've been taken for a ride," said the police officer. "We'll do our best to track this guy down, but for now, good luck."

They drove me back to the house and went in with me to be sure Jack hadn't come back, then I was alone in my house with the odor of Gladys' accident growing stronger by the minute.

To think I could have been so gullible, I thought. As I felt myself getting sick from the smell, as well as from my own stupidity, I ran for the bathroom and gave up the lovely dinner I had consumed not three hours ago.

"Did he ever come back?" Bertie asked.

"No. He knew better. But I'd learned my lesson, Bert. I had to be the worst judge of character God ever created. Three husbands, one as bad as the other, then Jack. From then on I decided I'd make all my own decisions, manage my own businesses, I wouldn't trust anyone. From that day to this I've stuck to that. I do trust Mr. Downing, my attorney, but I pay him for his advice. Nothing personal about it. Strictly business.

"After seeing what happened to Gladys Jordan when her husband died and then being left alone by her son, I started making plans for my own old age. I gave it a lot of thought, and decided I didn't want to live in the cold and snow when I got old. It'd be hard enough to take care of myself without sliding around on the ice during the cold winters in Chicago. So I did a complete turn-around and moved to Florida."

"For goodness sake, Maxine, jist like that, you moved? Why'd you pick Florida?"

"Because in the middle of my life before I married Frank, my grandfather died. My grandmother had been gone for years, but for their whole life, they had lived in some small town in Florida. I didn't know them, my parents and I never went to Florida, and the grandparents never came to Chicago, so I wouldn't have recognized them if we passed each other on the street. But let me go on tellin' this mess before I get tired of talking about it."

Thirty-Six

Maxine

SHORTLY AFTER FRANK AND I split up, I got a letter from my cousin Andy, my dad's brother's kid. It was a huge surprise to learn that he and his brother and I had inherited our grandparents' home in Florida. Cousins Andy and Marty grew up in Montana and they had no desire whatsoever to go live in Florida. Neither did I, so we put the place on the market. Kept it there for a couple of years but it didn't sell.

I decided to take a vacation and go down there to look it over, see for myself why no one wanted it. After looking at it in person, I knew why. The place was no prize. The grandparents had let it run down bad while they were sick, and then it sat empty after they died. It was in real bad shape. We all finally got tired of paying the taxes on the place, didn't know what to do about it. I called the real estate agent for advice. She told me we'd be lucky to get much out of it. The longer we continued to pay the taxes, the less we'd eventually recover of what we were paying into it. I called the boys, told them what the agent had told me. But I left out part of her information.

That realtor specialized in commercial property and acreage, and she felt the day was coming when our five acres would be worth something. Might be a few years, might be twenty, but eventually, the business world would work its way east and someday all this farmland could possibly turn into housing developments. She advised me to buy out the other two cousins, and then hang on to it for a while. So that's what I did. I paid each one of them three thousand dollars, and went back to Chicago and sat on it. Good thing I did, too, because after Jack left me to babysit with his mama, I'd had it with big city life.

I flew to Florida the week after Jack and Gladys left my life and checked out the old homestead. It was more dilapidated than the first time I'd seen it, but I'd tackled worse with the Chicago property so I knew I could do something with this one.

The day my return flight landed at O'Hare Airport, I put the strip mall and the big house on the market and hot-footed it out of town. That was twenty years ago, and I haven't looked back once.

"But this place is so nice, Maxine. Didn't you say it were all run down?"

"I did, Bert, and it was. First thing I did was rent a room at a local motel up by the highway. Got a cheap room at a weekly rate, asked around and found a farmer who agreed to come in with his hay mower. Took him six hours to mow the whole five acres. The weeds and underbrush had gotten so thick over the years it was hard for him to get through it. When he finished, he brought over his hay baler. He bundled it all up and hauled it away. Cost me a pretty penny, but it had to be done in order to get close enough to the house to start working on it. And a

THE MYSTERIES OF TREMONT MEADOW 233

benefit I hadn't even thought about made me real happy. The wild life living in that jungle ran for safety while he mowed. I never saw so many snakes in my life.

Then, once the land was cleared off, my realtor put me in contact with a neighbor. You'll meet him one of these days, he's a contractor here in Sarasota County. He brought his crew over here and we got to swinging sledgehammers and pounding nails. I jumped right in there with those guys, wore blue jeans and work shoes, I had a ball. We knocked out walls and rebuilt the inside of the house, put in modern plumbing, the works. The house you see here is the result of our hard work. Took six months. I set me up a bed in whatever room we weren't working in, ate all my meals at Slick's Diner in town. Used the outhouse until the plumbing got far enough along to use the indoor toilet. We all got to know each other so well during those six months that pretty soon the guys' wives were sending lunch for all of us as well as jugs of water. That was the best six months of my life, Bert."

"Well, I swear, it sure turned out pretty. It's a right cozy place, Maxine."

"Thank you, Bertie. I don't think I've ever been as comfortable or as content as I've been these last twenty years."

"But, I want to know how you got to ownin' the store, Maxine. Don't seem like somethin' a city lady like yourself would do, 'specially if you had enough money to live on without workin'."

"Well, the plain and simple truth is, I got tired of driving eleven miles to the closest store just to get a jug of milk and a loaf of bread. It wasn't like you had it, Bertie. I didn't have a milk cow and I didn't bake. So here's how it came to be."

I WAS COMING BACK from my milk run one day, feeling out of sorts and thinking how inconvenient it was to have to go all that way, and right about then, I went past the old fire station, about two miles from my house. Someone told me it'd been empty for a long time, ever since the new one got built, and it hit me just like that.

I pulled my car into the open bay where the fire engine used to sit, got out and inspected the place. The rest is history. I was on the Town Council by then, so at the meeting a few nights later, I brought up the idea of turning the old fire station into a store. Got all kinds of negative flak, like, who was going to turn it into a store, who would keep it stocked, who would run it. On and on, until someone finally tabled the subject and they went to the next item on the agenda. I could see there wasn't any real interest from the folks at that meeting. But I got more and more interested every time I drove past that empty firehouse.

I was in town, runnin' errands, when I passed City Hall a few weeks later. On an impulse I went in there and asked what it would take for someone to buy the old fire station. After being shuffled from one department to another, someone finally told me all it would take to buy the building was some money. No one knew how much, so I suggested they take bids. They put it in the local newspaper that bids were being taken on the old fire station, a deadline for submission of bids was set, I turned in my bid and sat back and waited. Two months later I got the news that I was the only one who bid on it, so I should come on down to City Hall with my check."

"Well, if you think about it, Maxine, who would want to buy a old fire station?"

"I did! You've seen it, you even go in there now and buy groceries with me. What do you think of it?"

"I think it's a right nice store. I think you had a good idea."

"You and lots of other folks, Bert. Sure cuts down on all the miles our neighbors used to put on their vehicles. And since we started the farm stand, people come from twenty, thirty miles away, sometimes farther, to buy dairy products and fresh produce that the local farmers bring in. Why, Homer was one of the first to bring his fruits and vegetables there.

"When I think back on it, Bertie, I feel such shame for letting you sit out there in the truck while Homer brought the crates in."

"Now you don't be gittin' on yourself so, Maxine. I growed up settin' outside ever' time I come into town with my daddy, so it warn't no different after I married Homer. You didn't know what. . ."

Maxine interrupted me. "No, now let me explain something here, Bertie. Shortly after I got settled into the house here in Creek, I got civic-minded, started going to Town Council meetings. Someone invited me to go to church with them. I still wasn't of a mind for going to church at that point, but it seemed like a good place to make new friends. So I went. It sure surprised me when the Holy Spirit took charge. I wound up joining the church, but more important than that, I wound up giving my life to Jesus. That was one of the best things I ever did. Studying His principles taught me so much about why my life had gone the way it did.

"I like to think I was a different person after I came to know the Lord, but I guess old ways die hard, because I let you down when you could have used some help. I'll always wonder what your life might have been like if I had gone over to that pickup truck and introduced myself, opened the truck door and talked with you. I should have done that every time you came to town. But I was afraid to do what that still, small voice was telling me to do. I owe you an apology. Maybe life would have been easier for you if I'd faced up to Mr. Homer Claxton."

"You cain't know what my life, or your's either, might of been like, Maxine, if you had done this thing or that thing. How do you think I'd feel right about now, if I'd stood up to my daddy and Homer? We have to take what we got an' work with that, not go to thinkin' about what things might of been like. So you don't owe me no apology, you hear?"

Before I could reply, the Sheriff's car pulled into the driveway. Leaning out the window of the patrol car, Sheriff Turner asked if it was too late for a visit.

"It's all right with me, if you don't mind me sittin' here in my pajamas," I said. "Come on up and have a seat. What's on your mind, Sheriff?"

Settling into the porch swing, Sheriff Turner cleared his throat a few times, trying to think how to start what he had to say.

"Oh, for Pete's sake, Sheriff, spit it out. I can't sit out here in the dark in my p.j.'s all night."

"Well, ever since the other day, when you two give me all that information, what Bertie thinks she remembers about her mama and daddy, I can't get it out of my mind. I set up a meetin' with your attorney, Mr. Downing, and Judge Colbert for today, and told them about the situation. I needed help deciding if this was anything that needed action, or what. They both agreed I should tell you, Bertie, that we're pretty much on the same page here with what we think should be done. I know it's after the fact, but I hope it's okay with you that I did this."

"Me an' Maxine were jist settin' here talkin' about what things might of been like if we'd done this or that, instead of that or this. So I'm not goin' to git my feathers ruffled over you doin' it without askin' me first. It's done, so we'll deal with it, right, Maxine?"

I agreed, and asked the Sheriff what Mr. Downing and Judge Colbert thought needed to be done, if anything.

"After all, Mr. Knight is dead. Even if he'd done something wrong, what could be done about it now?" I asked.

The Sheriff set us straight. "Legally, once the law knows about a crime or a possible crime, they're obligated to investigate it no matter what the timing. Most everyone who knew your ma and pa, Bertie, had an opinion about what happened. There's two or three ideas floatin around, but the real truth isn't known. It's my job to find out what that truth is.

"But important as the truth is, Bertie, someone owes your mama somethin'. If she did leave town that night, don't seem likely she'd never come back for her little girl, I think. And if she didn't leave town, then where is she, and what happened to her. If she was my mama, I'd want to make sure the truth got out, no matter what it is. How about it, Bertie?"

It seemed like Bertie was glad someone official had made a decision about this situation. It was real dark by now, but even with only the half moon for light, I could see tears running down Bertie's cheeks. I reached over and held her hand as she answered the Sheriff's question.

"I want to know what happened to my mama."

Thirty-Seven
Bertie

When I discovered my daddy's farm an' everthin' on it were mine now, it didn't hardly sink in. But after talkin' with Sheriff Turner an' learnin' they was goin' to search the property for any kind of evidence about my mama's disappearance, I started sortin' it all out in my mind.

The next Monday mornin' I showed up at the Mannings' condo to find Thad settin' by hisself at the kitchen table, sippin' a cup of coffee.

"Where's Grace at, Thad? Most mornin's she's up afore the chickens."

"I guess this is part of the process she's going to go through, Bertie. She slept until ten o'clock in the morning Saturday and Sunday, looks like she's going to do the same today. Pour yourself a cup and talk to me for a bit. Tell me what's happening with you and the sheriff."

I had told Thad I's nervous about my daddy's farm an' what they might find when they started searchin' it.

"Have you decided what you want to do with the property, Bertie? I know you told me you don't want to live in the house. Have you given any thought to selling it?"

"I surely have, Thad. I cain't do nothin' about it 'til the investigation is over with, but after that, I think I don't want to keep it. You know anyone might want to buy it?"

I set there lookin' into my coffee cup, tryin' not to smile.

"Actually," Thad said, jist as I started laughin'.

"What, what's funny?" he asked.

"Nothin'."

"Then why are you laughing?"

He knowed then I were foolin' with him.

"Why, you sly little country girl, you. Have you been thinking the same thing I have?"

"Maybe. Depends on what you been thinkin'."

"I've been thinking that the Knight farm and the Claxton farm, if combined, would make a wonderful place for a beautiful park-like setting for the new assisted living facility. Would you truly consider selling it to me, Bertie?"

"I would, an' I don't even care how much you give me for it, Thad. It'd make me feel right peaceful to know how many old folks would live out their life there. If you want it, it's yours. Jist git the papers made up, an' soon's the Sheriff's done there, we'll sign em."

It were eight-thirty in the mornin', an' sure enough, Grace's doin' jist what Thad said. I think the word he called her were unpredictable. She had walked into the kitchen holdin' her nightgown in her hand, lookin' confused.

Standin' in the doorway in her bare skin, Grace said, "I can't find my clothes, Dear."

Thad dropped his coffee cup on the table and run to help Grace to her bedroom.

A COUPLE OF DAYS later, I met Maxine in the kitchen after a mostly sleepless night. She warn't all the way to the stove to git her coffee when I blurted it out.

"You know what today is don't you, Maxine?"

"Yes, I do, Bertie. You okay? You planning on going out there?"

"Yes. I decided I want to know right away if they find anythin'. Can you come with me? I might not be s' brave as I think I am, once they git to diggin', if it comes to that."

"I have to open the store first, but yes, I'll come with you. We'll stop by the diner and get coffee for everyone and meet them over there."

"Who all's goin' to be there?"

"Let's see, Sheriff Turner, and his first deputy is comin' along. Jim Pritchett, the cemetery manager, and three of the guys that work for him will be there."

"You talkin' about the ones that digs graves, ain't you?"

"Yep. I heard the plan is to walk the farm, all of them in a row about an arm's length apart. Pritchett said they'll be looking for any kind of a depression or low spot that could indicate the ground had been dug up at some point in time. They're going to start with the meadow since that's where you remember your daddy carrying your mama the day she disappeared. Pritchett says if your daddy dug down very deep at all, the ground's most likely caved in by now. Says it shouldn't be hard to find."

Thirty-Eight
Thaddeus

THE SIX MEN STARTED at one end of the meadow, walking side by side to the farthest border of the fence. Turning around, they came back, then repeated the pattern again. On the fourth turn-around, one of the diggers walked into an impression up to his knees. The tall grass had hidden the low spot from sight, and since no one had gone into the meadow in years, it wouldn't have been found unless you were looking for it.

Mr. Pritchett drove a shovel into the ground to mark the spot, then walked back to the house where I had joined Bertie and Maxine. I came out and met him on the porch.

"Well, we found somethin'," Pritchett said. "There's a good-size dent in the ground. The hole's not the same shape a coffin would leave, but then I reckon he didn't bother with no box. Prob'ly just dumped 'er in and covered 'er up. You want us to start diggin'?" he asked.

The Sheriff had joined us on the porch. "You get the men goin' with the shovels, I'll go inside and let the ladies know what's happenin'. You all know what you're lookin' for, right?"

"Yeah," Mr. Pritchett said. "No casket, it'll just be bones after all this time, if we find anything at all."

"Okay. Oh, and one last instruction. The county coroner's in on this now, so if you find anything, you leave it there. Don't be handling it or moving things around. He'll tell us what to do next when he gets here. Got that?"

"Roger. I'll keep you posted."

Our little community of farm folks was shocked that something like that could happen right under their noses. Bertie's mother, Louise, had been murdered. Either that, or she had met death by way of a terrible accident of some kind. The coroner's report showed one side of her head was caved in, like she'd fallen from somewhere high up and landed on something headfirst. Or, it said, she got hit up alongside the head real hard. Also, over an undetermined period of time, Louise had suffered three broken ribs, a fractured collarbone, a dislocated jaw, and a fractured pelvis.

At the hearing a few months later, the judge stated that Louise Tremont Knight had died of a blow, or blows, to the head and other injuries of unknown origin sustained over a period of undetermined years. That evidence, coupled with Bertie's deposition, settled the matter. William S. Knight was found guilty, posthumously, of aggravated manslaughter in the first degree.

The judge explained to the curious neighbors and media reporters that aggravated manslaughter was defined as murder committed in the course of other crimes, such as injuries caused by beatings, resulting in unpremeditated death.

Speaking to the courtroom, which was filled to capacity with curious neighbors and media reporters, the judge said, "Although the jury has found the accused guilty, I will forego sentencing in this case, since I feel that Mr. Knight is already fulfilling his eternal life sentence in the worst maximum-security prison known to mankind. May God have mercy on his soul."

Outside the courthouse, Bertie stood on the sidewalk, crying, while we all tried to comfort her. Speaking to no one in particular, her voice came out in a horrible wail that I found difficult to bear, as she said, "How come nobody knowed he done it? I cain't remember anybody ever comin' to the house askin' about her. Seemed like she jist dropped out of sight with nobody gone lookin' for her!"

Thirty-Nine

Sheriff Turner

It would be real hard to go back sixty-five years to figure it out. A few people in town come up with bits and pieces of conversations they'd heard as youngsters. Whispered talk, the young'uns bein' shooed away when the ladies at the church picnic discovered the kids was listenin' to their gossip. Mr. Prichett's wife, Ruth, offered what she remembered of the situation.

"I was thirteen when all this was happenin', Sheriff. My folks talked a lot about it at the time. Word was that Mrs. Knight had finally got up enough gumption to leave her husband. Couple of months went by and she hadn't been seen sittin' outside the feed store in her husband's truck, waitin' for Mr. Knight to finish his shoppin' chores. When he showed up without his wife for the third month in a row, my father asked him outright where she was. Told him if she was sick or needed help of any kind, some of the ladies in town were willin' to go out to his place and do whatever needed to be done. Told him they were concerned about the little girl, Bertha.

"Accordin' to my father, Mr. Knight flared back at him real strong," Ruth said.

She went on givin' me her information.

"Mr. Knight was hollerin' real loud and told the people standin' around to mind their own business, and he'd mind his.

"Lookin' back, I think he was tellin' a story to cover up for his wife bein' gone," Ruth said.

"He told the crowd to go ahead an' talk about it after he left town, if they wanted to, but truth be told, his wife done left him. He said he didn't have to tell them nosy women that much, but he was wantin' to nip the tale tellin' in the bud. He said they didn't need to know more'n that, an' said his daughter was just fine."

Ruth said, "People was standin' around watchin' while he picked up the last sack of feed and throwed it in the truck. All this time little Bertie sat quiet, like she might be scared to move. I don't think I ever saw a child obey better than she did that day. She looked straight ahead without movin' while her daddy drove out of town and left us all standin' there wonderin' what we ought to do.

"It was the talk of the town for weeks," Ruth said. "Questions was raised, like, when did Louise leave? How'd she leave? Where'd she go? In the end, nobody had any answers.

"The biggest question was why would she leave little Bertha behind. It was suspected she didn't have a choice. Mr. Knight was a mean man. He could've stopped her from takin' the child with her. As to where she could've gone, some folks had known her grandma and grandpa a little bit, but they had died a while back, so there was no help to be got from them. Nobody knew where to start tryin' to track her down. They finally decided, like he told them, it wasn't none of their business."

One of the things that came out in the investigation of the death of Louise Knight was Bertie's birth date, which she had never been sure of. I had started my investigation with the oldest residents of the county, askin' anyone to step forward with information, no matter how unimportant it might seem to them.

David Johnson had lived in the same place his whole life. He was the first person to respond to my request.

"What you got for me, Davie?"

"Well, our family was in town, an' I remember it was two days before my eleventh birthday. Me an' some of the other kids was kickin' a ball in the street when Mr. Knight pulled into town. He was pickin' up a few bales of hay, so he was drivin his buckboard. We had to git out of the street to let him by. He hitched his horse up in front of the feed store where we'd been playin' and went in. We had to wait for him to come back out to go on with the game we was playin'.

"One of the boys saw Mrs. Knight holdin' a baby and wandered over to take a look at it. He told us he said to Mrs. Knight that he didn't know she had a baby, and she said she was just born eight days ago. After they left, we went back to playin' ball an' never give it another thought, forgot about it, like kids do.

"But later, back at home, I heard my ma and pa talkin' about the baby. My ma said, well, she can't be that old. I wonder when she was born. I run over to the table where they was settin' and said, I know when she was born! I remember bein' real proud that I could tell 'em that, made it seem like I was a grownup, takin' part in their conversation.

"My ma asked how in the world I would know something like that, so I told her about my friend, Oscar, going over to the wagon. Ma set there and figgered it out. Two days from that day I was havin' a birthday, and the baby was born eight days ago. So, on the day I turned eleven, Mrs. Knight's baby was ten days old."

"What day were you born on, Davie?" I asked.

"October eleven, nineteen-hunert and twenty-seven, Sheriff, and proud of it. Be eighty-two-year old next time."

"Happy Birthday," I said.

Doin' some quick figurin' in my head, it seemed her mama had brought Bertie into this world on October 1, 1928, just her and her little baby, all alone in the barn, out in the meadow on Mr. Knight's farm.

"You say your friend's name's Oscar? He still live around here? I don't know anyone by that name."

"Well, Oscar went and got hisself killed in the war. You know, WWII, back in '45, so he won't be any help to you, Sheriff. But my wife, Jennie, she was settin' on a pile of feed sacks watchin' us boys play ball. 'Course, she warn't my wife then, she was nine!" Davie stopped talking to laugh. "We got married when she turned sixteen. You might ask her if she remembers hearin' Oscar tell about the baby."

Jennie Johnson did remember. "Yes sir, Sheriff. Davie told you right. After Mrs. Knight went away, I remember hearing my folks talk about it. My mama said it seemed mighty strange to her that a body could just up and go away like that, and never be heard from again. But back in those days people had a hard enough time keepin' body and soul together and raisin' up their own younguns without solvin' everybody else's problems. After a while, it just wasn't talked about anymore."

"I guess I don't understand why it was, only a young boy went over to the wagon to talk to Mrs. Knight," I said.

"I didn't understand it for a long time, either," said Jennie. "But as I got older and heard the talk, it seemed like the women was timid and scared because of the way Mr. Knight was so mean. And the men. Well, you know men, Sheriff. They mostly keep to themselves and don't hardly talk to their own women, why would they go over there and talk to a woman who wasn't theirs, especially when that woman's husband had made it plain he didn't want nobody meddlin' in his business?"

From what Jennie told me I concluded that everyone had learned to keep their distance, and it seemed like Louise had learned to accept things the way they were, since she didn't make no effort to be friendly after that first year of bein' married to Bill Knight.

Forty

Thaddeus

"I can't thank you enough for staying tonight, Bertie. I'm sorry I'm so late. We're getting close to finalizing the plans for the new facility, and I didn't want to cut the meeting short. Are you certain you're okay now? The last few days have been hard for you. I don't think I could have handled it all as well as you have."

"Oh, I'm doin' fine, Thad, thank you. Hard as it's been, the good part is I'm finally gittin' some answers. An' I'm glad to help you, Thad. Grace didn't want to go to bed until she knowed you was home, but she finally got so sleepy she couldn't stay awake."

"You've been a Godsend to us, Bertie. I don't know what we would have done these past months if you hadn't come into our life. I want to thank you."

"Well, you are welcome. It's been a blessin' to me, too, havin' you an' Grace for friends. She been like a sister to me, an' you done showed me what a husband should be like. My daddy, an' Homer, they warn't any way like a man should be, they was both jist pitiful people. I don't fault either of 'em no more, they jist didn't know no better. So I thank you for bein' sech a good man to Grace, an' to me, too."

I cleared my throat and wiped my eyes on my shirtsleeve. "Well, that's enough of that, Ms. Claxton. Let's change the subject, shall we? Did you call Maxine and tell her you're staying here tonight?"

"I did. Since it's so late an' you got to be at the office to meet with the builder s' early an' all, she understood. It don't make no sense for you to leave Grace alone tonight to take me home, an' then Maxine have to bring me back first thing in the mornin'. I need to learn to drive an' git me a car."

"What you need to do, Bertie, is make the decision to move here. That unit next to us is still available. It's going to be at least a year getting the new facility built and operational, and as long as you insist on being Grace's companion it would be convenient for all of us to have you next door. Have you given it any more thought?"

"Me an Maxine was talkin' about it a few days ago. She hates for me to move out of her place, but she thinks I should do it. I been back an' forth in my mind, but I think I done decided. I'm gonna be your neighbor. Can I tell Grace in the mornin'?"

"Can you tell me what in the morning, Bertha?"

We turned around to find Grace standing in the doorway dressed in her best black suit, bedecked with every piece of jewelry she owned and wearing a feathered hat. Glancing at my wristwatch and noting the time, I tried to maintain my composure.

"Why, Grace, you look lovely. Are you going out?"

"Oh, Thaddeus, you always have been a joker. Hurry now and get ready, church will be starting soon and you know I dislike walking in after the service has started. Would you like to come with us, Bertha?"

The kitchen clock hanging on the wall over Grace's head showed the time.

It was midnight.

Forty-One
Bertie

TIME HAD COME TO clean out my daddy's house an I warn't lookin' forward to the chore. Me an' Maxine had took a quick look around the day we waited for the meadow to be searched an' discovered that everthin' had been left right where it were when my daddy died. I had tried to git Homer to let me go back to the house after the burial, but he refused. He said there warn't nothin' left there to worry about, an' I couldn't git him to change his mind. Maybe he done been right, I thought, but now I had to go see for myself. Maxine drove me out to the Knight farm, as we was all callin' it now.

"Are you sure you want to do this by yourself, Bert? I'd be more than happy to help. I don't feel right leaving you alone in the house for the whole day."

I reminded her the plumbers would be at the store that day, fixin' the old pipes that was leakin' real bad. They could break an' flood the store, an' I didn't want to take her away from what she had to do.

"You're right, I can't afford to have my stock ruined, Bertie. I better stay at the store. Plus, I have a Council meeting to attend in the afternoon, then back to the store to check on the plumbers. It'll be late by the time I get back out here to pick you up. What if you need help? What if you fall down the stairs? What if. . .?"

I interrupted her. "For heaven's sake, Maxine. I'll be fine. Now stop your worryin'."

Finally, Maxine give up. She handed me a brown bag with a san'wich, a apple, an' a carton of milk from her store.

"You're going to need to eat sometime today," she said, an' then she handed me a roll of toilet paper.

"Here. You forget this old house has no indoor plumbing. You'll need this. And watch out for snakes on your way to the outhouse. I'll see you later."

I knowed Maxine were upset at leavin' me alone for the day.

I had started talkin' to myself agin. I said out loud, "Okay, let's start with the attic an' work our way down."

Climbin' up the steep stairs to the second floor, I pulled on the rope hangin' from the ceilin'. The stair ladder should of come down, but it done been so long since it were used I had to pull real hard. It let go sudden-like an' if I hadn't been holdin' on to the rope I'd have broke my head fallin' backward. The steps lowered down real slow to the hallway floor. I looked up into the dark attic at the top of the steps, wishin' I had let Maxine come with me.

I's glad I had thought to bring a big flashlight along. Climbin' the steps, holdin' on to the side rail with one hand an' carryin' the light with the other, I made my way into the attic. It looked like ever'thin' ever been carried up them steps was still there.

I could stand up in the center of the attic with room to spare overhead. Settin' the light on a wooden box, I started lookin' at the attic contents.

They was a rockin' chair. Somethin' familiar about it. I set down cautious-like on the edge of the old cracked leather seat an' slid back to where the flat center panel pressed into my backbone. Placin' my elbows on the arm rests an' curlin' my fingers over the curved ends, I give a little push on the floor with my toes. The chair rocked back an' made a squeakin' sound. I knowed that sound. Where had I heard it afore? A picture come into my mind, an' I seen myself settin' in a woman's lap, warm arms holdin' me tight, someone kissin' my hair. I closed my eyes. I could almost make out the odor of this woman. I stood up quick out of the chair. Turnin' around fast, I left it rockin' back an' forth while I stared at it. What was it about that chair seemed so familiar?

Liftin' the light from the wooden box an' holdin' it high over my head, I peered into a corner of the attic. Pickin' my way through boxes, I come to a old wooden table covered with rags. Lookin' closer, I seen they warn't rags, they was a couple of quilts. One of them were finished, the other'n, half-done. So many years in a hot attic had rotted away the fabric though, an' they tore easy when I went to pick 'em up. Scoopin' my arms under the pile, I laid 'em off to one side real careful.

Turnin' back to the table, I got another picture in my head. A little girl standin' on tip-toe, holdin' on to the edge of the table top. Watchin' somebody workin' with – what? Bread dough. It seemed in my mind it were bread dough. *What is this,* I wondered. *What're them pictures in my head, why am I seein' them things?* I couldn't figger it out, all I knowed were I had to get out of this attic. Movin' fast as I could through the clutter, I made my way to the let-down steps. My legs was weak and real shaky as I climbed back down to the second floor of the house an' headed through the hallway to see what I would find in the two bedrooms.

They was a bed in one room. The frame were old black iron. The side rails an' slats was still in place, but the mattress done been chewed by mice an' squirrels an' mostly layin' on the floor under the bed.

This were my room all them years I done lived in this house. A dresser set against the wall next to the bed.

The other bedroom were empty. The dresser an' the bed done been moved to the livin' room. They was there the day I come here with Homer to see my daddy when he were dyin'.

I stood in the doorway lookin' into that empty room, an' all kind of thinkin' got to runnin' around in my head. Who took the furniture down there? Homer? An' how long were my daddy sick afore he died? Why hadn't he let me know? It come to me, things beginnin' to fall into place now that I knowed how my mama died. Daddy's guilty conscience kept him from contactin' me. Maybe he were afraid he would confess his sin to me agin. Maybe he thought it would be more awful for the truth to be knowed here on earth than to take his sins to his grave. The poor man couldn't of knowed I had no memory all that time about the things he told me when he were drinkin'. He must of been a tortured soul.

I couldn't remember my daddy ever mentionin' the name of Jesus 'cept in church. We went most ever' Sunday, but once we walked off the church lawn headed for home, he never mentioned God or religion. He kept me settin' next to him durin' the service. I pined to go into the Sunday School class with the other children, but he made me stay settin' with him. It turned out, stayin' in with the grown folks, I learned a lot about God an' Jesus from listenin' to the sermons.

I think I knowed now why my daddy didn't let me out of his sight all them years. He were fearful I'd be tellin' somebody what he had told me while he's drinkin' so bad. From what I learned in church settin' next to him, I guess my daddy must of gone straight to Hell when he died.

"An' a good place for 'im," I muttered into the bedroom he had shared with my mama until that terrible day she died.

I turned an' hurried down the stairs fast as my wobbly legs would take me, holdin' on to the wooden rail nailed to the wall. At the bottom of the stairs I found myself lookin' into the livin' room. There set the bed, right where it were the day my daddy died. I wondered, were that the same bed mama had died in? He said he woke up one mornin' an' she were jist layin' there with her eyes open, an' he knowed she were dead. So he took her outside to the meadow an' buried her.

All at once, my mind were full of rememberin'. Like the rockin' chair. It had set in the kitchen, pulled up close to the open fireplace. The warm arms I felt as I set in the rocker in the attic was my mama's arms, holdin' me close while she rocked us back an' forth, smellin' like fresh bread an' sweat built up atween one bath an' the next, whenever my daddy took the time to fill up the big round metal tub so we could take turns in it. First him, then me. Now I knowed my mama waited til last, so's

I would have water that only had my daddy's dirt in it, afore she added her week's worth to ours.

The table in the attic. Another memory comin' back to me. The little girl I seen in my mind holdin' on to the tabletop, watchin' somebody kneadin' dough. It were me. The woman were my mama.

The thing I remembered with the most strength, though, were the day my mama died, my mind all mixed up. Why am I rememberin' all this after so long a time? I didn't like thinkin' about it, but I couldn't make it stop. Somethin' had happened the day afore my mama died. Somethin' bad. I think she were tryin' to explain it to me. She said my daddy were pesterin' her. She's kneadin' bread dough when he come in from the field for lunch. He went upstairs, started callin' for her to come up there.

"Oh, I don't want to remember this," I cried out loud. But the memories wouldn't stop. Now they done got started, they was clear as day.

SHE HAD BEGGED HIM, please, to stop pesterin' her. Said she didn't want to go up there an' leave the child alone in the kitchen.

An' he had come flyin' down the stairs with his suspenders hangin' down around his hips an' told her to git upstairs right then or he would beat her within a inch of her life, an' she stood up straight as she could an' told him, 'Go ahead an' beat me, I'm not going up there with you ever again.'

He did what she told him to do. He beat her so bad she didn't even cry after a bit. She jist laid there on the floor an' looked up at me. I were too scared to cry. I backed up to the kitchen wall an' watched while he kept on hittin' my mama, then pulled his suspenders up over his shoulders an' slammed the kitchen door shut on his way out. Mama crawled over to the table an' pulled herself up an' sat down hard in the rocker, too bad hurt to take a full breath of air, jist lookin' at me an' tryin' to say somethin'.

The next mornin' I watched my daddy carry her out of the house, leavin' me settin' in the rocker where he put me, too afraid to move. That were the last I saw of my mama, an' pretty quick after it happened I didn't remember any of it. Until now.

Forty-Two
Maxine

WHEN I PULLED UP in front of the farmhouse, I found Bertie standing at the bottom of the porch steps waiting for me. She looked like she'd seen a ghost.

"What in the world is wrong, Bertie? Are you hurt? What's wrong?"

She held on to me real tight, mumbling into my shoulder about remembering some things.

"I want to go home, Maxine. After a bit I'll talk about it but right now I jist want to go home. I locked up the house, I didn't find nothin' I want to bring away with me. Let's jist go."

I took Bertie home and made her some hot tea. Then I coaxed her into the shower to wash off the grime collected as she rummaged through the old house. By then Bertie was exhausted. I put her to bed, staying beside her, talking about this and that and nothing in an effort to put her mind at rest. I asked if there was anything she needed to tell me right away, but Bertie said no it could wait til morning.

"I'm so tired, I jist want to go to sleep."

I sat by the bed for a while then I moved over to the recliner in the corner of Bertie's bedroom, pulled the footrest up, put a pillow under my head and fell into a fitful sleep. I was still there in the morning when Bertie woke up.

When she finished telling me about her memories from the day before, Bertie seemed as shaken as she had been when I found her sitting on the bottom step of the farmhouse porch.

"I'll tell you what I think about this, Bertie. You know, all those years I worked in hospitals, some of them I spent in psych wards, psychiatric wards, where people came to figure out what was bothering them so bad they had to be in a hospital. I learned a lot working in those places. One thing I learned is that people can forget the awful stuff that happened to them, almost forget it on purpose to protect themselves from hurting too bad in their hearts.

"Sometimes the stuff they've forgotten comes rushing back into their head for no reason at all, or maybe they get reminded somehow of what it was they're trying to forget. I think that's what happened to you yesterday. You've been in that house a couple of times since you left it to marry Homer, but you never went roaming around upstairs or in the attic. Lookin' at the stuff up there brought back to your mind the experiences your brain has worked so hard to forget. You understanding any of this, Bertie?"

"I think I do, but why were that stuff in the attic all them years? It must of been up there from right after my mama died. I don't recollect it bein' downstairs while I were growin' up."

"Well, it's just my opinion, but I believe your daddy couldn't stand to look at the things that belonged to your mother, Bertie.

Stuff she brought with her when she married him, like a dowry or something. From what you told us before, he didn't like anything that seemed worldly to him, so he put her furniture, her quilting, all the things she used trying to make his house look nice, he put it all away where he didn't have to look at it. I think he was trying to keep you as plain as he could, so he kept the house stripped down to a bare minimum. That way you wouldn't get any fancy ideas like he thought Louise had. Does that make sense to you?"

"It does. But you know what, Maxine? I'm goin' to fool my daddy, even if he won't know he's bein' fooled. I'm goin' to have somebody go in there an' git the things that are still worth savin', an' what I cain't use, I'm goin' to give to somebody what needs 'em. He'll turn over in his grave, but I don't care."

EARLY ONE MORNING THE next week, Bertie and I went to the Knight farm after I opened the store. We went through the house and picked out the things Bertie would be able to use in the condo. She would need a bed, and I convinced her that what she thought was an old black bed was really a very nice antique. So she kept it, plus her dresser from the bedroom. From the attic she kept the rocking chair and a wooden trunk she remembered seeing in the kitchen before her mama died.

When we opened the trunk, we gasped in astonishment. There, wrapped between two sun-bleached white sheets, surrounded by cedar chips and what must have been several gallons of lavender twigs, lay a beautiful hand-sewn quilt. The pattern was unique, designed in shades ranging from the palest pink to deep purple, sewn together at random to form what Bertie described as handfuls of field flowers. They were pieced together into a palette of color, laced together with leaves in every shade of green imaginable.

Between the folds of the quilt was an envelope. Opening it and taking out a piece of folded paper, Bertie saw her mother's handwriting for the first time.

For Bertie, her mother had written. We sat in the dim attic, unable to speak. When at last Bertie found her voice, she held the note to her cheek and whispered, "Thank you, Mama."

WHERE HER MOTHER HAD found fabric in all those colors, we had no idea. My guess was that Louise had brought the fabric with her as a young bride who looked forward to having a daughter one day. The quilt had most likely been pieced together in whatever moments Louise could steal out of every busy day. She had protected her gift for Bertie as best she knew how.

"Wouldn't your mama be pleased now, Bertie, to know that the quilt made it through all those years?"

"Yes, I think so. More'n that, Maxine, I think she'd be even happier to know that she give her growed-up little girl the best present she'll ever git for as long as she lives."

Forty-Three

Bertie

THE HIRED MEN LOADED my furniture on the truck. The bed, the trunk, the rocker an' the dresser goin' directly to the antique shop Thad had helped me find. He said Gil Pauley, the owner of the shop, were well known for the meticulous care he took with the objects that came to him for restoration. That's how he put it. I'm right proud I'm startin' to understand Thad when he talks like that. They was a time when that kind of talk would of sounded like a whole other language to me.

Anyhow, Mr. Pauley got real excited when he took his first look at the things I had brought to him.

He said, "Mrs. Claxton, your dresser is a beauty. From the style, I'm guessing it came from Virginia, somewhere around the eighteen hundreds. Is there any way you could verify that guess?"

"No sir," I said. "All I know is it used to be my mama's, now it's gonna be mine."

Mr. Pauley declared that the bed, the dresser, the rockin' chair an' the trunk was all worth keepin', for sure. The bed jist needed to be cleaned up an' rubbed down with some special solution that antique dealers use to clean iron beds. The dresser drawers could be sanded down a hair to make 'em slide smooth, an' then polished with a paste wax he put on old wood furniture. When he finished with the dresser, he said it would be beautiful. Because it had set in the same place for my whole life, an' a few years afore that without bein' moved, it had survived without no damage 'ceptin' for bein' dried out some. Mr. Pauley asked could he buy it from me, but I had decided to keep it.

The trunk turned out to be my favorite piece. Inside the lid was a inscription tellin' the name of the man who made the trunk. He were Henry Charles Tremont. The date aside his name told us he must of been my mama's granddaddy, an' my great-grandaddy. That figgered out to the trunk bein' somewhere around one-hundred-forty years old. There warn't a thing wrong with it, an' it still had its original handles an' hinges on it. Mr. Pauley called it hardware.

I declare, I love that trunk.

Forty-Four

Thaddeus

Tom's move from Hollywood, California, to Creek, Florida, went well. Some of his real estate sold almost before the ink dried on the listing contract. A few of his properties would take a while, but he could wait, he said. He didn't need the money. The Ohio property we owned jointly was for sale and had a contract on it. Life was looking good.

Tom's new condominium overlooked beautiful Sarasota Bay on one side, and downtown Sarasota on the other. He kept his "yacht", as he called his sailboat, anchored at Marina Jacks, which was within walking distance of his new digs. He'd declined my offer to stay with Grace and me.

"Naw, you guys need your privacy, and I need mine, Thad.

"Besides, I need to be close to the Marina. I'm taking lessons to learn how to handle the yacht. Now, if I'd gotten here in time, I woulda taken that condo next to yours, but Bertie got to it first. I think that's gonna work out real good for you three, though. As long as Bertie's gonna keep on staying with Grace, she might as well be close."

"You're right, Tom. Anyhow, construction is moving along faster than expected at the new facility. When are you going to come out and let me give you a tour?"

"I'm not doing anything this afternoon. You free?"

"I am. As a matter of fact, Grace wants to come out today. Why don't you join us for the grand tour?"

"Okey-doky, tell me what time and I'll meet you there. Can I bring a friend? I been tellin' her about you and Grace. I think she'd like to meet you."

"Sure, bring her along. Is this someone special, Tom, or is she one of your 'temporaries'?"

Tom laughed. "My what?"

"That's what Grace calls your lady friends, Tom. She came up with that name for the women who float in and out of your life on a regular basis without ever becoming permanent. She calls them your Temporaries."

"That is funny. Naw, she's not gonna make the grade, Thad. Not that there's anything wrong with her. Matter of fact, lots of my ladies have been great people. The problem is me. Every time I get close to one of them, I think about my ma and pa and how they had it so bad all them years. Trying to feed their kids, no room in that little apartment, no money, half the time no work for my pa at the wharf. Kinda soured me on marriage and havin' a family, you know? You were lucky, finding Grace. You took your time, though. I mean, thirty-seven's old to be gettin' married. I just never found the right lady, I guess. Now, I'm so old, who'd want me?"

I laughed, but I thought I detected a note of dejection in my friend's voice. "You're not that old, Tomasso Pelligrino. Clean up your act a little, give up the cursing, you never know. Some sweet thing might just fall for you one of these days."

That afternoon at the job site, Tom showed up alone. I didn't ask.

As we stood there watching the ongoing construction, Grace was the first one to comment on the progress.

"Well, Dear, I'm sure it's going to be lovely when it's finished, but right now it's just a pile of lumber and cement blocks."

"She's right, you know," Tom said. "We'll come back in two months, Grace, and maybe then he'll have something to show us. By the way, Thad, what's the name you've chosen for this old folks home?"

"I don't know, Tom. We've come up with several catchy names, but so far nothing's stuck. Everything in Florida has a name like Heron This, Dolphin That, Whitefish Something. I'm looking for, oh, I don't know what I'm looking for. I only know we haven't found it yet."

"I know what you can call it, Dear."

Tom and I looked at each other, then at Grace. Tom shrugged his shoulders as if to say, what could it hurt to hear it?

"What's your idea, Gracie Darling?"

"Well, you know how Bertha is looking for some way to honor her mother, and you know she's thinking of having her mother's remains reburied, but she's not sure where to do that?"

"Yes, I know all that."

"Well, I think she should have her reburied at the place where the creek goes around those big sycamore trees, just before it gets to the waterfall in the meadow, and then you should name the whole place after her."

"You mean, name it Louise's Place, or something like that? I don't think that's what we're looking for, Darling."

"No, I think since her mother's maiden name was Tremont, and if she's buried in the meadow where it's so peaceful and quiet, you should call the new facility Tremont Meadow."

Later, as Grace was napping, I told Tom, "All I can say is, I live with Grace and see how she's losing so many of her faculties, but when you least expect it, she's brilliant. I like it, it has a nice sound to it. I think it'll be a drawing point."

Tom's years of Hollywood hype and promotion came to the fore, and he filled my head full of brochures with pictures of the meadow, the waterfall, the trees, a memorial plaque to Louise.

"It can't miss, Thad. The place will fill up so fast, you'll have a two-year waiting list."

I told Bertie the next day about the name I wanted to use.

"How did you know my mama's last name were Tremont?"

"I hope you don't mind, Bertie. Grace told us. It was her idea to honor your mother by naming the facility after her. Can we do it?"

"I been tryin' to come up with some way to show my mama how much I love her, an' I cain't think of anythin' she would like better'n this. I'd be real proud to have it be called after her, Thad. I thank you, an' I know she'd say thank you if she were able to."

The next week a sign went up at the building site. It said:

Future Home

of

TREMONT MEADOW.

Bertie was so proud she felt like she was going to float away, as she put it.

Tom and I sat in the living room with the last cup of coffee for the night, while Grace busied herself in her room, reading, I supposed. I was grateful to Tom for the time he spent keeping me company in the evenings.

I said, "Even when she's awake, it's not the same as it used to be. We'd sit and visit in the evenings, tell each other about our day, watch a little TV, read a bit before going to bed. Now, it's hard to get her to sit still long enough to have a conversation. And if she does sit with me for a little bit, it's like her mind is blank, she has nothing she wants to talk about. I let her wander in and out of her room, check on her once in a while to make sure she's not getting into trouble of any kind. I mean it when I say you are appreciated more than you will ever know.

"But, enough of that, my friend. Do you miss the bright lights of Hollywood? I want to hear what keeps you busy these days. How's it going with your involvement in our community theater productions?"

Shortly after he got settled in Florida, Tom had joined the local theater group downtown. Always the thespian, he loved being on the stage. The women were drawn to the actor in him, giving him an edge over many of the other men in his age range. The Ladies' Man. He loved it. He was more popular here than in Hollywood.

There, he was one of many bit players, and not a very good one at that, to hear him tell it. Here, he's a Hollywood movie star. When that became known, he found himself being offered first choice of leading roles in many productions, even when someone else was better suited for it.

One thing that had changed in Tom recently, he'd begun to learn humility. I thought that might be the result of watching Grace humbly accepting what was happening to her and being kind and loving in spite of her ordeal.

Tom surprised himself the night he graciously refused the part of a leading man, suggesting that the role be given to a younger man whose audition was the best one. His magnanimity earned him points, and his popularity soared.

Forty-Five

Bertie

My brain had been workin' overtime. Maxine noticed I were quiet most of the time an' asked me about it.

"Are you still having a hard time with the memories, Bertie?"

"No, it's somethin' else, Maxine, but I don't want to talk about it. It's nothin' you can fix, so don't you worry over it, okay?"

The next time me an' Thad was together, he said Maxine done told him she were worried about me. She thought maybe he could ask me if ever'thin's okay.

"No, Thad, ever'thin' is not okay. I been wantin' to ask you somethin' but I didn't know how to say it, so I'm jist goin' to spit it out. I don't want my daddy's house tore down until after I die. You can do whatever you want with it then, but while I'm still livin', I want it left there an' I want nobody 'cept me allowed to go in it. I hope we can work that out, Thad. I'm right set on it, an' I don't want to talk about the 'whys' an' the 'what fors'. I hope you'll agree to it."

"It won't hurt anything for it to stay there, Bertie. We'll do it. I don't think I agree with your not wanting to talk about it, though. Why the big secret?"

"I told you, I don't want to talk about it. Besides, I told you didn't I, so that means it ain't no secret."

I had him there so he agreed. He give me the key an' asked me to let him know if he could help with this in any way, whatever it were.

"I surely will let you know, Thad. Thank you for lettin' me do this. I appreciate it."

Thad were walkin' away from me mumblin' somethin' under his breath. I didn't hear ever'thin' he said, but I got some of it. I think he said somethin' like, "I am baffled. Now I have two women on my hands who're acting strange."

Forty-Six

Maxine

IN THE DAYS PRECEDING William Knight's trial and sentencing, I drove Bertie here and there, pulling together the details for her mama's funeral.

"I think this is a wonderful thing you're doing, Bert. It's just too bad she can't stay on the farm, but the law says you can't bury people on private property."

"It turned out to be the best thing, Maxine. After I asked about leavin' her on the farm, I got to thinkin'. Some of them people who are goin' to live at Tremont Meadow might not like havin' a grave in their back yard. Too much of a reminder of where they're headed.

"What else made me be all right with that were knowin' how glad I had been to git away from Homer's farm after he died. I got to thinkin' my mama would want to be in a place that I pick for her, an' not have to stay where my daddy put her."

"I'll tell you what I think is the neatest part of her going to the cemetery, Bertie," I said. "Do you believe that God is in charge of our lives? I do. And you deciding to put your mama there was part of God's plan, I'm sure of it. Out of all the grave sites you looked at, it took old Mr. Pritchett to point out that there's two empty ones you hadn't seen, because we hadn't gone to that part of the cemetery yet."

"I knowed the minute he mentioned 'em what two he were talkin' about. I figgered they belonged to some family hadn't used 'em yet. Turns out, they warn't never sold to nobody. Jist settin' there empty, waitin' for my mama, an' someday me, to move in there next to Farley an' baby Tree.

"An' by the way, Maxine. I ain't never goin' to be able to thank you enough for takin' me out to the cemetery ever' once in a while to visit my baby's grave. Only other time I got to go there were afore Farley died an' he took me. It made me happy to clean away the leaves an' put flowers there."

It seemed that Bertie had more to say, so I stood quietly without speaking.

"Maxine, do you think my mama an' Farley are in Heaven takin' care of my baby?"

"I don't know, Bert. There's so much we aren't allowed to know about Heaven, and God. Did I ever tell you what I believe about why babies can't talk when they're first born?"

"No, you never did, Maxine. Why do you suppose they cain't talk?"

"Because they just came straight from Heaven, and if they could talk, they'd tell the rest of us what it's like there, and what God is like. They'd be able to describe the angels to us, they'd tell us things so wonderful we probably wouldn't believe them, we wouldn't want to stay here on Earth. So God makes them wait until the memory of those things begins to fade, and they start to replace those memories with earthly experiences, and then he lets them talk. That's what I believe."

"I like that idea, Maxine. An' since I don't know any better I'm goin' to believe what you say. Unless I find out different, I'm goin' to believe that my mama an' Farley an' Tree is together, waitin' for me to come up there an' be with 'em."

I fished my hankie out of the sleeve of my sweater and used it to mop the tears off my cheeks.

"I swan, Bertie, we can't stand here the rest of the day talking like this and bawling. We've got things to do. Come on. Hop in the car and let's get going."

We piled into my car and drove to Memorial Garden Cemetery. Farley's and Tree's graves were in Section A4 of the cemetery, up a small hill which overlooked the duck pond. Peaceful and serene, and wooded, Bertie had been drawn to the spot all those years ago, when first her baby died, then again a year later when her husband, Farley, was killed in the truck accident. She loved to go there now and sit under the trees and think about things.

Over in Section D2, however, the cemetery bordered the busy road that led into the main part of town. As I pulled up and Bertie climbed out of the car, I noticed the swish of traffic and emissions from the vehicles, which created a very different atmosphere for the graves of William Knight and Homer Claxton.

When William Knight died, Homer had chosen the least expensive site available in the cemetery for him, and when Homer died, Bertie did the same for him, not knowing that she could now afford the most expensive site. Her newly acquired wealth became known to her only after the dirt had settled over Homer's casket.

I stayed in the car after I turned off the ignition.

"Ain't you comin' with me?" Bertie asked.

"No, I'll sit here and let you have a few minutes to yourself, Bert. Just come on back when you're ready to go."

"I need you to go over there with me, Maxine. I reckon I got to do this, but it sure would be helpful to have a arm to lean on, in case it gits to me too bad."

We walked off the paved roadway into the grass. After a few minutes of searching, we found Bertie's father's grave marker.

"The day my daddy got buried, Mr. Pritchett an' the grave diggers kept back a ways from where me an' Homer stood. I knowed they's wonderin' when I were goin' to leave, I stayed so long. I watched while they lowered his casket into the ground, an' when they throwed shovels full of dirt an' it landed with a thump on top of it, I stood there until they was done.

"Homer finally took my arm an' made me git in the truck. He drove us home an' I cooked supper like it were any other day. He never talked to me about my daddy from that time on. He were jist gone."

I let her stand and look at his grave for a few minutes. She wasn't showing any signs of leaving, so I took the initiative. "Are you ready to go to Homer's grave now, Bertie? I'll drive you over there."

"No, let me walk it, Maxine. It's only twenty, thirty feet across the grass. I'll be okay now, let me go over there by myself."

She was crying as she walked away from the car, and I was afraid of another episode like the one at the Knight farm, the day I left her there by herself. After she'd been gone about ten minutes, I started the car and eased it around the bend in the road, coming to a stop on the narrow pavement that passed for a road next to Homer's grave. Sitting in the car, I waited a few minutes for Bertie to get in. When she made no move in my direction, I sighed, got out of the car and walked across a couple of graves to where Bertie stood.

"Let's go home, Bert. No use standing here looking at what's done."

"I jist had to see for myself that he's really under that dirt an' ain't never comin' back. This is where he's goin' to be from now on, this is his new sleepin' quarters. That dirt looks like his old brown wool blanket, coverin' him up.

"I used to think what it'd be like to wake up of a mornin' an' Homer not be there. I'd be settin' for a bit on the front porch while I waited for the bread to come out of the oven, thinkin' how I'd be, what I'd do first thing, if he warn't around. I'm standin' here now tryin' to think what I'm goin' to do this afternoon, an' for the life of me, I cain't think of nothin'. Ain't that the berries?"

She turned away from the grave and looked at me. Tears spilled out of both our eyes, but in spite of my sympathy for Bertie and her situation, I burst into laughter at her remarks. It was contagious. The laughter that Bertie had kept inside for so long burst out of her now, with no one to criticize her.

She was free as the birds who were circling above our heads, waiting for us to leave so they could resume their search for fat worms and tasty bugs in the loose dirt scattered over Homer. It would be easy pickings for their evening meal before they roosted for the night in the trees above the grave, resting up for the morning's flight to some unknown destination.

The drive home was quiet, each of us lost in our own thoughts. In an effort to pull Bertie away from memories of her father and Homer, I was the first one to speak.

"Say, Bert. With all the story telling we've done, the one thing I wonder about from time to time is how did you meet Farley? I mean, your father kept you on such a short leash, you didn't go anywhere without him, how'd you have the chance to have a boyfriend?"

Bertie laughed for the second time that day. "My daddy, he thought he's keepin' me stuck at home where I couldn't meet no boys. Guess the one place he never give no thought to? Church. We met at church."

I hooted. "Church? Bet he was surprised at that, wasn't he?"

"He surely were, an' me, too. It happened so sudden-like, I think we was all surprised. We's leavin' the church that day, same as ever' Sunday, an' Daddy stopped on the steps to tell the minister them same words he always said, 'Nice sermon, Pastor.' This one were a fairly new pastor, only been with us a few months, his wife dead an' his children growed up an' gone on with their own lives, so we hadn't met none of his family yet. That day, though, there's this boy, a man I should say, standin' aside the Pastor, shakin' hands with ever'one an' smilin' at all of us. Pastor Kenner in'erduced him to us an' said he were his brother's son, come to hear his uncle preach at the new church. His name were Farley Kenner.

"He had his arm hung over Pastor Kenner's shoulders, give him a hug an' said that were the best sermon he had heard since he were six years old. Pastor said that's because he hadn't been in a church since he were six. They laughed real big at the joke, but my daddy didn't laugh, he didn't hold with joke tellin', 'specially in church. It kinda put a damper on them laughin' when Daddy stood there so sober, an' it made me uneasy. So when Farley asked his uncle what he were doin' for lunch, could he take him out to eat, I guess I's tryin' to make up for Daddy bein' rude. To this day, I don't know where it come from, but I spoke out an' said, 'If you ain't got plans, there's more'n enough for two people waitin' at home. Why don't you come an' eat with us?'

"My daddy liked to choke. He said he's sure they must of made plans, said they wouldn't want to eat no plain food like we eat. 'Ain't that right, Pastor,' he said, thinkin' he got out of that real easy.

"But the Pastor looked at my daddy, an' then at Farley, like he were askin' him what he thought about the invitation. Farley smiled right at me an' said they would love to come for dinner.

"They follered us home in their car, an' while the men set on the porch steps an' talked about farmin' an' Farley's college courses in agriculture, I put dinner on the table an' called 'em in to eat it.

"Sometime later, when me an' Farley been married for a while, Uncle Kenner told me while they drove home after dinner that day, Farley said he were goin' to marry me. He told his uncle that I were quiet, sweet, not gaudy like lots of the girls at college, said our house were clean an' peaceful. Said he's so full he prob'ly wouldn't eat agin for a week.

"I done had a piece of beef roastin' in the oven while we was in church, an' soon as we come in the door I fixed mashed taters an' gravy, green beans with bacon an' fresh vegetables from my garden. For desert I had a apple pie I'd baked the day afore. Farley only had a week til he went back to college to graduate, but he come to our house ever' night for supper afore he left, an' his uncle come with him. Seemed like Pastor Kenner had a way of makin' my daddy think he done invited them back for a visit the next night. I kept on cookin', Farley an' the Pastor kept on eatin', an' my daddy kept mumblin' somethin' about his bein' glad when that boy went back to college.

"He about had a fit on the last night when Farly an' Uncle Kenner talked to him alone while I were cleanin' up after supper. Farley asked my daddy if he could marry me. Jist like that. He hadn't even asked me yet."

"And your daddy said. . .?"

Bertie's eyes sparkled. "Uncle Kenner didn't give him the chance to say no. Said since I were twenty-three, there warn't nothin' my daddy could do to stop us gittin' married, if that's what I agreed to, an' said he'd help us do it, if he had to. One thing I found out about my daddy as he got older, if somebody stood up to him, he'd back down pretty quick. He warn't like that when my mama's still livin'."

"You suppose he had a guilty conscience? Even though no one else knew what he'd done, he did, and felt like he needed to back off," Maxine said.

"Yes, I guess that's what were happenin' to him. No matter what, he let me marry Farley the month after he graduated. Farley already had rented a farm farther over in East Manatee County, so we was all set. An' then, afore summer were over, we found out we was havin' a baby."

"Do you mind talking about him, Bert? It must be hard for you to remember all this."

"Like I told you afore, Maxine, you're the first one I ever talked to like this about any of the stuff what's happened to me. It's been so long ago now, I guess it's easier than it would of been, tryin' to talk about it at first. No, I don't mind. In fact, I appreciate that you're lettin' me go on this way, talkin' an' talkin'. My daddy didn't want to hear it, so I never said nary a word to him, or to Homer, either, about my feelin's.

"I had a few people, nurses at the hospital, an' the funeral home, they told me that lots of times a first baby dies when it's born, but that didn't bring no comfort to me. All I knowed, I couldn't hold him, he were in that tiny grave over at the cemetery. Me an' Farley had a hard time with it. I didn't know how to tell him the way I were feelin', an' he didn't either. He tried to talk to me about havin' another baby, but I were afraid to, afraid the same thing would happen. I knowed I'd never be able to bear it if I lost another baby. I told him, maybe next year. But you know how that turned out. Farley got killed, an' they warn't never another baby after that.

"An' if all that warn't bad enough, Pastor Kenner retired an' moved to Michigan. Then I truly were alone in the world, 'cept for William Knight."

Forty-Seven
Thaddeus

"Tom, you know I appreciate you staying with Grace today, don't you?"

"Sure, sure I know it, Thad. Any time. I guess Bertie's up to her ears with moving in next door, sorting through the two farmhouses and getting rid of stuff."

"Yes, but that's not the biggest job she's working on right now. The coroner's released her mother's remains, and Bertie needs to make a decision about what to do with them. I told her it would be okay to rebury them in the meadow, but evidently it's against the law to bury human remains on private property. She and Maxine are at the cemetery right now, making arrangements for the burial to take place there. I guess tomorrow they'll be meeting with the funeral home to plan for a service in about two weeks."

"Why is she waiting so long? I'd think she'd want to get it over with," Tom said.

"Well, she wasn't sure when the coroner would be finished doing the autopsy and releasing the body, so she picked a date far enough in the future to give him time to accomplish it all.

In the meantime, we made appointments for other things that need to happen."

"Such as?" Tom asked.

"Well, one day next week, my friend, Gil Pauley, is going out to both houses to see if there's anything worth putting in his antique shop. According to Maxine, the attic at the Knight farm is loaded with furniture, knick-knacks, boxes Bertie hasn't even opened yet. After the traumatic day she had there a few weeks ago, she's afraid of what she might find if she continues rummaging around up there. I offered to help sort stuff out. Want to come and help?"

"I'd love to, Thad, but you forget. If we're all over at the farm, who's goin' to stay with Grace?"

"Yikes, I did forget. You know what, Tom, I think I'm just going to hire someone to stay with her that day and see how she does. Bertie can't do this forever, we're going to have to make a change one of these days. This might be a good test to see how it goes."

"If you're sure, Thad. I don't mind staying with her, although I'll admit, sometimes I'm at a loss for knowing what to talk to her about. We've played a lot of *Scrabble*, but I'm getting tired of losing all the time."

We laughed. Grace might be regressing in her ability to remember the details of daily living, but her competitive spirit and intelligence emerged whenever Tom brought out the *Scrabble* board or a deck of cards. She beat him at everything.

Forty-Eight

Bertie

GIL PAULEY PICKED THROUGH the Knight barn an' both houses in about three hours. He brung one of his employees to help with the heavy liftin'.

"Land's sake," I said to him, "who'd of thought them old wooden tools an' farm machines was worth anythin'?"

"You can't believe what people collect, Mrs. Claxton. City folks come out to the country and buy up this stuff to decorate their houses. I'm sorry you're keeping the one iron bedstead. That and the other one would have made a great pair, even if they don't match. People like to mix their furniture up. But I understand it was your bed from the time you were a young girl."

He looked at his watch. "Wow, look at the time. I need to get back to the shop. That's where the real work is. What we did here this morning is not work for me, it's fun. You take care, you hear, and if you find anything else you decide to get rid of, just give me a call."

"I will, Mr. Pauley. Thanks for helpin' me clean out the houses."

As he were drivin' away, I stood there lookin' at the check he give me. "My word," I said to no one in particular. "I cain't hardly believe that stuff is worth this much money. I sure hope Mr. Pauley knows what he's doin'."

My move done been made to Egret Gardens. Ever' mornin' I would walk down the hall an' meet up with Grace an' Thad for breakfast afore he headed to the office an' the construction site at Tremont Meadow. Then Grace an' me would spend a few hours in the library, practicin' my readin'.

"You are becoming quite the reader, Bertha," Grace told me one morning. "Pretty soon, you won't need any more lessons. What will I do when you don't come to see me anymore?"

"Oh, I'll still come to see you, Grace. I figger it'll be a spell til I can read good as you, an' I still want to learn to talk better'n I do. I'm startin' to work on that jist as soon's I git everthin' else done. Once my mama is buried proper, an' I feel settled in my new home, that's when I'm goin' to start."

"Do you have a curriculum planned yet, Bertha?"

"What in the world is a curric, um, how do you say that word, Grace?"

"Curr-ic-u-lum. Curriculum, Bertha. It means a course of study, a plan for how you're going to go about it."

"No, I ain't give no thought how to go about it, 'cept I figgered I'd jist choose me one word at a time an' start tryin' to say it right til I finally don't say it wrong no more."

"Well, Bertha. That is a curriculum. You see, you're so much more intelligent than you give yourself credit for. I'd be happy to continue helping you with that even if we don't need to keep on with the reading lessons. Would you like that?"

"I sure would, Grace. Maybe we don't need to wait to git started. Why don't we pick a word, an' I'll start with that one right now. You got a suggestion?"

"Yes, I do. Let's start with one that's really easy. And."

"An' what," I asked.

"Just the word 'and'."

"Don't I say it right?"

"No, you always leave the letter "d" off the end. It comes out sounding like 'an'."

I thought for a few seconds. "Well, I never noticed that, but I believe you are right, Grace. An' I'll - oops - let me say that right. And I'll start practicin' it this very minute. An' you, well there I go agin." I started over. "And you make me stop an', and say it right ever' time, you hear?"

Grace said she had her work cut out for her, whatever that meant.

IT SEEMED LIKE MY life had been full of buryin' people. First my baby son. Then my husband, Farley. Next my daddy. The last one were my old husband, Homer Claxton. Now, sixty-five years after she died, I's plannin' a funeral for my mama. There warn't much left to bury by now, jist bones. But at least there would be a casket.

Maxine drove me to Shadley's Funeral Home to meet with Mr. Shadley, the owner. He were also the funeral director.

"Would it be okay, Maxine, if I meet with Mr. Shadley by myself?"

"Oh, sure, Bert, that'd be fine. I expect you've got some things you want to talk to him about in private. I'll just go out in the lobby and read one of those magazines out there."

Soon as Maxine shut the door behind her, I went straight to the point. I's learnin' from her.

"You'll excuse me, sir, if I come across kind of blunt-like. I used to have nothin' to say, mostly, but I'm gittin' too old to beat around the bush anymore. Now, you know I'm here to pick out a casket for my mama to be buried in. But there's somethin' else I need to do, an', and I don't want anyone to hear about this, 'cept you and me. You understand?"

"Why, of course, Mrs. Claxton. Anything we talk about here today is strictly confidential. How can I help you?"

MAXINE WERE SNORIN' REAL loud, and had a thin line of drool at the side of her mouth. I nudged her awake.

"What," Maxine said, settin' up real quick.

"It's time to go. I got ever'thin' settled with the funeral director."

"Gosh, that didn't take any time at all, did it," she said.

I didn't tell her she had been sleepin' for more'n an hour. I also didn't tell her why it took that long. She'll find out soon enough, I thought, unless she goes afore I do. I hoped that wouldn't be the case. I loved Maxine so much. I didn't think I could stand to lose her, too.

MAXINE DROPPED ME OFF at the Knight farm a few days later. Mr. Pauley and his men had brought all the boxes from the attic to the livin' room and left 'em there for me to go through. I dug into the first one.

What I found in them boxes give me a whole new life. Afore, when Homer were livin', the only family I had were him. I didn't know what I's goin' to do with the information I jist dug out of these boxes, but at least now I had a idea where my family come from and who they was, 'cause somewhere along the way, my mama must of had the notion she warn't goin' to be around to tell me what I needed to know about her family, so she wrote it down. Lookin' through one of them boxes, I come across a notebook full of writin'. I couldn't make it all out, so I give it to Maxine to read to me when we got back to her place that night.

"Bertie. This is like a diary of your mama's family history all the way back to the seventeen-hundreds. Mr. Pauley's guess about where the furniture came from and how old it is was pretty accurate. He must really know his stuff where antiques are concerned. This is amazing.

"You want me to read this to you right now?" she asked. "It's kind of long."

"Go on ahead and read it, Maxine. I ain't goin nowhere else tonight."

I set real still while she read. Seemed to me like my mama had some poor feelin's for William Knight. Writin' stuff down were prob'ly her way to git shed of the resentment she held against him, I think, because some of what she wrote explained the kind of person my daddy were.

Maxine read to me what my mama had wrote.

My great-grandmother Prudence Adams came from Virginia to Florida as a seventeen-year-old pilgrim with her twenty-year-old husband, Jacob Adams, in 1875, his intention being to make his fortune as a fisherman. Lacking the means to put together a fishing crew, let alone buy a fishing vessel, he did what many men did back then. He joined a bunch of cowmen and started rounding up scrub cows for a ranch owner he met up with. He settled into it thinking someday he would give it up because those little cows were tough. Even with the dogs they used to round up the cows, and the long whips they cracked above the cows' heads to keep them in line, it was dangerous work. It was because of those whips that these poor, rough-natured men became known as Florida Crackers.

Jacob Adams died out in the brush trying to round up an ornery bull that didn't want to get caught. The bull turned on him, causing his cow pony to buck him off, and the bull trampled him to death while he lay injured on the ground. This left my great-grandmother, Prudence, with two small children to raise by herself. One of them was my grandmother, Abigail.

The family had been poor before my great-grandfather's death, but his being gone made it real hard for my great-grandmother and her two children, Abigail and Benjamin. Prudence took to doing laundry for the cowmen and kept a garden. The children ate a lot of citrus fruit and caught fish from a nearby stream. Times were hard but they got by.

Years later, Abigail married Henry Charles Tremont and gave birth to a daughter, Martha. When Martha turned eighteen, she ran off with an itinerant preacher from Georgia. He brought her back and left her with her mother when he found out she was having a baby. Said it wasn't his and he wouldn't do for it nohow.

That baby was me, Louise. A few months after I was born, my mama, Martha, just up and left. My grandmother, Abigail Tremont, wound up raising me, after she had already raised her own children.

My grandmother was a tough lady. She came from a good Virginia family who always made sure their children got as much education as possible in spite of their pioneer life. She didn't take no guff from anybody, so after I was grown and William Knight started coming around, she let him know right off what was what. She said you don't take my granddaughter off this porch unless you see the preacher first. We done had enough of that stuff in this family.

I wasn't even sure I wanted to marry William. All we knew about him was he owned a piece of land out the eastern part of the county. When he tried talking to me about marrying him, I told him I had to stay with my grandmother and pay her back for raising me all those years.

William got sort of rude then and said he was doing me a favor asking me to marry him. Said I was twenty-two and should have been married a long time ago. Said I ought to be grateful he wanted to marry me, seeing as how the whole county knowed my mama was never married to my daddy.

When my grandmother heard I wasn't of a mind to get married, she set me down and talked real strong to me. She said you look here, Louise Tremont, you know I'm not long for this world. I'm leavin' pretty soon to be with your grandpa in Heaven, and I need to know you're taken care of before I go. That man standin' out there on the porch isn't the best thing ever created, but he's got a farm and a couple horses, he could provide for you real good, I think. You'd better get out there and tell him you'll marry him.

I did marry William Knight, and my grandmother died the next year, just before my own child, Bertha, was born.

I believe William heard my grandmother talk like that about him, and he never did like her after that. Said she was a snooty so and so, reading books and teaching me stuff I would never have any use for living on a farm. Said she thinks because her family lived in Virginia all the way back to when the first boat came over here, they were something special, but the truth, he said, our family was descended from nothing but a Florida Cracker and my own mama had run off and left me. I think he said those things to get even for what he heard Grandma say about him while he was standing out there on the porch.

Maxine stopped readin'. We looked at each other like we was both thinkin' the same thing. If it really happened afore that a mother had run off an' left her child behind, maybe my daddy thought it would do for explainin' where my mama went.

For all them years, it did do for a explanation. But then Homer died, and now the truth were comin' out.

THE ONLY PEOPLE AT my mama's funeral were me, Maxine, Thad and Grace, Tom, the pastor, the sheriff, Mr. Pritchett and his wife, the gravediggers, the coroner, and a newspaper reporter who learned about the event from somethin' he overheard at Maxine's store.

It were a fine funeral. Maxine had helped plan it and ordered flowers. The first time my mama got buried, my daddy did it alone. He prob'ly picked a spot in the middle of the meadow so he wouldn't have to dig around any tree roots. This time she would be buried in the cemetery in a grave next to her grandson, Tree, and his daddy, where a big sycamore give off shade for most of the day. Her headstone wouldn't be ready for a few months, but the way I looked at it, she had waited all them years to be buried proper, she could wait a little while longer for a grave marker. The pastor couldn't say much since no one knew a lot about my mama, but he read out of the Bible, and then he prayed some.

When the reporter heard the information that Louise Tremont Knight had died sixty-five years ago and her remains was bein' reburied in a different place today, he come lookin' for a story. He were fidgety and kept lookin' at the ground or the trees, anywhere 'cept at us. We all talked about that later an' figgered he felt out of place bein' at the funeral uninvited. He tried to make light of the occasion, laughin' nervous-like and jokin' around. Said he were at the cemetery to start diggin' for the facts. Sheriff Turner told him to behave or he'd be asked to leave.

When the pastor said the final prayer, the grave diggers let down the ropes and my mama were back in the ground agin. We filed past the open grave and each of us pitched a handful of dirt over that casket full of bones.

Later that day, Grace told me I should write all this down, what my life had been like. She thought I owed it to my mama to finish the story she had started so long ago. Seems like that might be a hard thing to do, but I told her I would think about it.

Forty-Nine
Thaddeus

THE DECISION TO NAME the new senior housing facility after Louise Tremont Knight had been an easy one. My wife, Grace, had suggested Bertie's mama's name, and right away I knew it was the only name that really suited the place. Grace said it would honor Louise and restore dignity to her after being abused and treated in such a way that it had actually caused her to lose her life.

Bertie had been Grace's companion and caregiver for almost two years, and in that time they had grown to be great friends and shared many parts of their lives with one another. It disturbed Grace that her friend's mother had been buried without a funeral or a minister, even without a casket. Just Bertie's father, taking her out to the meadow, digging a hole and burying her in it, with no one there to honor her existence. Bertie agreed to the name, telling me she couldn't remember a time when she had felt pride as she felt it now, not for herself, but for the mother she had almost no memory of, but suddenly felt very close to.

The interior designers were in the process of decorating, but otherwise Tremont Meadow was finished. Two floors, consisting of the main lobby and three wings, housed apartments with enough space to accommodate a maximum of one-hundred-fifty people. The two wings on the ground floor to the right of the lobby were for folks who could still manage on their own in an independent living lifestyle. Fifty-six fully equipped units, each with a small patio off the living room, joined a lawn that sloped gently down to the creek where rocks, polished smooth by years of running water, showed through the clear liquid as plain as if they were on the lawn instead of being submerged. For the safety of the residents, access to the creek was restricted by an ornamental wrought iron fence.

Smaller apartments in the first-floor wing to the left of the lobby were the assisted living section, for people who needed help with daily living needs but were not seriously ill. They also had patios so the residents could sit outside and enjoy the scenery.

The floor above the assisted living wing was reserved for any of the residents who would eventually need full-time, skilled nursing care, or Extended Care, as it would be known.

I reserved the first apartment past the main hallway in the Independent Living section, overlooking the creek, for Grace. I had made the decision to keep her there even though her diagnosis qualified her for Extended Care on the upper floor. Her apartment had been equipped with everything she might need as her health deteriorated in the future. This would allow Grace to stay in the same place until she died, a thought that I could hardly bear to face. I was trying to learn to live with that idea, but the only comfort I found in any of it was that Grace would not have to live out her life alone. She certainly would die before I did, and this kept me going in spite of the grief I felt over knowing I would lose her.

The location of the apartment put her right next to the nurse's office, and across the hall from the clinic where the doctors would preside over visits with residents who used their services in lieu of going out of the building to see doctors farther away.

I had tried, as closely as possible, to duplicate the interior of our condominium at Egret Gardens in the hope that when the time came to move Grace into the new facility it would make the transition easier for her. Change was hard on her these days. Bertie, along with Grace's part-time caregivers, varied her daily routine as little as possible, making it easier for her to cope with everything. Bertie had been keeping Grace company since the early days of her illness, but the two of them were aging together, and Bertie began having a hard time keeping up with Grace's daily struggles.

The day came when I had to break the news to Grace that Bertie wouldn't be coming to see her every day. At first Grace regressed, withdrawing into herself as she mourned the loss of her friend's everyday presence. When Bertie showed up after being gone for three days in a row, Grace would have nothing to do with her.

"Please, Grace, don't be mad at me," Bertie pleaded. "I'm not able to take care of you anymore like I used to. Somebody else is goin' to be here with you when I cain't come, but I surely will visit you whenever I can. Come and sit with me, Grace, and tell me about what's been happenin' while I was gone."

Grace was at the kitchen sink, getting a drink of water, as Bertie turned to walk into the living room. Picking up the dish cloth, she held it under the faucet and then heaved it toward Bertie's retreating figure. It hit Bertie square in the back of the head. She screamed out in terror, staggering forward into the arms of the nurse who was on duty that day. She reached back to take the unknown object off her head, whirling around to see who had done this terrible thing to her. There stood Grace, as frightened as Bertie was at what she had done. In a moment of lucidity, coming out of the fog of her tortured mind, Grace cried out, "Oh, Bertha, I'm so sorry, I don't know why I did such a terrible thing to you. Oh, oh, Bertha..."

Bertie put her arms around Grace and they stood there, wrapped in their friendship, trembling from fright and crying. We figured out later, after we settled both ladies down, why Grace had done this. It was the only way she knew to express her confusion and anger at her friend for leaving her alone for so long.

When their tears subsided, Grace pleaded, "You know, don't you Bertha, I would never hurt you on purpose. Please forgive me, won't you?"

"I know you wouldn't never hurt me on purpose, Grace. It's just your illness makes you like this. You won't even remember it, like as not, in the mornin'. So don't you fret any, and we'll just go on and forget it ever happened."

That was the incident that caused me to make the decision to get full-time, professional help for Grace. The nurses worked in shifts, three to a day, supplemented by Bertie's faithful visits. Grace came to accept the situation with more aplomb than anyone thought she would, which made life easier for me. I hadn't been feeling all that well myself for quite a while. Tired all the time, I chalked it up to the work involved in getting Tremont Meadow up and running so Grace could move into a more controlled atmosphere and lighten up Bertie's feelings of responsibility for this woman she had learned to love like the sister she never had. I thought once we were all settled in the new facility I would cut back and start taking it easier. Might want to see a doctor, myself.

Fifty

Tomasso

I'D MADE THE DECISION to move to Tremont Meadow. At this point in my life, I was in pretty good shape, but I had to face the fact that I was gettin' old, along with my high school friend, Thad. We'd been through a lot together over the years, and the way I figured, we might as well go through the rest of it the same way.

Thad was excited about the prospect of me bein' so close. Until I made that decision and we were all settled in at Tremont Meadow, I spent lots of time at the Manning's, a few miles from my rented high-rise apartment. Once Grace was in bed, the night got longer and emptier for Thad, and he was grateful that I hung around to keep him company.

So here I was, an aging former movie star, at loose ends, spending the evenings with my childhood friend and his sick wife. Moving into Tremont Meadow held the promise of meeting new people and living a different kind of life than I'd known before.

Speaking of meeting people and making new friends, a lady named Hannah Billings showed up in the dining room one evening looking uncertain about seating arrangements. As she stood in the doorway looking lost, I stood up and called out to her.

"Hey, over here. Come and sit with us if you want."

Hannah turned out to be a good friend to Bertie and Maxine. And to me.

Fifty-One
Hannah

My husband, Carl, had died of a heart attack at the age of sixty-five, leaving me a small insurance policy, eight-hundred dollars in the bank, some debts that needed to be paid, and a small house.

The house was paid for until two years ago, when Carl refinanced it, taking out extra money to put on a new roof and pay off several credit cards that were maxed out and overdue. The mortgage payment amounted to over half of the social security check I received each month, leaving me with precious little money to buy food and medicine. Most of the insurance money went to pay for Carl's cremation, and I was now in dire straits. I had no option except to call my daughter, Madeline, a retired Navy officer, who lived several thousand miles away from my home.

I placed the call reluctantly. Madeline had come to Florida for her father's funeral last year, and I felt I was placing a burden on her by asking her to come back again so soon, but I didn't know what to do about my situation.

"Can't you come, just for a few days?" I pleaded. "Just come and see what needs to be done here. Please?"

MADELINE TOOK A HARD look at her modest childhood home, seeing it now for what it really was. Run down and probably not worth much on the open market, she supposed it might be worth something eventually. Many of the homes and farms in the eastern part of Sarasota County were being bought up by developers and turned into office complexes or housing developments.

Madeline got busy on the phone the day after she arrived, calling local realtors. From the facts she gathered that day, my property wouldn't be desirable for that sort of thing for quite a few years yet. Commercial development hadn't reached out as far as where my house sat. I needed money now, though, so Madeline made the decision to put the house up for sale and get what we could for it.

"But where will I live, Madeline? Where will I go?" I'd never been alone in my whole life, and my limited prospects for the future had me terrified.

"Now, take it easy, Mom. We'll figure something out. But we have to start somewhere, and the fact is you can't afford to stay in this house. By the time you pay the mortgage and buy your medicine, you barely have enough money for groceries each month. What if you need new glasses or dental work? What about car insurance and gasoline? And that's another thing, Mom. The car is old. It's going to quit on you one of these days. What will you do then for transportation?

"Let's talk about the house itself. You can't even change a light bulb in the chandelier because you're not supposed to climb ladders with your poor sense of balance. There are so many things you can't do in the way of housekeeping chores. And the lawn, who's going to mow the lawn? How will you get to the store to buy groceries when you can't drive anymore?"

"I can drive! It's just that the doctor won't let me," I said.

"He won't let you because of your heart condition. If you pass out at the wheel and kill yourself, that's one thing, Mom. But what if you run into someone else in the process and kill them, too? You want to answer to God for murdering some innocent person, huh?"

I protested. I cried. I refused to move out of my house. But in the end, I knew my daughter was right. We started looking the next day for a new home for me. After checking out a few places, we called it a day. Discouraged, we stopped for groceries. Madeline said she needed something to read to get her mind off things and bought a newspaper.

Half listening to the late news on television, Madeline was relaxing on the sofa, leafing through the newspaper. When she got to the real estate section, an ad jumped out at her. A place called Tremont Meadow was having an open house the next day to introduce a new facility to the public. Pictures accompanied the full-page ad, which read:

COME AND SEE YOUR NEW HOME. Live independently for as long as you are able, then move up to our beautiful Assisted Living area where your daily needs will be met with kindly compassion. If the need arises, without leaving the premises of our Nature Reserve Compound, our on-site medical staff will give you the loving care your special situation requires.

COME AND SEE WHAT WE HAVE TO OFFER. Spend a few hours meeting our friendly staff and touring our lovely apartments. We'll be serving an assortment of delicious appetizers and liquid refreshments, a sampling of our Afternoon Tea menu, offered to residents and their guests every Saturday afternoon. We hope to meet you tomorrow.

We were there when the doors opened the next morning. When we left the grounds several hours later, we were both convinced that if there was any way to swing it financially, I would be living at Tremont Meadow as soon as possible.

Madeline called a realtor that afternoon. The agent pounded a for sale sign into the front yard lawn that evening. Because of the age of the house, and the needed repairs, the listing price was lower than I had hoped it would be but given the fact that I needed to sell it quickly, I didn't argue the point.

The house sold within the week. The buyer was probably an investor, Madeline said. He paid full price without any negotiations, and the cashier's check cleared the bank with no problem in just a few days. Now we were left with the task of clearing thirty-two years of detritus out of the house. The new owner was kind and understood our dilemma, so instead of asking for immediate possession, he gave us thirty days to vacate the house.

"The money won't last long, Mom," Madeline said. "One year, maybe two. If you're frugal, adding your social security check to what you have left after paying off the mortgage and the other bills you had after Dad died, it might even stretch out a little longer than that."

"What will I do then?" I was horrified to think I would run out of money that soon. "How will I live?"

"Well, one of the things I discovered in talking with the lady in the office at Tremont Meadow was this. Once you're an established resident who pays their own way for one year, if you then run out of money you can stay there as a Medicaid recipient. Medicaid allows you to keep your car and your home plus $2,000 in cash reserves, in case your situation changes and you're able to live on your own again. But in your case, you can't keep the house. You need the money you'll get from selling it to pay your way at Tremont Meadow, and you can't keep the car because you can't afford the insurance or the upkeep, even if you were medically fit to drive it, which you aren't."

I was bewildered by all this information, but having no other choice, I put my trust in my daughter. Before the month was out, I had settled in at Tremont Meadow. What few pieces of furniture I needed from home, my clothes and my personal items came with me. The rest of my belongings were sold at auction. The money from the proceeds of the sale were added to the balance of my new money market account to keep me going financially for as long as possible. A few days after the auction, Madeline returned to her home in rain-saturated Portland, Oregon, leaving me behind to start my new life on my own.

THE DINING ROOM LOOKED empty and unfriendly the day I walked into it to eat my first meal there. New residents were arriving on a daily basis to occupy their apartments in the independent living section of Tremont, the name having already been shortened before the facility was fully opened for business. I was a firm believer that things should be called by their proper name, and the shorter name was not to my liking.

The assisted living and extended care sections were not quite finished, the developer having made the decision to open this wing before the others. It would be several weeks before they opened, so the dining room had plenty of seats available. I stood uncertainly in the doorway.

A voice called out. "Hey, over there. Come and sit with us if you want."

I looked in the direction of the voice and saw a man and a woman sitting at a four top table. Not knowing how to avoid the invitation, I walked hesitantly over to their table. The man immediately walked around to my chair and pulled it back from the table, indicating that I should sit down.

I found myself seated at a table elegantly set with china, linen napkins and candles. The man leaned over slightly at the waist, picked up my napkin and draped it across my lap.

"My name is Tomasso Pellegrino, known to my friends as Tom, and my dinner companion is Maxine Monk. May I ask wit' whom we have the honor of sharin' our table?"

The woman, Maxine, rolled her eyes and laughed at his obvious display of theatrical formality.

Embarrassed and shy, I looked away as I told them my name. An awkward silence surrounded us. I had nothing to say, as usual, and Tom and Maxine were affected by the strained atmosphere that I brought with me to their table.

It was Tom who broke the silence. "So, Hannah, tell us about yourself. How do you come to be at Tremont?"

"My husband died." It was the only thing I could think of to say.

"I'm so sorry," said Maxine. "Was it recent, or have you had time to adjust to being alone yet?"

Unlike me, Maxine didn't seem a bit shy.

All my life I had done the bidding of others, let them be in charge of my life, for the most part. I felt obligated to answer when I was spoken to, and hadn't learned the art of evasion yet, didn't know how to turn the conversation in another direction. So as usual, I answered the question that had been put before me.

"I guess I'm getting used to it. He's been gone long enough that it doesn't seem strange anymore."

Maxine looked like she picked up on something right away. Without realizing it, I had yet to refer to my husband by his name. And I didn't say I missed him, just that it seemed strange not to have him around anymore. I guess maybe it sounded like I didn't really love my husband all that much. Probably didn't hate him, or wish him dead, just didn't love him like a wife should love her husband. What was wrong with me, I wondered? It wasn't like me to let my feelings out like this. How embarrassed I felt.

Fifty-Two
Maxine

I turned the conversation in a direction that I thought Hannah would feel more comfortable with.

"I guess we're the official welcoming committee for Tremont Meadow, Mrs. Billings. Which do you prefer, Hannah or Mrs. Billings?"

"I prefer Hannah, thank you. Should I call you both by your first names, too?"

"By all means, yes," I said. I felt my motherly nature emerging, wanting to put Hannah's uneasiness to rest. "Tom was the third resident to move into Tremont, right behind Grace Manning and Bertie Claxton. Bertie's having lunch today with Grace in her apartment. You'll meet her later. Grace is the wife of the developer of Tremont, and Bertie is her best friend and faithful companion. The land this facility sits on used to be Bertie's farm. Well, truth be told, part of it was her father's farm and part of it was Bertie's husband's farm. They're both gone to glory, as Bertie puts it. Bertie sold the whole shebang to Mr. Manning, and he built this beautiful place.

"It seemed natural that Bertie would move in here, especially when Mr. Manning planned to move his wife here. I guess it's okay for me to tell you about Grace, since you'll find it out on your own anyhow. Grace has Alzheimer's, but before she got real sick, she and Bertie became good friends, and Mr. Manning asked Bertie if she would agree to stay close by Grace so she wouldn't feel too displaced, leaving her home and moving into Tremont. Of course Bertie said yes. Grace has pretty much become Bertie's whole life. I worry what will happen to Bertie when Grace goes."

"Oh, my," said Hannah. "Is there a chance that Mrs. Manning might die any time soon?"

Tom answered her question. "Well, let me say this, no one can predict when it will be someone's turn, and this disease is unpredictable. Sometimes it goes quickly, sometimes it takes years and years to do its damage. In Grace's case, it seems to be going quickly, which is not good. Thad, Mr. Manning, isn't dealing with her illness very well. They've been everything to each other for almost forty years, and this has hit him hard. it's a painful process to watch, especially when it's someone you love."

I spoke to Tom now, forgetting for a minute that Hannah was at the table with us.

"Have you noticed anything different about Thad lately, Tom? He seems more distracted than usual, more concerned about Grace's future. He's losing weight, and I've watched him picking at his food. Almost like he doesn't have an appetite anymore. Is it just me, or have you spotted any of this?"

"No, I haven't seen what you have, Maxine, but I'll pay attention and see if I notice anything. He's probably overloaded, what with trying to get Tremont open, moving Grace into her new apartment here. Lots of changes happening, lots going on. It's enough to worry any man. He'll be okay as soon as things settle down.

"Anyhow, Hannah, back to you. What are your plans for the future? You got anything to keep you busy? Life here will be full of action, they've hired an activity director, I hear she's one of the best. She's already got a schedule of events posted in the craft room. There's enough stuff on that schedule, a person could stay busy every waking hour of every single day, going somewhere, doing one thing or another. I'm afraid though, that's not my style. I prefer quiet days. I love to read. Do you read, Hannah?" Tom asked.

Hannah responded quickly to Tom's question.

"Actually, I do love to read. I also write. I've been writing since I was a young child."

"Have you ever published anything?"

"Oh, no," she said.

"You seem embarrassed by that question, Hannah. Why is that?"

"My writing's not very good, Tom. I just write for myself. It was a way to fill in a lot of lonely hours when I was growing up."

"I'd like to read some of your writing sometime, Hannah. Could I? Hah, I have a few connections with some people in Hollywood, maybe I'll find something in your writing that I could send to them, get someone interested enough, maybe they'll make a motion picture from one of your books."

Tom said this with a twinkle in his eye, winking at me as he spoke. He was a great joker and all his friends knew this, but Hannah had just met him, so she wasn't aware that he was kidding her.

"Oh, no, Tom. I wouldn't even consider such a thing. I'm sure if you read my little stories, you'll agree they're the simple musings of a silly woman."

I spoke up. "Don't lose any sleep thinking about Tom's offer, Hannah. He's the biggest joker in the world. Doesn't mean anything by it, he just loves to tease people. Ignore him."

Hannah watched Tom as he winked at me again. Her face registered a puzzled look that quickly turned to embarrassment as she realized she had reacted far too seriously to what was meant to be a joke. Looking at the napkin in her lap, picking at the hem around the edge of the white linen fabric, she said, "Oh."

Tom had a rare flash of genuine insight into someone's insecurity, and responded with a compassion that showed me a side of Tom that I hadn't been aware of until now. He apologized to Hannah for offending her, but he spoiled the moment by sprinkling curse words throughout his apology and using the Lord's name in the wrong way several times.

Hannah spoke up immediately. "I'm not one to press my religious beliefs on other people, Tom, but after living with a cursing husband for forty-five years, I feel I need to say something. First, thank you for the apology. It made me angry that you would patronize my writing, something I'm very sensitive about. I let that go, but then to have you take the Lord's name in vain and curse, well, I had to speak up.

"I guess I need to learn some new ways and not be so serious all the time. I suppose I'll get used to your jokes after a while, but in the meantime, could I ask you for a favor?"

"Sure, anything," Tom said, eager to make amends.

"Well, if we're to be friends, and I would like that, could you possibly save your cursing for a time when I'm not around you?"

"Oh, hey, I don't mean anything by that kind of talk, Hannah. But if it bothers you, I'll try to hold back when you're around. You just remind me if I get out of hand again, will you?"

I had known Tom for several years now, ever since he moved to Florida to be near his old friends, Grace and Thad. Because of my strong friendship with Bertie, I became involved in their life, too. When Tom came along, he and I also became good friends.

As our friendship deepened and we spent a good deal of time together, I'd accepted his profanity, shame on me. I'd been known to let a swear word slip out once in a while myself, if I was angry or upset. It was the bane of my Christian existence, and I worked hard at watching what came out of my mouth. But since leaving Chicago and starting over in Florida, the anger and upheaval of my former life had pretty much disappeared, so it was a rare occasion to hear me curse.

However, listening to Hannah's request to Tom, I resolved to watch what I said from now on. *I guess we never really know how we sound, or what impression we're making on other people,* I thought.

I also realized you can't tell what a person is like by looking at them. I never would have guessed that this shy lady would be the kind to speak out to an aggressive man like Tom and tell him in so many words to clean up his language when he's around her.

You just never know, do you? I thought to myself in amusement, as I watched Tom squirming in his seat. Deciding to leave him alone with our new friend, and his discomfort, I excused myself from the table.

"I'm afraid I have to go, Hannah. I have dogs at home waiting to be fed, and I have a Council meeting tonight. Better get at it."

"Oh, you don't live here?" Hannah said.

"Goodness, no. I have a small farm a few miles from here. Used to belong to my grandparents. I've been there close to twenty years now. I'm going to have to give it up someday, I suppose, but not quite yet. Not as long as I have the energy to keep it going, with a bit of help from the hired hand that does most of the work. It's getting close, though. I'll probably be here in a few years. In the meantime, I plan on coming to have lunch with Tom and Bertie every chance I get. I'll see you, too, once in a while."

I put my hand on Tom's head and turned his face to look at me. "You take good care of her, Tom, you hear? And watch your mouth, boy."

"Yes, Mom," Tom said, rolling his eyes around in their sockets and looking at Hannah with a meek grin on his face.

I saw Hannah smile at him in spite of herself. He had a way about him that drew a person in. Hannah was going to like it here.

"Say, Thad, do you have a minute to talk?" I caught him coming out of his office a few days later.

"Sure, Maxine. What is it?"

"How we doing outside by now? Is the area down by the waterfall finished?"

"Yes. They finished mowing the new sod yesterday. The only thing missing is the benches. They should be here in a few days, then it'll be up and running, ready to go. Why do you ask?"

"Well, shortly after we met, Bertie told me how she and her first husband, young Farley, liked to go on picnics. They had one planned the day he was killed in that accident. I'd like to give her that lost picnic, and I want to do it at the waterfall. That's another thing she didn't get to do. Said she sat under the trees there one day, after she threw the squash into the creek, and..."

"Wait. What squash? And why'd she throw squash in the creek? You're not making sense, Maxine."

Laughing, I told him, "Thad, you have to get Bertie to tell you herself about the squash, it's too funny. Anyhow, she wanted to go back there some day when she could sit under the trees and read a book without worrying about having chores to do, or have Homer...oh, shoot, Thad. Just trust me on this and stay with me here while I tell you what I want to do."

THE NEXT WEEK I cornered Bertie and told her to come with me.

"I'm taking you to lunch," I told her.

"I was thinkin' I would eat in the dinin' room with Hannah today," Bertie said.

"Now, don't argue with me, Bertie. Close your eyes and get in the golf cart. I'm taking you for a ride and you're not to look until we get there, you hear me?"

"I hear you, Maxine, but I don't understand what you're doin'."

"You don't have to understand everything, Bert. Just do what I tell you to do, and be quiet. Get in the golf cart."

"Well, I thought you said we were goin' to lunch."

"We are. Now get in the golf cart."

"We're eatin' in the golf cart?"

"No, we're not eating in the golf cart. I swan, Bertha, you get more stubborn all the time. I think I liked it better when you did whatever you were told to do and didn't ask any questions. *Now, get in the golf cart!*"

"Land's sake, I'm getting in the golf cart. You don't need to holler at me. I got my eyes closed. How long do I have to keep 'em closed?"

"Until I tell you to open them. Now hold on, we're going for a ride."

I took off, the golf cart bouncing along the dirt berm leading up to the newly paved path that branched off here and there to various parts of the compound. The path I veered onto would take us to the grove of trees and saw palmettos that bordered the creek and shaded the waterfall where it spilled over into the pond a few feet below.

I heard voices and hoped to goodness the rest of the people involved in this shindig would stop talking before we got close, or Bertie was likely to get suspicious. As we rounded the bend, they saw me and Bertie coming, and started shushing each other.

Pulling the cart next to the little group, I said, "On the count of three, Bertie, you open your eyes. One, two. . ." I waved my arm in the air like an orchestra conductor, and on the down stroke, as planned, everyone yelled, *THREE!*

Startled, Bertie opened her eyes and looked around, confused. "What in the world?"

Tom scrambled to his feet and offered his hand to help Hannah stand up from her seat on the grass. Thad helped Grace out of her lawn chair, and they all gathered around the golf cart, everyone talking at once. I held up my hand for silence. Clearing my throat, I tried to talk, but my voice wouldn't work. I motioned to Thad to take over while I wiped the tears out of my eyes.

"This is a picnic for you, Bertie," Thad said. "Maxine shared with me how you missed the last picnic you had planned, and how you wanted, someday, to sit in this very spot and have nothing else to do except relax with a good book.

"This one won't replace the picnic you were going to have, but it's a picnic. And we wanted you to be the first resident of Tremont Meadow to enjoy your favorite spot, right here under the trees by the waterfall. Thank you, Bertie, for making this lovely place possible."

Tom had his back to the rest of us by then, mopping his eyes with his handkerchief. Hannah and I were crying outright, with no effort being made to hide the tears, while Grace looked confused and asked what was wrong, why was everyone crying?

Her question brought laughter and smiles all around, and with that, Hannah said, "Oh, Bertie. When I heard you wanted to come here and read, I bought you a book. The name of it is *Prayers Written at Vailima* and it was written by Robert Louis

Stevenson. I'd like to read one of his prayers that I think speaks to each of us here today. May I?"

"I'd like that," Bertie said.

"Thank you, Bertie. It goes like this," Hannah said. She read Stevenson's prayer in a soft voice.

"'Lord, behold our family here assembled. We thank Thee for this place in which we dwell; for the love that unites us; for the peace accorded us this day; for the hope with which we expect the morrow; for the health, the work, the food, and the bright skies, that make our lives delightful; for our friends in all parts of the earth, and our friendly helpers in this foreign isle. Let peace abound in our small company. Purge out of every heart the lurking grudge. Give us grace and strength to forbear and to persevere. Offenders, give us the grace to accept and to forgive offenders. Forgetful ourselves, help us to bear cheerfully the forgetfulness of others. Give us courage and gaiety and the quiet mind. Spare to us our friends, soften to us our enemies. Bless us, if it may be, in all our innocent endeavours. If it may not, give us the strength to encounter that which is to come, that we be brave in peril, constant in tribulation, temperate in wrath, and in all changes of fortune, and, down to the gates of death, loyal and loving one to another. As the clay to the potter, as the windmill to the wind, as children of their sire, we beseech of Thee this help and mercy for Christ's sake. Amen.'"

"I believe that prayer says it all, as far as our small company goes," said Thad. "We are all so proud of you, Bertie, for the progress you've made in your efforts to gain the education you were denied as a child. For the good spirit that resides in you in spite of the hardships you've endured. But more than any other accomplishment you've made, Bertie, we thank you for the love you show to each one of us, for your courage, your grace and strength. I think," and as Thad looked around the group, they nodded in agreement, "that you have been the glue that has held us together in the face of obstacles, rejection, fear, and uncertainty for our future. You have brought joy and laughter into our midst, Bertie, and we thank you for being our friend. How about it, everyone?"

Even Grace clapped her hands together, and did a little dance on the grass, which ended the solemn part of our gathering with more laughter.

"Hey," Tom called out, "who brought the corkscrew? I need to get this bottle of sparkling grape juice open."

I walked up to him, took the bottle, and twisted the cap. It came right off. "You spent too many years drinking that other stuff, Tom. You don't need a corkscrew for these bottles."

Tom poured the juice into paper cups and distributed them. Holding his high in the air, he started to make a toast. Bertie interrupted him.

"Maxine, do you remember the time we made a toast? I hadn't never heard of doin' such a thing, so I don't think I did it right. Can I make another one before Tom does his?"

"Absolutely," I said. You don't mind, do you, Tom?"

"You go right ahead, Bert. It's your party. I mean, it's your picnic."

"Well, the last time, I made a toast to my daddy and Homer. I don't hate 'em anymore like I did then, I just think what they did was wrong, but like Mr. Stevenson said in his prayer, we should have the grace to forgive our offenders. I believe he must've been a Bible reader, because that's the same thing Jesus told us to do.

"So today, I'm makin' it official. I forgive my daddy and Homer for the bad things they did to me and to my mama. But the toast I want to make is this. Here's to my mama, and the part of me that's like she was, whatever that might be, because if I'm different from my daddy, it must be that I'm like her. So I thank you, Mama, for my quilt, I feel your love ever' time I snuggle up underneath it, and we all thank you for this beautiful place we live in that's been given your name. Drink up, ever'body."

"Okay, Tom," Thad said, after we all took a sip. "Give us your toast now."

Tom seemed to be having a difficult time today controlling his tear ducts, because he stood at the edge of the group with his back turned to us, and muttered over his shoulder, "I think Bertie covered it all, Thad, thanks."

The loud honk into his handkerchief brought on some more laughter, and with that, we dug into the fried chicken picnic that had been prepared by the kitchen staff at Tremont Meadow.

THE CHICKEN WAS GONE, a few missed baked beans clung to the side of the bowl, and a spoonful of potato salad lingered in the corner of its container. Tom reached for the last stuffed egg, beating Thad to it by a two second margin. More laughter.

"Well," said Thad, standing and stretching his arms over his head. "We have got to get going. Grace has a doctor's appointment in half an hour, and I have two meetings back-to-back after that."

"I have a Council meeting scheduled," I said. "Better get going. By the time I get home and change, I'll just make it. Tom, help me get this stuff packed up and in the golf cart. Leave a little room for Bertie to sit on the front seat, though."

"If you all don't mind," said Bertie, "I'd like to stay here for a while, just sit and listen to the water and the birds. You go on ahead and I'll walk back."

Hannah looked concerned. She knew Bertie was having trouble with her knees. "You know what, Bertie? Why don't I stay with you for a little while and I'll read some from your new book? Or, you can read to me. I'd love for you to read some to me. Would that be all right with you?"

Fifty-Three
Bertie

I THOUGHT THAT WOULD be just fine. I told the rest of the crowd to go on. If we warn't back in time for supper they should send someone on the golf cart to get us.

Me and Hannah spent the rest of the afternoon readin' to each other, watchin' the water spill over the rocks, splashin' into the small pool below, and talkin'.

"I envy Maxine, Bertie," Hannah said.

"You do? She'd be surprised to hear that, Hannah. She wishes her life had been more like yours. You had a husband, a home, your children for all them years. Your kids call you all the time to make sure you're doin' okay here. They send you stuff in the mail. Maxine don't have none of that, so why would you envy her?"

She faced me and worked up her courage.

"I envy her because she's had you for a friend all this time. I know you told me last week that you never had any friends until after your husband died, and you were pretty amazed to learn that the same thing was kind of true about me."

"Yes, Hannah, but you told me that for many years you had your parents and your aunt in your life, and then the children were born. You had family. Maxine had her children, but she raised 'em up pretty much on her own. Now, her boy is dead, and her girl lives in Alaska and she don't even call Maxine once in a while. Just because Maxine and me are friends, that don't make up for all the years she's been so lonely."

"Oh, forgive me, Bertie. I didn't mean to upset you. You've had a hard time of it yourself, and I shouldn't envy either of you just because you're good friends."

"I want to tell you somethin', Hannah. Maxine and me both like you a lot. If you give us the chance, we'd like for you to be our friend, too. But you got to quit actin' so shy-like, and skittish. Just pretend like we's always knowed each other, and let it all hang out."

"Another thing. You got to stop holdin' Thad and Tom at arm's length. I don't know why you're so afraid of them, but you act like they're goin' to bite you. They ain't–oh, darn, there I go again with talking funny, let me say it over – they aren't going to hurt you. In fact, I think Tom might even like you for more than a friend. I see him looking at you, and he talks real nice about you to me sometimes. So just let us all be your friends, Hannah, and you won't have any need to envy nobody."

"Why do you think Tom likes me, uhm, in that way, Bertie. I haven't done anything to encourage him."

"You remember that first day you met Tom, Hannah, and you asked him to not curse or use the Lord's name in vain when he's around you? You stood up to him and showed some spunk.

You let him know in a nice way what was what, and I think he admires you for that."

"Yes, but. . ."

"Yes, but nothing. I warn't there, I was havin lunch with Grace that day, but Maxine told me later, Tom got meek as a kitty cat when you talked to him like that, and he's been so polite ever since, not just in front of you, but around the rest of us, too. You made him take a second look at hisself, and I don't think he liked what he saw. He told Maxine if some woman had stood up to him like that before, he prob'ly would have been married a long time ago.

"What? What are you thinkin', Hannah? You got a funny look on your face."

"You've made me realize something, Bertie. All those years I put up with my husband's nonsense, maybe he was waiting for me to stand up to him. Why didn't I ever know this before? Maybe he would have been a better person if I had just stood up to him."

"Well, you can spend the rest of your life wonderin' if this, and if that. But I like to think about frogs whenever I get to sayin' if, if, if."

"What do you mean, about frogs?"

"You know," I said. "Life would be a lot easier for a frog if it had wings, because it wouldn't bump its behind ever' time it jumped."

Hannah laughed. "You are funny, Bertie."

"I'm glad I was able to make you laugh again, Hannah. We done had some really good laughs today, haven't we?"

"We have," Hannah said.

"By the way, how do you like the benches? Thad was goin' to get the cement ones, said they'd last longer, but I talked him into the cedar ones with these nice fat, waterproof cushions. They're prettier, but the best part about them, they're comfortable."

"They're very pretty, Bertie. I like them. Not to change the subject, but I want to ask if you mind that I stayed with you after the others left? I've been wondering if you maybe wanted some quiet time alone, instead of listening to me talk."

"Hannah, you ain't said much at all today, but even if you was a big talker, I wouldn't care. I spent too many years mostly alone, now I love to talk to people. Even better, I love to listen to people. Me and Maxine have spent hours and hours yakkin' at each other. Why, I guess the only one knows more about the other one is God hisself. We done told each other everything."

"Truly? You've told each other everything about yourself?"

"Yep, far as I know. I told Maxine ever' detail I could remember about my life, and she says she done the same. So unless one of us is fibbin', we're startin' over with a clean slate. No secrets between us, and we still love each other." I cackled with delight. "It's a good feelin' to know you got nothing to hide."

"Oh, come on Bertie, what could you possibly have done in your life that you had to hide? I've heard your story, what kind of sins could you have committed?"

"I know what you're thinkin', Hannah. The ten commandments, right? Well, if I recall what Jesus said, he said, there ain't, I mean isn't, any sin that's worse than the next one. Sin is sin. So, no matter what it is you done, it's just as bad as what someone else done. And no matter what sin someone else done committed, it's no worse than what the other guy did. And that's that.

"So, let me tell you, my biggest sin for a long time was hatin' my daddy, and then addin' Homer to that same list. I even hated my mama for most of my life, until I found out she didn't go away and leave me behind on purpose. Then there was the sin of tellin' lies. Well, I didn't actually tell the lie, but I planned on it, the day I threw the squash in the creek. I intended to lie, which is about as bad as doin' it.

"But the worst sin I ever did was hatin' God for a while. That happened after I found out what my daddy did to my mama. I had to live that awful life, with a mean man like my daddy was, and without a mama to love me, and I could not understand why God would let me have to live that way. I listened good when I was in church with my daddy all them years, and I kept hearin' that God is good, he's kind, he cares about us. I just couldn't figure out, if he was all them things, why he wasn't bein' good and kind to me. Seemed like he didn't care nothing about Bertha, so I started in hatin' Him. Put Him right up there at the top of that hate list. Almost the worst sin anyone could ever commit, and I did it."

"But Bertie, it doesn't seem like you hate God."

"Oh, I don't now. Of all people, it was Sheriff Turner that set me straight. He was behind me and Maxine as we was leavin' the church one Sunday after they found my mama's grave. He had been there that day when I was carryin' on so, askin' why God would let such a bad thing happen to her, why I had to live such a sad life. I was askin' all kinds of questions, like how could our preacher say God was good. Questions like that.

"Sheriff Turner said he didn't know if it would help me see things in the right light, but he'd like to talk to me for a few minutes. He told Maxine to go on home, he'd bring me later.

"Pretty much what he told me that day was God doesn't make us do anything. He gives us our freedom to choose if we want to follow Him, or not. If we choose not to follow Him, we break his laws, and when we do that, other people can suffer, because what we do always affects others. So the things my daddy did affected my mama, and she died. What he did affected me because I had to grow up without her.

"Ever'thing changes, dependin' not only on what we do, but what other people do, too. So I wasn't to blame God for my daddy's poor behavior. When I thought about what Sheriff Turner said to me that day, I knowed he was right. So I stopped hatin' God, and started loving Him again."

Hannah sat quiet for a bit. I think she was tryin' to soak up Sheriff Turner's advice to me. When she did start talkin', she seemed real sad.

"I have to believe that God has forgiven you for that, Bertie. He knows what your life was like. But He knew your heart, too. You have a good heart, and you're kind. You care about people. You're like Him, Bertie.

"On the other hand, my sins were terrible. I've done things I've never told to anyone. Terrible sins. Some of what I did, everyone knew about at the time. They haunt me something terrible. How do you get to the point where you feel truly forgiven, Bertie?"

I said a silent prayer for help. *Oh God, I don't know what to tell Hannah. You know her sins, you know her needs. If there's anythin' I can do to help her accept your forgiveness, tell me what it is, put it in my mind what I should say.*

"Well, Hannah, here's what me and Maxine did. We decided we needed to get it all out in the open, tell someone what troubled us, and then each of us forgive the other, and then ask God to forgive us for all the bad we'd done. It worked."

"You mean, I'd have to tell someone? I don't know if I can do that. I'd be so ashamed."

"You think on it, Hannah, and pray about it. If you decide you want to do what we done, I'd be right proud to be the one you choose to help you through it. You know it would be between you and me and God, no one else. In the meantime, we got to get off our behinds and head for home."

We got as far as the bend in the path when Tom rolled into sight with the golf cart. "Hey ladies, how about a lift? Looks like it might rain any time now. Hop up here, just squeeze in tight. I think we'll all fit."

I pushed Hannah toward the cart, makin' sure she got in first. Then I climbed aboard and complained that I didn't have room on the seat.

"Move over some more, Hannah, I'm goin' to fall out of this contraption and break a leg."

Tom put his right arm over Hannah's shoulders and grabbed hold of my sweater. "You're okay, Bert, I got you. Hang on, girls, here we go."

I think Hannah liked sittin' close to Tom, laughin' as we whizzed along at top speed, headed for a hot meal and then a few hours in front of the TV in the media room, watchin' a movie with some of the other residents at Tremont.

Fifty-Four
Hannah

I DECIDED THAT DAY I wanted to be Tom's friend. But the really amazing thing I was discovering about myself was my developing ability to express a personal preference about something, as I had done when I asked Tom to be careful with his speech and to have respect for God's name. As we watched the movie that night, I realized I wanted to talk with Bertie about the things in my life that bothered me so badly. What in the world was happening to me, I wondered? I had begun to think about how people get connected to each other sometimes. I had been a plain, not really pretty teenager, shy to the point of being backward. I belonged to no clubs in high school, didn't date. How did I ever wind up with Carl Billings? Now that he was gone, I'd blossomed, due to Bertie's and Maxine's perseverance. They kept at me, drawing me out of my shell, until I began to respond to their efforts.

Maxine and Bertie, I thought. *So different, yet best friends.*

And here I was, Hannah Banana, as the kids in school had called me, being accepted into the circle of friendship they shared with the Mannings, and Tom. My life had changed so much in the past six months, sometimes it seemed as if I were a different person from the girl who had married Carl all those years ago.

THE NEXT MORNING, MY doorbell rang and shook me out of my daydream. "Who is it?"

"It's me, Hannah. Bertie."

I hoped everything was all right. Bertie wasn't in the habit of dropping in unannounced. I pulled the door open quickly and asked, "What's wrong? Are you okay?"

"Yes, I am, but I came to see if you were. You warn't at breakfast. Are you sick?"

"No. I just have a lot on my mind. I didn't feel like eating."

"It's about our conversation yesterday, isn't it? I been thinkin' about the things I said to you, Hannah. I want to apologize if I was pushy, sayin' all them things to you."

"You weren't pushy, Bertie. In fact, I've thought a lot about what you told me, about you and Maxine talking. I haven't known you long at all, but if there's anyone I feel I could trust, it would be you. I've decided I want to tell you something, try to understand myself why my life has been the way it's been. Do you have some time to spare right now, to come in and sit for a while?"

"All I got is time, Hannah. Now that Grace has nurses with her around the clock, I got lots of spare time. I don't go see her too often anymore. She remembers my name sometimes, but mostly she don't know who I am. It's so sad.

"Sometimes I want to share with her the results of all the hard work she put into helpin' me with my learnin', but I don't think she'd even know what I'm talkin' about."

"Well, I've noticed the difference, Bertie. In the short time I've known you, your way of speaking has changed,"

"Oh, I know, and I'm excited about it, Hannah. I've made a real effort to say the words "of", "get", "was", and some others, the right way. I'm real proud, not that I talk good, but because I set me a goal and I'm keepin' to it. Helps me know I'm smart. Before Grace, I figgered I was dumb, like my daddy always told me."

"Bertie, there is more to being smart than using good speech. You are one of the smartest people I've ever met. You seem to know things about life that some folks are ignorant about. And I admire you for your courage and determination."

"Well, I thank you for them kind words, Hannah."

I got Bertie to sit down, and offered her a cup of tea, which she declined.

"No, I had a big breakfast a hour ago. I'm all tea'd out, but thanks anyway."

"Well, I thank you for coming to see me. I wish I knew where to start telling you what's on my mind, Bertie."

"Maxine and me, we always say, just start at the beginning. Works for us."

So I spent the next hour describing my childhood to Bertie. It seemed once I got started, the words came tumbling out so fast, Bertie was having trouble following along. It was a sad story she heard that day.

I WAS SHY FROM birth. My only sibling, a sister, was sixteen years old when I came along, so by the time I turned two, my sister was at college, then married and living far away. We never really knew each other, and I was raised as though I was an only child.

Starting with first grade, school had been hard on me because of my shyness. At home, there was nothing to object to. My parents and my widowed aunt who lived with us, doted on me. In a house full of sober adults, life was quiet and orderly. I had no playmates to quarrel with or share my things with, so life went along smooth as glass until I started school.

On the first day of first grade, one of my classmates hit me over the head with his lunch box. The teacher didn't see it happen. When I didn't object, the boy bit me on the back of my hand. When I pulled my hand away, and looked imploringly in the direction of the teacher, the boy kicked me in the leg. But her back was turned to the class while she wrote on the blackboard. At this last indignity, I finally objected, and shoved the boy, just as the teacher turned around to face the class and saw him land smack dab on his behind. The boy screamed bloody murder. The teacher took me by the arm and sat me down hard at my desk, and told me that was a mean thing to do. She said she didn't want to see me do anything like that again or she would spank me.

I learned that day that shoving someone in self-defense equated to objecting, for which a person got punished. Since there was no need to object to anything at home, therefore never getting punished, and since objecting to something at school meant getting punished, the lesson was learned. Don't object to anything unless you want to get punished and stay away from anyone who showed the slightest interest in causing trouble. Walk away, and don't complain.

This was how I lived my life from then on. Consequently, I had no real friends, because at that age there was always someone causing trouble, fighting over toys, grabbing cookies out of each other's hands, pulling hair and biting, shoving each other all over the place. I stayed away from them as much as possible.

As I grew older and the girls began to gossip about one another and get mad at each other over the smallest things, I kept my distance. I didn't want to be the one they gossiped about, I didn't want anyone thinking I had gossiped about them, so I avoided the other girls. That wasn't hard to do, since none of them paid any attention to me, anyhow. They were too busy dating and competing to see who had the nicest clothes, the prettiest hair. I avoided the whole scene and stayed away from them.

It was a lonely way to grow up, but I was used to being lonely at home, and truth be told, I preferred the quietness that reigned there. School was a loud, noisy place, with yelling and shouting, bells ringing. And the cafeteria. You couldn't hear yourself think in there, so I tried to always find a quiet spot on the school lawn and sat with my lunch, reading a book.

It was there, in the fall of my senior year of high school, that I met Carl.

As I sat reading under the shade of the old elm tree at the back edge of the school lawn, a pair of feet came into view in front of me. Looking up, I saw a tall young man standing there with a smile on his face.

"Can I help you with something?"

"No. I mean, um, I've noticed you sitting here almost every day by yourself, reading. I'm a great reader myself, so I thought I'd come over and see what you're reading today."

I blushed. There seemed to be no way to get out of showing him the book, but what would he think of my choice of reading material? Too shy, too used to doing what I was told at home, I held the book out to him and looked away.

He burst out laughing. "The dictionary?" His loud laughter caught the attention of some passing students, who looked in our direction as they went by.

"Oh, please be quiet," I said. Being noticed by the other students was a great embarrassment to me. I wanted to hide somewhere. "Please, just give it back."

He handed the book to me. "I'd like to sit down if that's okay with you."

I was totally flustered by then. "I, uh, I, uh," I stammered, not looking at him. "Yes, if you want to, you can."

"Say, listen, I didn't mean to embarrass you, but I've never seen anyone just sit and read the dictionary. The only time I open up that book is if I need to look up a word. Do you actually just read it?"

"Yes." Not knowing what else to say, I said nothing.

He wouldn't let me off the hook so easily. "Why would you want to sit all by yourself on a beautiful fall day like this, and read the dictionary just for the heck of it? Come on, you can tell me, I'd love to know why. Come on, tell me."

"I want to be a writer someday. I mean, I write now, but someday, I want to publish my writing in books. I read the dictionary to learn new words. It's very interesting, really."

"I never thought about that. I guess it would be interesting. By the way, I guess if we're going to be friends we ought to know each other's names. I'm Carl Billings. Who're you?"

Friends, I thought. *I don't have any friends, not really.* "Why do you want to be friends," I said. "We don't even know each other."

"We know each other. We're sitting here talking, and you know my name, so if you tell me your name, then we'll be friends. Don't you want me for a friend? Come on, tell me your name." He looked at me as if to say it was a very normal thing for a boy to walk up and sit down beside me and say he wanted to be my friend. He made it sound so reasonable, so I told him.

"I'm Hannah. Hannah Barker."

"There, that didn't hurt a bit, did it? Tell me now, what kinds of things do you write? Mysteries? No, I bet you write love stories, you have that dreamy, faraway look about you, so I bet you write love stories, filled with passion and romance."

I gasped. Never had anyone talked to me about such things. I didn't know what to say in reply to him. I blushed, and started to stand up, intending to leave him sitting there, but I dropped my dictionary. As I leaned to pick it up, Carl took hold of my wrist and stopped my movement, leaving me half standing, half stooping, not knowing what to do next.

"Look, I'm sorry, I guess I didn't know how shy you really are. The other kids, they talk, you know? They think you're a stuck up snob, the way you stay away from everyone, That's not it, is it?"

I was horrified. "They talk about me? Why would they even care?" Tears were gathering in my eyes, and I had started to shake.

"Hey, hey, sit down before you fall down, Hannah. Good grief, they're goofballs, all of them. A clique of jealous, malicious girls who don't have the sense to see past the outside of someone. Ignore them, Hannah. You're fine just the way you are. I bet if they got to know you, they'd want you for their friend, too."

Carl turned out to be my first real friend, or so I thought at the time. He pestered me to open up and let some of the others in besides himself, but it was too ingrained in my teenaged mind to change my outlook on life. The only reason I accepted Carl was that he wouldn't give up on me. He continued looking for me at lunch time, sitting with me and bringing me books to read. Some of them were not the kind of books I thought I should be reading, but in order to not hurt Carl's feelings, I leafed through them, skipping over anything that looked like it was leading to a suggestive scene.

Once in a while, Carl showed up with one of his girlfriends, thinking he could persuade me to talk to someone other than himself. We had conversations about school subjects, my piano lessons, which composer I was studying at the time. We talked about anything that came up, as long as it wasn't personal. I was an extremely private person, Carl discovered, and I wanted to keep my life to myself.

The truth was, though, I didn't have a real life of my own. All I knew to talk about was other people, usually dead people, historical figures who were written about in the history books and biographies I'd read.

One day, I asked Carl why he bothered with me. "What can I possibly be to you that you keep coming around me, neglecting your other friends in order to eat lunch with me under this tree. What do you want from me, Carl?"

I sat with my hands in my lap, leaning slightly forward in his direction, looking earnestly into his face.

"I don't know" was his reply. "I started out just being curious about you. Hearing the other kids talk about you like you were someone very strange made me want to know if the things they said were true. I found out they aren't true. So now my curiosity is satisfied. So I should go away, right?"

Again, I was at a loss for words, as so often was the case when I was with Carl. He was a curiosity himself. In the few months he'd been hanging around me at lunch, we had become friends, of a sort. But I really wanted to know now what he wanted from me. I was totally confused.

Carl sat back against the tree trunk and looked at me. I wasn't what a person would call beautiful, not even pretty, in the usual way that girls are thought to be pretty. I had flawless skin, the result, I suppose, of never having worn makeup. My hair was thick and black, but straight as a stick. I thought it was ugly, but my father said it was my best feature.

It embarrassed me to have Carl looking at me, so I turned my head, watching some of the other students engaging in horseplay on the other side of the school lawn, waiting for Carl to tell me what it was he wanted from me.

Suddenly, Carl reached over and touched my cheek. I jumped in surprise and turned to ask him what he was doing. I was totally unprepared for what he did next.

Carl put his hand under my hair at the back of my neck, and leaned over and kissed me. I didn't object. I simply stood, picked up my books, and did what I was used to doing when it appeared that trouble loomed. I turned my back and walked away.

"Here's the part that leads up to the start of my sinning, Bertie. I had never kissed a boy before that day. We didn't kiss each other at home, my parents weren't open with their feelings for each other, or for me. Anyway, I didn't go back to school for the next three days. Carl got scared and went to the school office and asked if they could tell him where I lived. Of course they told him no. They're not allowed to give out personal information, but when Carl told the principal that he thought he had offended me, and that's why I wasn't coming to school, the principal became concerned and asked what he did to offend me. Carl explained what had been going on, and that he had kissed me. Since I hadn't come back to school after that, Carl told them it must be his fault."

Later, my father faulted the principal for letting Carl contact me with the school's help. The principal defended himself by saying he couldn't imagine a simple kiss would be the cause of my absence. He did agree that maybe he should have telephoned my father instead of sending the truant officer to our house to investigate the situation. He also admitted that allowing Carl to send a note to me with the truant officer might have been out of line.

"What did the note say, Hannah,? Bertie asked.

"Carl asked me to call him. He wrote his family's telephone number in the note and apologized for upsetting me.

"The horrible part of all this, Bertie, was that in order to keep my parents from knowing I wasn't going to school, I'd spent three days in the public library. When the truant officer showed up at our door, my mother almost fainted. She called my father home from work. They were waiting for me when I walked through the door that afternoon. Of course he had read Carl's note and they knew I hadn't been in school, so they wanted to know what this boy had done to upset me. I made some excuse that he had bothered me while I was reading at lunchtime and in order to keep it from happening again I decided to stay away from school for a few days.

My father sent me back to school the next day with orders to stay away from Carl. If he bothered me again I was to go straight to the principal and report him.

"I went back. I dreaded facing my teachers and the other students. I especially dreaded seeing Carl, but I had to. He had to hear my terrible news."

"What could have been so awful, Hannah?" Bertie asked.

"I had to tell Carl that I was pregnant."

"Oh, mercy, Hannah. Oh, my." Bertie was at a loss for words, until I laughed.

"Why are you laughing? What could have been funny about that?"

"Because I wasn't pregnant, Bertie. None of this was funny then, and now I can't believe how stupid I was. You see, my mother was so afraid to tell me the facts of life, all she could bring herself to tell me was to stay away from boys, never let a boy kiss me, because that's what caused girls to get in the family way."

"That's it? That's all she told you?"

"Yes. So when Carl kissed me, I thought I had gotten pregnant. I was terrified. Of course, Carl knew it couldn't be his baby, but he also found my news hard to believe. Before the day was over, I'd been educated to the real facts of life."

When I told Carl I was pregnant, he said 'what do you mean you're going to have a baby?' He wanted to know who the father was. He asked what the heck I was talking about. He said I had told him I'd never even been out on a date, how could I be pregnant!

I explained to him that you don't have to go out on a date to have a baby and asked him hadn't anyone ever explained these things to him. My mother had told me about it a few years ago and I couldn't believe Carl didn't know.

"Listen Hannah, are you sure about this? Something isn't adding up here. I know you said you don't date. Why do you think you're pregnant?"

"Because you kissed me, and then it happened."

"What happened? You're not making any sense. What did your mother tell you when she explained where babies come from?"

When Carl stopped laughing, he took one look at my face and sobered up. He said, "Look, we need to talk. Come with me, and I don't want to hear you say a word until I'm finished talking."

He took me around the corner to an empty lot where the kids hung out after school. We sat in the grass facing each other, and he told me things I'd never heard before. He said, "Now, Hannah, get ready for some really heavy stuff here, because I'm going to tell you the real truth about babies. You don't get pregnant just because some boy kisses you. I know your mother meant well. She wanted to make sure her little girl grew up safe and sound, and telling you that when a boy kisses a girl, that's what causes a baby to grow, was her way of trying to protect you. But I'm going to tell you the real truth."

I was so embarrassed, but I sat there and let him tell me the facts of life. When I couldn't listen anymore, I put my hands over my ears, but Carl just pulled them away and went on talking. I was crying by the time he finished.

I asked him if everyone else knew this stuff. Was I the only one so stupid to think a person could get pregnant from a kiss? I felt like such an idiot.

"You're not an idiot," Carl said. "You've been sheltered by your family because they love you and wanted you to stay safe. But you're almost eighteen years old. Don't you think it's time you started making some of your own decisions? Like for instance, how about going to the Christmas dance with me next month?"

"I couldn't, Carl. My father would have a fit. Even if I was allowed to go, what would I wear? I only have school clothes and church clothes. And I don't know how to dance."

"Hey, I don't hear you saying no! All your objections can be overcome. First of all, just tell your father you're going. If he tries to stop you, go anyhow. Next, my sister has lots of dresses. You can borrow one of them. She and her friends are always trading clothes. And you don't know how to dance? Stand up and I'll show you. It's easy."

So, in the middle of an empty lot around the corner from school, Carl taught me the facts of life, I learned how to dance, and I got my second kiss from a boy.

"Yes, but Hannah, kissing a boy ain't a sin," Bertie said.

"I know that now, Bertie. But you'll see that my mother wasn't wrong in telling me what she did. Let me go on while I'm still brave enough to tell you what happened."

"I'll be still," said Bertie.

BY JANUARY, MY FATHER and Carl were at a standoff. Dad knew in another month when I turned eighteen he wouldn't be able to tell me what to do anymore, so in the meantime he figured he might as well let me see Carl. At least he seemed like a decent young man, my father said.

But Dad forgot to figure in the hormone factor. I had fallen in love with Carl and started to trust him. I allowed him to kiss me, often. At first I was ashamed of how it made me feel when he kissed me, but once he had explained that you can't get pregnant from a kiss, I wasn't afraid of him anymore, and the shame went away. I liked the way his kisses made me feel. However, I hadn't given any thought to the fact that my mother was right, after all. It was the feeling you got from kissing, not the kiss itself, that led to having babies. In February, the night of the Valentine Sweetheart Dance, I found this out in the back seat of Carl's father's car, parked behind the school gymnasium, while our classmates were inside, dancing.

"Oh, dear," Bertie said. It was becoming her favorite phrase. "I don't know what to say, Hannah."

"There's nothing to say, Bertie. Even after Carl had told me the facts of life, the reality of it hadn't sunk into my brain. I think in looking back over it all, I was so in love, things were so different from my life at home, I just didn't think about it. It felt so good to have someone show their love for me."

"I can understand that," Bertie said. "After all them years living with my daddy, I turned into a whole other person once I was married to Farley, my first husband. I know how you was feelin', Hannah. Go on and finish your story."

THE SAD PART IS that if Carl had ever been truly in love with me, it didn't last. He broke up with me in March, and it wasn't until May, a month before graduation, that my mother confronted me. She was waiting for me when I got home from school. She told me we needed to talk and invited me into the study with her. She closed the door and turned around and just looked at me. I knew she was angry, but she managed to stay her usual calm self. Nobody in our family ever showed anger or raised their voice. But I knew something was brewing from the look on her face.

She wanted to know who did this to me. She stood and waited but I didn't know what she was talking about. I truly didn't know. She said she was not a fool, she could see how my body was changing. She knew I had missed several of my monthly times.

I was so naïve it hadn't sunk in. I was sick and I wondered how my mother knew but was suddenly glad that she did.

"Oh, Mother, I've wanted to say something, but we don't talk about such personal things in our family, and I didn't know how to tell you. I feel sick all the time and I've thrown up almost every morning for a week now. All I want to do is sleep. I think I may be dying."

She stood there in disbelief. She asked if I really thought I was sick, did I not know what the problem was.

I didn't know, but she thought I was lying. It was painful for her, but she asked me some horrible questions.

"Hannah, I need to ask you something now that I fear will be painful for both of us. Will you answer me honestly?"

I told her of course I would, why would I lie to her about being sick? I was so confused. I couldn't have begun to imagine the questions she asked me then. She asked me if anyone, a boy, had ever..."

I stopped talking and looked away from Bertie.

"It's all right, Hannah," Bertie said. "I can guess what your mama must of asked you."

"Oh, Bertie, I was so ashamed, so ashamed. But the worst part wasn't my shame. The worst part was that she didn't really care about me, or how it was all going to affect my life. Do you know what she said, Bertie?"

Without waiting for an answer, I angrily spit out my mother's words. She said, "You're going to have a baby. How could you do this to me, Hannah?"

"Well, I declare," said Bertie. "Didn't she take on any of the blame for not tellin you the whole story? How'd your father take the news?"

"My mother was afraid to tell him. She said he would turn me out of the house. She was so afraid that she sent me to school the next day with orders to not let on to anyone what was happening. She was trying to figure out how to tell my father and aunt about this horrible tragedy I had brought on our family."

I was a mess that day. Several of my teachers asked me if I needed to go home. I guess I looked terrible, but I was trying to follow my mother's instructions to act normal. But when I saw Carl coming toward me in the hallway between classes, I forgot my instructions to keep things to myself. Carl had been avoiding me since we broke up, but I walked into his path and told him I needed to talk to him after school.

"Can't we talk now?"

Oh, Bertie, I was so scared, I blurted it out right there. "I'm going to have a baby, Carl." I was terrified of his reaction. And rightly so, it turned out."

Carl said, "Right. Like you were the last time you told me that. And if you are, what do you want me to do about it?"

I fainted right there in the hallway. He grabbed me before I hit the floor, and a passing student ran for the school nurse. They took me to her office and put me on a cot, revived me with smelling salts. I mumbled something about not feeling well and needing to go home. Once the nurse was sure I could walk, the principal excused us both for the rest of the day and told Carl to drive me home and deliver the nurse's note to my mother. As we were leaving, I saw the nurse and the principal look at each other and shake their heads. I knew what they were thinking, and I was ashamed.

Carl didn't even go in the house with me. He dropped me off a few doors down from my house and waited there until I went in, then drove away real fast.

My mother was in the process of telling my father why I had come home from school early when our doorbell rang that evening. He was already very, very angry when he opened the door to see Carl and his father standing there. He started yelling at Mr. Billings like it was his fault. Mr. Billings let him yell until he ran out of insults, then asked if he and Carl could come inside and discuss this like we were all adults. I thought my father was going to hit him. But he let them come in.

My mother kept saying things like what will the neighbors think, the scandal will kill your aunt. She carried on something awful, but the worst was yet to come.

Carl had gone to his father for help. He was truly frightened. He told him he didn't want to get married. It was a terrible evening. Mr. Billings started out by saying he was sure I must be a nice girl, but sometimes when a young lady finds herself in this position, she picks the most likely candidate and says the fault is his. He wondered if that could be the case here?

My mother almost fainted again at the insinuation, and my father started yelling again. To his credit, Carl broke into the noise and assured Mr. Billings there was no need for that. The baby was his, I was telling the truth.

"Well, at least he stood up for you, Hannah," Bertie said.

"Yes, I appreciated that. But the evening kept getting worse and worse."

Right in front of me and my parents, Mr. Billings bawled Carl out for being such an idiot. He said if Carl was going to fool around, he should have picked some trashy girl farther away from home. And then he asked Carl how long this had been going on. I wanted to die, Bertie. My father spoke up and told Mr. Billings to be quiet. He said 'what difference does that make? The point here is that your son has been abusing my daughter.'

Before my father finished speaking, Carl stood up and started waving his hands around in the air, looking flustered, and said he hadn't been abusing me, we only did it that one time.

I learned that night that Mr. Billings was a crude person. He winked at my father as he said, "It only takes one time to get the job done, Son. Looks like you were one of the lucky ones. Now, if you don't want to marry this girl, you say the word. I'll pull some strings and see what we can do. No sense you being miserable for the rest of your life."

"For goodness' sake, Hannah. You mean you married this boy anyhow, with a father like that? What was the matter with your parents, they'd let you marry him after them treatin' you so bad?"

"My parents were afraid of what people would think, afraid of the gossip. None of it was about me, Bertie, it was all about them, and their reputation. They were upstanding members of the community, good Christian people. All they wanted was for me to be safely married so my baby would not be born out of wedlock. When he was born too soon after the wedding, they lied and said he was premature, but another embarrassing and shameful fact was, everybody knew it was a lie."

I've often wondered why I didn't see things for what they were. But I didn't. When Carl explained the facts of life to me, he told me what he knew about the basics. He told me about getting pregnant, but what he didn't know to tell me were the facts of being pregnant. So, morning sickness, and the physical symptoms were mistaken for illness. I learned that Carl knew a little, but he didn't know enough. I also learned that although he seemed sincere in his feelings for me, it wasn't love. He was just a boy intent on getting his way. Once he'd accomplished it, I was so ashamed of my part in it, I wouldn't even let him put his arm around my waist, or hold my hand. I stopped kissing him and became more distant every day. By the first of March, Carl told me if that was how I was going to be, there was no sense in us seeing each other anymore. He broke up with me. Then he went back to seeing his former girlfriend, Margie. The news I gave him that day at school ruined that relationship for him.

"No," Bertie said, "the news didn't ruin no relationship, Hannah. Carl ruined it by behavin' like he did with you."

"I guess you're right, Bertie. What Carl never knew, because I didn't tell him, was that Margie stopped me on the street a few days later and told me what happened when Carl told her about me."

She said Carl didn't intend to marry me, he wanted to continue dating her. She said she'd been watching him with me for the past few months, and wondered what he thought he was doing. She said she knew I was a meek little thing and Carl had it all planned and knew where it would lead. Now he got caught, and he didn't like it one little bit and wanted out. She told him all she could think of was what if it had been her instead of me and told him, 'do Hannah a favor and don't marry her.' She said she slapped his face and called him scum before she walked away.

"Good for her. I don't hold with hittin' people, but I have to say he deserved that," said Bertie. "How you doin' tellin' me all this, Hannah? So far, the only sin I think you committed was givin' in to Carl when he, well, you know. The Bible tells us that is a sin. Did you ever ask God to forgive you?"

"Yes, many times. The problem is, I couldn't forgive myself, and I didn't understand how God could forgive me. For years, I resisted accepting His forgiveness for that sin. Then I committed a sin that I have never asked forgiveness for. That's why I'm talking to you now. I don't know if I can even tell you about it, it's so bad."

"Nobody's sins is any worse than somebody else's, Hannah. It's just in our own minds that ours is the worst."

"Oh, Bertie. I was so unhappy with Carl. By the time we'd been married for ten years, he'd started drinking a lot, and staying away from home. He said awful things to me, he blamed me for having our son, and then our two daughters. He said if it hadn't been for us he would have gone to college and made something of himself. He said if it wasn't for us, he would be a free man."

"What a terrible thing to say to you, Hannah. Didn't he ever think he was responsible for his part in bringin' those babies into the world?"

"No. He blamed me every time we had another baby. When I found out I was in the family way again, our youngest child was only one year old."

"Oh dear, Hannah. How did he take the news?"

"I never told him. I had an abortion. Oh, Bertie, how can I expect God to forgive me for that?"

"He will. You just have to ask Him."

"How will I know if He's really listening, how will I know if He's heard Me? How does a person know, Bertie?"

"Well, I could go on and on about forgiveness, what Jesus said about it, how it works. Instead, I want to tell you about the results of bein' forgiven and ask you one question. How long's it been since you felt full of happiness and joy?"

"What does that have to do with God's forgiveness?"

"Just answer the question, and then I'll tell you."

"I've never been truly happy, Bertie. For as far back as I can remember, my childhood was unhappy. I couldn't do anything right, not at home, not at school. I've always felt so out of things. Then, when I thought I was happy, being in love with Carl, I sinned with him, and he left me. I felt used, and then to be expecting a baby without being married. I know many people in today's world think there's nothing wrong with that, but in my day, it was a sin. I still think it's a sin."

"Do you read the Bible, Hannah? Psalm fifty-one is about David and how he repented of his terrible sins, and asked God to forgive him. He believed God forgave him, but he was feelin' right poorly about things, so he asked God to restore to him the joy of His salvation.

"There's more to it, you should read the whole psalm sometime, and you should read the thirty-second Psalm, too, because in that one, God answered David's prayer and told him he would bless the person whose sins are forgiven, because their guilt would be gone.

"That's how you'll know God has forgiven you, Hannah. And that's how you'll know you done accepted His forgiveness, because the guilt will be gone, you'll feel happy and joyful inside, and it will show on the outside."

"I guess I don't look happy on the outside, do I, Bertie? I sure know I don't feel joyful or happy on the inside. My children have often told me that I'm a miserable person. I know they love me, but I think sometimes they don't like me. How can I change that?"

"You got to ask God to forgive you, and you got to believe He will. You already live your life like He told us to, you know, that scripture verse where He told the sinful woman to go, and sin no more. Now all you got to do, close as I can tell, is truly believe that He has forgiven you.

"That's the hard part, because if we can't put our hands on something, we can't see it, how do we know it's real? How can we believe God and Jesus are real when we can't see 'em with our eyes? Here's how I get past that. I heard a sermon once about Helen Keller, you probably know about her. She was blind, and she was deaf. Now, if she couldn't see or hear, how do you suppose she had any idea about anything?

"I got to thinkin' about her one day when I was havin' trouble believing God was real. I mean, I couldn't see Him, I couldn't hear him. I asked God to help me with the problem I was havin' with that. He answered me. He told me to put myself in Helen Keller's place, and remember that she couldn't see her mother or her father, but she knew they was real. He said I should talk to Him and believe like Helen did, and I'd get my answers.

"So, I started talkin' to God. I was prayin' real hard about how Homer was treatin' me, and askin' God how was I goin' to stand it, livin' with Homer for the rest of my life. Then I set real still and waited. I knew I wouldn't be able to hear Him if He talked to me, and I wondered how in the world would I know if He answered my prayer, because, remember, right then I was blind and deaf like Helen Keller was."

I was leaning forward in my chair, my hands clasped tightly in my lap. I asked Bertie, "Did He answer you?"

"Yes, He did, Hannah. Now, you got to know me good enough to trust that I don't make up stories and try to pass 'em off as true."

"I do know that about you, Bertie. What happened?"

"Just as plain as if it was wrote on a blackboard in front of my open eyes, I saw words in my brain that I haven't never forgotten, all these years. Here's what the words said: *I will make all things right in the end.*

"I knew it was God speakin' to me. I was filled with such peace, I can't explain it, it was like nothing I felt before then, or ever since.

"Now, I don't know if that's how He's goin' to answer your prayers, Hannah. He's full of surprises. But I do believe if you trust Him, He's goin' to do something wonderful for you."

"But Bertie, I don't know how to pray like you do. I could learn, I guess, but I don't want to wait, I want Him to know now that I want to be forgiven, and that I want to accept His forgiveness, and I want to forgive myself."

"You can learn, Hannah. I'll help you. But in the meantime, would you like me to say the words for you?"

"Can you do that, Bertie?"

"I surely could. I heard a sermon once, tellin' us to bear each other's burdens and to pray for one another. Would you like me to pray for you about this?"

"Yes. What do I have to do?"

"Well, if we were younger, and our knees worked like they did way back when, I'd say let's kneel on the floor. Since there's no one here to haul us up and get us back on our feet, let's just sit where we are and hold hands. I'll do the prayin' and you do the believin'."

We held hands and closed our eyes, and Bertie asked our Heavenly Father's forgiveness on behalf of me, his daughter, Hannah Billings.

Fifty-Five

Sheriff Turner

THAD ANSWERED HIS PHONE on the first ring. I got right to the Point.

"Thad, I think we got us a problem."

"What is it, Sheriff?"

"You know my grandson, Hugh, right? He's tellin me a story I don't know what to do with, but it concerns the old Knight farm you bought from Bertie Claxton."

"What, did we find another body out there, Sheriff?"

"Under the recent circumstances, Thad, that probably ain't funny."

"I'm sorry, Sheriff. Just trying to make a joke. Guess I didn't think first. What's the problem?"

"We all know how boys is, Thad, always tryin' to do the other boys one up. Hugh come home from school this afternoon and told his ma that some of his classmates were out at the Knight farm over the weekend, they say they didn't do nothin' wrong, just roastin' wieners, campin' out in the woods behind the creek, poking around, no harm meant. These kids live in town, sometimes they don't have enough to do. I'm signing my grandson up with 4H, maybe that'll keep him out of trouble."

"I'm sure that'll be good for him, Sheriff, but what about the Knight farm?"

"Oh, yeah. Well, I don't know if there's any truth to what these boys are sayin', but if there is, I don't know what to make of it. They're saying they was lookin' in the windows out there at the farm, and they seen a casket in the kitchen."

"What?"

"You heard me, Thad. They say there's a casket settin' right there in the kitchen. You couldn't see it right off because you got the windows all boarded up, but one of them pieces of plywood's got a big knothole down in the corner. Jed Parker's boy, Nate, stood on an old bucket they found out in the yard and looked through that hole. When he seen that casket settin' there, he forgot he was up on a bucket and turned to run. Fell off and about broke his neck, I guess.

"Anyhow, the other boys had to get up there and have a look. There's three of 'em, and they're all tellin' the same story.

"'Course they had to tell their tale, so half the school knows about it by now. My grandson told me because he's afraid maybe someone's hidin' a body in there."

"Oh, for Pete's sake, Sheriff, who'd hide a body in someone's kitchen?"

"Well, Thad, you got to admit. We already found one body out there."

"I know, but the last time I was at the farm was when we boarded up the windows. There wasn't any casket out there..." Thad stopped talking.

"What you thinkin', Thad?" I asked.

"How soon can you meet me at Tremont Meadow? I think we need to talk to Bertie. She might be able to shed some light on this situation, Sheriff."

Bertie and Maxine were eating their supper in the dining room at Tremont when Thad and I walked in.

"Evenin', ladies. Mind if we join you for a cup of coffee?"

"Shoot, no, Sheriff," said Maxine. "What brings you to our part of the country at suppertime?" Looking at Thad, Maxine's face took on a questioning look.

"Hey, Sheriff. Everything okay? You ought to be home with your family, eating supper. What's up?"

Thad was looking at Bertie, who looked back at him with curiousity.

"Is Grace all right, Thad, she seemed fine when I left her a hour ago," Bertie said. "Why're you lookin' at me that way? Did I do something wrong?"

"I don't know Bertie. I think we need to talk, though. Can you come with us to the office for a few minutes?" Putting his hand on Maxine's shoulder, Thad said, "Stay here, Maxine. I'll let you know if we need you."

SHERIFF TURNER CLOSED THE office door and turned to Bertie.

"You have anything you want to tell us, Bertie?"

"About what? I don't know what this is about."

Looking at Thad, Bertie asked for help. "Can you give me a hint, Thad?"

I spoke before Thad could answer. "You know how boys is, Bertie. They don't mean no harm, but they get to nosin' around in other people's business, the next thing you know, we got a problem. My grandson's tellin' me a story about the old Knight farm. You know anything about anything out there?"

I guessed from the look on her face that Bertie knew something. I was afraid to ask what it was she knew. But I had to.

"Let me help you out here, Bert. The boys found a knothole in one of the boards that covers the kitchen window. They looked through the hole. Do you have any idea what they saw?"

"Well, shoot. They warn't nobody supposed to know about that until after I died."

"So you know there's a casket in there," said Thad.

"Yes, I know that. I had it put there. It's for me, Thad, when I die."

Neither of us could think what to say to that revelation. Bertie helped us out.

"It seems like I been burying people off and on most of my life. First my baby, then his daddy. Then my daddy, then Homer. I was the only one to do that for each of them. When it come time to bury my mama proper, there for sure warn't nobody but me to do it for her. Now, I ain't got no husband, no child, no mama or daddy, and when I was planning my mama's funeral, it come to me to plan my own, so nobody else would have to do it."

"Bertie, you're a long way away from dying," Thad said. "But even if you do die any time soon, you've got all of us."

"I can't count on that, Thad. Grace is sick, you're not lookin real good yourself lately, Maxine's just a few years younger'n I am, and so forth and so on. None of us knows who's goin' to be the first to go, or the last. I aim to be ready so I don't have to worry about it. I got everything planned out and paid for, and I was restin' easy until those boys got to trespassin' on private property."

We saw that she was getting upset. Thad said, "You sit here with the Sheriff for a minute, Bertie. I'll be right back."

"Do you suppose she's sick, Thad?" When he told Maxine about the casket, that was the first thing she thought of.

"I don't know, but we're going to find out. Come on to the office with me, Maxine. I think you'll be able to calm her down. She's real upset that we found out what she's done."

Fifty-Six

Maxine

"You know, Bert, there's only been one other time where you and me had words with each other. It was when you didn't trust me to help you with selling Homer's farm, remember? You thought I wanted something out of it and you couldn't understand why that wasn't true. You didn't know to trust anyone yet. I thought we got past that. Seems like I was wrong."

Bertie started to cry. She covered her face with her hands and let the tears fall through her fingers onto her lap.

"Oh, Maxine, I'm sorry. It ain't that I didn't trust you, I just, I just, I guess I just. . .oh, I don't know what I was thinkin'. Remember when we first met, I told you nobody had ever done anything for me? I still think, sometimes, that if I don't do it for myself, it won't get done. I guess that means I don't trust anyone, don't it?"

"We're a pair, aren't we, my friend? You don't trust anyone and I've spent a great deal of my life trusting everyone. You think you have to do everything yourself, and I often thought it was okay to let someone else do for me what I should have done for myself. You think we're either one ready to learn from our mistakes?"

"Well, you're bein' kind, Maxine. You learned your lesson a long time ago, I'm just now catchin' on. But I'm ready now."

"I surely hope so, Bert. What I want to know, though, is when did you arrange all this? You must have had to do some real sneaking around. I didn't have a clue."

"I didn't do no sneaking around, Maxine. You helped me do it. Do you remember the day you took me to Shadley's Funeral Home to plan for my mama to be buried?"

"Aha. That's when you did it, right? But how on earth did you get the casket into the kitchen with no one knowing? And why would you want to do such a thing? That's the biggest question I have about all this."

Fifty-Seven

Bertie

I HAD BEEN HOPIN' to be dead and under the ground myself afore the questions got started. Warn't no one else's business, I figgered, what I decided to do with my remains, long as they just had to call Mr. Shadley to send the hearse to get me.

When Maxine asked why, though, it got me to feelin' poorly about the way I done it. She'd been real good to me and we loved each other now, so it come to me that I wasn't takin' into consideration how my plans might make her feel. And now that I'm thinkin' about it, I'm realizin' there's other people in this world who loves me.

One more thing I got to learn in my old age; after all them years of havin' nobody to love me, now I am blessed with friends who do love me, and they deserve to have me love them back. So I told Maxine about how I done took stock of my life a few weeks ago. Seemed to me like I been buryin' my family for most of my life, and it's not a pleasant chore. I buried Farley, our baby, my daddy, Homer, and finally my mama. They all had me to do the job, but I had no family left to do the same for me. So, I planned it out in my head, and told it to Mr. Shadley.

Maxine set real still, lookin' serious, while I told her about that day at Shadley's.

"I WANT TO PAY you for two caskets, Mr. Shadley. I want the nicest ones you got, and I'll pay you for both of them today. One of them is for my mama to be buried in, and I want the other'n delivered to the address I'm going to give you. I need to know when you're goin' to deliver it so I can be there alone. Can you do that?"

"Why, certainly, Mrs. Claxton. But may I ask, who is the second casket to be used for? Has someone else died?"

"Not yet, but you never know, do you? I'm gettin' older by the day and my time could be right around the corner! I figure if my own funeral is planned and paid for I'll sleep better at night. Part of that plannin' is buyin' me a casket and arranging everything with you so when it happens I'll be set."

"Well, this is a bit unusual. I've never been called on to do anything like this before, but I guess there's nothing wrong with it. Let me get out the order forms and we'll get started. I know your mama's casket will stay here for her funeral, but I'll need to know what you want me to do with the other one."

Mr. Shadley set his pen on top of the form and took hold of my hand across the desk, real kind like.

He said, "You know, don't you, Mrs. Claxton, that I could keep your casket here until you, uhm, until you're, uh, well, until you need it?"

"Yes sir, I do know that. But this is how I planned it out, and I'm stickin' with that. I know you mean to be helpful to me, but after all these years of doin' what somebody else tells me to do, I aim to foller through with my own thinking about things."

"I'll abide by that," he said. "Where would you like the other one sent. I assume you have a place in mind?"

"Yes. I want it delivered to my property out past town, the old Knight farm. I done sold the land to Manning Development, but the house is goin' to be mine until I die.

"I got the agreement with me, it's signed by me and Mr. Manning. I want the other casket delivered there and put in the kitchen. It's big enough to hold something that size and still leave room to walk around in. There's nobody livin' there, so it won't be in the way, and the will I leave'll have instructions about my funeral. I'm goin' to be buried next to my mama in the cemetery, and Mr. Manning can tear the house down if he wants, after I'm gone."

Mr. Shadley said, "Well."

He swallered hard like he had somethin' stuck in his throat and said it again.

"Well."

"And I was in his reception room reading a magazine while all this was going on?" said Maxine.

"I don't know about no magazine, Maxine. When I come out of his office, you was sound asleep and snorin'. I had to shake your shoulder to wake you up."

We all laughed at Maxine, includin' her.

"ANYHOW, THE DAY THEY were delivering the casket, I had you drive me out to the farm and leave me there. I said I was goin' to go through the boxes Mr. Pauley's men had brung down from the attic.

"The part I didn't tell you about that was happening that day was what me and Mr. Shadley talked about when we were arrangin' my mama's funeral."

I looked at Thad and Sheriff Turner to say this next part.

"I want you to know Maxine warn't all that happy leavin' me there alone, but I told her I'd be okay, I was getting used to all that was happening in my life. I done got cried out, I told her, and now I'm movin' on."

Maxine said, "That's what we agreed to do, right Bertie? Move on? Good for you."

"Anyhow, I don't want you to think poorly of Maxine. She left me there by myself because that's how I wanted it to be. And since you all is so interested in ever'thing, I might's well tell you the rest of the darn story!"

THE TRUCK FROM DANES Casket Company drove up to the front door at Knight's farmhouse at ten o'clock that mornin'. I held the screen door open while they worked the heavy casket into the house and wheeled it to the kitchen at the end of the hall where I showed I wanted it.

The delivery man looked around like he thought I was kiddin' and asked if that's where I really wanted them to put it. "Ain't it gonna be in your way?"

"No, it ain't going to be in my way. Just cozy it right over there along that empty wall. You can see for yourself this is a big kitchen. Even with that casket in here, it's got lots of room left.

"Now, Mr. Shadley says you fellers is real good at keepin' stuff confidential, so I'm countin' on you to keep this to yourselves, you hear? And I thank ya'll for delivering it way out here in the country."

I still had a few hours afore Maxine would be back to pick me up, so I got busy doin' what I had said I come here to do. I opened the first box and dug in.

"I'll say this for you, Bertie," Sheriff Turner said, "when you make up your mind to somethin', you stick with it."

I did stick with it for the whole afternoon, sortin' through boxes and throwin' junk away. I shut the door and locked it that night and was waitin' on the porch when Maxine come to pick me up. I never give it no thought that somebody would go out there and see what I had done.

Now I'm wonderin' what are the others goin' to think when they find out.

Fifty-Eight
Maxine

"Well, we're not going to tell Grace, that's for sure," I said. "Even if we did, she wouldn't remember it tomorrow. That's one advantage of being in her shoes. As for Tom, he's a bit on the shallow side sometimes, Bert. He won't think a thing of it. Hannah, now there's the only problem I see. She's so insecure, she hasn't caught on yet that we love her. She's the one that might feel real left out here."

"You did what?" Hannah laughed out loud. "I think that's the funniest thing I've heard in all my born days. A casket in the kitchen? Sounds like the title of a book, if you ask me. A good Halloween murder mystery, maybe."

Tom picked up on Hannah's remarks. "Yeah. Or a movie. I can see it on the big screen now, a semi-dark kitchen with the camera focused on the eyeball in the knothole, a casket looming in the background. Eerie organ music playing for the opening scene."

"Oh, stop it, you two," I said, laughing. "Such imaginations. No wonder you get along so well, you both have demented minds."

We had all gathered in Tom's apartment at Tremont to hear Bertie's story. When she was finished, Thad breathed a sigh of relief at everyone's reactions, and said, "That went well," and this time we all laughed.

"Okay, I'll be serious," said Tom. "I think what we ought to do is turn the farmhouse into a mortuary. We'll all buy a casket and store them in the kitchen with Bertie's, and as we each die, we'll have the funeral there, then the rest of us will go out to the park by the waterfall and throw a picnic for all the residents. You know, life hasn't exactly been a picnic for any of us, so we'll have one as we leave this old world behind."

"I knew when you said you'd be serious, you weren't going to be serious, Tom," I said. "That is one whacky idea."

Thad stood up and said, "Wait a minute, wait a minute," as he paced around the floor, running his hands through his hair. "Wait a minute. Tom, you may be on to something here." Sitting back down on Tom's couch, Thad perched on the edge of the cushion and looked at each one of us before he continued.

"I've been considering that old house, wondering what to eventually do with it. Several thoughts have come to mind, but nothing stuck. Stay with me for a few minutes and let me know what you think when I'm through telling you what just came into my mind as Tom was talking.

"I hate the thought of destroying all the gingerbread trim on that house. And they don't build porches like that anymore, wrapped around three sides of the house, ten feet wide with an overhanging roof. The old glass in the windows can't be replaced. And the oak floors. Wow, they need to be refinished, but they could be beautiful. If we renovated the whole house, put in plumbing and central heat and air, it could be a showplace. I'm thinking, like, a chapel."

Thad sat back and looked at the group, watching for reactions. Bertie was the first to speak.

"All them years my mama suffered in that house, and me right after her, livin' with that sinful man that was my daddy. I used to not care if I ever went back in there, once I left it. But like God forgives us for our sins, and gives us a new heart, He could give that beat-up old house a new heart, couldn't He? It could be used for a good purpose, finally."

We heard a sniffle and turned as one in the direction of the sound. Tom stood at the sliding door to his patio with his back to us, fishing in his rear pants pocket for the handkerchief he had used so frequently, recently.

"I hope that's a clean hankie, Tom," said Maxine, and everyone, including Tom, burst into laughter.

Fifty-Nine

Bertie

SOMETIME LATER THAT NIGHT, just as I pulled one of my new nighties, as Maxine calls 'em, over my head, I was inspired by the Holy Spirit.

Now, most people would tell me I was a religious fanatic for thinkin' such things. But I believe Jesus meant it when He said He was going to send us a Helper. And part of the Holy Spirit's job as the Helper is to help us figger things out when we don't know what to do.

I had been praying every day since that time in the parkin' lot at the diner when I told Maxine about how I wanted to help some little girl have a better life than I done had, praying that I would know when the time come what I should do with all this money bein' give to me from Homer and from sellin' the two farms.

Now, there ain't no accountin' for how or when the Spirit chooses to help us. I do know this much, though. God's timin' is always perfect. He made me wait these last few years 'til things fell into place for me to be inspired. Here's how I see it now, just plain as them stars I can see out my bedroom window.

First, Homer's farm burnt. Then I found out my daddy's farm been settin' there all them years waiting for me. Next Thaddeus come along and bought the whole shebang for a lot of money, and last, he left the Knight house standin' when I asked him to instead of tearing it down. And now, I been given this wonderful plan about how to help not one little girl, but a bunch of them. I ain't gonna wait until morning, I'm goin' to call a meetin' right now"

Sixty

Thaddeus

I WAS STILL AT my office at eight o'clock that night when I got the call. I always jump when the phone rings at night, my first thought being, *Grace, something's happened with Grace*.

But it was Bertie, telling me, not asking, but telling me, I had to come to her apartment right away. She told me to call Tom and Hannah, she would call Maxine and Sheriff Turner, and we were to meet at her place within the hour.

"Just give Maxine time to drive in from her house, and then we're havin' a meetin'."

"Can you tell me what it's about?"

"No, you all will hear at the same time what I got to say."

Sixty-One
Bertie

ONE HOUR LATER, AT nine o'clock in the evenin', I stood in front of everybody in my bathrobe and said, "Creekside House."

I just stood there, smilin', until Maxine said, "You called us here to say Creekside House? What's that mean, Bertie? Are you okay? I mean, you're in your bathrobe, for Pete's sake. Your hair is hanging down your back. You never go out in public looking like this. What's wrong, Bert?"

"Well, in the first place, I'm not out in public, I'm in my own home. Next, thank you everybody for coming. I just couldn't wait until tomorrow. I knew Thad would have appointments, Maxine has the store to open, you all have stuff to do of a morning, and I didn't want this to wait 'til tomorrow was half over afore tellin' you this news.

"Remember, Maxine, when we was first getting acquainted, I told you about wantin' to help some little girl so she wouldn't have to grow up like I did?"

"Yeah, I do remember that, Bert."

"Okay. About a hour ago, I got the answer to my prayers, how I should go about doin' that. The answer is Creekside House."

They were all lookin' at each other like I had gone daft. "Hear me out, now. Earlier, we thought we had a good idea what to do with the Knight farmhouse. Turn it into a chapel, a place to hold funerals for the residents at Tremont Meadow. Seems to me that wouldn't benefit nobody except dead people and them that come to mourn over them. God knows that I have had enough mourning. He is going to give a new heart to that house and we are going to celebrate life in it, according to the instructions that the Holy Spirit give to me. Here's what we're going to do."

Sixty-Two
Sheriff Turner

WHEN WE FINISHED WITH our meetin', I hung back and let the others leave Bertie's apartment so I could talk to her alone. Figured the decision I was gonna put to her ought to be made with no one there to influence her, since she'd been doin' such a good job being on her own lately.

"I'm gonna give you the information I got from my grandson, Hugh, Bertie, and let you think on it for a while before you tell me what you want to do about it. That be all right with you?"

"Sounds serious, Sheriff. This is something I got to decide?"

"I think it is. Here's the thing, Bert. While my grandson was tellin' me about the casket in the kitchen, he also told me somethin' else. I figured one thing at a time was enough for you to handle, so I didn't tell the rest of his story until I had a chance to check it out.

"I'm tellin' you now. You haven't had boys of your own, so you might have trouble understandin' how they think. But I'll fill you in a little bit, since I used to be a boy myself."

Bertie laughed, and said, "Ain't you a boy now, Sheriff? Bigger, but you're still a boy."

"Yeah, we're all still little boys underneath our beards, Bertie. Scared to admit it when we done somethin' wrong, like these boys are feelin'. So keep that in mind when you hear this.

"Remember when we was all eatin' pumpkin pie and drinkin' coffee Thanksgiving Day? I asked about Homer having any enemies?"

"Yes, I do remember you asking me that."

"You gave me permission to go lookin' around, see if I came up with anything that might explain the fire that night. I used the word arson. Well, turns out it was arson, but it wasn't."

"How could it be both, Sheriff?"

"Seems Homer had caught some of the boys from town swimmin' in the creek on his farm a few times that summer. The last time he chased 'em out, he did a lot of yellin', makin' threats about what he'd do if he caught 'em there again, you know? And boys bein' boys, they decided a few weeks later to show Homer a thing or three. At the time, they didn't know Homer had died. They didn't think about the consequences of their actions. That's another thing about boys, Bert. Lots of times we don't think things through real good.

"Anyhow, they went back and set a fire on purpose. That's arson. They only meant to burn out some underbrush, make a little smoke. So I call it a prank, what they were trying to do. What they didn't figure on was how dry everything was that late in the year. When the fire started to get out of hand they tried putting it out with creek water, but they didn't have buckets.

Used their hands, their shoes, tryin' to get water on the fire, but it went out of control. They panicked and ran.

Fortunately your neighbor, Jed Bailey, smelled the smoke and called the fire department. Since you weren't hurt, Bertie, the boys decided to keep their secret about startin' the fire.

"Course, we all know about secrets, don't we Bertie? The truth always comes out, one way or another. I won't give you all the details, I'll just tell you their parents know about it now.

"Here's where you come in. You have a case. You lost the barn and outbuildings, the house was damaged. They caused destruction of property, grief and inconvenience. The question is, Bertie, do you want to press charges?"

Sixty-Three

Bertie

I DIDN'T TAKE LONG to decide.

"All I can think about right now, Sheriff, is what if one of them boys was my son, Tree? I'd want him to know he done something real bad, but I would like for him to have a chance to make up for it somehow.

"We're gettin' ready to start fixin' up the Knight farmhouse. I know there's goin' to be more work there than you can shake a stick at. Nails to be pounded, shingles to be carried, that kind of thing. I believe aside from bein' hard work for boys that age to do it would teach them what it's like to make up for what they done, even though it's been a while since they did it. I'd like to hope they might see their work taking shape and turning into something they could maybe be proud to say they helped make beautiful.

"I say put 'em to work on Creekside House, give 'em a curfew for a good long time. And they got to come and tell me what they done so I can forgive 'em to their faces. That's important, Sheriff, 'cause if they don't know they been forgiven, they's always going to feel guilty.

"I don't think they's bad boys, Sheriff. I think they just need to grow up some. Let's help 'em do that."

Sixty-Four
Maxine

THE NEXT DAY, LUNCHTIME found the Sheriff, Tom, Hannah, and I gathered in the private dining room at Tremont Meadow, waiting for Bertie to show up for the first organizational meeting for Creekside House. Thad would join us shortly with answers to his initial phone inquiries about how to proceed with Bertie's plan.

Each one of us, per Bertie's instructions, came to the meeting with a pad of paper and some pens. We were also prepared to share with the group what we each thought we might be able to contribute to Creekside House. I was excited.

We chit-chatted and threw some ideas around as we ate lunch. Thad had gotten there in time to have coffee and dessert. Bertie arrived after her lunch visit with Grace just as the table was being cleared. She asked Thad to take charge of the meeting and fill us in on what he'd been able to learn that morning.

"Well, first, Bertie, let me say that initially last night I wasn't certain about the feasibility of your idea."

"Warn't my idea. Was my Helper's idea, the Holy Spirit."

"Yes. Ahem. Well. After sleeping on it, if you can call what I did during the night sleeping, I was just plain eager to get on the phone this morning. I even called a few of my business contacts at their homes. Couldn't wait for them to open their offices. I got some good advice, some solid leads as to how to proceed.

"Things are in the works. Sam Jones from the County Building Department is checking on permits and zoning restrictions, things like that. Harry Fein, my chief electrician and a friend of his who is a plumber will be meeting me at the Knight farm this afternoon to assess what needs to be done in those areas. I'll be hearing back from County Water and Sewer today, and the heating and air people are out there right now. I met them there before I came to lunch. While they were looking at the logistics of installing a heat and air system, I checked out the roof. Needs a new one. We'll preserve as many of the original windows as possible, and the floors are solid, Just need refinishing. And, the whole house needs to be insulated."

"That sounds like a lot of work," said Hannah.

"Not so much," Thad said. "It goes fast when the house is empty. All I just mentioned can be accomplished in a matter of a few months, once all the permits are in place. With my connections as a general contractor and real estate developer for all these years, I see no problem with permits.

"The only thing I think might set us back some is finding the people we need to run the place. They'll all have to be degreed or certified, depending on the position they fill. I'll get personnel from Tremont Meadow to help with that. Also, anyone who works there will need to be run through the legal system. That's where you come in, Sheriff."

"I'm ready and waitin'. Bring 'em on," he said.

"Okay, Bertie, I'm turning the meeting over to you now. Get on up here and act like a businesswoman."

Tom shouted out, "Let's hear it for Bertha Claxton, CEO!"

Sixty-Five

Bertie

"Well, I declare, y'all. There warn't no need for all that clappin' and whistlin'. But I thank you anyhow.

"I never did anything like this afore, so just bear with me. I guess the best way to do this is to ask for a volunteer to start us off. Who wants to be the first to tell what they plan on bringin' to Creekside House?"

I was real surprised to see Hannah stand up right away. Seems like her shyness got left outside somewhere.

"I'm goin' to sit down while y'all speak, so come up here to the head of the table, Hannah."

She had it all down on paper and held it out in front of her. But after readin' a few words, she looked up with tears in her eyes and started speakin' without the paper.

"I grew up in a home with people who loved me. I'm grateful for that. But my family were people who lived according to rigid rules, with no encouragement to be anything other than what they were raised to be. I doubt that any of them knew of my desire to write. If they did, they never acknowledged it. Who knows who I might have been if my gifts and talents had been nurtured? It's only because of the love and acceptance that each of you has shown me that I am finally able to be proud of my writing. I hope I still have enough time left on earth to do something with it.

"That's what I would like to bring to Creekside House. I love to write, and I want to share that with the students. I want to acknowledge the gifts of those who will live there and encourage them to develop their talents."

Tom barely waited for Hannah to sit down before he come up to take her place.

"I understand where Hannah's coming from. It's not that I wasn't encouraged to go into acting. While I was a kid, no one, not my family, not even me, ever thought I would be a movie star. When I found myself involved in theater, and then movies, I was totally unprepared for that life. I did lots of things wrong, and I didn't live up to my potential. I wasted that opportunity, for the most part.

"So, what I want to bring to Creekside is an awareness of all the possibilities that exist out there in this big, old world we live in. Not just acting, but all the arts. After all, if you don't know what's available, how can you take advantage of it? I'll teach acting, from behind the wings out to the stage, from painting sets to makin' costumes. Everything. Who knows, maybe we'll discover the next Shirley Temple!"

More clapping and cheering. Things was heatin' up. Maxine come up front next.

"I fell asleep early this morning after wondering most of the night what I might contribute to this effort. I finally decided to get in the bed and try to sleep because I had a store to open in a few hours. That's when it hit me. The store.

"Writing and acting are wonderful professions. Where would we be without books and entertainment? Life would be dull, indeed. However, writers and actors need to be fed. So my contribution to Creekside House is to teach what it takes to get the food from the farm to the store. To display it. To market it. To make sure there's good, wholesome produce and meat and cheese for people to eat. I run a tight store, make a good profit, so I must know what I'm doing. I'd like to pass that knowledge on to the next generation so they can maybe find their way in the world of commerce."

What Maxine had to say went right along with what I had been thinkin about my part in this. So I took her place and spoke my piece.

"I always thought of myself as just a housewife. I ain't educated, I can't sing or dance. I don't know how Maxine does all she does, being on the Town Council, runnin' a store. Everybody here has a gift, some God-given talent they can share. If Homer hadn't of died and left me some money, if I hadn't been able to sell two farms to Thad, how would I ever have been able to provide for myself?

"When I found myself alone with no house to clean, nothin' to do all day, I learned I had a gift for takin' care of someone who couldn't do for herself anymore. And I believe I did a good job takin' care of my friend. Maybe I can teach our girls about takin' care of people.

"I know how to keep a house clean and get dirt out of work pants. I know how to milk a cow and raise a garden. I know how to bake bread and can and freeze food and make pickles. Them's all things a woman ought to know how to do.

"Now that I'm off the farm and out in the world, so to speak, I seen how so many young ladies don't know nothin' about any of this. That bothers me, because what if a time comes when the world changes and we all have to grow our own food or go hungry? I think these are all good things to know. Surrounding Creekside House we got all this land goin' to waste. I want to get our girls out into the fresh air and sunshine and teach 'em how to grow good food on their land. I want to teach them to take care of this beautiful earth God done give us to live on."

Thad walked over and put his arms around me and give me a long hug.

"If everyone in the world could be like you, Bertie, it would be a lovely place in which to live. You are precious, and you are loved."

Everybody started clappin' again. Land's sake, you'd think Tom was puttin' on one of his stage plays and it was the end of act nine. I set down, trying not to let the tears run down my face.

"Well, as long as I'm on my feet," Thad said, "I'll tell about my contribution. And Grace's. I include her because even though she never had to work for a living, she raised children and kept house and did many things Bertie just talked about. She supported me in my efforts to build Manning Development, and we've been fortunate to be in a position to invest in Bertie's idea. So our contribution will be just that. A contribution.

"Whatever it takes financially to get Creekside House started, whatever it takes to maintain it until it becomes self-sustaining, the money will be there. A trust fund will be set up and a board of directors will be formed. Each of you will be a member of that board, and we'll fill in the empty seats on the board with people who are knowledgable about running a facility such as Creekside House will be.

"I'm going to sit down now and let Sheriff Turner speak. Sheriff."

The Sheriff took his time gettin' up out of his chair. It took even longer for him to get his voice to work. Somethin' was botherin' him real bad, I could tell. He stood lookin' at all of us for a bit and then he started talkin'.

"I'm a small-town sheriff. Not too much goes on here that on the surface most of the citizens don't know about. But I see the rest of it. Kids abused, abandoned, neglected, some of them from so-called good families, and the general public don't know about it because the families, sometimes the law, covers it up. Ask Bertie about that. She'll tell you. These kids are helpless. They're angry. Some of them turn out bad. Some grow up to be prison inmates.

"One of the ways I try livin' a Christian life is to visit the juvenile detention facility downstate once a month. Try to talk some sense into a kid that has no one else to do that. It's not enough. What we need is a place for these kids to live where they'll get what you folks are willin' to give them, plus lots more. I know who these kids are. Many of them are little girls who are livin' in foster homes where they're sometimes worse off than they were at home. If you folks succeed in getting Creekside House certified as a home for these little girls, I believe I can fill it up a couple times over with kids who don't belong in a facility, little girls who would thrive in the environment you all are willin' to provide.

"Let me know when you're ready. I'll be lookin' through the records and pullin' some strings. You'll have all the young ladies you can handle.

"And in case no one here has thought of it, there's a whole lot of folks gonna be livin' at Tremont Meadow might be happy to act as grandmas and grandpas to the little girls livin' just a few acres away."

The Sheriff turned to take his seat, but hesitated. Facing his friends, he zeroed in on me.

"Just so you know, Ms. Claxton, I already talked with Mr. Shadley. He said he expects you got a lot of years left before you're ready for it, but in the meantime there's room in the warehouse, so he's sendin' the truck out tomorrow to get the casket out of the kitchen."

Epilogue
SEVEN YEARS LATER

"Good afternoon. My name is Marion Paige. I'm the Executive Director of Creekside House and I want to thank you all for being with us. At the end of today's ceremony, you are invited to stay for refreshments that have been prepared for us by the girls from our home economics class, with a little help from our kitchen staff. You'll be served selections of pastries and hors d'Oeuvres that are part of the culinary class at Creekside, and are included in our catering package that we offer to the public. We hope you enjoy them!

"I've been asked to preside over today's ceremony in which we are celebrating five years of new life in this beautiful facility. The auditorium we're sitting in is part of Creekside Academy, financed from the trust fund set up by Thaddeus Manning shortly after the idea for Creekside House came into being. Along with the auditorium, the Academy consists of a gymnasium, a natatorium, the kitchen where today's delicious refreshments were prepared, and, of course, the classrooms. Designed with growth in mind, the Academy will eventually be able to hold up to sixty students.

"As part of the renovation of the original house, a small wing of bedrooms was added to the south side of the main building, Bertie will tell you about future plans for housing.

"Later, for anyone who is interested, a tour will be given of the entire campus of Creekside Academy and Creekside House. Please gather on the front lawn after this ceremony, and a guide will take you around in small groups.

"But now, the real reason for today's gathering. We are here to honor its founder, Bertha Louise Knight Kenner Claxton, affectionately known to all of us as Granny Bert."

Many of the attendees began applauding. I held up my hand for quiet.

"Before we get too far into the ceremony, I'm going to ask her to come and have a seat on the stage."

A commotion in the audience interrupted the proceedings. It seemed one of the youngest residents of Creekside House had to be persuaded to let our guest of honor be escorted to the stage.

"No," the little one cried out, "she's sitting here, I want her to sit by me!"

Sheriff Turner came to the rescue and took Bertie's place, lifting the child onto his knee and bouncing her up and down, allowing Bertie to exit her seat and head to the front of the room.

My testimonial had been upstaged by that of a five-year-old before the ceremony had even started. Once the laughter, and more applause, subsided, I began again. By now, Bertie was settled in her chair on the stage, and I continued with the planned program.

"Everyone here is familiar with our founder's story. We all know and love her. She is the glue that holds this place together.

She is one of the finest examples of integrity and generosity most of us have ever known. She will not claim these attributes for herself, so today we're here to do it for her.

"Granny Bert, as she's known to her girls, doesn't put much store in awards for herself. There's a plaque with her name on it that will be preserved in the trophy case in the entry hall of our beautiful facility. You're welcome to look at it later if you like. But right now, we're going to let her know how we feel about the work she's done and all that she's contributed to the lives of the young women here at Creekside. Let's put our hands together and hear it for Granny Bert Claxton."

The applause and whistles and shouted accolades lasted for three minutes.

As the applause faded away, two young ladies came forward from the wings. Residents of Creekside House from the beginning, they were recent graduates of the Academy. Currently enrolled in nursing courses at the local college, they were working their way through the program as part of Creekside's housekeeping staff.

Assisting eighty-one-year-old Bertie from her seat on the stage, they escorted her to the podium where she was asked to say a few words.

Epilogue

Bertie

"I'D LIKE TO SPEAK about my friends who helped make my dream for Creekside House come true.

"We started out all them years ago with six good friends decidin' to give a couple of little girls a place to live, and makin' sure they got an education. Out of those six, four of us is still hangin' on. We're older, not so on top of things like we used to be. But until we can't get up and at 'em anymore, we aim to keep doing what we can to help as many young'uns as possible get a good start in life.

"My dear friend, Maxine Monk, isn't here today. She's in the hospital recovering from a bad fall. That's one of the problems with gettin' old. Sometimes your feet don't do what your brain tells 'em to do."

I waited for the laughin' to stop so I could go on.

"Two of the original bunch is here with me, though. That would be Tom and Hannah Pelligrino, sittin' down there in the front row, holdin' hands. They started this project as single people, but somewhere along the way they run off to Vegas and got married! Best thing ever happened to either one of 'em, far as I can tell."

Tom stood and pulled Hannah to her feet, raising their hands over their heads and kissing her cheek, ever the showman. I had to wait again for the laughin' and clappin' and hootin' to stop so I could go on talkin'.

"The saddest part of today is that our dear friend, Grace Manning, left us behind three years ago to continue our work without her. Her sweet husband, Thaddeus, fought a hard fight, but the cancer got him anyhow. He followed his lovely Grace home to Heaven just one year ago. I don't know enough words to tell how much they are missed.

"Before he left, Thad made sure funding was in place for the next phase of building, planned for next year. That will be an addition of six more dormitory bedrooms and bathrooms to the main house, followed by a second phase to build a common area that will house a library, media room, theater, and dining hall. We have a waitin' list of girls that's growin' longer by the month, and this new addition can't get done too soon. For their faith in what we were planning, for their belief in the future of Creekside, and for making it possible financially, we thank Thad and Grace Manning.

"There's someone else who was an important part of getting Creekside House started. At the beginning, we pulled Sheriff Joe Turner into our efforts. He'd been part of all six of our lives for a while and he wanted to help. He and Maxine had been friends for many years. He's an easy man to get to know and love. If my son Tree had lived, I like to think he would've been a good, kind man like Joe Turner. He's responsible for a whole lot more'n I am for this place. He's the one got it filled up the first time, and he's the one talked to the people at Tremont Meadow about bein' grandmas and grandpas over here at Creekside.

"There was some negative talk in the community about where our girls were going to come from, and a lot of questions about how us run-down, burned-out, old geezers would do, taking on these girls at such a late time in our life. But we went ahead with it anyhow, and now the only way I can think to sum up the success of Sheriff Turner's suggestion is to tell you what happened shortly after the first girls were settled in their new home here. It went somethin' like this:

"Quicker than a jack rabbit can run, a path was wore down between us old folks and them young'uns. That path through the meadow is still there and gets used every day. We all are forever grateful to our Sheriff for knowin' what them girls needed. And it sure didn't hurt us old folks, either."

The audience started clapping again. When they quit, I said, "I'm going to ask all them folks from Tremont Meadow who been acting as grandmas and grandpas to stand up by their chairs so we can thank them."

It took a minute of chairs scraping and feet shuffling for all of them to stand.

"Look at that," I said. "If we were to count 'em, I'd say half of the residents at Tremont Meadow has more grandkids than they can count. Let's give them some of that clappin' and say thank you to them for the girls they've loved over the past five years. While we're at it, we sure can't forget our young ladies. We are thankful for these beautiful girls who let us love them, and we're proud of every one. Let's give them a round of clappin'. Stand up with your grandmas and grandpas, girls!"

I stood quietly until the noise died down, then I went on bein' grateful.

"It took a whole crew of us to get the job done and I thank every one of you!" I had to wait a bit because my voice kind of quit workin' all of a sudden. The audience set quiet, waitin' until somewhere from the back someone yelled out "Hey, Granny Bert!"

This time the clappin' was mixed in with a lot of laughter and cheerin'!

Finally everybody got back in their seats and settled down so I could go on with what I wanted to make sure they heard.

"We're real proud of the hard work and commitment it took from our whole community to make Creekside House a reality.

"But more'n any of us, there's someone else needs to be praised, because without Him and His Crew, it wouldn't have gotten done. Today we dedicate *Tremont Meadow* and *Creekside House* to them.

"I hope everybody here today will join in with me when I say thank you to Our Heavenly Father, His Son Jesus, and our Helper, The Holy Spirit!

"Can I hear an amen?"

And everybody there got to their feet and said,

"AMEN!"

Acknowledgements

There are many people to thank for their part in producing an accounting of Bertie Claxton's life. First on the list is my friend Bona Lee who, in the 1980's, talked me into attending a writer's workshop with her. At this workshop Bertie became a character that waited all these years for her story to unfold in my mind. The mid-2000's found me entered in the National Novel Writing Month, (a.k.a. NaNoWriMo), a 50,000-word self-imposed month-long competition. Coached and cheered on by NaNoWriMo's founder, coach, and head cheerleader, Chris Baty, I closed the door behind me, hung a "Do Not Disturb" sign on the door and attacked the keyboard. Bertie used every word of her allotted 50,000 and then some, and at the end of the month her story was told. So, thank you, Chris Baty for telling us our story didn't have to be perfect at the beginning, it just had to have a beginning! From that beginning, Bertie finally became tired of waiting and we began in earnest putting her story on paper. The result of our effort is this book.

I want to thank my husband for his trips in and out of my workspace, bringing me sandwiches and cups of hot tea. I would have starved otherwise. And my children – at various times over the years, one or the other of them would ask if

I finished that book yet. Thank you all for remembering that Bertie was still trying to tell me something.

That brings us to today, 2023, and the leader of our Adult Writing Group at Massillon Public Library. Thank you, Rachel Ketler, CEO of Queen Anne's Lace, for sharing your knowledge of prose, poetry, publishing and the world of literature in general. Your editing and critique of my manuscript added much to the telling of Bertie's life.

To my fellow wordsmiths in our writing group, thank you for your support as we share our writing with each other.

I give thanks to my Beta Readers: Jackie, Mickey, Summer, and Rachel for "test reading" Bertie's story.

And to my baby sister, Julianne, I thank her for her unwavering confidence that someone, somewhere, will be blessed by something they read here.

I thank you all, and ask God's blessings on each of you.

About the Author

MKS Cooper began composing poetry at the age of ten.

A number of those early, handwritten poems were preserved by her grandmother and mother. Though old, tattered, and somewhat faded, they are some of her favorite treasures.

As an adult, she added short stories and novels to her repertoire. *The Mysteries of Tremont Meadow* is her debut novel and is available through Amazon, as is her children's illustrated book, *The Christmas Horse*.

Ms. Cooper lives in Ohio with her husband. They share a family of children, grandchildren, and great-grandchildren who are scattered around the country in Ohio, Illinois, Florida, Georgia, and California. In her spare time, she enjoys reading, knitting, crocheting, crossword and jigsaw puzzles, and both classical and Golden Oldies music.

She can be contacted at Cooperbooks72@yahoo.com.

Two more manuscripts are in the works.

Learn more at Cooperbooks72.com